A SILVER CLASSIC

W9-ARB-918

Classic
Short
Stories

SILVER BURDETT COMPANY
Morristown, New Jersey
Glenview, Illinois · Palo Alto · Dallas · Atlanta

The stories in this edition are complete and unabridged
except "The Man Without a Country,"
which is slightly abridged.

Acknowledgment Pages 278–283: "A Work of Art" from *The Stories of Anton Chekhov*, by Anton Chekhov, edited by Robert Linscott. Copyright © 1932 and renewed 1960 by The Modern Library, Inc. Reprinted by permission of Random House, Inc.

Library of Congress Card Number 80–54129

ISBN 0–382–03444–9

CONTENTS

THEME

───

What does the story mean? What idea is the author trying to convey? A story's central idea is called its theme. But an author does not want to pound the theme into your head; instead, he or she tries to entice, or tempt, you to reach a conclusion from the story.

To practice finding and stating the theme of a story, read "The Death of the Dauphin," the first story in this section. What is the story about? It is about death, of course, but death is the topic, not the theme. The theme must be a more complete idea, such as "Death is not so bad after all" or "Death is not painful for those who are powerful." Neither of these theme statements is fitting for this story. It will be up to you to read the story, to decide what is the main idea, or theme (what the author is trying to say about death), and to state the theme accurately, as you see it.

Stating a story theme is not always easy. A theme may be as plain as ordinary daylight or as elusive as a shadow. And as you read and reread stories, you will find that any statement of theme falls short, just as one sentence about someone you know is no substitute for being with that person. There is certainly more to any story than its theme, but understanding the theme is essential to understanding the story.

"Then don't cry, Madame my Queen; you forget that I am the Dauphin, and that Dauphins cannot die like this."

THE DEATH OF THE DAUPHIN

Alphonse Daudet

The little Dauphin is ill; the little Dauphin is dying. In all the churches of the kingdom, the Blessed Sacrament remains exposed night and day, and great candles burn for the recovery of the royal child. The streets of the old capital are sad and silent; the bells no longer ring; carriages move at the pace of a walk. Around the palace curious townspeople watch, through the iron railings, the guards with gilded paunches who are conversing in the courtyard with an air of importance.

The whole castle is aquiver. Chamberlains and majordomos run up and down the marble staircases. The galleries are filled with pages and courtiers in silken garments going from one group to another, asking for news in low voices. On the wide porticos tearful ladies-in-waiting exchange deep curtsies and wipe their eyes with dainty embroidered handkerchiefs.

In the Orangery is a large assemblage of doctors in their robes. They can be seen through the windows waving their long black sleeves and nodding their periwigged heads knowingly. The prince's tutor and squire are pacing before the door, awaiting the decision of the Faculty. Scullions pass them without bowing. The squire swears like a pagan; the tutor recites lines from Horace. And during all this time, from the stables over there, is heard a long and plaintive neighing. It is

4 the little Dauphin's sorrel pony, forgotten by the grooms, and whinnying sadly before its empty manger.

And the King? Where is his Majesty the King? The King has locked himself up in a room at a remote end of the castle. Their Majesties do not like to be seen weeping. As for the Queen, that is another matter. Seated by the little Dauphin's bedside, her beautiful face is bathed in tears, and she sobs aloud before everybody, just as any tailor's wife might do.

In his small lace-trimmed bed, the Dauphin, whiter than the pillows on which he lies, is resting with his eyes closed. They think he is sleeping; but, no, the little Dauphin is not asleep. He turns toward his mother, and seeing her tears, he says to her:

"Madame my Queen, why are you weeping? Do you really believe I am going to die?"

The Queen tries to answer. Sobs prevent her from speaking.

"Then don't cry, Madame my Queen; you forget that I am the Dauphin, and that Dauphins cannot die like this."

The Queen sobs more bitterly still, and the prince begins to feel frightened.

"Wait!" he says, "I will not let Death come and take me away. I will find a way to prevent him from coming here. Send, at once, for forty of our strongest soldiers to keep guard around our bed! Have a hundred cannon keep watch night and day, with fuses lit, under our windows! And woe to Death if he should dare come near us!"

To humor the royal child, the Queen makes a sign. Immediately the great cannon are heard rolling in the courtyard; and the forty tall soldiers, halberds in hand, take up formation around the room. They are all old soldiers with grizzled mustaches. The Dauphin claps his hands on seeing them. He recognizes one and calls to him:

"Lorrain! Lorrain!"

The old soldier takes a step toward the bed.

"I love you very much, my old Lorrain. Let me see your big

sword. If Death comes to fetch me, we must kill him, mustn't we?"

Lorrain replies, "Yes, my Lord." And two great tears roll down his weathered cheeks.

At this moment the chaplain approaches the little Dauphin and talks to him at length in a hushed voice while showing him a crucifix. The Dauphin listens with a stunned expression, then interrupts him suddenly:

"I understand very well what you are saying, Reverend Father; but, after all, could not my little friend Beppo die in my place if he were given a great sum of money?"

The chaplain continues to speak to him in a low voice, and the little Dauphin looks more and more astonished.

When the chaplain has finished, the Dauphin resumes with a heavy sigh:

"All that you tell me is very sad, Reverend Father, but one thing consoles me; it is that up there, in the paradise of the stars, I shall still be the Dauphin. I know that God is my cousin and cannot fail to treat me according to my rank."

Then he adds, turning toward his mother:

"Have them bring me my finest clothes: my white ermine doublet and my velvet pumps! I want to look gallant to the angels and to enter heaven dressed as a Dauphin."

Again, for the third time, the chaplain bends over the little Dauphin and talks to him softly for a long time. In the middle of his discourse, the royal child interrupts him angrily:

"But then," he cries, "to be Dauphin, why, it is nothing at all!"

And, refusing to hear anything more, the little Dauphin turns toward the wall and weeps bitterly.

Now, the point of the story is this: Did the tiger come out of that door, or did the lady?

———————

THE LADY OR THE TIGER?

Frank Stockton

In the very olden time, there lived a semibarbaric king, whose ideas, though somewhat polished and sharpened by the progressiveness of distant Latin neighbors, were still large, florid, and untrammeled, as became the half of him which was barbaric. He was a man of exuberant fancy, and, withal, of an authority so irresistible that, at his will, he turned his varied fancies into facts. He was greatly given to self-communing; and when he and himself agreed upon any thing, the thing was done. When every member of his domestic and political systems moved smoothly in its appointed course, his nature was bland and genial; but whenever there was a little hitch, and some of his orbs got out of their orbits, he was blander and more genial still, for nothing pleased him so much as to make the crooked straight and crush down uneven places.

Among the borrowed notions by which his barbarism had become semified was that of the public arena, in which, by exhibitions of manly and beastly valor, the minds of his subjects were refined and cultured.

But even here the exuberant and barbaric fancy asserted itself. The arena of the king was built, not to give the people an opportunity of hearing the rhapsodies of dying gladiators, nor to enable them to view the inevitable conclusion of a conflict between religious opinions and hungry jaws, but for purposes far better adapted to widen and develop the mental energies of the people. This vast amphitheater, with its encircling galleries, its mysterious vaults, and its unseen passages, was an agent of poetic justice, in which crime was punished, or virtue rewarded, by the decrees of an impartial and incorruptible chance.

When a subject was accused of a crime of sufficient importance to interest the king, public notice was given that on an appointed day the fate of the accused person would be decided in the king's arena—a structure which well deserved its name; for although its form and plan were borrowed from afar, its purpose emanated solely from the brain of this man, who, every barleycorn a king, knew no tradition to which he owed more allegiance than pleased his fancy, and who ingrafted on every adopted from of human thought and action the rich growth of his barbaric idealism.

When all the people had assembled in the galleries, and the king, surrounded by his court, sat high up on his throne of royal state on one side of the arena, he gave a signal, a door beneath him opened, and the accused subject stepped out into the amphitheater. Directly opposite him, on the other side of the enclosed space, were two doors, exactly alike and side by side. It was the duty and the privilege of the person on trial to walk directly to these doors and open one of them. He could open either door he pleased. He was subject to no guidance or influence but that of the aforementioned impartial and incorruptible chance. If he opened the one, there came out of it a hungry tiger, the fiercest and most cruel that could be procured, which immediately sprang upon him and tore him to pieces as a punishment for his guilt. The moment that the case of the criminal was thus decided, doleful iron bells were clanged, great wails went up from the hired mourners posted on the outer rim of the arena, and the vast audience, with bowed heads and downcast hearts, wended slowly their home-

8 ward way, mourning greatly that one so young and fair, or so old and respected, should have merited so dire a fate.

But if the accused person opened the other door, there came forth from it a lady, the most suitable to his years and station that his majesty could select among his fair subjects; and to this lady he was immediately married as a reward of his innocence. It mattered not that he might already possess a wife and family, or that his affections might be engaged upon an object of his own selection. The king allowed no such subordinate arrangements to interfere with his great scheme of retribution and reward. The exercises, as in the other instance, took place immediately and in the arena. Another door opened beneath the king, and a priest, followed by a band of choristers and dancing maidens blowing joyous airs on golden horns and treading an epithalamic measure, advanced to where the pair stood, side by side; and the wedding was promptly and cheerily solemnized. Then the gay brass bells rang forth their merry peals, the people shouted glad hurrahs, and the innocent man, preceded by children strewing flowers on his path, led his bride to his home.

This was the king's semibarbaric method of administering justice. Its perfect fairness is obvious. The criminal could not know out of which door would come the lady. He opened either he pleased, without having the slightest idea whether, in the next instant, he was to be devoured or married. On some occasions the tiger came out of one door, and on some out of the other. The decisions of this tribunal were not only fair, they were positively determinate. The accused person was instantly punished if he found himself guilty; and if innocent, he was rewarded on the spot, whether he liked it or not. There was no escape from the judgments of the king's arena.

The institution was a very popular one. When the people gathered together on one of the great trial days, they never knew whether they were to witness a bloody slaughter or a hilarious wedding. This element of uncertainty lent an interest to the occasion which it could not otherwise have attained. Thus the masses were entertained and pleased, and the thinking part of the community could bring no charge of unfairness against this plan; for did not the accused person have the whole matter in his own hands?

This semibarbaric king had a daughter as blooming as his most florid fancies and with a soul as fervent and imperious as his own. As is usual in such cases, she was the apple of his eye and was loved by him above all humanity. Among his courtiers was a young man of that fineness of blood and lowness of station common to the conventional heroes of romance who love royal maidens. This royal maiden was well satisfied with her lover, for he was handsome and brave to a degree unsurpassed in all this kingdom; and she loved him with an ardor that had enough of barbarism in it to make it exceedingly warm and strong. This love affair moved on happily for many months until one day the king happened to discover its existence. He did not hesitate nor waver in regard to his duty in the premises. The youth was immediately cast into prison, and a day was appointed for his trial in the king's arena. This, of course, was an especially important occasion; and his majesty, as well as all the people, was greatly interested in the workings and development of this trial. Never before had such a case occurred; never before had a subject dared to love the daughter of a king. In after-years such things became commonplace enough; but then they were, in no slight degree, novel and startling.

The tiger cages of the kingdom were searched for the most savage and relentless beasts from which the fiercest monster might be selected for the arena; and the ranks of maiden youth and beauty throughout the land were carefully surveyed by competent judges in order that the young man might have a fitting bride in case fate did not determine for him a different destiny. Of course, everybody knew that the deed with which the accused was charged had been done. He had loved the princess, and neither he, she, nor anyone else thought of denying the fact; but the king would not think of allowing any fact of this kind to interfere with the workings of the tribunal, in which he took such great delight and satisfaction. No matter how the affair turned out, the youth would be disposed of; and the king would take an aesthetic pleasure in watching the course of events which would determine whether or not the young man had done wrong in allowing himself to love the princess.

The appointed day arrived. From far and near the people gathered and thronged the great galleries of the arena; and crowds, unable to gain admittance, massed themselves against its outside walls. The king and his court were in their places, opposite the twin doors—those fateful portals, so terrible in their similarity.

All was ready. The signal was given. A door beneath the royal party opened, and the lover of the princess walked into the arena. Tall, beautiful, fair, his appearance was greeted with a low hum of admiration and anxiety. Half the audience had not known so grand a youth had lived among them. No wonder the princess loved him! What a terrible thing for him to be there!

As the youth advanced into the arena, he turned, as the custom was, to bow to the king. But he did not think at all of that royal personage; his eyes were fixed upon the princess, who sat to the right of her father. Had it not been for the moiety of barbarism in her nature, it is probable that lady would not have been there; but her intense and fervid soul would not allow her to be absent on an occasion in which she was so terribly interested. From the moment that the decree had gone forth that her lover should decide his fate in the king's arena, she had thought of nothing, night or day, but this great event and the various subjects connected with it. Possessed of more power, influence, and force of character than anyone who had ever before been interested in such a case, she had done what no other person had done—she had possessed herself of the secret of the doors. She knew in which of the two rooms that lay behind those doors stood the cage of the tiger, with its open front, and in which waited the lady. Through these thick doors, heavily curtained with skins on the inside, it was impossible that any noise or suggestion should come from within to the person who should approach to raise the latch of one of them. But gold—and the power of a woman's will—had brought the secret to the princess.

And not only did she know in which room stood the lady ready to emerge, all blushing and radiant, should her door be opened, but she knew who the lady was. It was one of the fairest and loveliest of the damsels of the court who had been selected as the reward of the accused youth, should he be proved innocent of the crime of aspiring to one so far above him; and the princess hated her. Often had she seen, or imagined that she had seen, this fair creature throwing glances of admiration upon the person of her lover, and sometimes she thought these glances were perceived and even returned. Now and then she had seen them talking together; it was but for a moment or two, but much can be said in a brief space. It may have been on most unimportant topics, but how could she know that? The girl was lovely, but she had dared to raise her eyes to the loved one of the princess; and with all the intensity of the savage blood transmitted to her through long lines of wholly barbaric ancestors, she hated the woman who blushed and trembled behind that silent door.

When her lover turned and looked at her, and his eye met hers as she sat there paler and whiter than anyone in the vast ocean of anxious faces about her, he saw, by that power of quick perception which is given to those whose souls are one, that she knew behind which door crouched the tiger, and behind which stood the lady. He had expected her to know it. He understood her nature, and his soul was assured that she would never rest until she had made plain to herself this thing, hidden to all other lookers-on, even to the king. The only hope for

12   the youth in which there was any element of certainty was based upon the success of the princess in discovering this mystery; and the moment he looked upon her, he saw she had succeeded, as in his soul he knew she would succeed.

Then it was that his quick and anxious glance asked the question: "Which?" It was as plain to her as if he shouted it from where he stood. There was not an instant to be lost. The question was asked in a flash; it must be answered in another.

Her right arm lay on the cushioned parapet before her. She raised her hand and made a slight, quick movement toward the right. No one but her lover saw her. Every eye but his was fixed on the man in the arena.

He turned, and with a firm and rapid step he walked across the empty space. Every heart stopped beating, every breath was held, every eye was fixed immovably upon that man. Without the slightest hesitation he went to the door on the right and opened it.

· · ·

Now, the point of the story is this: Did the tiger come out of that door, or did the lady?

The more we reflect upon this question, the harder it is to answer. It involves a study of the human heart which leads us through devious mazes of passion, out of which it is difficult to find our way. Think of it, fair reader, not as if the decision of the question depended upon yourself, but upon that hot-blooded, semibarbaric princess, her soul at a white heat beneath the combined fires of despair and jealousy. She had lost him, but who should have him?

How often, in her waking hours and in her dreams, had she started in wild horror and covered her face with her hands as she thought of her lover opening the door on the other side of which waited the cruel fangs of the tiger!

But how much oftener had she seen him at the other door! How in her grievous reveries had she gnashed her teeth and torn her hair when she saw his start of rapturous delight as he opened the door of the lady! How her soul had burned in agony when she had seen him rush to meet that woman, with her flushing cheek and sparkling eye of triumph; when she had seen him lead her forth, his whole frame kindled with the joy of recovered life; when she had heard the glad shouts from the multitude and the wild ringing of the happy bells; when she had seen the priest, with his joyous followers, advance to the couple and make them man and wife before her very eyes; and when she had seen them walk away together upon their path of flowers, followed by the tremendous shouts of the hilarious multitude, in which her one despairing shriek was lost and drowned!

Would it not be better for him to die at once and go to wait for her in the blessed regions of semibarbaric futurity?

And yet, that awful tiger, those shrieks, that blood!

Her decision had been indicated in an instant, but it had been made after days and nights of anguished deliberation. She had known she would be asked, she had decided what she would answer, and without the slightest hesitation she had moved her hand to the right.

The question of her decision is one not to be lightly considered, and it is not for me to presume to set myself up as the one person able to answer it. And so I leave it with all of you: Which came out of the opened door—the lady or the tiger?

But would the Beautiful Idea ever be yielded to his hand . . . ?

THE ARTIST OF THE BEAUTIFUL

Nathaniel Hawthorne

An elderly man, with his pretty daughter on his arm, was passing along the street, and emerged from the gloom of the cloudy evening into the light that fell across the pavement from the window of a small shop. It was a projecting window; and on the inside were suspended a variety of watches—pinchbeck, silver, and one or two of gold—all with their faces turned from the street, as if churlishly disinclined to inform the wayfarers what o'clock it was. Seated within the shop, sidelong to the window, with his pale face bent earnestly over some delicate piece of mechanism on which was thrown the concentrated lustre of a shade lamp, appeared a young man.

"What can Owen Warland be about?" muttered old Peter Hovenden, himself a retired watchmaker, and the former master of this same young man, whose occupation he was now wondering at. "What can the fellow be about? These six months past, I have never come by his shop without seeing him just as steadily at work as now. It would be a flight beyond his usual foolery to seek for the perpetual motion. And yet I know enough of my old business to be certain that what he is now so busy with is no part of the machinery of a watch."

"Perhaps, Father," said Annie, without showing much interest in the question, "Owen is inventing a new kind of timekeeper. I am sure he has ingenuity enough."

"Poh, child! He has not the sort of ingenuity to invent any-thing better than a Dutch toy," answered her father, who had formerly been put to much vexation by Owen Warland's ir-regular genius. "A plague on such ingenuity! All the effect that ever I knew of it was to spoil the accuracy of some of the best watches in my shop. He would turn the sun out of its orbit and derange the whole course of time, if, as I said before, his inge-nuity could grasp anything bigger than a child's toy!"

"Hush, Father! He hears you," whispered Annie, pressing the old man's arm. "His ears are as delicate as his feelings, and you know how easily disturbed they are. Do let us move on."

So Peter Hovenden and his daughter Annie plodded on, without further conversation, until, in a by-street of the town, they found themselves passing the open door of a blacksmith's shop. Within was seen the forge, now blazing up and illumi-nating the high and dusky roof, and now confining its lustre to a narrow precinct of the coal-strewn floor, according as the breath of the bellows was puffed forth or again inhaled into its vast leathern lungs. In the intervals of brightness, it was easy to distinguish objects in remote corners of the shop, and the horseshoes that hung upon the wall; in the momentary gloom, the fire seemed to be glimmering amidst the vagueness of unenclosed space. Moving about in this red glare and alternate dusk was the figure of the blacksmith, well worthy to be viewed in so picturesque an aspect of light and shade, where the bright blaze struggled with the black night, as if each would have snatched his comely strength from the other. Anon, he drew a white-hot bar of iron from the coals, laid it on the anvil, uplifted his arm of might, and was soon enveloped in the myriads of sparks which the strokes of his hammer scat-tered into the surrounding gloom.

"Now, that is a pleasant sight," said the old watchmaker. "I know what it is to work in gold, but give me the worker in iron, after all is said and done. He spends his labor upon a

16 reality. What say you, daughter Annie?"

"Pray don't speak so loud, Father," whispered Annie. "Robert Danforth will hear you."

"And what if he should hear me?" said Peter Hovenden. "I say again, it is a good and a wholesome thing to depend upon main strength and reality, and to earn one's bread with the bare and brawny arm of a blacksmith. A watchmaker gets his brain puzzled by his wheels within a wheel, or loses his health or the nicety of his eyesight, as was my case, and finds himself at middle age, or a little after, past labor at his own trade, and fit for nothing else, yet too poor to live at his ease. So, I say once again, give me main strength for my money. And then, how it takes the nonsense out of a man! Did you ever hear of a blacksmith being such a fool as Owen Warland, yonder?"

"Well said, Uncle Hovenden!" shouted Robert Danforth, from the forge, in a full, deep, merry voice that made the roof re-echo. "And what says Miss Annie to that doctrine? She, I suppose, will think it a genteeler business to tinker up a lady's watch than to forge a horseshoe or make a gridiron!"

Annie drew her father onward, without giving him time for reply.

But we must return to Owen Warland's shop, and spend more meditation upon his history and character than either Peter Hovenden, or probably his daughter Annie, or Owen's old schoolfellow, Robert Danforth, would have thought due to so slight a subject. From the time that his little fingers could grasp a penknife, Owen had been remarkable for a delicate ingenuity, which sometimes produced pretty shapes in wood, principally figures of flowers and birds, and sometimes seemed to aim at the hidden mysteries of mechanism. But it was always for purposes of grace, and never with any mockery of the useful. He did not, like the crowd of schoolboy artisans, construct little windmills on the angle of a barn, or watermills across the neighboring brook. Those who discovered such peculiarity in the boy as to think it worth their while to observe him closely sometimes saw reason to suppose that he was attempting to imitate the beautiful movements of Nature, as exemplified in the flight of birds or the activity of little animals. It seemed, in fact, a new development of the love of the Beautiful, such as might have made him a poet, a painter, or a sculptor, and which was as completely refined from all utilitarian coarseness as it could have been in either of the fine arts. He looked with singular distaste at the stiff and regular processes of ordinary machinery. Being once carried to see a steam engine, in the expectation that his intuitive comprehension of mechanical principles would be gratified, he turned pale and grew sick, as if something monstrous and unnatural had been presented to him. This horror was partly owing to the size and terrible energy of the iron laborer; for the character of Owen's mind was microscopic, and tended naturally to the minute, in accordance with his diminutive frame, and the marvelous smallness and delicate power of his fingers. Not that his sense of beauty was thereby diminished into a sense of prettiness. The Beautiful Idea has no relation to size, and may be as perfectly developed in a space too minute for any but microscopic investigation as within the ample verge that is measured by the arc of the rainbow. But, at all events, this characteristic minuteness in his objects and accomplishments made the world even more incapable than it might otherwise have been of appreciating Owen Warland's genius. The boy's relatives saw nothing better to be done—as perhaps there was not—than to bind him apprentice to a watchmaker, hoping that his strange ingenuity might thus be regulated and put to utilitarian purposes.

Peter Hovenden's opinion of his apprentice has already been expressed. He could make nothing of the lad. Owen's apprehension of the professional mysteries, it is true, was inconceivably quick. But he altogether forgot or despised the grand object of a watchmaker's business, and cared no more for the measurement of time than if it had been merged into eternity.

18 So long, however, as he remained under his old master's care,
Owen's lack of sturdiness made it possible, by strict injunctions
and sharp oversight, to restrain his creative eccentricity within
bounds. But when his apprenticeship was served out, and he
had taken the little shop which Peter Hovenden's failing eyesight compelled him to relinquish, then did people recognize
how unfit a person was Owen Warland to lead old blind Father
Time along his daily course. One of his most rational projects
was to connect a musical operation with the machinery of his
watches so that all the harsh dissonances of life might be rendered tuneful, and each flitting moment fall into the abyss of
the past in golden drops of harmony. If a family clock was entrusted to him for repair—one of those tall, ancient clocks that
have grown nearly allied to human nature by measuring out
the lifetime of many generations—he would take upon himself
to arrange a dance or funeral procession of figures across its
venerable face, representing twelve mirthful or melancholy
hours. Several freaks of this kind quite destroyed the young
watchmaker's credit with that steady and matter-of-fact class
of people who hold the opinion that time is not to be trifled
with, whether considered as the medium of advancement and
prosperity in this world or preparation for the next. His custom
rapidly diminished—a misfortune, however, that was probably
reckoned among his better accidents by Owen Warland, who
was becoming more and more absorbed in a secret occupation
which drew all his science and manual dexterity into itself,
and likewise gave full employment to the characteristic ten-
dencies of his genius. This pursuit had already consumed many
months.

After the old watchmaker and his pretty daughter had gazed
at him out of the obscurity of the street, Owen Warland was
seized with a fluttering of the nerves, which made his hand
tremble too violently to proceed with such delicate labor as he
was now engaged upon.

"It was Annie herself!" murmured he. "I should have known

it, by this throbbing of my heart, before I heard her father's voice. Ah, how it throbs! I shall scarcely be able to work again on this exquisite mechanism tonight. Annie! Dearest Annie! Thou shouldst give firmness to my heart and hand, and not shake them thus; for if I strive to put the very spirit of Beauty into form and give it motion, it is for thy sake alone. Oh, throbbing heart, be quiet! If my labor be thus thwarted, there will come vague and unsatisfied dreams, which will leave me spiritless tomorrow."

As he was endeavoring to settle himself again to his task, the shop door opened and gave admittance to no other than the stalwart figure which Peter Hovenden had paused to admire, as seen amid the light and shadow of the blacksmith's shop. Robert Danforth had brought a little anvil of his own manufacture, and peculiarly constructed, which the young artist had recently bespoken. Owen examined the article and pronounced it fashioned according to his wish.

"Why, yes," said Robert Danforth, his strong voice filling the shop as with the sound of a bass viol, "I consider myself equal to anything in the way of my own trade; though I should have made but a poor figure at yours, with such a fist as this," added he, laughing, as he laid his vast hand beside the delicate one of Owen. "But what then? I put more main strength into one blow of my sledgehammer than all that you have expended since you were a 'prentice. Is not that the truth?"

"Very probably," answered the low and slender voice of Owen. "Strength is an earthly monster. I make no pretensions to it. My force, whatever there may be of it, is altogether spiritual."

"Well, but, Owen, what are you about!" asked his old schoolfellow, still in such a hearty volume of tone that it made the artist shrink; especially as the question related to a subject so sacred as the absorbing dream of his imagination. "Folks do say that you are trying to discover the perpetual motion."

"The perpetual motion? Nonsense!" replied Owen Warland,

20 with a movement of digust; for he was full of little petulances. "It can never be discovered! It is a dream that may delude men whose brains are mystified with matter, but not me. Besides, if such a discovery were possible, it would not be worth my while to make it, only to have the secret turned to such purposes as are now effected by steam and water power. I am not ambitious to be honored with the paternity of a new kind of cotton machine."

"That would be droll enough!" cried the blacksmith, breaking out into such an uproar of laughter that Owen himself and the bell glasses on his workboard quivered in unison. "No, no, Owen! No child of yours will have iron joints and sinews. Well, I won't hinder you any more. Good night, Owen, and success; and if you need any assistance, so far as a downright blow of hammer upon anvil will answer the purpose, I'm your man!"

And with another laugh the man of main strength left the shop.

"How strange it is," whispered Owen Warland to himself, leaning his head upon his hand, "that all my musings, my purposes, my passion for the Beautiful, my consciousness of power to create it—a finer, more ethereal power, of which this earthly giant can have no conception—all, all, look so vain and idle, whenever my path is crossed by Robert Danforth! He would drive me mad, were I to meet him often. His hard, brute force darkens and confuses the spiritual element within me. But I, too, will be strong in my own way. I will not yield to him!"

He took from beneath a glass a piece of minute machinery, which he set in the condensed light of his lamp, and looking intently at it through a magnifying glass, proceeded to operate with a delicate instrument of steel. In an instant, however, he fell back in his chair and clasped his hands, with a look of horror on his face that made its small features as impressive as those of a giant would have been.

"Heaven! What have I done!" exclaimed he. "The vapor— the influence of that brute force—it has bewildered me and obscured my perception. I have made the very stroke—the fatal stroke—that I have dreaded from the first! It is all over—the toil of months—the object of my life! I am ruined!"

And there he sat, in strange despair, until his lamp flickered in the socket and left the Artist of the Beautiful in darkness.

Thus it is that ideas which grow up within the imagination and appear so lovely to it, and of a value beyond whatever men call valuable, are exposed to be shattered and annihilated by contact with the Practical. It is requisite for the ideal artist to possess a force of character that seems hardly compatible with its delicacy; he must keep his faith in himself while the incredulous world assails him with its utter disbelief; he must stand up against mankind and be his own sole disciple, both as respects his genius and the objects to which it is directed.

For a time, Owen Warland succumbed to this severe but inevitable test. He spent a few sluggish weeks with his head so continually resting in his hands that the townspeople had scarcely an opportunity to see his countenance. When at last it was again uplifted to the light of day, a cold, dull, nameless change was perceptible upon it. In the opinion of Peter Hovenden, however, and that order of sagacious understandings who think that life should be regulated like clockwork, with leaden weights, the alteration was entirely for the better. Owen now, indeed, applied himself to business with dogged industry. It was marvelous to witness the obtuse gravity with which he would inspect the wheels of a great, old silver watch; thereby delighting the owner, in whose fob it had been worn till he deemed it a portion of his own life, and was accordingly jealous of its treatment. In consequence of the good report thus acquired, Owen Warland was invited by the proper authorities to regulate the clock in the church steeple. He succeeded so admirably in this matter of public interest that the merchants gruffly acknowledged his merits on 'Change; the nurse whispered his praises as she gave the potion in the sick chamber; the lover blessed him at the hour of appointed inter-

view; and the town in general thanked Owen for the punc-
tuality of dinner time. In a word, the heavy weight upon his
spirits kept everything in order, not merely within his own system, but wheresoever the iron accents of the church clock
were audible. It was a circumstance, though minute, yet characteristic of his present state, that when employed to engrave
names or initials on silver spoons, he now wrote the requisite
letters in the plainest possible style, omitting a variety of fanciful flourishes that had heretofore distinguished his work in
this kind.

One day, during the era of this happy transformation, old
Peter Hovenden came to visit his former apprentice.

"Well, Owen," said he, "I am glad to hear such good accounts of you from all quarters, and especially from the town
clock yonder, which speaks in your commendation every hour
of the twenty-four. Only get rid altogether of your nonsensical
trash about the Beautiful, which I, nor nobody else, nor yourself to boot, could ever understand—only free yourself of that,
and your success in life is as sure as daylight. Why, if you go on
in this way, I should even venture to let you doctor this precious old watch of mine; though, except my daughter Annie, I
have nothing else so valuable in the world."

"I should hardly dare touch it, sir," replied Owen in a depressed tone; for he was weighed down by his old master's
presence.

"In time," said the latter, "in time, you will be capable of
it."

The old watchmaker, with the freedom naturally con-
sequent on his former authority, went on inspecting the work
which Owen had in hand at the moment, together with other
matters that were in progress. The artist, meanwhile, could
scarcely lift his head. There was nothing so antipodal to his nature as this man's cold, unimaginative sagacity, by contact
with which everything was converted into a dream except the
densest matter of the physical world. Owen groaned in spirit

and prayed fervently to be delivered from him.

"But what is this?" cried Peter Hovenden abruptly, taking up a dusty bell glass, beneath which appeared a mechanical something, as delicate and minute as the system of a butterfly's anatomy. "What have we here? Owen! Owen! There is witchcraft in these little chains, and wheels, and paddles! See! With one pinch of my finger and thumb I am going to deliver you from all future peril."

"For heaven's sake," screamed Owen Warland, springing up with wonderful energy, "as you would not drive me mad—do not touch it! The slightest pressure of your finger would ruin me forever."

"Aha, young man! And is it so?" said the old watchmaker, looking at him with just enough of penetration to torture Owen's soul with the bitterness of worldly criticism. "Well, take your own course. But I warn you again that in this small piece of mechanism lives your evil spirit. Shall I exorcise him?"

"You are my evil spirit," answered Owen, much excited·"you, and the hard, coarse world! The leaden thoughts and the despondency that you fling upon me are my clogs. Else, I should long ago have achieved the task that I was created for."

Peter Hovenden shook his head with the mixture of contempt and indignation which mankind, of whom he was partly a representative, deem themselves entitled to feel towards all simpletons who seek other prizes than the dusty one along the highway. He then took his leave with an uplifted finger and a sneer upon his face that haunted the artist's dreams for many a night afterwards. At the time of his old master's visit, Owen was probably on the point of taking up the relinquished task; but by this sinister event he was thrown back into the state whence he had been slowly emerging.

But the innate tendency of his soul had only been accumulating fresh vigor during its apparent sluggishness. As the summer advanced, he almost totally relinquished his business and permitted Father Time, so far as the old gentleman was represented by the clocks and watches under his control, to stray at random through human life, making infinite confusion among the train of bewildered hours. He wasted the sunshine, as people said, in wandering through the woods and fields and along the banks of streams. There, like a child, he found amusement in chasing butterflies, or watching the motions of water insects. There was something truly mysterious in the intentness with which he contemplated these living playthings as they sported on the breeze; or examined the structure of an imperial insect whom he had imprisoned. The chase of butterflies was an apt emblem of the ideal pursuit in which he had spent so many golden hours. But would the Beautiful Idea ever be yielded to his hand, like the butterfly that symbolized it? Sweet, doubtless, were these days, and congenial to the artist's soul. They were full of bright conceptions, which gleamed through his intellectual world as the butterflies gleamed through the outward atmosphere and were real to him for the instant, without the toil, and perplexity, and many disappointments of attempting to make them visible to the sensual eye. Alas, that the artist, whether in poetry or whatever other material, may not content himself with the inward enjoyment of the Beautiful, but must chase the flitting mystery beyond the verge of his ethereal domain and crush its frail being in seizing it with a material grasp. Owen Warland felt the impluse to give external reality to his ideas as irresistibly as any of the poets or painters, who have arrayed the world in a dimmer and fainter beauty, imperfectly copied from the richness of their visions.

The night was now his time for the slow progress of re-creating the one idea to which all his intellectual activity referred itself. Always at the approach of dusk, he stole into the town, locked himself within his shop, and wrought with patient delicacy of touch for many hours. Sometimes he was startled by the rap of the watchman, who, when all the world should be asleep, had caught the gleam of lamplight through the crevices of Owen Warland's shutters. Daylight, to the morbid sensibility of his mind, seemed to have an intrusiveness that interfered with his pursuits. On cloudy and inclement days, therefore, he sat with his head upon his hands, muffling, as it were, his sensitive brain in a mist of indefinite musings; for it was a relief to escape from the sharp distinctness with which he was compelled to shape out his thoughts during his nightly toil.

From one of these fits of torpor, he was aroused by the entrance of Annie Hovenden, who came into the shop with the freedom of a customer, and also with something of the familiarity of a childish friend. She had worn a hole through her silver thimble and wanted Owen to repair it.

"But I don't know whether you will condescend to such a task," said she, laughing, "now that you are so taken up with the notion of putting spirit into machinery."

"Where did you get that idea, Annie?" said Owen, starting in surprise.

"Oh, out of my own head," answered she, "and from something that I heard you say, long ago, when you were but a boy and I a little child. But come! Will you mend this poor thimble of mine?"

"Anything for your sake, Annie," said Owen Warland— "anything; even were it to work at Robert Danforth's forge."

"And that would be a pretty sight!" retorted Annie, glancing with imperceptible slightness at the artist's small and slender frame. "Well, here is the thimble."

"But that is a strange idea of yours," said Owen, "about the spiritualization of matter."

And then the thought stole into his mind that this young girl possessed the gift to comprehend him better than all the world beside. And what a help and strength would it be to him, in his lonely toil, if he could gain the sympathy of the only being whom he loved! To persons whose pursuits are insulated from

26 the common business of life—who are either in advance of mankind or apart from it—there often comes a sensation of moral cold that makes the spirit shiver, as if it had reached the frozen solitudes around the pole. What the prophet, the poet, the reformer, the criminal, or any other man with human yearnings, but separated from the multitude by a peculiar lot, might feel, poor Owen Warland felt.

"Annie," cried he, growing pale as death at the thought, "how gladly would I tell you the secret of my pursuit! You, methinks, would estimate it rightly. You, I know, would hear it with a reverence that I must not expect from the harsh, material world."

"Would I not? To be sure I would!" replied Annie Hovenden, lightly laughing. "Come; explain to me quickly what is the meaning of this little whirligig, so delicately wrought that it might be a plaything for Queen Mab. See, I will put it in motion."

"Hold!" exclaimed Owen, "hold!"

Annie had but given the slightest possible touch, with the point of a needle, to the same minute portion of complicated machinery which has been more than once mentioned, when the artist seized her by the wrist with a force that made her scream aloud. She was affrighted at the convulsion of intense rage and anguish that writhed across his features. The next instant he let his head sink upon his hands.

"Go, Annie," murmured he, "I have deceived myself and must suffer for it. I yearned for sympathy—and thought—and fancied—and dreamed—that you might give it me. But you lack the talisman, Annie, that should admit you into my secrets. That touch has undone the toil of months and the thought of a lifetime! It was not your fault, Annie—but you have ruined me!"

Poor Owen Warland! He had indeed erred, yet pardonably; for if any human spirit could have sufficiently reverenced the processes so sacred in his eyes, it must have been a woman's.

Even Annie Hovenden, possibly, might not have disappointed him had she been enlightened by the deep intelligence of love.

The artist spent the ensuing winter in a way that satisfied any persons who had hitherto retained a hopeful opinion of him that he was, in truth, irrevocably doomed to inutility as regarded the world and to an evil destiny on his own part. The decease of a relative had put him in possession of a small inheritance. Thus freed from the necessity of toil, and having lost the steadfast influence of a great purpose—great, at least to him—he abandoned himself to habits from which, it might have been supposed, the mere delicacy of his organization would have availed to secure him. But when the ethereal portion of a man of genius is obscured, the earthly part assumes an influence the more uncontrollable, because the character is now thrown off the balance to which Providence had so nicely adjusted it, and which, in coarser natures, is adjusted by some other method. Owen Warland made proof of whatever show of bliss may be found in riot. He looked at the world through the golden medium of wine, and contemplated the visions that bubble up so gaily around the brim of the glass, and that people the air with shapes of pleasant madness, which so soon grow ghostly and forlorn. Even when this dismal and inevitable change had taken place, the young man might still have continued to quaff the cup of enchantments, though its vapor did but shroud life in gloom and fill the gloom with spectres that mocked at him. There was a certain irksomeness of spirit, which, being real, and the deepest sensation of which the artist was now conscious, was more intolerable than any fantastic miseries and horrors that the abuse of wine could summon up. In the latter case, he could remember, even out of the midst of his trouble, that all was but a delusion; in the former, the heavy anguish was his actual life.

From this perilous state he was redeemed by an incident which more than one person witnessed, but of which the shrewdest could not explain or conjecture the operation on

28 Owen Warland's mind. It was very simple. On a warm afternoon of spring, as the artist sat among his riotous companions with a glass of wine before him, a splendid butterfly flew in at the open window and fluttered about his head.

"Ah!" exclaimed Owen, who had drank freely, "are you alive again, child of the sun, and playmate of the summer breeze, after your dismal winter's nap? Then it is time for me to be at work!"

And leaving his unemptied glass upon the table, he departed and was never known to sip another drop of wine.

And now, again, he resumed his wanderings in the woods and fields. It might be fancied that the bright butterfly, which had come so spiritlike into the window as Owen sat with the rude revellers, was indeed a spirit, commissioned to recall him to the pure, ideal life that had so etherealized him among men. It might be fancied that he went forth to seek this spirit in its sunny haunts; for still, as in the summertime gone by, he was seen to steal gently up wherever a butterfly had alighted, and lose himself in contemplation of it. When it took flight, his eyes followed the winged vision, as if its airy track would show the path to heaven. But what could be the purpose of the unseasonable toil, which was again resumed, as the watchman knew by the lines of lamplight through the crevices of Owen Warland's shutters? The townspeople had one comprehensive explanation of all these singularities. Owen Warland had gone mad! How universally efficacious—how satisfactory, too, and soothing to the injured sensibility of narrowness and dullness—is this easy method of accounting for whatever lies beyond the world's most ordinary scope! From Saint Paul's days, down to our poor little Artist of the Beautiful, the same talisman has been applied to the elucidation of all mysteries in the words or deeds of men who spoke or acted too wisely or too well. In Owen Warland's case, the judgment of his townspeople may have been correct. Perhaps he was mad. The lack of sympathy—that contrast between himself and his neighbors which took away the restraint of example—was enough to make him so. Or possibly, he had caught just so much of ethereal radiance as served to bewilder him, in an earthly sense, by its intermixture with the common daylight.

One evening, when the artist had returned from a customary ramble and had just thrown the lustre of his lamp on the delicate piece of work, so often interrupted but still taken up again, as if his fate were embodied in its mechanism, he was surprised by the entrance of old Peter Hovenden. Owen never met this man without a shrinking of the heart. Of all the world, he was most terrible, by reason of a keen understanding which saw so distinctly what it did see, and disbelieved so uncompromisingly in what it could not see. On this occasion, the old watchmaker had merely a gracious word or two to say.

"Owen, my lad," said he, "we must see you at my house tomorrow night."

The artist began to mutter some excuse.

"Oh, but it must be so," quoth Peter Hovenden, "for the sake of the days when you were one of the household. What, my boy, don't you know that my daughter Annie is engaged to Robert Danforth? We are making an entertainment, in our humble way, to celebrate the event."

"Ah!" said Owen.

That little monosyllable was all he uttered; its tone seemed cold and unconcerned to an ear like Peter Hovenden's; and yet there was in it the stifled outcry of the poor artist's heart, which he compressed within him like a man holding down an evil spirit. One slight outbreak, however, imperceptible to the old watchmaker, he allowed himself. Raising the instrument with which he was about to begin his work, he let it fall upon the little system of machinery that had, anew, cost him months of thought and toil. It was shattered by the stroke!

Owen Warland's story would have been no tolerable representation of the troubled life of those who strive to create the Beautiful, if, amid all other thwarting influences, love had not

30 interposed to steal the cunning from his hand. Outwardly, he had been no ardent or enterprising lover; the career of his passion had confined its tumults and vicissitudes so entirely within the artist's imagination that Annie herself had scarcely more than a woman's intuitive perception of it. But, in Owen's view, it covered the whole field of his life. Forgetful of the time when she had shown herself incapable of any deep response, he had persisted in connecting all his dreams of artistical success with Annie's image; she was the visible shape in which the spiritual power that he worshipped, and on whose altar he hoped to lay a not unworthy offering, was made manifest to him. Of course he had deceived himself; there were no such attributes in Annie Hovenden as his imagination had endowed her with. She, in the aspect which she wore to his inward vision, was as much a creation of his own as the mysterious piece of mechanism would be were it ever realized. Had he become convinced of his mistake through the medium of successful love; had he won Annie to his bosom, and there beheld her fade from angel into ordinary woman, the disappointment might have driven him back, with concentrated energy, upon his sole remaining object. On the other hand, had he found Annie what he fancied, his lot would have been so rich in beauty that out of its mere redundancy he might have wrought the Beautiful into many a worthier type than he had toiled for. But the guise in which his sorrow came to him, the sense that the angel of his life had been snatched away and given to a rude man of earth and iron, who could neither need nor appreciate her ministrations; this was the very perversity of fate, that makes human existence appear too absurd and contradictory to be the scene of one other hope or one other fear. There was nothing left for Owen Warland but to sit down like a man that had been stunned.

He went through a fit of illness. After his recovery, his small and slender frame assumed an obtuser garniture of flesh than it had ever before worn. His thin cheeks became round; his delicate little hand, so spiritually fashioned to achieve fairy task-work, grew plumper than the hand of a thriving infant. His aspect had a childishness, such as might have induced a stranger to pat him on the head—pausing, however, in the act, to wonder what manner of child was here. It was as if the spirit had gone out of him, leaving the body to flourish in a sort of vegetable existence. Not that Owen Warland was idiotic. He could talk, and not irrationally. Somewhat of a babbler, indeed, did people begin to think him; for he was apt to discourse at wearisome length of marvels of mechanism that he had read about in books, but which he had learned to consider as absolutely fabulous. Among them he enumerated the Man of Brass, constructed by Albertus Magnus, and the Brazen Head of Friar Bacon; and, coming down to later times, the automata of a little coach and horses, which, it was pretended, had been manufactured for the Dauphin of France; together with an insect that buzzed about the ear like a living fly and yet was but a contrivance of minute steel springs. There was a story, too, of a duck that waddled, and quacked, and ate; though, had any honest citizen purchased it for dinner, he would have found himself cheated with the mere mechanical apparition of a duck.

"But all these accounts," said Owen Warland, "I am now satisfied, are mere impositions."

Then, in a mysterious way, he would confess that he once thought differently. In his idle and dreamy days, he had considered it possible, in a certain sense, to spiritualize machinery and to combine with the new species of life and motion, thus produced, a beauty that should attain to the ideal which Nature has proposed to herself in all her creatures, but has never taken pains to realize. He seemed, however, to retain no very distinct perception either of the process of achieving this object or of the design itself.

"I have thrown it all aside now," he would say. "It was a dream, such as young men are always mystifying themselves with. Now that I have acquired a little common sense, it makes me laugh to think of it."

Poor, poor, and fallen Owen Warland! These were the symptoms that he had ceased to be an inhabitant of the better sphere that lies unseen around us. He had lost his faith in the invisible and now prided himself, as such unfortunates invariably do, in the wisdom which rejected much that even his eye could see, and trusted confidently in nothing but what his hand could touch. This is the calamity of men whose spiritual part dies out of them and leaves the grosser understanding to assimilate them more and more to the things of which alone it can take cognizance. But in Owen Warland the spirit was not dead, nor passed away; it only slept.

How it awoke again is not recorded. Perhaps the torpid slumber was broken by a convulsive pain. Perhaps, as in a former instance, the butterfly came and hovered about his head and reinspired him—as, indeed, the creature of the sunshine had always a mysterious mission for the artist—reinspired him with the former purpose of his life. Whether it were pain or happiness that thrilled through his veins, his first impluse was to thank heaven for rendering him again the being of thought, imagination, and keenest sensibility that he had long ceased to be.

"Now for my task," said he. "Never did I feel such strength for it as now."

Yet, strong as he felt himself, he was incited to toil the more diligently by an anxiety lest death should surprise him in the midst of his labors. This anxiety, perhaps, is common to all men who set their hearts upon anything so high, in their own view of it, that life becomes of importance only as conditional to its accomplishment. So long as we love life for itself, we seldom dread the losing it. When we desire life for the attainment of an object, we recognize the frailty of its texture. But side by side with this sense of insecurity, there is a vital faith in our invulnerability to the shaft of death, while engaged in any task that seems assigned by Providence as our proper thing to do, and which the world would have cause to mourn for, should we leave it unaccomplished. Can the philosopher, big with the inspiration of an idea that is to reform mankind, believe that he is to be beckoned from this sensible existence at the very instant when he is mustering his breath to speak the word of light? Should he perish so, the weary ages may pass away—the world's whole life-sand may fall, drop by drop—before another intellect is prepared to develop the truth that might have been uttered then. But history affords many an example where the most precious spirit, at any particular epoch manifested in human shape, has gone hence untimely, without space allowed him, so far as mortal judgment could discern, to perform his mission on the earth. The prophet dies; and the man of torpid heart and sluggish brain lives on. The poet leaves his song half-sung, or finishes it, beyond the scope of mortal ears, in a celestial choir. The painter—as Allston did—leaves half his conception on the canvas, to sadden us with its imperfect beauty, and goes to picture forth the whole, if it be no irreverence to say so, in the hues of heaven. But, rather, such incomplete designs of this life will be perfected nowhere. This so frequent abortion of man's dearest projects must be taken as a proof that the deeds of earth, however etherealized by piety or genius, are without value, except as exercises and manifestations of the spirit. In heaven, all ordinary thought is higher and more melodious than Milton's song. Then, would he add another verse to any strain that he had left unfinished here?

But to return to Owen Warland. It was his fortune, good or ill, to achieve the purpose of his life. Pass we over a long space of intense thought, yearning effort, minute toil, and wasting anxiety, succeeded by an instant of solitary triumph; let all this be imagined; and then behold the artist, on a winter evening, seeking admittance to Robert Danforth's fireside circle. There he found the man of iron, with his massive substance thor-

34 oughly warmed and attempered by domestic influences. And
there was Annie, too, now transformed into a matron, with
much of her husband's plain and sturdy nature, but imbued, as
Owen Warland still believed, with a finer grace that might enable her to be the interpreter between Strength and Beauty. It
happened, likewise, that old Peter Hovenden was a guest this
evening at his daughter's fireside; and it was his well-remem-
bered expression of keen, cold criticism that first encountered
the artist's glance.

"My old friend Owen!" cried Robert Danforth, starting up,
and compressing the artist's delicate fingers within a hand that
was accustomed to gripe bars of iron. "This is kind and neighborly, to come to us at last! I was afraid your perpetual motion
had bewitched you out of the remembrance of old times."

"We are glad to see you!" said Annie, while a blush reddened her matronly cheek. "It was not like a friend, to stay
from us so long."

"Well, Owen," inquired the old watchmaker, as his first
greeting, "how comes on the Beautiful? Have you created it at
last?"

The artist did not immediately reply, being startled by the
apparition of a young child of strength that was tumbling
about on the carpet—a little personage who had come myster-
iously out of the infinite, but with something so sturdy and real
in his composition that he seemed moulded out of the densest
substance which earth could supply. This hopeful infant
crawled towards the newcomer, and setting himself on end—as
Robert Danforth expressed the posture—stared at Owen with a
look of such sagacious observation that the mother could not
help exchanging a proud glance with her husband. But the artist was disturbed by the child's look, as imagining a resemblance between it and Peter Hovenden's habitual expression.
He could have fancied that the old watchmaker was compressed into this baby shape, and looking out of those baby
eyes, and repeating—as he now did—the malicious question:

"The Beautiful, Owen! How comes on the Beautiful? Have you succeeded in creating the Beautiful?"

"I have succeeded," replied the artist, with a momentary light of triumph in his eyes and a smile of sunshine, yet steeped in such depth of thought that it was almost sadness. "Yes, my friends, it is the truth. I have succeeded!"

"Indeed!" cried Annie, a look of maiden mirthfulness peeping out of her face again. "And is it lawful, now, to inquire what the secret is?"

"Surely; it is to disclose it that I have come," answered Owen Warland. "You shall know, and see, and touch, and possess the secret! For Annie—if by that name I may still address the friend of my boyish years—Annie, it is for your bridal gift that I have wrought this spiritualized mechanism, this harmony of motion, this Mystery of Beauty! It comes late, indeed; but it is as we go onward in life, when objects begin to lose their freshness of hue and our souls their delicacy of perception, that the spirit of Beauty is most needed. If—forgive me, Annie—if you know how to value this gift, it can never come too late!"

He produced, as he spoke, what seemed a jewel box. It was carved richly out of ebony by his own hand, and inlaid with a fanciful tracery of pearl, representing a boy in pursuit of a butterfly, which, elsewhere, had become a winged spirit and was flying heavenward; while the boy, or youth, had found such efficacy in his strong desire that he ascended from earth to cloud, and from cloud to celestial atmosphere, to win the Beautiful. This case of ebony the artist opened, and bade Annie place her finger on its edge. She did so, but almost screamed as a butterfly fluttered forth, and alighting on her finger's tip, sat waving the ample magnificence of its purple and gold-speckled wings, as if in prelude to a flight. It is impossible to express by words the glory, the splendor, the delicate gorgeousness which were softened into the beauty of this object. Nature's ideal butterfly was here realized in all its per-

36 fection; not in the pattern of such faded insects as flit among earthly flowers, but of those which hover across the meads of paradise, for child-angels and the spirits of departed infants to disport themselves with. The rich down was visible upon its wings; the lustre of its eyes seemed instinct with spirit. The firelight glimmered around this wonder—the candles gleamed upon it—but it glistened apparently by its own radiance and illuminated the finger and outstretched hand on which it rested with a white gleam like that of precious stones. In its perfect beauty, the consideration of size was entirely lost. Had its wings overreached the firmament, the mind could not have been more filled or satisfied.

"Beautiful! Beautiful!" exclaimed Annie. "Is it alive? Is it alive?"

"Alive? To be sure it is," answered her husband. "Do you suppose any mortal has skill enough to make a butterfly, or would put himself to the trouble of making one, when any child may catch a score of them in a summer's afternoon? Alive? Certainly! But this pretty box is undoubtedly of our friend Owen's manufacture; and really it does him credit."

At this moment, the butterfly waved its wings anew, with a motion so absolutely lifelike that Annie was startled, and even awestricken; for, in spite of her husband's opinion, she could not satisfy herself whether it was indeed a living creature or a piece of wondrous mechanism.

"Is it alive?" she repeated, more earnestly than before.

"Judge for yourself," said Owen Warland, who stood gazing in her face with fixed attention.

The butterfly now flung itself upon the air, fluttered round Annie's head, and soared into a distant region of the parlor, still making itself perceptible to sight by the starry gleam in which the motion of its wings enveloped it. The infant on the floor followed its course with his sagacious little eyes. After flying about the room, it returned, in a spiral curve, and settled again on Annie's finger.

"But is it alive?" exclaimed she again; and the finger on which the gorgeous mystery had alighted was so tremulous that the butterfly was forced to balance himself with his wings. "Tell me if it be alive, or whether you created it?"

"Wherefore ask who created it, so it be beautiful?" replied Owen Warland. "Alive? Yes, Annie; it may well be said to possess life, for it absorbed my own being into itself; and in the secret of that butterfly, and in its beauty—which is not merely outward, but deep as its whole system—is represented the intellect, the imagination, the sensibility, the soul of an Artist of the Beautiful! Yes, I created it. But"—and here his countenance somewhat changed—"this butterfly is not now to me what it was when I beheld it afar off, in the daydreams of my youth."

"Be it what it may, it is a pretty plaything," said the blacksmith, grinning with childlike delight. "I wonder whether it would condescend to alight on such a great clumsy finger as mine? Hold it hither, Annie!"

By the artist's direction, Annie touched her finger's tip to that of her husband; and, after a momentary delay, the butterfly fluttered from one to the other. It preluded a second flight by a similar, yet not precisely the same, waving of wings as in the first experiment; then, ascending from the blacksmith's stalwart finger, it rose in a gradually enlarging curve to the ceiling, made one wide sweep around the room, and returned with an undulating movement to the point whence it had started.

"Well, that does beat all nature!" cried Robert Danforth, bestowing the heartiest praise that he could find expression for; and, indeed, had he paused there, a man of finer words and nicer perception could not easily have said more. "That goes beyond me, I confess! But what then? There is more real use in one downright blow of my sledgehammer than in the whole five years' labor that our friend Owen has wasted on this butterfly!"

38   Here the child clapped his hands and made a great babble of indistinct utterance, apparently demanding that the butterfly should be given him for a plaything.

Owen Warland, meanwhile, glanced sidelong at Annie, to discover whether she sympathized in her husband's estimate of the comparative value of the Beautiful and the Practical. There was, amid all her kindness towards himself, amid all the wonder and admiration with which she contemplated the marvelous work of his hands and incarnation of his idea, a secret scorn—too secret, perhaps, for her own consciousness and perceptible only to such intuitive discernment as that of the artist. But Owen, in the latter stages of his pursuit, had risen out of the region in which such a discovery might have been torture. He knew that the world, and Annie as the representative of the world, whatever praise might be bestowed, could never say the fitting word nor feel the fitting sentiment which should be the perfect recompense of an artist who, symbolizing a lofty moral by a material trifle—converting what was earthly to spiritual gold—had won the Beautiful into his handiwork. Not at this latest moment was he to learn that the reward of all high performance must be sought within itself, or sought in vain. There was, however, a view of the matter, which Annie and her husband, and even Peter Hovenden, might fully have understood, and which would have satisfied them that the toil of years had here been worthily bestowed. Owen Warland might have told them that this butterfly, this plaything, this bridal gift of a poor watchmaker to a blacksmith's wife, was, in truth, a gem of art that a monarch would have purchased with honors and abundant wealth, and have treasured it among the jewels of his kingdom as the most unique and wondrous of them all! But the artist smiled and kept the secret to himself.

"Father," said Annie, thinking that a word of praise from the old watchmaker might gratify his former apprentice, "do come and admire this pretty butterfly!"

"Let us see," said Peter Hovenden, rising from his chair,

with a sneer upon his face that always made people doubt, as he himself did, in everything but a material existence. "Here is my finger for it to alight upon. I shall understand it better when once I have touched it."

But, to the increased astonishment of Annie, when the tip of her father's finger was pressed against that of her husband, on which the butterfly still rested, the insect drooped its wings and seemed on the point of falling to the floor. Even the bright spots of gold upon its wings and body, unless her eyes deceived her, grew dim, and the glowing purple took a dusky hue, and the starry lustre that gleamed around the blacksmith's hand became faint and vanished.

"It is dying! It is dying!" cried Annie, in alarm.

"It has been delicately wrought," said the artist calmly. "As I told you, it has imbibed a spiritual essence—call it magnetism, or what you will. In an atmosphere of doubt and mockery, its exquisite susceptibility suffers torture, as does the soul of him who instilled his own life into it. It has already lost its beauty; in a few moments more its mechanism would be irreparably injured."

"Take away your hand, Father!" entreated Annie, turning pale. "Here is my child; let it rest on his innocent hand. There, perhaps, its life will revive, and its colors grow brighter than ever."

Her father, with an acrid smile, withdrew his finger. The butterfly then appeared to recover the power of voluntary motion; while its hues assumed much of their original lustre, and the gleam of starlight, which was its most ethereal attribute, again formed a halo round about it. At first, when transferred from Robert Danforth's hand to the small finger of the child, this radiance grew so powerful that it positively threw the little fellow's shadow back against the wall. He, meanwhile, extended his plump hand as he had seen his father and mother do and watched the waving of the insect's wings with infantine delight. Nevertheless, there was a certain odd expression of sa-

40   gacity that made Owen Warland feel as if here were old Peter Hovenden, partially, and but partially, redeemed from his hard skepticism into childish faith.

"How wise the little monkey looks!" whispered Robert Danforth to his wife.

"I never saw such a look on a child's face," answered Annie, admiring her own infant, and with good reason, far more than the artistic butterfly. "The darling knows more of the mystery than we do."

As if the butterfly, like the artist, were conscious of something not entirely congenial in the child's nature, it alternately sparkled and grew dim. At length, it arose from the small hand of the infant with an airy motion that seemed to bear it upward without an effort, as if the ethereal instincts with which its master's spirit had endowed it impelled this fair vision involuntarily to a higher sphere. Had there been no obstruction, it might have soared into the sky and grown immortal. But its lustre gleamed upon the ceiling; the exquisite texture of its wings brushed against that earthly medium; and a sparkle or two, as of stardust, floated downward and lay glimmering on the carpet. Then the butterfly came fluttering down and instead of returning to the infant was apparently attracted towards the artist's hand.

"Not so, not so!" murmured Owen Warland, as if his handiwork could have understood him. "Thou hast gone forth out of thy master's heart. There is no return for thee!"

With a wavering movement and emitting a tremulous radiance, the butterfly struggled, as it were, towards the infant and was about to alight upon his finger. But while it still hovered in the air, the little child of strength, with his grandsire's sharp and shrewd expression in his face, made a snatch at the marvelous insect, and compressed it in his hand. Annie screamed! Old Peter Hovenden burst into a cold and scornful laugh. The blacksmith, by main force, unclosed the infant's hand and found within the palm a small heap of glittering fragments, whence the Mystery of Beauty had fled forever. And as for Owen Warland, he looked placidly at what seemed the ruin of his life's labor, and which was yet no ruin. He had caught a far other butterfly than this. When the artist rose high enough to achieve the Beautiful, the symbol by which he made it perceptible to mortal senses became of little value in his eyes, while his spirit possessed itself in the enjoyment of the reality.

SETTING

Since people do not move about in a timeless, spaceless void, an author has to select a particular time and place for a story's characters. The time and place make up the setting of the story. The setting should serve to make everything in the story believable.

The author can choose an actual place or a purely imaginary one. For example, "A White Heron" takes place in a woodland near the sea, a setting similar to the Maine the author knew. But the setting of "The Lady or the Tiger?" is more like the "once upon a time in a kingdom far away" of a fairy tale. The historical context of "The Pit and the Pendulum" gives the story's terror a framework of reality. In "The Outcasts of Poker Flat," the hostility of the natural environment parallels the hostility and intolerance of the townspeople. The time and place of a story can even be psychological, existing within a character's mind.

Setting is crucial to a story. In many cases, changing the setting would greatly alter what a story's characters could or could not do. The stories in this section rely heavily on setting. The reader should try to see how the settings influence the characters and their actions and judge whether each author has created a world that seems real.

A WHITE HERON

Sarah Orne Jewett

1

The woods were already filled with shadows one June evening,
just before eight o'clock, though a bright sunset still glimmered faintly among the trunks of the trees. A little girl was
driving home her cow, a plodding, dilatory, provoking creature
in her behavior, but a valued companion for all that. They
were going away from the western light, and striking deep into
the dark woods, but their feet were familiar with the path, and
it was no matter whether their eyes could see it or not.

There was hardly a night the summer through when the old
cow could be found waiting at the pasture bars; on the contrary, it was her greatest pleasure to hide herself away among
the high huckleberry bushes, and though she wore a loud bell
she had made the discovery that if one stood perfectly still it
would not ring. So Sylvia had to hunt for her until she found
her, and call Co'! Co'! with never an answering Moo, until her
childish patience was quite spent. If the creature had not
given good milk and plenty of it, the case would have seemed
very different to her owners. Besides, Sylvia had all the time
there was, and very little use to make of it. Sometimes in pleasant weather it was a consolation to look upon the cow's pranks
as an intelligent attempt to play hide-and-seek, and as the
child had no playmates she lent herself to this amusement with

46   a good deal of zest. Though this chase had been so long that the wary animal herself had given an unusual signal of her whereabouts, Sylvia had only laughed when she came upon Mistress Moolly at the swamp-side, and urged her affectionately homeward with a twig of birch leaves. The old cow was not inclined to wander farther; she even turned in the right direction for once as they left the pasture, and stepped along the road at a good pace. She was quite ready to be milked now, and seldom stopped to browse. Sylvia wondered what her grandmother would say because they were so late. It was a great while since she had left home at half past five o'clock, but everybody knew the difficulty of making this errand a short one. Mrs. Tilley had chased the hornéd torment too many summer evenings herself to blame anyone else for lingering, and was only thankful as she waited that she had Sylvia, nowadays, to give such valuable assistance. The good woman suspected that Sylvia loitered occasionally on her own account; there never was such a child for straying about out-of-doors since the world was made! Everybody said that it was a good change for a little maid who had tried to grow for eight years in a crowded manufacturing town, but, as for Sylvia herself, it seemed as if she never had been alive at all before she came to live at the farm. She thought often with wistful compassion of a wretched dry geranium that belonged to a town neighbor.

" 'Afraid of folks,' " old Mrs. Tilley said to herself, with a smile, after she had made the unlikely choice of Sylvia from her daughter's houseful of children, and was returning to the farm. " 'Afraid of folks,' they said! I guess she won't be troubled no great with 'em up to the old place!" When they reached the door of the lonely house and stopped to unlock it, and the cat came to purr loudly and rub against them—a deserted pussy, indeed, but fat with young robins—Sylvia whispered that this was a beautiful place to live in, and she never should wish to go home.

. . .

The companions followed the shady woodroad, the cow taking slow steps, and the child very fast ones. The cow stopped
long at the brook to drink, as if the pasture were not half a
swamp, and Sylvia stood still and waited, letting her bare feet
cool themselves in the shoal water, while the great twilight
moths struck softly against her. She waded on through the
brook as the cow moved away, and listened to the thrushes
with a heart that beat fast with pleasure. There was a stirring
in the great boughs overhead. They were full of little birds and
beasts that seemed to be wide awake, and going about their
world, or else saying good-night to each other in sleepy twit-
ters. Sylvia herself felt sleepy as she walked along. However, it
was not much farther to the house, and the air was soft and
sweet. She was not often in the woods so late as this, and it
made her feel as if she were a part of the gray shadows and the
moving leaves. She was just thinking how long it seemed since
she first came to the farm a year ago, and wondering if everything went on in the noisy town just the same as when she was
there; the thought of the great red-faced boy who used to
chase and frighten her made her hurry along the path to escape from the shadow of the trees.

Suddenly this little woods-girl is horror-stricken to hear a
clear whistle not very far away. Not a bird's whistle, which
would have a sort of friendliness, but a boy's whistle, determined, and somewhat aggressive. Sylvia left the cow to whatever sad fate might await her, and stepped discreetly aside
into the bushes, but she was just too late. The enemy had discovered her, and called out in a very cheerful and persuasive
tone, "Halloa, little girl, how far is it to the road?" and trembling Sylvia answered almost inaudibly, "A good ways."

She did not dare to look boldly at the tall young man, who
carried a gun over his shoulder, but she came out of her bush
and again followed the cow, while he walked alongside.

"I have been hunting for some birds," the stranger said kindly, "and I have lost my way, and need a friend very much. Don't be afraid," he added gallantly. "Speak up and tell me what your name is, and whether you think I can spend the night at your house, and go out gunning early in the morning."

Sylvia was more alarmed than before. Would not her grandmother consider her much to blame? But who could have foreseen such an accident as this? It did not appear to be her fault, and she hung her head as if the stem of it were broken, but managed to answer "Sylvy" with much effort when her companion again asked her name.

Mrs. Tilley was standing in the doorway when the trio came into view. The cow gave a loud moo by way of explanation.

"Yes, you'd better speak up for yourself, you old trial! Where'd she tucked herself away this time, Sylvy?" Sylvia kept an awed silence; she knew by instinct that her grandmother did not comprehend the gravity of the situation. She must be mistaking the stranger for one of the farmer lads of the region.

The young man stood his gun beside the door and dropped a heavy game bag beside it; then he bade Mrs. Tilley good-evening, and repeated his wayfarer's story, and asked if he could have a night's lodging.

"Put me anywhere you like," he said. "I must be off early in the morning, before day; but I am very hungry, indeed. You can give me some milk at any rate, that's plain."

"Dear sakes, yes," responded the hostess, whose long-slumbering hospitality seemed to be easily awakened. "You might fare better if you went out on the main road a mile or so, but you're welcome to what we've got. I'll milk right off, and you make yourself at home. You can sleep on husks or feathers," she proffered graciously. "I raised them all myself. There's good pasturing for geese just below here towards the ma'sh. Now step round and set a plate for the gentleman, Sylvy!" And Sylvia promptly stepped. She was glad to have something to do, and she was hungry herself.

It was a surprise to find so clean and comfortable a little dwelling in this New England wilderness. The young man had known the horrors of its most primitive housekeeping and the dreary squalor of that level of society which does not rebel at the companionship of hens. This was the best thrift of an old-fashioned farmstead, though on such a small scale that it seemed like a hermitage. He listened eagerly to the old woman's quaint talk; he watched Sylvia's pale face and shining gray eyes with ever-growing enthusiasm, and insisted that this was the best supper he had eaten for a month; then, afterward, the new-made friends sat down in the doorway together while the moon came up.

Soon it would be berry time, and Sylvia was a great help at picking. The cow was a good milker, though a plaguy thing to keep track of, the hostess gossiped frankly, adding presently that she had buried four children, so that Sylvia's mother and a son (who might be dead) in California were all the children she had left. "Dan, my boy, was a great hand to go gunning," she explained sadly. "I never wanted for pa'tridges or gray squer'ls while he was to home. He's been a great wand'rer, I expect, and he's no hand to write letters. There, I don't blame him, I'd ha' seen the world myself if it had been so I could.

"Sylvia takes after him," the grandmother continued affectionately, after a minute's pause. "There ain't a foot o' ground she don't know her way over, and the wild creatur's counts her one o' themselves. Squer'ls she'll tame to come an' feed right out o' her hands, and all sorts o' birds. Last winter she got the jaybirds to bangeing here, and I believe she'd 'a' scanted herself of her own meals to have plenty to throw out amongst 'em, if I hadn't kep' watch. Anything but crows, I tell her, I'm willin' to help support—though Dan he went an' tamed one o' them that did seem to have reason same as folks. It was round here a good spell after he went away. Dan an' his father they didn't hitch—but he never held up his head ag'in after Dan had dared him an' gone off."

50   The guest did not notice this hint of family sorrows in his eager interest in something else.

"So Sylvy knows all about birds, does she?" he exclaimed, as he looked round at the little girl who sat, very demure but increasingly sleepy, in the moonlight. "I am making a collection of birds myself. I have been at it ever since I was a boy." (Mrs. Tilley smiled.) "There are two or three very rare ones I have been hunting for these five years. I mean to get them on my own ground if they can be found."

"Do you cage 'em up?" asked Mrs. Tilley doubtfully, in response to this enthusiastic announcement.

"Oh, no, they're stuffed and preserved, dozens and dozens of them," said the ornithologist, "and I have shot or snared every one myself. I caught a glimpse of a white heron three miles from here on Saturday, and I have followed it in this direction. They have never been found in this district at all. The little white heron, it is," and he turned again to look at Sylvia with the hope of discovering that the rare bird was one of her acquaintances.

But Sylvia was watching a hoptoad in the narrow footpath.

"You would know the heron if you saw it," the stranger continued eagerly. "A queer tall white bird with soft feathers and long thin legs. And it would have a nest perhaps in the top of a high tree, made of sticks, something like a hawk's nest."

Sylvia's heart gave a wild beat; she knew that strange white bird, and had once stolen softly near where it stood in some bright-green swamp grass, away over at the other side of the woods. There was an open place where the sunshine always seemed strangely yellow and hot, where tall, nodding rushes grew, and her grandmother had warned her that she might sink in the soft black mud underneath and never be heard of more. Not far beyond were the salt marshes and beyond those was the sea, the sea which Sylvia wondered and dreamed about, but never had looked upon, though its great voice could often be heard above the noise of the woods on stormy nights.

"I can't think of anything I should like so much as to find that heron's nest," the handsome stranger was saying. "I would give ten dollars to anybody who could show it to me," he added desperately, "and I mean to spend my whole vacation hunting for it if need be. Perhaps it was only migrating, or had been chased out of its own region by some bird of prey."

Mrs. Tilley gave amazed attention to all this, but Sylvia still watched the toad, not divining, as she might have done at some calmer time, that the creature wished to get to its hole under the doorstep, and was much hindered by the unusual spectators at that hour of the evening. No amount of thought, that night, could decide how many wished-for treasures the ten dollars, so lightly spoken of, would buy.

• • •

The next day the young sportsman hovered about the woods, and Sylvia kept him company, having lost her first fear of the friendly lad, who proved to be most kind and sympathetic. He told her many things about the birds and what they knew and where they lived and what they did with themselves. And he gave her a jackknife, which she thought as great a treasure as if she were a desert-islander. All day long he did not once make her troubled or afraid except when he brought down some unsuspecting singing creature from its bough. Sylvia would have liked him vastly better without his gun; she could not understand why he killed the very birds he seemed to like so much. But as the day waned, Sylvia still watched the young man with loving admiration. She had never seen anybody so charming and delightful; the woman's heart, asleep in the child, was vaguely thrilled by a dream of love. Some premonition of that great power stirred and swayed these young foresters who traversed the solemn woodlands with soft-footed silent care. They stopped to listen to a bird's song; they pressed forward again eagerly, parting the branches—speaking to each other rarely and in whispers; the young man going first and Sylvia follow-

52 ing, fascinated, a few steps behind, with her gray eyes dark with excitement.

She grieved because the longed-for white heron was elusive, but she did not lead the guest, she only followed, and there was no such thing as speaking first. The sound of her own unquestioned voice would have terrified her—it was hard enough to answer yes or no when there was need of that. At last evening began to fall, and they drove the cow home together, and Sylvia smiled with pleasure when they came to the place where she heard the whistle and was afraid only the night before.

2

Half a mile from home, at the farther edge of the woods, where the land was highest, a great pine tree stood, the last of its generation. Whether it was left for a boundary mark, or for what reason, no one could say; the woodchoppers who had felled its mates were dead and gone long ago, and a whole forest of sturdy trees, pines and oaks and maples, had grown again. But the stately head of this old pine towered above them all and made a landmark for sea and shore miles and miles away. Sylvia knew it well. She had always believed that whoever climbed to the top of it could see the ocean; and the little girl had often laid her hand on the great rough trunk and looked up wistfully at those dark boughs that the wind always stirred, no matter how hot and still the air might be below. Now she thought of the tree with a new excitement, for why, if one climbed it at break of day, could not one see all the world, and easily discover whence the white heron flew, and mark the place, and find the hidden nest?

What a spirit of adventure, what wild ambition! What fancied triumph and delight and glory for the later morning when she could make known the secret! It was almost too real and too great for the childish heart to bear.

All night the door of the little house stood open, and the whippoorwills came and sang upon the very step. The young sportsman and his old hostess were sound asleep, but Sylvia's great design kept her broad awake and watching. She forgot to think of sleep. The short summer night seemed as long as the winter darkness, and at last when the whippoorwills ceased, and she was afraid the morning would after all come too soon, she stole out of the house and followed the pasture path through the woods, hastening toward the open ground beyond, listening with a sense of comfort and companionship to the drowsy twitter of a half-awakened bird, whose perch she had jarred in passing. Alas, if the great wave of human interest which flooded for the first time this dull little life should sweep away the satisfactions of an existence heart to heart with nature and the dumb life of the forest!

There was the huge tree asleep yet in the paling moonlight, and small and hopeful Sylvia began with utmost bravery to mount to the top of it, with tingling, eager blood coursing the channels of her whole frame, with her bare feet and fingers that pinched and held like bird's claws to the monstrous ladder reaching up, up, almost to the sky itself. First she must mount the white oak tree that grew alongside, where she was almost lost among the dark branches and the green leaves heavy and wet with dew; a bird fluttered off its nest, and a red squirrel ran to and fro and scolded pettishly at the harmless house-breaker. Sylvia felt her way easily. She had often climbed there, and knew that higher still one of the oak's upper branches chafed against the pine trunk, just where its lower boughs were set close together. There, when she made the dangerous pass from one tree to the other, the great enterprise would really begin.

She crept out along the swaying oak limb at last, and took the daring step across into the old pine tree. The way was harder than she thought; she must reach far and hold fast, the sharp dry twigs caught and held her and scratched her like angry talons, the pitch made her thin little fingers clumsy and stiff as she went round and round the tree's great stem, higher and higher upward. The sparrows and robins in the woods below were beginning to wake and twitter to the dawn, yet it seemed much lighter there aloft in the pine tree, and the child knew that she must hurry if her project were to be of any use.

The tree seemed to lengthen itself out as she went up, and to reach farther and farther upward. It was like a great mainmast to the voyaging earth; it must truly have been amazed that morning through all its ponderous frame as it felt this determined spark of human spirit creeping and climbing from higher branch to branch. Who knows how steadily the least twigs held themselves to advantage this light, weak creature on her way! The old pine must have loved his new dependent. More than all the hawks, and bats, and moths, and even the sweet-voiced thrushes, was the brave, beating heart of the solitary gray-eyed child. And the tree stood still and held away the winds that June morning while the dawn grew bright in the east.

Sylvia's face was like a pale star, if one had seen it from the ground, when the last thorny bough was passed, and she stood trembling and tired but wholly triumphant, high in the treetop. Yes, there was the sea with the dawning sun making a golden dazzle over it, and toward that glorious east flew two hawks with slow-moving pinions. How low they looked in the air from that height when before one had only seen them far up, and dark against the blue sky. Their gray feathers were as soft as moths; they seemed only a little way from the tree, and Sylvia felt as if she too could go flying away among the clouds. Westward, the woodlands and farms reached miles and miles into the distance; here and there were church steeples, and white villages; truly it was a vast and awesome world.

The birds sang louder and louder. At last the sun came up bewilderingly bright. Sylvia could see the white sails of ships out at sea, and the clouds that were purple and rose-colored and yellow at first began to fade away. Where was the white heron's nest in the sea of green branches, and was this wonderful sight and pageant of the world the only reward for having climbed to such a giddy height? Now look down again, Sylvia, where the green marsh is set among the shining birches and dark hemlocks; there where you saw the white heron once you will see him again; look, look! a white spot of him like a single floating feather comes up from the dead hemlock and grows larger, and rises, and comes close at last, and goes by the landmark pine with steady sweep of wing and outstretched slender neck and crested head. And wait! wait! do not move a foot or a finger, little girl; do not send an arrow of light and consciousness from your two eager eyes, for the heron has perched on a pine bough not far beyond yours, and cries back to his mate on the nest, and plumes his feathers for the new day!

The child gives a long sigh a minute later when a company of shouting catbirds comes also to the tree; and vexed by their fluttering and lawlessness, the solemn heron goes away. She knows his secret now: the wild, light, slender bird that floats and wavers, and goes back like an arrow presently to his home in the green world beneath. Then Sylvia, well satisfied, makes her perilous way down again, not daring to look far below the branch she stands on, ready to cry sometimes because her fingers ache and her lamed feet slip—wondering over and over again what the stranger would say to her, and what he would think when she told him how to find his way straight to the heron's nest.

* * *

"Sylvy, Sylvy!" called the busy old grandmother again and again, but nobody answered, and the small husk bed was

56 empty, and Sylvia had disappeared.

The guest waked from a dream, and remembering his day's pleasure, hurried to dress himself that it might sooner begin. He was sure from the way the shy little girl looked once or twice yesterday that she had at least seen the white heron, and now she must really be persuaded to tell. Here she comes now, paler than ever, and her worn old frock is torn and tattered, and smeared with pine pitch. The grandmother and the sportsman stand in the door together and question her, and the splendid moment has come to speak of the dead hemlock tree by the green marsh.

But Sylvia does not speak after all, though the old grandmother fretfully rebukes her, and the young man's kind appealing eyes are looking straight in her own. He can make them rich with money; he has promised it, and they are poor now. He is so well worth making happy, and he waits to hear the story she can tell.

No, she must keep silence! What is it that suddenly forbids her and makes her dumb? Has she been nine years growing, and now, when the great world for the first time puts out a hand to her, must she thrust it aside for a bird's sake? The murmur of the pine's green branches is in her ears, she remembers how the white heron came flying through the golden air and how they watched the sea and the morning together, and Sylvia cannot speak; she cannot tell the heron's secret and give its life away.

. . .

Dear loyalty, that suffered a sharp pang as the guest went away disappointed later in the day, that could have served and followed him and loved him as a dog loves! Many a night Sylvia heard the echo of his whistle haunting the pasture path as she came home with the loitering cow. She forgot even her sorrow at the sharp report of his gun and the piteous sight of thrushes and sparrows dropping silent to the ground, their songs hushed and their pretty feathers stained and wet with blood. Were the birds better friends than their hunter might have been—who can tell? Whatever treasures were lost to her, woodlands and summertime, remember! Bring your gifts and graces and tell your secrets to this lonely country child!

Of the dungeons there had been strange things narrated—
fables I had always deemed them—but yet strange, and
too ghastly to repeat, save in a whisper.

THE PIT AND THE PENDULUM

Edgar Allan Poe

I was sick—sick unto death with that long agony; and when
they at length unbound me, and I was permitted to sit, I felt
that my senses were leaving me. The sentence—the dread sentence of death—was the last of distinct accentuation which
reached my ears. After that, the sound of the inquisitorial
voices seemed merged in one dreamy indeterminate hum. It
conveyed to my soul the idea of *revolution*—perhaps from its
association in fancy with the burr of a mill wheel. This only for
a brief period; for presently I heard no more. Yet, for a while, I
saw; but with how terrible an exaggeration! I saw the lips of
the black-robed judges. They appeared to me white—whiter
than the sheet upon which I trace these words—and thin even
to grotesqueness; thin with the intensity of their expression of
firmness—of immovable resolution—of stern contempt of human torture. I saw that the decrees of what to me was Fate
were still issuing from those lips. I saw them writhe with a
deadly locution. I saw them fashion the syllables of my name;
and I shuddered because no sound succeeded. I saw, too, for a
few moments of delirious horror, the soft and nearly imperceptible waving of the sable draperies which enwrapped the walls
of the apartment. And then my vision fell upon the seven tall
candles upon the table. At first they wore the aspect of charity

and seemed white slender angels who would save me; but then, all at once, there came a most deadly nausea over my spirit, and I felt every fiber in my frame thrill as if I had touched the wire of a galvanic battery, while the angel forms became meaningless spectres, with heads of flame, and I saw that from them there would be no help. And then there stole into my fancy, like a rich musical note, the thought of what sweet rest there must be in the grave. The thought came gently and stealthily, and it seemed long before it attained full appreciation; but just as my spirit came at length properly to feel and entertain it, the figures of the judges vanished, as if magically, from before me; the tall candles sank into nothingness; their flames went out utterly; the blackness of darkness supervened; all sensations appeared swallowed up in a mad rushing descent as of the soul into Hades. Then silence, and stillness, and night were the universe.

I had swooned; but still will not say that all of consciousness was lost. What of it there remained I will not attempt to define, or even to describe; yet all was not lost. In the deepest slumber—no! In delirium—no! In a swoon—no! In death—no! even in the grave all *is not* lost. Else there is no immortality for man. Arousing from the most profound of slumbers, we break the gossamer web of *some* dream. Yet in a second afterward, (so frail may that web have been) we remember not that we have dreamed. In the return to life from the swoon there are two stages; first, that of the sense of mental or spiritual; secondly, that of the sense of physical, existence. It seems probable that if, upon reaching the second stage, we could recall the impressions of the first, we should find these impressions eloquent in memories of the gulf beyond. And that gulf is—what? How at least shall we distinguish its shadows from those of the tomb? But if the impressions of what I have termed the first stage are not, at will, recalled, yet, after long interval, do they not come unbidden, while we marvel whence they come? He who has never swooned is not he who finds strange palaces and wildly familiar faces in coals that glow; is not he who beholds floating in midair the sad visions that the many may not view; is not he who ponders over the perfume of some novel flower; is not he whose brain grows bewildered with the meaning of some musical cadence which has never before arrested his attention.

Amid frequent and thoughtful endeavors to remember; amid earnest struggles to regather some token of the state of seeming nothingness into which my soul had lapsed, there have been moments when I have dreamed of success; there have been brief, very brief periods when I have conjured up remembrances which the lucid reason of a later epoch assures me could have had reference only to that condition of seeming unconsciousness. These shadows of memory tell, indistinctly, of tall figures that lifted and bore me in silence down—down—still down—till a hideous dizziness oppressed me at the mere idea of the interminableness of the descent. They tell also of a vague horror at my heart, on account of that heart's unnatural stillness. Then comes a sense of sudden motionlessness throughout all things; as if those who bore me (a ghastly train!) had outrun, in their descent, the limits of the limitless, and paused from the wearisomeness of their toil. After this I call to mind flatness and dampness; and then all is *madness*—the madness of a memory which busies itself among forbidden things.

Very suddenly there came back to my soul motion and sound—the tumultuous motion of the heart, and, in my ears, the sound of its beating. Then a pause in which all is blank. Then again sound, and motion, and touch—a tingling sensation pervading my frame. Then the mere consciousness of existence, without thought—a condition which lasted long. Then, very suddenly, *thought,* and shuddering terror, and earnest endeavor to comprehend my true state. Then a strong desire to lapse into insensibility. Then a rushing revival of soul and a successful effort to move. And now a full memory of the trial, of the judges, of the sable draperies, of the sentence, of the sickness, of the swoon. Then entire forgetfulness of all that followed; of all that a later day and much earnestness of endeavor have enabled me vaguely to recall.

So far, I had not opened my eyes. I felt that I lay upon my back, unbound. I reached out my hand, and it fell heavily upon something damp and hard. There I suffered it to remain for many minutes, while I strove to imagine where and *what* I could be. I longed, yet dared not, to employ my vision. I dreaded the first glance at objects around me. It was not that I feared to look upon things horrible, but that I grew aghast lest there should be *nothing* to see. At length, with a wild desperation at heart, I quickly unclosed my eyes. My worst thoughts, then, were confirmed. The blackness of eternal night encompassed me. I struggled for breath. The intensity of the darkness seemed to oppress and stifle me. The atmosphere was intolerably close. I still lay quietly and made effort to exercise my reason. I brought to mind the inquisitorial proceedings and attempted from that point to deduce my real condition. The sentence had passed; and it appeared to me that a very long interval of time had since elapsed. Yet not for a moment did I suppose myself actually dead. Such a supposition, notwithstanding what we read in fiction, is altogether inconsistent with real existence—but where and in what state was I? The condemned to death, I knew, perished usually at the *autos-da-fé,* and one of these had been held on the very night of the day of my trial. Had I been remanded to my dungeon to await the next sacrifice, which would not take place for many months? This I at once saw could not be. Victims had been in immediate demand. Moreover, my dungeon, as well as all the condemned cells at Toledo, had stone floors, and light was not altogether excluded.

A fearful idea now suddenly drove the blood in torrents upon my heart, and for a brief period, I once more relapsed into insensibility. Upon recovering, I at once started to my feet, trembling convulsively in every fiber. I thrust my arms wildly above and around me in all directions. I felt nothing yet dreaded to move a step, lest I should be impeded by the walls of a *tomb*. Perspiration burst from every pore and stood in cold big beads upon my forehead. The agony of suspense grew at length intolerable, and I cautiously moved forward, with my arms extended, and my eyes straining from their sockets, in the hope of catching some faint ray of light. I proceeded for many paces; but still all was blackness and vacancy. I breathed more freely. It seemed evident that mine was not, at least, the most hideous of fates.

And now, as I still continued to step cautiously onward, there came thronging upon my recollection a thousand vague rumors of the horrors of Toledo. Of the dungeons there had been strange things narrated—fables I had always deemed them—but yet strange, and too ghastly to repeat, save in a whisper. Was I left to perish of starvation in this subterranean world of darkness; or what fate, perhaps even more fearful, awaited me? That the result would be death, and a death of more than customary bitterness, I knew too well the character of my judges to doubt. The mode and the hour were all that occupied or distracted me.

My outstretched hands at length encountered some solid obstruction. It was a wall, seemingly of stone masonry—very smooth, slimy, and cold. I followed it up, stepping with all the careful distrust with which certain antique narratives had inspired me. This process, however, afforded me no means of ascertaining the dimensions of my dungeon, as I might make its circuit and return to the point whence I set out without being aware of the fact, so perfectly uniform seemed the wall. I therefore sought the knife which had been in my pocket when led into the inquisitorial chamber; but it was gone; my clothes had been exchanged for a wrapper of coarse serge. I had thought of forcing the blade in some minute crevice of the masonry, so as to identify my point of departure. The difficulty, nevertheless, was but trivial; although, in the disorder of my fancy, it seemed at first insuperable. I tore a part of the hem from the robe and placed the fragment at full length and at right angles to the wall. In groping my way around the prison, I could not fail to encounter this rag upon completing the circuit. So, at least I thought; but I had not counted upon the extent of the dungeon, or upon my own weakness. The ground was moist and slippery. I staggered onward for some time, when I stumbled and fell. My excessive fatigue induced me to remain prostrate; and sleep soon overtook me as I lay.

Upon awaking, and stretching forth an arm, I found beside me a loaf and a pitcher with water. I was too much exhausted to reflect upon this circumstance, but ate and drank with avidity. Shortly afterward, I resumed my tour around the prison, and with much toil, came at last upon the fragment of the serge. Up to the period when I fell I had counted fifty-two paces, and upon resuming my walk, I had counted forty-eight more—when I arrived at the rag. There were in all, then, a hundred paces; and admitting two paces to the yard, I presumed the dungeon to be fifty yards in circuit. I had met, however, with many angles in the wall, and thus I could form no guess at the shape of the vault; for vault I could not help supposing it to be.

I had little object—certainly no hope—in these researches; but a vague curiosity prompted me to continue them. Quitting the wall, I resolved to cross the area of the enclosure. At first I proceeded with extreme caution, for the floor, although seemingly of solid material, was treacherous with slime. At length, however, I took courage and did not hesitate to step firmly, endeavoring to cross in as direct a line as possible. I had advanced some ten or twelve paces in this manner, when the remnant of the torn hem of my robe became entangled between my legs. I stepped on it, and fell violently on my face.

In the confusion attending my fall, I did not immediately apprehend a somewhat startling circumstance, which yet, in a few seconds afterward, and while I still lay prostrate, arrested my attention. It was this: my chin rested upon the floor of the prison, but my lips and the upper portion of my head, although seemingly at a less elevation than the chin, touched nothing. At the same time my forehead seemed bathed in a clammy vapor, and the peculiar smell of decayed fungus arose to my nostrils. I put forward my arm, and shuddered to find that I had fallen at the very brink of a circular pit, whose extent, of course, I had no means of ascertaining at the moment. Groping about the masonry just below the margin, I succeeded in dislodging a small fragment, and let it fall into the abyss. For many seconds I hearkened to its reverberations as it dashed against the sides of the chasm in its descent; at length there was a sullen plunge into water, succeeded by loud echoes. At the same moment there came a sound resembling the quick opening, and as rapid closing, of a door overhead, while a faint gleam of light flashed suddenly through the gloom, and as suddenly faded away.

I saw clearly the doom which had been prepared for me, and congratulated myself upon the timely accident by which I had escaped. Another step before my fall, and the world had seen me no more. And the death just avoided was of that very character which I had regarded as fabulous and frivolous in the tales respecting the Inquisition. To the victims of its tyranny, there was the choice of death with its direst physical agonies, or death with its most hideous moral horrors. I had been reserved for the latter. By long-suffering my nerves had been unstrung, until I trembled at the sound of my own voice and had become in every respect a fitting subject for the species of torture which awaited me.

Shaking in every limb, I groped my way back to the wall, resolving there to perish rather than risk the terrors of the wells, of which my imagination now pictured many in various positions about the dungeon. In other conditions of mind I might have had courage to end my misery at once by a plunge into one of these abysses; but now I was the veriest of cowards. Neither could I forget what I had read of these pits—that the *sudden* extinction of life formed no part of their most horrible plan.

Agitation of spirit kept me awake for many long hours; but at length I again slumbered. Upon arousing, I found by my side, as before, a loaf and a pitcher of water. A burning thirst consumed me, and I emptied the vessel at a draught. It must have been drugged; for scarcely had I drunk before I became irresistibly drowsy. A deep sleep fell upon me—a sleep like that of death. How long it lasted, of course I know not; but when, once again, I unclosed my eyes, the objects around me were visible. By a wild sulphurous lustre, the origin of which I could not at first determine, I was enabled to see the extent and aspect of the prison.

In its size I had been greatly mistaken. The whole circuit of its walls did not exceed twenty-five yards. For some minutes this fact occasioned me a world of vain trouble; vain indeed! for what could be of less importance, under the terrible circumstances which environed me, than the mere dimensions of my dungeon? But my soul took a wild interest in trifles, and I busied myself in endeavors to account for the error I had committed in my measurement. The truth at length flashed upon me. In my first attempt at exploration I had counted fifty-two paces, up to the period when I fell; I must then have been within a pace or two of the fragment of serge; in fact, I had nearly performed the circuit of the vault. I then slept, and upon awaking, I must have returned upon my steps—thus supposing the circuit nearly double what it actually was. My confusion of mind prevented me from observing that I began my tour with the wall to the left, and ended it with the wall to the right.

I had been deceived, too, in respect to the shape of the enclosure. In feeling my way I had found many angles and thus deduced an idea of great irregularity; so potent is the effect of total darkness upon one arousing from lethargy or sleep! The angles were simply those of a few slight depressions, or niches, at odd intervals. The general shape of the prison was square. What I had taken for masonry seemed now to be iron, or some other metal, in huge plates, whose sutures or joints occasioned the depression. The entire surface of this metallic enclosure was rudely daubed in all the hideous and repulsive devices to which the charnel superstition of the monks has given rise. The figures of fiends in aspects of menace, with skeleton forms and other more really fearful images, overspread and disfigured the walls. I observed that the outlines of these monstrosities were sufficiently distinct, but that the colors seemed faded and blurred, as if from the effects of a damp atmosphere. I now noticed the floor, too, which was of stone. In the center yawned the circular pit from whose jaws I had escaped; but it was the only one in the dungeon.

All this I saw indistinctly and by much effort; for my personal condition had been greatly changed during slumber. I now lay upon my back, and at full length, on a species of low framework of wood. To this I was securely bound by a long strap resembling a surcingle. It passed in many convolutions about my limbs and body, leaving at liberty only my head and my left arm to such extent that I could, by dint of much exertion, supply myself with food from an earthen dish which lay by my side on the floor. I saw, to my horror, that the pitcher had been removed. I say to my horror; for I was consumed with intolerable thirst. This thirst it appeared to be the design of my persecutors to stimulate: for the food in the dish was meat pungently seasoned.

Looking upward, I surveyed the ceiling of my prison. It was some thirty or forty feet overhead and constructed much as the side walls. In one of its panels a very singular figure riveted my whole attention. It was the painted figure of Time as he is commonly represented, save that, in lieu of a scythe, he held what, at a casual glance, I supposed to be the pictured image of a huge pendulum such as we see on antique clocks. There was something, however, in the appearance of this machine which caused me to regard it more attentively. While I gazed directly upward at it (for its position was immediately over my own) I fancied that I saw it in motion. In an instant afterward the fancy was confirmed. Its sweep was brief, and of course slow. I watched it for some minutes, somewhat in fear, but more in wonder. Wearied at length with observing its dull movement, I turned my eyes upon the other objects in the cell.

A slight noise attracted my notice, and looking to the floor, I saw several enormous rats traversing it. They had issued from the well, which lay just within view to my right. Even then, while I gazed, they came up in troops, hurriedly, with ravenous eyes, allured by the scent of the meat. From this it required much effort and attention to scare them away.

It might have been half an hour, perhaps even an hour, (for I could take but imperfect note of time) before I again cast my eyes upward. What I then saw confounded and amazed me. The sweep of the pendulum had increased in extent by nearly a yard. As a natural consequence, its velocity was also much greater. But what mainly disturbed me was the idea that it had perceptibly *descended*. I now observed—with what horror it is needless to say—that its nether extremity was formed of a crescent of glittering steel, about a foot in length from horn to horn; the horns upward, and the under edge evidently as keen as that of a razor. Like a razor also, it seemed massy and heavy, tapering from the edge into a solid and broad structure above. It was appended to a weighty rod of brass, and the whole *hissed* as it swung through the air.

I could no longer doubt the doom prepared for me by monkish ingenuity in torture. My cognizance of the pit had become known to the inquisitorial agents—*the pit* whose horrors had been destined for so bold a recusant as myself—*the pit*, typical of hell, and regarded by rumor as the Ultima Thule of all their punishments. The plunge into this pit I had avoided by the merest of accidents, and I knew that surprise, or entrap-

68 ment into torment, formed an important portion of all the grotesquerie of these dungeon deaths. Having failed to fall, it was no part of the demon plan to hurl me into the abyss; and thus (there being no alternative) a different and a milder destruction awaited me. Milder! I half-smiled in my agony as I thought of such application of such a term.

What boots it to tell of the long, long hours of horror more than mortal, during which I counted the rushing vibrations of the steel! Inch by inch—line by line—with a descent only appreciable at intervals that seemed ages—down and still down it came! Days passed—it might have been that many days passed—ere it swept so closely over me as to fan me with its acrid breath. The odor of the sharp steel forced itself into my nostrils. I prayed—I wearied heaven with my prayer for its more speedy descent. I grew frantically mad and struggled to force myself upward against the sweep of the fearful scimitar. And then I fell suddenly calm, and lay smiling at the glittering death, as a child at some rare bauble.

There was another interval of utter insensibility; it was brief; for, upon again lapsing into life there had been no perceptible descent in the pendulum. But it might have been long; for I knew there were demons who took note of my swoon and who could have arrested the vibration at pleasure. Upon my recovery, too, I felt very—oh, inexpressibly sick and weak, as if through long inanition. Even amid the agonies of that period, the human nature craved food. With painful effort I outstretched my left arm as far as my bonds permitted, and took possession of the small remnant which had been spared me by the rats. As I put a portion of it within my lips, there rushed to my mind a half-formed thought of joy—of hope. Yet what business had *I* with hope? It was, as I say, a half-formed thought—man has many such which are never completed. I felt that it was of joy—of hope; but I felt also that it had perished in its formation. In vain I struggled to perfect—to regain it. Long-suffering had nearly annihilated all my ordinary powers of mind. I was an imbecile—an idiot.

The vibration of the pendulum was at right angles to my length. I saw that the crescent was designed to cross the region of the heart. It would fray the serge of my robe—it would return and repeat its operations—again—and again. Notwithstanding its terrifically wide sweep (some thirty feet or more) and the hissing vigor of its descent, sufficient to sunder these very walls of iron, still the fraying of my robe would be all that, for several minutes, it would accomplish. And at this thought I paused. I dared not go farther than this reflection. I dwelt upon it with a pertinacity of attention—as if, in so dwelling, I could arrest *here* the descent of the steel. I forced myself to ponder upon the sound of the crescent as it should pass across the garment—upon the peculiar thrilling sensation which the friction of cloth produces on the nerves. I pondered upon all this frivolity until my teeth were on edge.

Down—steadily down it crept. I took a frenzied pleasure in contrasting its downward with its lateral velocity. To the right—to the left—far and wide—with the shriek of a damned spirit; to my heart with the stealthy pace of the tiger! I alternately laughed and howled as the one or the other idea grew predominant.

Down—certainly, relentlessly down! It vibrated within three inches of my bosom! I struggled violently, furiously, to free my left arm. This was free only from the elbow to the hand. I could reach the latter, from the platter beside me, to my mouth, with great effort, but no farther. Could I have broken the fastenings above the elbow, I would have seized and attempted to arrest the pendulum. I might as well have attempted to arrest an avalanche!

Down—still unceasingly—still inevitably down! I gasped and struggled at each vibration. I shrunk convulsively at its every sweep. My eyes followed its outward or upward whirls with the eagerness of the most unmeaning despair; they closed themselves spasmodically at the descent, although death would have been a relief, oh! how unspeakable! Still I quivered in every nerve to think how slight a sinking of the machinery would precipitate that keen, glistening axe upon my bosom. It was *hope* prompted the nerve to quiver—the frame to shrink. It was *hope*—the hope that triumphs on the rack—that whispers to the death-condemned even in the dungeons of the Inquisition.

I saw that some ten or twelve vibrations would bring the steel in actual contact with my robe, and with this observation there suddenly came over my spirit all the keen, collected calmness of despair. For the first time during many hours—or perhaps days—I *thought*. It now occurred to me that the bandage, or surcingle, which enveloped me, was *unique*. I was tied by no separate cord. The first stroke of the razorlike crescent athwart any portion of the band would so detach it that it might be unwound from my person by means of my left hand. But how fearful, in that case, the proximity of the steel! The result of the slightest struggle how deadly! Was it likely, moreover, that the minions of the torturer had not foreseen and provided for this possibility! Was it probable that the bandage crossed my bosom in the track of the pendulum? Dreading to find my faint, and, as it seemed, my last hope frustrated, I so far elevated my head as to obtain a distinct view of my breast. The surcingle enveloped my limbs and body close in all directions—*save in the path of the destroying crescent.*

Scarcely had I dropped my head back into its original position when there flashed upon my mind what I cannot better describe than as the unformed half of that idea of deliverance to which I have previously alluded, and of which a moiety only floated indeterminately through my brain when I raised food to my burning lips. The whole thought was now present—feeble, scarcely sane, scarcely definite—but still entire. I proceeded at once, with the nervous energy of despair, to attempt its execution.

For many hours the immediate vicinity of the low framework upon which I lay had been literally swarming with rats. They were wild, bold, ravenous—their red eyes glaring upon me as if they waited but for motionlessness on my part to make me their prey. "To what food," I thought, "have they been accustomed in the well?"

They had devoured, in spite of all my efforts to prevent them, all but a small remnant of the contents of the dish. I had fallen into an habitual seesaw, or wave of the hand about the platter; and, at length, the unconscious uniformity of the movement deprived it of effect. In their voracity the vermin frequently fastened their sharp fangs in my fingers. With the particles of the oily and spicy viand which now remained, I thoroughly rubbed the bandage wherever I could reach it; then, raising my hand from the floor, I lay breathlessly still.

At first the ravenous animals were startled and terrified at the change—at the cessation of movement. They shrank alarmedly back; many sought the well. But this was only for a moment. I had not counted in vain upon their voracity. Observing that I remained without motion, one or two of the boldest leaped upon the framework and smelt at the surcingle. This seemed the signal for a general rush. Forth from the well they hurried in fresh troops. They clung to the wood—they overran it and leaped in hundreds upon my person. The measured movement of the pendulum disturbed them not at all. Avoiding its strokes they busied themselves with the anointed bandage. They pressed—they swarmed upon me in ever accumulating heaps. They writhed upon my throat; their cold lips sought my own; I was half-stifled by their thronging pressure; disgust, for which the world has no name, swelled my bosom, and chilled, with a heavy clamminess, my heart. Yet one minute, and I felt that the struggle would be over. Plainly I perceived the loosening of the bandage. I knew that in more than one place it must be already severed. With a more than human resolution I lay *still*.

Nor had I erred in my calculations—nor had I endured in

72   vain. I at length felt that I was *free*. The surcingle hung in
ribands from my body. But the stroke of the pendulum already
pressed upon my bosom. It had divided the serge of the robe. It
had cut through the linen beneath. Twice again it swung, and
a sharp sense of pain shot through every nerve. But the moment of escape had arrived. At a wave of my hand my deliv-
erers hurried tumultuously away. With a steady movement—
cautious, sidelong, shrinking, and slow—I slid from the embrace of the bandage and beyond the reach of the scimitar. For
the moment, at least, *I was free.*

Free!—and in the grasp of the Inquisition! I had scarcely
stepped from my wooden bed of horror upon the stone floor of
the prison when the motion of the hellish machine ceased and
I beheld it drawn up, by some invisible force, through the ceiling. This was a lesson which I took desperately to heart. My
every motion was undoubtedly watched. Free!—I had but escaped death in one form of agony, to be delivered unto worse
than death in some other. With that thought I rolled my eyes
nervously around on the barriers of iron that hemmed me in.
Something unusual—some change which, at first, I could not
appreciate distinctly—it was obvious, had taken place in the
apartment. For many minutes of a dreamy and trembling ab-
straction, I busied myself in vain, unconnected conjecture.
During this period, I became aware, for the first time, of the
origin of the sulphurous light which illumined the cell. It proceeded from a fissure, about half an inch in width, extending
entirely around the prison at the base of the walls, which thus
appeared and were completely separated from the floor. I endeavored, but of course in vain, to look through the aperture.

As I arose from the attempt, the mystery of the alterations in
the chamber broke at once upon my understanding. I have observed that although the outlines of the figures upon the walls
were sufficiently distinct, yet the colors seemed blurred and indefinite. These had now assumed, and were momentarily as-
suming, a startling and most intense brilliancy that gave to the

spectral and fiendish portraitures an aspect that might have thrilled even firmer nerves than my own. Demon eyes, of a wild and ghastly vivacity, glared upon me in a thousand directions, where none had been visible before, and gleamed with the lurid lustre of a fire that I could not force my imagination to regard as unreal.

Unreal!—Even while I breathed there came to my nostrils the breath of the vapor of heated iron! A suffocating odor pervaded the prison! A deeper glow settled each moment in the eyes that glared at my agonies! A richer tint of crimson diffused itself over the pictured horrors of blood. I panted! I gasped for breath! There could be no doubt of the design of my tormentors—oh! most unrelenting! oh! most demoniac of men! I shrank from the glowing metal to the center of the cell. Amid the thought of the fiery destruction that impended, the idea of the coolness of the well came over my soul like balm. I rushed to its deadly brink. I threw my straining vision below. The glare from the enkindled roof illumined its inmost recesses. Yet, for a wild moment, did my spirit refuse to comprehend the meaning of what I saw. At length it forced—it wrestled its way into my soul—it burned itself in upon by shuddering reason. Oh! for a voice to speak!—oh! horror!—oh! any horror but this! With a shriek, I rushed from the margin and buried my face in my hands—weeping bitterly.

The heat rapidly increased, and once again I looked up, shuddering as with a fit of the ague. There had been a second change in the cell—and now the change was obviously in the *form.* As before, it was in vain that I at first endeavored to appreciate or understand what was taking place. But not long was I left in doubt. The inquisitorial vengeance had been hurried by my twofold escape, and there was to be no more dallying with the King of Terrors. The room had been square. I saw that two of its iron angles were now acute—two, consequently, obtuse. The fearful difference quickly increased with a low rumbling or moaning sound. In an instant the apartment had

74 shifted its form into that of a lozenge. But the alteration stopped not here—I neither hoped nor desired it to stop. I could have clasped the red walls to my bosom as a garment of eternal peace. "Death," I said, "any death but that of the pit!" Fool! might I have not known that *into the pit* it was the object of the burning iron to urge me? Could I resist its glow? or, if even that, could I withstand its pressure? And now, flatter and flatter grew the lozenge, with a rapidity that left me no time for contemplation. Its center, and of course its greatest width, came just over the yawning gulf. I shrank back—but the closing wall pressed me resistlessly onward. At length for my seared and writhing body there was no longer an inch of foothold on the firm floor of the prison. I struggled no more, but the agony of my soul found vent in one loud, long, and final scream of despair. I felt that I tottered upon the brink—I averted my eyes—

There was a discordant hum of human voices! There was a loud blast as of many trumpets! There was a harsh grating as of a thousand thunders! The fiery walls rushed back! An outstretched arm caught my own as I fell, fainting, into the abyss. It was that of General Lasalle. The French army had entered Toledo. The Inquisition was in the hands of its enemies.

The exiles were forbidden to return at the peril of their lives.

THE OUTCASTS OF POKER FLAT

Bret Harte

As Mr. John Oakhurst, gambler, stepped into the main street of Poker Flat on the morning of the twenty-third of November, 1850, he was conscious of a change in its moral atmosphere since the preceding night. Two or three men, conversing earnestly together, ceased as he approached, and exchanged significant glances. There was a Sabbath lull in the air, which, in a settlement unused to Sabbath influences, looked ominous.

Mr. Oakhurst's calm, handsome face betrayed small concern in these indications. Whether he was conscious of any predisposing cause was another question. "I reckon they're after somebody," he reflected; "likely it's me." He returned to his pocket the handkerchief with which he had been whipping away the red dust of Poker Flat from his neat boots, and quietly discharged his mind of any further conjecture.

In point of fact, Poker Flat was "after somebody." It had lately suffered the loss of several thousand dollars, two valuable horses, and a prominent citizen. It was experiencing a spasm of virtuous reaction, quite as lawless and ungovernable as any of the acts that had provoked it. A secret committee had determined to rid the town of all improper persons. This was done permanently in regard of two men who were then hanging from the boughs of a sycamore in the gulch, and tem-

76 porarily in the banishment of certain other objectionable characters. I regret to say that some of these were ladies. It is but due to the sex, however, to state that their impropriety was professional, and it was only in such easily established standards of evil that Poker Flat ventured to sit in judgment.

Mr. Oakhurst was right in supposing that he was included in this category. A few of the committee had urged hanging him as a possible example, and a sure method of reimbursing themselves from his pockets of the sums he had won from them. "It's agin justice," said Jim Wheeler, "to let this yer young man from Roaring Camp—an entire stranger—carry away our money." But a crude sentiment of equity residing in the breasts of those who had been fortunate enough to win from Mr. Oakhurst overruled this narrower local prejudice.

Mr. Oakhurst received his sentence with philosophic calmness, none the less coolly that he was aware of the hesitation of his judges. He was too much of a gambler not to accept Fate. With him life was at best an uncertain game, and he recognized the usual percentage in favor of the dealer.

A body of armed men accompanied the deported wickedness of Poker Flat to the outskirts of the settlement. Besides Mr. Oakhurst, who was known to be a coolly desperate man, and for whose intimidation the armed escort was intended, the expatriated party consisted of a young woman familiarly known as "The Duchess"; another, who had won the title of "Mother Shipton"; and "Uncle Billy," a suspected sluice-robber and confirmed drunkard. The cavalcade provoked no comments from the spectators, nor was any word uttered by the escort. Only, when the gulch which marked the uttermost limit of Poker Flat was reached, the leader spoke briefly and to the point. The exiles were forbidden to return at the peril of their lives.

As the escort disappeared, their pent-up feelings found vent in a few hysterical tears from the Duchess, some bad language from Mother Shipton, and a Parthian volley of expletives from Uncle Billy. The philosophic Oakhurst alone remained silent. He listened calmly to Mother Shipton's desire to cut somebody's heart out, to the repeated statements of the Duchess that she would die in the road, and to the alarming oaths that seemed to be bumped out of Uncle Billy as he rode forward. With the easy good humor characteristic of his class, he insisted upon exchanging his own riding horse, "Five Spot," for the sorry mule which the Duchess rode. But even this act did not draw the party into any closer sympathy. The young woman readjusted her somewhat draggled plumes with a feeble, faded coquetry; Mother Shipton eyed the possessor of "Five Spot" with malevolence, and Uncle Billy included the whole party in one sweeping anathema.

The road to Sandy Bar—a camp that, not having as yet experienced the regenerating influences of Poker Flat, consequently seemed to offer some invitation to the emigrants—lay over a steep mountain range. It was distant a day's severe travel. In that advanced season, the party soon passed out of the moist, temperate regions of the foothills into the dry, cold, bracing air of the Sierras. The trail was narrow and difficult. At noon the Duchess, rolling out of her saddle upon the ground, declared her intention of going no farther, and the party halted.

The spot was singularly wild and impressive. A wooded amphitheater, surrounded on three sides by precipitous cliffs of naked granite, sloped gently toward the crest of another precipice that overlooked the valley. It was, undoubtedly, the most suitable spot for a camp, had camping been advisable. But Mr. Oakhurst knew that scarcely half the journey to Sandy Bar was accomplished, and the party were not equipped or provisioned for delay. This fact he pointed out to his companions curtly, with a philosophic commentary on the folly of "throwing up their hand before the game was played out." But they were furnished with liquor, which in this emergency stood them in place of food, fuel, rest, and prescience. In spite of his remonstrances, it was not long before they were more or less under its influence. Uncle Billy passed rapidly from a bellicose state into one of stupor, the Duchess became maudlin, and Mother Shipton snored. Mr. Oakhurst alone remained erect, leaning against a rock, calmly surveying them.

Mr. Oakhurst did not drink. It interfered with a profession which required coolness, impassiveness, and presence of mind, and, in his own language, he "couldn't afford it." As he gazed at his recumbent fellow exiles, the loneliness begotten of his pariah trade, his habits of life, his very vices, for the first time seriously oppressed him. He bestirred himself in dusting his black clothes, washing his hands and face, and other acts characteristic of his studiously neat habits, and for a moment forgot his annoyance. The thought of deserting his weaker and more pitiable companions never perhaps occurred to him. Yet he could not help feeling the want of that excitement which, singularly enough, was most conducive to that calm equanimity for which he was notorious. He looked at the gloomy walls that rose a thousand feet sheer above the circling pines around him; at the sky, ominously clouded; at the valley below, already deepening into shadow. And, doing so, suddenly he heard his own name called.

A horseman slowly ascended the trail. In the fresh, open face of the newcomer Mr. Oakhurst recognized Tom Simson, otherwise known as "The Innocent" of Sandy Bar. He had met him some months before over a "little game," and had, with perfect equanimity, won the entire fortune—amounting to some forty dollars—of that guileless youth. After the game was finished, Mr. Oakhurst drew the youthful speculator behind the door and thus addressed him: "Tommy, you're a good little man, but you can't gamble worth a cent. Don't try it over again." He then handed him his money back, pushed him gently from the room, and so made a devoted slave of Tom Simson.

There was a remembrance of this in his boyish and enthusiastic greeting of Mr. Oakhurst. He had started, he said, to go to Poker Flat to seek his fortune. "Alone?" No, not exactly alone; in fact (a giggle), he had run away with Piney Woods. Didn't Mr. Oakhurst remember Piney? She that used to wait on the table at the Temperance House? They had been engaged a long time, but old Jake Woods had objected, and so they had run away, and were going to Poker Flat to be married, and here they were. And they were tired out, and how lucky it was they had found a place to camp and company. All this the Innocent delivered rapidly, while Piney, a stout, comely damsel of fifteen, emerged from behind the pine tree, where she had been blushing unseen, and rode to the side of her lover.

Mr. Oakhurst seldom troubled himself with sentiment, still less with propriety; but he had a vague idea that the situation was not fortunate. He retained, however, his presence of mind sufficiently to kick Uncle Billy, who was about to say something, and Uncle Billy was sober enough to recognize in Mr. Oakhurst's kick a superior power that would not bear trifling. He then endeavored to dissuade Tom Simson from delaying further, but in vain. He even pointed out the fact that there was no provision, nor means of making a camp. But, unluckily, the Innocent met this objection by assuring the party that he was provided with an extra mule loaded with provisions, and by the discovery of a rude attempt at a log house near the trail. "Piney can stay with Mrs. Oakhurst," said the Innocent, pointing to the Duchess, "and I can shift for myself."

Nothing but Mr. Oakhurst's admonishing foot saved Uncle Billy from bursting into a roar of laughter. As it was, he felt compelled to retire up the canyon until he could recover his gravity. There he confided the joke to the tall pine trees, with many slaps of his leg, contortions of his face, and the usual profanity. But when he returned to the party, he found them seated by a fire—for the air had grown strangely chill and the sky overcast—in apparently amicable conversation. Piney was actually talking in an impulsive, girlish fashion to the Duchess, who was listening with an interest and animation she had not shown for many days. The Innocent was holding forth, apparently with equal effect, to Mr. Oakhurst and Mother Shipton, who was actually relaxing into amiability. "Is this yer a d—d picnic?" said Uncle Billy, with inward scorn, as he surveyed the sylvan group, the glancing firelight, and the tethered animals in the foreground. Suddenly an idea mingled with the alcoholic fumes that disturbed his brain. It was apparently of a jocular nature, for he felt impelled to slap his leg again and cram his fist into his mouth.

As the shadows crept slowly up the mountain, a slight breeze rocked the tops of the pine trees and moaned through their long and gloomy aisles. The ruined cabin, patched and covered with pine boughs, was set apart for the ladies. As the lovers parted, they unaffectedly exchanged a kiss, so honest and sincere that it might have been heard above the swaying pines. The frail Duchess and the malevolent Mother Shipton were probably too stunned to remark upon this last evidence of simplicity, and so turned without a word to the hut. The fire was replenished, the men lay down before the door, and in a few minutes were asleep.

Mr. Oakhurst was a light sleeper. Toward morning he awoke benumbed and cold. As he stirred the dying fire, the wind, which was now blowing strongly, brought to his cheek that which caused the blood to leave it—snow!

He started to his feet with the intention of awakening the sleepers, for there was no time to lose. But turning to where Uncle Billy had been lying, he found him gone. A suspicion leaped to his brain and a curse to his lips. He ran to the spot where the mules had been tethered; they were no longer there. The tracks were already rapidly disappearing in the snow.

The momentary excitement brought Mr. Oakhurst back to the fire with his usual calm. He did not waken the sleepers. The Innocent slumbered peacefully, with a smile on his good-humored, freckled face; the virgin Piney slept beside her frailer sisters as sweetly as though attended by celestial guardians, and Mr. Oakhurst, drawing his blanket over his shoulders, stroked his mustaches and waited for the dawn. It came slowly in a whirling mist of snowflakes that dazzled and confused the eye. What could be seen of the landscape appeared magically changed. He looked over the valley and summed up the present and future in two words: "Snowed in!"

A careful inventory of the provisions, which, fortunately for the party, had been stored within the hut, and so escaped the felonious fingers of Uncle Billy, disclosed the fact that with care and prudence they might last ten days longer. "That is," said Mr. Oakhurst, *sotto voce* to the Innocent, "if you're willing to board us. If you ain't—and perhaps you'd better not—you can wait till Uncle Billy gets back with provisions." For some occult reason, Mr. Oakhurst could not bring himself to disclose Uncle Billy's rascality, and so offered the hypothesis that he had wandered from the camp and had accidentally stampeded the animals. He dropped a warning to the Duchess and Mother Shipton, who of course knew the facts of their associate's defection. "They'll find out the truth about us *all* when they find out anything," he added, significantly, "and there's no good frightening them now."

Tom Simson not only put all his worldly store at the disposal of Mr. Oakhurst, but seemed to enjoy the prospect of their enforced seclusion. "We'll have a good camp for a week, and then the snow'll melt, and we'll all go back together." The cheerful gaiety of the young man and Mr. Oakhurst's calm infected the others. The Innocent, with the aid of pine boughs,

82 extemporized a thatch for the roofless cabin, and the Duchess directed Piney in the rearrangement of the interior with a taste and tact that opened the blue eyes of that provincial maiden to their fullest extent. "I reckon now you're used to fine things at Poker Flat," said Piney. The Duchess turned away sharply to conceal something that reddened her cheeks through its professional tint, and Mother Shipton requested Piney not to "chatter." But when Mr. Oakhurst returned from a weary search for the trail, he heard the sound of happy laughter echoed from the rocks. He stopped in some alarm, and his thoughts first naturally reverted to the whiskey, which he had prudently cached. "And yet it don't somehow sound like whiskey," said the gambler. It was not until he caught sight of the blazing fire through the still-blinding storm and the group around it that he settled to the conviction that it was "square fun."

Whether Mr. Oakhurst had cached his cards with the whiskey as something debarred the free access of the community, I cannot say. It was certain that, in Mother Shipton's words, he "didn't say cards once" during that evening. Haply the time was beguiled by an accordion, produced somewhat ostentatiously by Tom Simson from his pack. Notwithstanding some difficulties attending the manipulation of this instrument, Piney Woods managed to pluck several reluctant melodies from its keys, to an accompaniment by the Innocent on a pair of bone castinets. But the crowning festivity of the evening was reached in a rude camp-meeting hymn, which the lovers, joining hands, sang with great earnestness and vociferation. I fear that a certain defiant tone and Covenanter's swing to its chorus, rather than any devotional quality, caused it speedily to infect the others, who at last joined in the refrain:

> I'm proud to live in the service of the Lord,
> And I'm bound to die in His army.

The pines rocked, the storm eddied and whirled above the miserable group, and the flames of their altar leaped heavenward, as if in token of the vow.

At midnight the storm abated, the rolling clouds parted, and the stars glittered keenly above the sleeping camp. Mr. Oakhurst, whose professional habits had enabled him to live on the smallest possible amount of sleep, in dividing the watch with Tom Simson somehow managed to take upon himself the greater part of that duty. He excused himself to the Innocent by saying that he had "often been a week without sleep." "Doing what?" asked Tom. "Poker!" replied Oakhurst sententiously. "When a man gets a streak of luck, he don't get tired. The luck gives in first. Luck," continued the gambler reflectively, "is a mighty queer thing. All you know about it for certain is that it's bound to change. And it's finding out when it's going to change that makes you. We've had a streak of bad luck since we left Poker Flat—you come along, and slap, you get into it, too. If you can hold your cards right along you're all right. For," added the gambler with cheerful irrelevance:

> "I'm proud to live in the service of the Lord,
> And I'm bound to die in His army."

The third day came, and the sun, looking through the white-curtained valley, saw the outcasts divide their slowly decreasing store of provisions for the morning meal. It was one of the peculiarities of that mountain climate that its rays diffused a kindly warmth over the wintry landscape, as if in regretful commiseration of the past. But it revealed drift on drift of snow piled high around the hut—a hopeless, uncharted, trackless sea of white lying below the rocky shores to which the castaways still clung. Through the marvelously clear air, the smoke of the pastoral village of Poker Flat rose miles away. Mother Shipton saw it, and from a remote pinnacle of her

84 rocky fastness hurled in that direction a final malediction. It was her last vituperative attempt, and perhaps for that reason was invested with a certain degree of sublimity. It did her good, she privately informed the Duchess. "Just you go out there and cuss, and see." She then set herself to the task of amusing "the child," as she and the Duchess were pleased to call Piney. Piney was no chicken, but it was a soothing and original theory of the pair thus to account for the fact that she didn't swear and wasn't improper.

When night crept up again through the gorges, the reedy nodes of the accordion rose and fell in fitful spasms and long-drawn gasps by the flickering campfire. But music failed to fill entirely the aching void left by insufficient food, and a new diversion was proposed by Piney—storytelling. Neither Mr. Oakhurst nor his female companions caring to relate their personal experiences, this plan would have failed, too, but for the Innocent. Some months before he had chanced upon a stray copy of Mr. Pope's ingenious translation of the *Iliad*. He now proposed to narrate the principal incidents of that poem—having thoroughly mastered the argument and fairly forgotten the words—in the current vernacular of Sandy Bar. And so for the rest of that night the Homeric demigods again walked the earth. Trojan bully and wily Greek wrestled in the winds, and the great pines in the canyon seemed to bow to the wrath of the son of Peleus. Mr. Oakhurst listened with quiet satisfaction. Most especially was he interested in the fate of "Ash-heels," as the Innocent persisted in denominating the "swift-footed Achilles."

So with small food and much of Homer and the accordion, a week passed over the heads of the outcasts. The sun again forsook them, and again from leaden skies the snowflakes were sifted over the land. Day by day, closer around them drew the snowy circle, until at last they looked from their prison over drifted walls of dazzling white that towered twenty feet above their heads. It became more and more difficult to replenish their fires, even from the fallen trees beside them, now half-hidden in the drifts. And yet no one complained. The lovers turned from the dreary prospect and looked into each other's eyes, and were happy. Mr. Oakhurst settled himself coolly to the losing game before him. The Duchess, more cheerful than she had been, assumed the care of Piney. Only Mother Shipton—once the strongest of the party—seemed to sicken and fade. At midnight on the tenth day she called Oakhurst to her side. "I'm going," she said, in a voice of querulous weakness, "but don't say anything about it. Don't waken the kids. Take the bundle from under my head and open it." Mr. Oakhurst did so. It contained Mother Shipton's rations for the last week, untouched. "Give 'em to the child," she said, pointing to the sleeping Piney. "You've starved yourself," said the gambler. "That's what they call it," said the woman querulously, as she lay down again, and, turning her face to the wall, passed quietly away.

The accordion and the bones were put aside that day, and Homer was forgotten. When the body of Mother Shipton had been committed to the snow, Mr. Oakhurst took the Innocent aside and showed him a pair of snowshoes which he had fashioned from the old packsaddle. "There's one chance in a hundred to save her yet," he said, pointing to Piney. "But it's there," he added, pointing toward Poker Flat. "If you can reach there in two days she's safe." "And you?" asked Tom Simson. "I'll stay here," was the curt reply.

The lovers parted with a long embrace. "You are not going, too?" said the Duchess, as she saw Mr. Oakhurst apparently waiting to accompany him. "As far as the canyon," he replied. He turned suddenly and kissed the Duchess, leaving her pallid face aflame and her trembling limbs rigid with amazement.

Night came, but not Mr. Oakhurst. It brought the storm again and the whirling snow. Then the Duchess, feeding the fire, found that someone had quietly piled beside the hut enough fuel to last a few days longer. The tears rose to her eyes, but she hid them from Piney.

The women slept but little. In the morning, looking into each other's faces, they read their fate. Neither spoke; but Piney, accepting the position of the stronger, drew near and placed her arm around the Duchess's waist. They kept this attitude for the rest of the day. That night the storm reached its greatest fury, and, rending asunder the protecting pines, invaded the very hut.

Toward morning they found themselves unable to feed the fire, which gradually died away. As the embers slowly blackened, the Duchess crept closer to Piney and broke the silence of many hours: "Piney, can you pray?" "No, dear," said Piney simply. The Duchess, without knowing exactly why, felt relieved, and, putting her head upon Piney's shoulder, spoke no more. And so reclining, the younger and purer pillowing the head of her soiled sister upon her virgin breast, they fell asleep.

The wind lulled as if it feared to waken them. Feathery drifts of snow, shaken from the long pine boughs, flew like white-winged birds, and settled about them as they slept. The moon through the rifted clouds looked down upon what had been the camp. But all human stain, all trace of earthly travail, was hidden beneath the spotless mantle mercifully flung from above.

They slept all that day and the next, nor did they awaken when voices and footsteps broke the silence of the camp. And when pitying fingers brushed the snow from their wan faces, you could scarcely have told from the equal peace that dwelt upon them which was she that had sinned. Even the law of Poker Flat recognized this, and turned away, leaving them still locked in each other's arms.

But at the head of the gulch, on one of the largest pine trees, they found the deuce of clubs pinned to the bark with a bowie knife. It bore the following, written in pencil, in a firm hand:

✝

BENEATH THIS TREE
LIES THE BODY
OF
JOHN OAKHURST,
WHO STRUCK A STREAK OF BAD LUCK
ON THE 23D OF NOVEMBER, 1850,
AND
HANDED IN HIS CHECKS
ON THE 7TH DECEMBER, 1850.

☨

And pulseless and cold, with a derringer by his side and a bullet in his heart, though still calm as in life, beneath the snow lay he who was at once the strongest and yet the weakest of the outcasts of Poker Flat.

PLOT

A story does not include every thought, word, and deed in a fictional character's life. It does include those events, thoughts, and dialogue that the author feels will enliven the characters and the theme. This carefully selected series of actions is the story's plot.

Plot is a tightened spring waiting to uncoil. The author builds a controlled tension by letting the reader share in the main character's problems. The reader expects and wants something to result from these conflicts. As the author reveals events, the spring unwinds, the tension is released, and the story reaches its conclusion.

Several kinds of conflicts are possible. Two characters may be at odds in personality or values (Captain Jolliffe and his wife in "To Please His Wife"). A character may differ from society as represented by other characters (Soapy and the police in "The Cop and the Anthem"). There may even be conflicts within a character (Owen and self-doubt in "The Artist of the Beautiful").

Whatever the conflict, the reader wants a solution. A story usually has a high point of dramatic tension, the climax. The rising action is what leads to this turning point. The denouement is the final release or explanation of the story's resolution. Thus, in "A White Heron" many readers would call Sylvia's sighting of the heron the climax. Many would identify the denouement as her hinted-at decision on whether to tell of the bird's whereabouts.

Authors vary in their methods of building and releasing tension brought about by conflict. But a measure of their success or failure with plot is the reader's level of satisfaction.

And he began to tell the story of the string. They did not believe him. They laughed.

THE PIECE OF STRING

Guy de Maupassant

It was market day, and over all the roads around Goderville the peasants and their wives were coming toward the town. The men walked easily, lurching the whole body forward at every step. Their long legs were twisted and deformed by the slow, painful labors of the country; by bending over to plow, which is what also makes their left shoulders too high and their figures crooked; and by reaping corn, which obliges them for steadiness' sake to spread their knees too wide. Their starched blue blouses, shining as though varnished, ornamented at collar and cuffs with little patterns of white stitchwork, and blown up big around their bony bodies, seemed exactly like balloons about to soar, but putting forth a head, two arms, and two feet.

Some of these fellows dragged a cow or a calf at the end of a rope. And just behind the animal, beating it over the back with a leaf-covered branch to hasten its pace, went their wives, carrying large baskets from which came forth the heads of chickens or the heads of ducks. These women walked with steps far shorter and quicker than the men; their figures, withered and upright, were adorned with scanty little shawls pinned over their flat bosoms; and they enveloped their heads each in a white cloth, closely fastened around the hair and surmounted by a cap.

Then a wagon passed by at the jerky trot of a nag, shaking up strangely the two men on the seat and the woman at the bottom of the cart, who held fast to its sides to lessen the hard joltings.

In the marketplace at Goderville was a great crowd, a mingled multitude of men and beasts. The horns of cattle, the high and long-napped hats of wealthy peasants, the headdresses of the women came to the surface of that sea. And voices clamorous, sharp, shrill, made a continuous and savage din. Above it a huge burst of laughter from the robust lungs of a merry countryman would sometimes sound, or sometimes the long lowing of a cow tied fast to the wall of a house.

It all smelled of the stable, of milk, of hay, and of sweat, giving off that half-human, half-animal odor which is peculiar to the people of the fields.

Maître Hauchecorne, of Bréauté, had just arrived at Goderville and was making his way toward the square when he perceived on the ground a little piece of string. Maître Hauchecorne, economical, like all true Normans, reflected that everything was worth picking up that could be of any use; and he stooped down painfully, for he suffered from rheumatism. He took the bit of thin cord from the ground and was carefully preparing to roll it up when he saw Maître Malandain, the harness-maker, on his doorstep, looking at him. They had once had a quarrel about a halter, and they had remained angry, bearing malice on both sides. Maître Hauchecorne was overcome with a sort of shame at being seen thus by his enemy, looking in the dirt for a bit of string. He quickly hid his find beneath his blouse; then in the pocket of his breeches; then pretended to be still looking for something on the ground which he did not discover; and at last went off toward the marketplace with his head bent forward and a body almost doubled in two by rheumatic pains.

He lost himself immediately in the noisy and slow crowd, which was agitated by interminable haggling. The peasants examined the cows, went off, came back, always in great perplexity and fear of being cheated, never quite daring to decide, spying at the eye of the seller, trying ceaselessly to discover the tricks of the man and the defect in the beast.

The women, having placed their great baskets at their feet, had pulled out the poultry that lay upon the ground, tied by the legs, with scared eyes and scarlet combs.

They listened to offers, maintained their prices with a dry manner, with an impassive face; or, suddenly, perhaps, deciding to take the lower price which was offered, they cried out to the customer, who was departing slowly:

"All right, I'll let you have them, Maître Anthime."

Then, little by little, the square became empty, and when the Angelus rang at noon, those who lived at a distance poured into the inns.

At Jourdain's the great room was filled with people eating, just as the vast court was filled with vehicles of every sort—carts, cabs, wagons, carriages, tilt-carts which have no name, yellow with mud, misshapen, pieced together, raising their shafts to heaven like two arms, or it may be with their nose in the dirt and their rear in the air.

Just opposite to where the diners were at table the huge fireplace, full of clear flame, threw a lively heat on the backs of those who sat along the right. Three spits were turning, loaded with chickens, pigeons, and with joints of mutton; and a delectable odor of roast meat, and of gravy gushing over crisp brown skin, took wing from the hearth, kindled merriment, caused mouths to water.

All the aristocracy of the plow were eating there, at Maître Jourdain's, the innkeeper's, a dealer in horses also, and a sharp fellow who had made a pretty penny in his day.

The dishes were passed around, were emptied, with jugs of yellow cider. Everyone told of his affairs, of his purchases and his sales. They asked news about the crops. The weather was good for green stuffs, but a little wet for wheat.

All of a sudden the drum rolled in the court before the house. Everyone, except some of the most indifferent, was on his feet at once, and ran to the door, to the windows, with his mouth still full and his napkin in his hand.

When the public crier had finished his drumroll, he called forth in a jerky voice, making his pauses out of time:

"Be it known to the inhabitants of Goderville, and in general to all persons present at the market, that there has been lost this morning, on the Beuzeville road, between nine and ten o'clock, a pocketbook of black leather, containing five hundred francs and business papers. You are requested to return it to the mayor's office, at once, or to Maître Fortuné Houlbrèque, of Manneville. There will be twenty francs' reward."

Then the man departed. They heard once more at a distance the dull beatings on the drum and the faint voice of the crier.

Then they began to talk of this event, reckoning up the chances which Maître Houlbrèque had of finding or of not finding his pocketbook again. And the meal went on. They were finishing their coffee when the corporal of the gendarmes appeared on the threshold.

"Is Maître Hauchecorne, of Bréauté, here?" he asked.

Maître Hauchecorne, seated at the other end of the table, answered, "Here I am."

And the corporal resumed:

"Maître Hauchecorne, will you have the kindness to come with me to the mayor's office? The mayor would like to speak to you."

The peasant, surprised and uneasy, gulped down his little glass of cognac, got up, and even worse bent over than in the morning, since the first steps after a rest were always particularly difficult, started off, repeating:

"Here I am, here I am."

And he followed the corporal.

The mayor was waiting for him, seated in an armchair. He was the notary of the place, a tall, grave man of pompous speech.

"Maître Hauchecorne," said he, "this morning, on the Beuzeville road, you were seen to pick up the pocketbook lost by Maître Houlbrèque, of Manneville."

The countryman, speechless, regarded the mayor, frightened already by this suspicion which rested on him—he knew not why.

"I, I picked up that pocketbook?"

"Yes, you."

"I swear I didn't even know nothing about it at all."

"You were seen."

"They saw me, me? Who says he saw me?"

"Monsieur Malandain, the harness-maker."

Then the old man remembered, understood, and, reddening with anger: "Ah! He saw me, did he, the rascal? He saw me picking up this string here, M'sieu' the Mayor."

And fumbling at the botton of his pocket, he pulled out of it the little end of string. But the mayor incredulously shook his head. "You will not make me believe, Maître Hauchecorne, that Monsieur Malandain, who is a man worthy of credit, has mistaken this string for a pocketbook."

The peasant, furious, raised his hand and spit as if to attest his good faith, repeating:

"For all that, it is God's truth, the blessed truth, M'sieu' the Mayor. There! On my soul and my salvation I repeat it."

The mayor continued:

"After having picked up the thing in question, you even looked for some time in the mud to see if a piece of money had not dropped out of it."

The good man was suffocated with indignation and with fear.

"If they can say!—if they can say . . . such lies as that to slander an honest man! If they can say!—"

He could protest all he wanted; nobody believed him.

He was confronted with Monsieur Malandain, who repeated and sustained his testimony. They abused one another for an hour. At his own request Maître Hauchecorne was searched. Nothing was found upon him. At last, the mayor, much perplexed, sent him away, warning him that he would inform the public prosecutor and ask for orders.

The news had spread. When he left the mayor's office, the old man was surrounded, interrogated with a curiosity which was serious or mocking as the case might be, but into which no indignation entered. And he began to tell the story of the string. They did not believe him. They laughed.

He passed on, buttonholed by everyone, himself buttonholing his acquaintances, beginning over and over again his tale and his protestations, showing his pockets turned inside out to prove that he had nothing.

They said to him, "You old rogue, go on!"

And he grew angry, exasperated, feverish, in despair at not being believed, and always telling his story.

Night came. It was time to go home. He set out with three of his neighbors, to whom he pointed out the place where he had picked up the end of string; and all the way he talked of his adventure.

That evening he made the round in the village of Bréauté, so as to tell everyone. He met only unbelievers.

It made him sick all night long.

The next day, about one in the afternoon, Marius Paumelle, a farmhand of Maître Breton, the market grower at Ymauville, returned the pocketbook and its contents to Maître Houlbrèque, of Manneville.

This man claimed that indeed he had found it on the road; but not knowing how to read, he had carried it home and given it to his master.

The news spread throughout the vicinity. Maître Hauchecorne was informed. He put himself at once upon the go, and began to relate his story as completed by the denouement. He triumphed.

"What grieved me," said he, "was not the thing itself, do you understand; but it was the lies. There's nothing does you so much harm as being in disgrace for lying."

All day he talked of his adventure, he told it on the roads to the people who passed; at the cabaret to the people who drank; and the next Sunday, when they came out of church. He even stopped strangers to tell them about it. He was easy, now, and yet something worried him without his knowing exactly what it was. People had a joking manner while they listened. They did not seem convinced. He seemed to feel their gossip behind his back.

On Tuesday of the next week he went to market at Goderville, prompted entirely by the need of telling his story. Malandain, standing on his doorstep, began to laugh as he saw him pass. Why?

He accosted a farmer of Criquetot, who did not let him finish, but giving him a punch in the pit of his stomach, cried in his face, "Get out of here, you scoundrel!" and then took to his heels.

Maître Hauchecorne remained speechless and grew more and more uneasy. Why had he been called a scoundrel?

When seated at table in Jourdain's tavern, he began again to explain the whole affair. A horse dealer from Montivilliers shouted at him, "Get out, get out, you old scamp! I know all about your piece of string!"

Hauchecorne stammered, "But since they found it again, the pocketbook!"

But the other continued, "Hold your tongue, Papa. There's one who finds it and there's another who returns it. Anyway, you're tangled up with it."

The peasant was choked. He understood at last. They accused him of having had the pocketbook brought back by an accomplice, by a confederate. He tried to protest. The whole table began to laugh. He could not finish his dinner and went away amid a chorus of jeers.

He went home, ashamed and indignant, choked with rage, with confusion, dumbfounded all the more because by his Norman cunning he was perhaps capable of having done what they accused him of, and even of boasting of it as a good trick. His innocence dimly seemed to him impossible to prove, his craftiness being so well-known. And he felt himself struck to the heart by the injustice of the suspicion.

Then he began anew to tell of his adventure, lengthening his recital every day, each time adding new proofs, more energetic protestations, and more solemn oaths which he thought of, which he prepared in his hours of solitude, his mind being entirely occupied by the story of the string. The more complicated his defense and the more artful his arguments, the less he was believed.

"Those are liars' proofs," they said behind his back.

He felt this; it preyed upon his heart. He exhausted himself in useless efforts.

He was visibly wasting away.

The jokers now made him tell the story of "The Piece of String" to amuse them, just as you make a soldier who has been on a campaign tell his story of the battle. His mind, struck at the root, grew weak.

About the end of December he took to his bed.

He died early in January, and in the delirium of his death agony he protested his innocence, repeating:

"A little piece of string—a piece of string—see, here it is, M'sieu' the Mayor."

TO PLEASE HIS WIFE

Thomas Hardy

1

The interior of St. James's Church, in Havenpool Town, was slowly darkening under the close clouds of a winter afternoon. It was Sunday—service had just ended, the face of the parson in the pulpit was buried in his hands, and the congregation, with a cheerful sigh of release, were rising from their knees to depart.

For the moment the stillness was so complete that the surging of the sea could be heard outside the harbor-bar. Then it was broken by the footsteps of the clerk going towards the west door to open it in the usual manner for the exit of the assembly. Before, however, he had reached the doorway, the latch was lifted from without, and the dark figure of a man in a sailor's garb appeared against the light.

The clerk stepped aside, the sailor closed the door gently behind him, and advanced up the nave till he stood at the chancel step. The parson looked up from the private little prayer which, after so many for the parish, he quite fairly took for himself, rose to his feet, and stared at the intruder.

"I beg your pardon, sir," said the sailor, addressing the minister in a voice distinctly audible to all the congregation. "I have come here to offer thanks for my narrow escape from shipwreck. I am given to understand that it is a proper thing to do, if you have no objection?"

The parson, after a moment's pause, said hesitatingly, "I have no objection; certainly. It is usual to mention any such wish before service, so that the proper words may be used in the General Thanksgiving. But, if you wish, we can read from the form for use after a storm at sea."

"Aye, sure; I ain't particular," said the sailor.

The clerk thereupon directed the sailor to the page in the prayer book where the collect of thanksgiving would be found, and the rector began reading it, the sailor kneeling where he stood, and repeating it after him word by word in a distinct voice. The people, who had remained agape and motionless at the proceeding, mechanically knelt down likewise; but they continued to regard the isolated form of the sailor, who, in the precise middle of the chancel step, remained fixed on his knees, facing the east, his hat beside him, his hands joined, and he quite unconscious of his appearance in their regard.

When his thanksgiving had come to an end he rose; the people rose also; and all went out of church together. As soon as the sailor emerged, so that the remaining daylight fell upon his face, old inhabitants began to recognize him as no other than Shadrach Jolliffe, a young man who had not been seen at Havenpool for several years. A son of the town, his parents had died when he was quite young, on which account he had early gone to sea, in the Newfoundland trade.

He talked with this and that townsman as he walked, informing them that, since leaving his native place years before, he had become captain and owner of a small coasting ketch, which had providentially been saved from the gale as well as himself. Presently he drew near to two girls who were going out of the churchyard in front of him; they had been sitting in the nave at his entry and had watched his doings with deep interest, afterwards discussing him as they moved out of church together. One was a slight and gentle creature, the other a tall, large-framed, deliberative girl. Captain Jolliffe regarded the loose curls of their hair, their backs and shoulders, down to their heels, for some time.

"Who may them two maids be?" he whispered to his neighbor.

"The little one is Emily Hanning; the tall one Joanna Phippard."

"Ah! I recollect 'em now, to be sure."

He advanced to their elbow and genially stole a gaze at them.

"Emily, you don't know me?" said the sailor, turning his beaming brown eyes on her.

"I think I do, Mr. Jolliffe," said Emily shyly.

The other girl looked straight at him with her dark eyes.

"The face of Miss Joanna I don't call to mind so well," he continued. "But I know her beginnings and kindred."

They walked and talked together, Jolliffe narrating particulars of his late narrow escape, till they reached the corner of Sloop Lane, in which Emily Hanning dwelt, when, with a nod and smile, she left them. Soon the sailor parted also from Joanna, and, having no especial errand or appointment, turned back towards Emily's house. She lived with her father, who called himself an accountant, the daughter, however, keeping a little stationery shop as a supplemental provision for the gaps of his somewhat uncertain business. On entering, Jolliffe found father and daughter about to begin tea.

"Oh, I didn't know it was teatime," he said, "Aye, I'll have a cup with much pleasure."

He remained to tea and long afterwards, telling more tales of his seafaring life. Several neighbors called to listen and were asked to come in. Somehow Emily Hanning lost her heart to the sailor that Sunday night, and in the course of a week or two there was a tender understanding between them.

One moonlight evening in the next month Shadrach was ascending out of the town by the long straight road eastward, to an elevated suburb where the more fashionable houses stood—

if anything near this ancient port could be called fashionable—
when he saw a figure before him whom, from her manner of
glancing back, he took to be Emily. But, on coming up, he
found she was Joanna Phippard. He gave a gallant greeting
and walked beside her.

"Go along," she said, "or Emily will be jealous!"

He seemed not to like the suggestion, and remained.

What was said and what was done on that walk never could
be clearly recollected by Shadrach; but in some way or other
Joanna contrived to wean him away from her gentler and
younger rival. From that week onwards, Jolliffe was seen more
and more in the wake of Joanna Phippard and less in the company of Emily; and it was soon rumored about the quay that
old Jolliffe's son, who had come home from sea, was going to
be married to the former young woman, to the great disappointment of the latter.

Just after this report had gone about, Joanna dressed herself
for a walk one morning and started for Emily's house in the
little cross street. Intelligence of the deep sorrow of her friend
on account of the loss of Shadrach had reached her ears also,
and her conscience reproached her for winning him away.

Joanna was not altogether satisfied with the sailor. She liked
his attentions, and she coveted the dignity of matrimony; but
she had never been deeply in love with Jolliffe. For one thing,
she was ambitious, and socially his position was hardly so good
as her own, and there was always the chance of an attractive
woman mating considerably above her. It had long been in her
mind that she would not strongly object to give him back again
to Emily if her friend felt so very badly about him. To this end
she had written a letter of renunciation to Shadrach, which
letter she carried in her hand, intending to send it if personal observation of Emily convinced her that her friend was
suffering.

Joanna entered Sloop Lane and stepped down into the
stationery shop, which was below the pavement level. Emily's

TO PLEASE HIS WIFE

father was never at home at this hour of the day, and it seemed as though Emily were not at home either, for the visitor could make nobody hear. Customers came so seldom hither that a five minutes' absence of the proprietor counted for little. Joanna waited in the little shop, where Emily had tastefully set out—as women can—articles in themselves of slight value, so as to obscure the meagerness of the stock-in-trade; till she saw a figure pausing without the window apparently absorbed in the contemplation of the sixpenny books, packets of paper, and prints hung on a string. It was Captain Shadrach Jolliffe, peering in to ascertain if Emily were there alone. Moved by an impulse of reluctance to meet him in a spot which breathed of Emily, she slipped through the door that communicated with the parlor at the back. Joanna had frequently done so before, for in her friendship with Emily she had the freedom of the house without ceremony.

Jolliffe entered the shop. Through the thin blind which screened the glass partition, she could see that he was disappointed at not finding Emily there. He was about to go out again, when Emily's form darkened the doorway, hastening home from some errand. At sight of Jolliffe she started back as if she would have gone out again.

"Don't run away, Emily; don't!" said he. "What can make ye afraid?"

"I'm not afraid, Captain Jolliffe. Only—only I saw you all of a sudden, and—it made me jump!" Her voice showed that her heart had jumped even more than the rest of her.

"I just called as I was passing," he said.

"For some paper?" She hastened behind the counter.

"No, no, Emily; why do you get behind there? Why not stay by me? You seem to hate me."

"I don't hate you. How can I?"

"Then come out, so that we can talk like Christians."

Emily obeyed with a fitful laugh, till she stood again beside him in the open part of the shop.

"There's a dear," he said.

"You mustn't say that, Captain Jolliffe; because the words belong to somebody else."

"Ah! I know what you mean. But, Emily, upon my life I didn't know till this morning that you cared one bit about me, or I should not have done as I have done. I have the best of feelings for Joanna, but I know that from the beginning she hasn't cared for me more than in a friendly way; and I see now the one I ought to have asked to be my wife. You know, Emily, when a man comes home from sea after a long voyage he's as blind as a bat—he can't see who's who in women. They are all alike to him, beautiful creatures, and he takes the first that comes easy, without thinking if she loves him, or if he might not soon love another better than her. From the first I inclined to you most, but you were so backward and shy that I thought you didn't want me to bother ye, and so I went to Joanna."

"Don't say any more, Mr. Jolliffe, don't!" said she, choking. "You are going to marry Joanna next month, and it is wrong to—to—"

"Oh, Emily, my darling!" he cried, and clasped her little figure in his arms before she was aware.

Joanna, behind the curtain, turned pale, tried to withdraw her eyes, but could not.

"It is only you I love as a man ought to love the woman he is going to marry; and I know this from what Joanna has said, that she will willingly let me off! She wants to marry higher I know, and only said 'Yes' to me out of kindness. A fine, tall girl like her isn't the sort for a plain sailor's wife—you be the best suited for that."

He kissed her and kissed her again, her flexible form quivering in the agitation of his embrace.

"I wonder—are you sure—Joanna is going to break off with you? Oh, are you sure? Because—"

"I know she would not wish to make us miserable. She will release me."

"Oh, I hope—I hope she will! Don't stay any longer, Captain Jolliffe!"

He lingered, however, till a customer came for a penny stick of sealing wax, and then he withdrew.

Green envy had overspread Joanna at the scene. She looked about for a way of escape. To get out without Emily's knowledge of her visit was indispensable. She crept from the parlor into the passage, and thence to the back door of the house, where she let herself noiselessly into the street.

The sight of that caress had reversed all her resolutions. She could not let Shadrach go. Reaching home, she burnt the letter, and told her mother that if Captain Jolliffe called she was too unwell to see him.

Shadrach, however, did not call. He sent her a note expressing in simple language the state of his feelings, and asked to be allowed to take advantage of the hints she had given him that her affection, too, was little more than friendly by cancelling the engagement.

Looking out upon the harbor and the island beyond, he waited and waited in his lodgings for an answer that did not come. The suspense grew to be so intolerable that after dark he went up the High Street. He could not resist calling at Joanna's to learn his fate.

Her mother said her daughter was too unwell to see him, and to his questioning admitted that it was in consequence of a letter received from himself, which had distressed her deeply.

"You know what it was about, perhaps, Mrs. Phippard?" he said.

Mrs. Phippard owned that she did, adding that it put them in a very painful position. Thereupon Shadrach, fearing that he had been guilty of an enormity, explained that if his letter had pained Joanna it must be owing to a misunderstanding, since he had thought it would be a relief to her. If otherwise, he would hold himself bound by his word, and she was to think of the letter as never having been written.

Next morning he received an oral message from the young woman, asking him to fetch her home from a meeting that evening. This he did, and while walking from the Town Hall to her door, with her hand in his arm, she said:

"It is all the same as before between us, isn't it, Shadrach? Your letter was sent in mistake?"

"It is all the same as before," he answered, "if you say it must be."

"I wish it to be," she murmured, with hard lineaments, as she thought of Emily.

Shadrach was a religious and scrupulous man, who respected his word as his life. Shortly afterwards the wedding took place, Jolliffe having conveyed to Emily as gently as possible the error he had fallen into when estimating Joanna's mood as one of indifference.

2

A month after the marriage Joanna's mother died, and the couple were obliged to turn their attention to very practical matters. Now that she was left without a parent, Joanna could not bear the notion of her husband going to sea again, but the question was, What could he do at home? They finally decided to take on a small grocer's shop in High Street, the goodwill and stock of which were waiting to be disposed of at that time. Shadrach knew nothing of shopkeeping, and Joanna very little, but they hoped to learn.

To the management of this grocery business they now devoted all their energies and continued to conduct it for many succeeding years, without great success. Two sons were born to them, whom their mother loved to idolatry, although she had never passionately loved her husband; and she lavished upon them all her forethought and care. But the shop did not thrive, and the large dreams she had entertained of her sons' education and career became attenuated in the face of realities. Their schooling was of the plainest, but, being by the sea, they grew alert in all such nautical arts and enterprises as were attractive to their age.

The great interest of the Jolliffes' married life, outside their own immediate household, had lain in the marriage of Emily. By one of those odd chances which lead those that lurk in unexpected corners to be discovered, while the obvious are passed by, the gentle girl had been seen and loved by a thriving merchant of the town, a widower, some years older than herself, though still in the prime of life. At first Emily had declared that she never, never could marry anyone; but Mr. Lester had quietly persevered, and had at last won her reluctant assent. Two children also were the fruit of this union, and, as they grew and prospered, Emily declared that she had never supposed that she could live to be so happy.

The worthy merchant's home, one of those large, substantial brick mansions frequently jammed up in old-fashioned towns, faced directly on the High Street, nearly opposite to the grocery shop of the Jolliffes, and it now became the pain of Joanna to behold the woman whose place she had usurped out of pure covetousness, looking down from her position of comparative wealth upon the humble shop window with its dusty sugarloaves, heaps of raisins, and canisters of tea, over which it was her own lot to preside. The business having so dwindled, Joanna was obliged to serve in the shop herself, and it galled and mortified her that Emily Lester, sitting in her large drawing room over the way, could witness her own dancings up and down behind the counter at the beck and call of wretched twopenny customers, whose patronage she was driven to welcome gladly—persons to whom she was compelled to be civil in the street, while Emily was bounding along with her children and her governess, and conversing with the genteelest people of the town and neighborhood. This was what she had

108 gained by not letting Shadrach Jolliffe, whom she had so faintly loved, carry his affection elsewhere.

Shadrach was a good and honest man, and he had been faithful to her in heart and in deed. Time had clipped the wings of his love for Emily in his devotion to the mother of his boys: he had quite lived down that impulsive earlier fancy, and Emily had become in his regard nothing more than a friend. It was the same with Emily's feelings for him. Possibly, had she found the least cause for jealousy, Joanna would almost have been better satisfied. It was in the absolute acquiescence of Emily and Shadrach in the results she herself had contrived that her discontent found nourishment.

Shadrach was not endowed with the narrow shrewdness necessary for developing a retail business in the face of many competitors. Did a customer inquire if the grocer could really recommend the wondrous substitute for eggs which a persevering bagman had forced into his stock, he would answer that "when you did not put eggs into a pudding it was difficult to taste them there"; and when he was asked if his "real Mocha coffee" was real Mocha, he would say grimly, "as understood in small shops." The way to wealth was not by this route.

One summer day, when the big brick house opposite was reflecting the oppressive sun's heat into the shop, and nobody was present but husband and wife, Joanna looked across at Emily's door, where a wealthy visitor's carriage had drawn up. Traces of patronage had been visible in Emily's manner of late.

"Shadrach, the truth is, you are not a businessman," his wife sadly murmured. "You were not brought up to shopkeeping, and it is impossible for a man to make a fortune at an occupation he had jumped into, as you did into this."

Jolliffe agreed with her, in this as in everything else. "Not that I care a rope's end about making a fortune," he said cheerfully. "I am happy enough, and we can rub on somehow."

She looked again at the great house through the screen of

bottled pickles.

"Rub on—yes," she said bitterly. "But see how well off Emmy Lester is, who used to be so poor! Her boys will go to college, no doubt; and think of yours—obliged to go to the parish school!"

Shadrach's thoughts had flown to Emily.

"Nobody," he said good-humoredly, "ever did Emily a better turn than you did, Joanna, when you warned her off me and put an end to that little simpering nonsense between us, so as to leave it in her power to say 'Aye' to Lester when he came along."

This almost maddened her.

"Don't speak of bygones!" she implored, in stern sadness. "But think, for the boys' and my sake, not for your own, what are we to do to get richer?"

"Well," he said, becoming serious, "to tell the truth, I have always felt myself unfit for this business, though I've never liked to say so. I seem to want more room for sprawling; a more open space to strike out in than here among friends and neighbors. I could get rich as well as any man, if I tried my own way."

"I wish you would! What is your way?"

"To go to sea again."

She had been the very one to keep him at home, hating the semiwidowed existence of sailors' wives. But her ambition checked her instincts now, and she said:

"Do you think success really lies that way?"

"I am sure it lies in no other."

"Do you want to go, Shadrach?"

"Not for the pleasure of it, I can tell ye. There's no such pleasure at sea, Joanna, as I can find in my back parlor here. To speak honest, I have no love for the brine. I never had much. But if it comes to a question of a fortune for you and the lads, it is another thing. That's the only way to it for one born and bred a seafarer as I."

"Would it take long to earn?"

"Well, that depends; perhaps not."

The next morning Shadrach pulled from a chest of drawers the nautical jacket he had worn during the first months of his return, brushed out the moths, donned it, and walked down to the quay. The port still did a fair business in the New-foundland trade, though not so much as formerly.

It was not long after this that he invested all he possessed in purchasing a part ownership in a brig, of which he was appointed captain. A few months were passed in coast trading, during which interval Shadrach wore off the land rust that had accumulated upon him in his grocery phase; and in the spring the brig sailed for Newfoundland.

Joanna lived on at home with her sons, who were now growing up into strong lads, and occupying themselves in various ways about the harbor and quay.

"Never mind, let them work a little," their fond mother said to herself. "Our necessities compel it now, but when Shadrach comes home they will be only seventeen and eighteen, and they shall be removed from the port, and their education thoroughly taken in hand by a tutor; and with the money they'll have they will perhaps be as near to gentlemen as Emmy Lester's precious two, with their algebra and their Latin!"

The date for Shadrach's return drew near and arrived, and he did not appear. Joanna was assured that there was no cause for anxiety, sailing ships being so uncertain in their coming; which assurance proved to be well-grounded, for late one wet evening, about a month after the calculated time, the ship was announced as at hand, and presently the slipslop step of Shadrach as the sailor sounded in the passage, and he entered. The boys had gone out and had missed him, and Joanna was sitting alone.

As soon as the first emotion of reunion between the couple had passed, Jolliffe explained the delay as owing to a small speculative contract, which had produced good results.

"I was determined not to disappoint ye," he said; "and I think you'll own that I haven't!"

With this he pulled out an enormous canvas bag, full and rotund as the money bag of the giant whom Jack slew, untied it, and shook the contents out into her lap as she sat in her low chair by the fire. A mass of sovereigns and guineas (there were guineas on the earth in those days) fell into her lap with a sudden thud, weighing down her gown to the floor.

"There!" said Shadrach complacently. "I told ye, dear, I'd do it; and have I done it or no?"

Somehow her face, after the first excitement of possession, did not retain its glory.

"It is a lot of gold, indeed," she said. "And—is this *all*?"

"All? Why, dear Joanna, do you know you can count to three hundred in that heap? It is a fortune!"

"Yes—yes. A fortune—judged by sea; but judged by land—"

However, she banished considerations of the money for the nonce. Soon the boys came in, and next Sunday Shadrach returned thanks to God—this time by the more ordinary channel of the italics in the General Thanksgiving. But a few days after, when the question of investing the money arose, he remarked that she did not seem so satisfied as he had hoped.

"Well you see, Shadrach," she answered, "*we* count by hundreds; *they* count by thousands" (nodding towards the other side of the street). "They have set up a carriage-and-pair since you left."

"Oh, have they?"

"My dear Shadrach, you don't know how the world moves. However, we'll do the best we can with it. But they are rich, and we are poor still!"

The greater part of a year was desultorily spent. She moved sadly about the house and shop, and the boys were still occupying themselves in and around the harbor.

"Joanna," he said, one day, "I see by your movements that it is not enough."

"It is not enough," said she. "My boys will have to live by steering the ships that the Lesters own; and I was once above her!"

Jolliffe was not an argumentative man, and he only murmured that he thought he would make another voyage. He meditated for several days, and coming home from the quay one afternoon said suddenly:

"I could do it for ye, dear, in one more trip, for certain, if— if—"

"Do what, Shadrach?"

"Enable ye to count by thousands instead of hundreds."

"If what?"

"If I might take the boys."

She turned pale.

"Don't say that, Shadrach," she answered hastily.

"Why?"

"I don't like to hear it! There's danger at sea. I want them to be something genteel, and no danger to them. I couldn't let them risk their lives at sea. Oh, I couldn't ever, ever!"

"Very well, dear, it shan't be done."

Next day, after a silence, she asked a question:

"If they were to go with you, it would make a great deal of difference, I suppose, to the profit?"

"'Twould treble what I should get from the venture single-handed. Under my eye they would be as good as two more of myself."

Later on she said: "Tell me more about this."

"Well, the boys are almost as clever as master mariners in handling a craft, upon my life! There isn't a more cranky place in the northern seas than about the sandbanks of this harbor, and they've practiced here from their infancy. And they are so steady. I couldn't get their steadiness and their trustworthiness in half a dozen men twice their age."

"And is it *very* dangerous at sea; now, too, there are rumors of war?" she asked uneasily.

"Oh, well, there be risks. Still . . ."

The idea grew and magnified, and the mother's heart was crushed and stifled by it. Emmy was growing *too* patronizing; it could not be borne. Shadrach's wife could not help nagging him about their comparative poverty. The young men, amiable as their father when spoken to on the subject of a voyage of enterprise, were quite willing to embark; and though they, like their father, had no great love for the sea, they became quite enthusiastic when the proposal was detailed.

Everything now hung upon their mother's assent. She withheld it long, but at last gave the word: the young men might accompany their father. Shadrach was unusually cheerful about it: Heaven had preserved him hitherto, and he had uttered his thanks. God would not forsake those who were faithful to him.

All that the Jolliffes possessed in the world was put into the enterprise. The grocery stock was pared down to the least that possibly could afford a bare sustenance to Joanna during the absence, which was to last through the usual "Newf'nland spell." How she would endure the weary time she hardly knew, for the boys had been with her formerly; but she nerved herself for the trial.

The ship was laden with boots and shoes, ready-made clothing, fishing tackle, butter, cheese, cordage, sailcloth, and many other commodities; and was to bring back oil, furs, skins, fish, cranberries, and what else came to hand. But much speculative trading to other ports was to be undertaken between the voyages out and homeward, and thereby much money made.

3

The brig sailed on a Monday morning in spring; but Joanna did not witness its departure. She could not bear the sight that she

114 had been the means of bringing about. Knowing this, her husband told her overnight that they were to sail sometime before noon next day; hence when awakening at five the next morning she heard them bustling about downstairs, she did not hasten to descend, but lay trying to nerve herself for the parting, imagining they would leave about nine, as her husband had done on his previous voyage. When she did descend she beheld words chalked upon the sloping face of the bureau; but no husband or sons. In the hastily scrawled lines Shadrach said they had gone off thus not to pain her by a leave-taking; and the sons had chalked under his words: "Good-bye, Mother!"

She rushed to the quay and looked down the harbor towards the blue rim of the sea, but she could only see the masts and bulging sails of the *Joanna;* no human figures. "'Tis I have sent them!" she said wildly, and burst into tears. In the house the chalked "Good-bye" nearly broke her heart. But when she had re-entered the front room, and looked across at Emily's, a gleam of triumph lit her thin face at her anticipated release from the thraldom of subservience.

To do Emily Lester justice, her assumption of superiority was mainly a figment of Joanna's brain. That the circumstances of the merchant's wife were more luxurious than Joanna's, the former could not conceal; though whenever the two met, which was not very often now, Emily endeavored to subdue the difference by every means in her power.

The first summer lapsed away; and Joanna meagerly maintained herself by the shop, which now consisted of little more than a window and a counter. Emily was, in truth, her only large customer; and Mrs. Lester's kindly readiness to buy anything and everything without questioning the quality had a sting of bitterness in it, for it was the uncritical attitude of a patron, and almost of a donor. The long dreary winter moved on; the face of the bureau had been turned to the wall to protect the chalked words of farewell, for Joanna could never bring herself to rub them out; and she often glanced at them with wet eyes. Emily's handsome boys came home for the Christmas holidays; the university was talked of for them; and still Joanna subsisted as it were with held breath, like a person submerged. Only one summer more, and the "spell" would end. Towards the close of the time Emily called on her quondam friend. She had heard that Joanna began to feel anxious; she had received no letter from husband or sons for some months. Emily's silks rustled arrogantly when, in response to Joanna's almost dumb invitation, she squeezed through the opening of the counter and into the parlor behind the shop.

"*You* are all success, and *I* am all the other way!" said Joanna.

"But why do you think so?" said Emily. "They are to bring back a fortune, I hear."

"Ah! will they come? The doubt is more than a woman can bear. All three in one ship—think of that! And I have not heard of them for months!"

"But the time is not up. You should not meet misfortune halfway."

"Nothing will repay me for the grief of their absence!"

"Then why did you let them go? You were doing fairly well."

"I *made* them go!" she said, turning vehemently upon Emily. "And I'll tell you why! I could not bear that we should be only muddling on, and you so rich and patronizing! Now I have told you, and you may hate me if you will!"

"I shall never hate you, Joanna."

And she proved the truth of her words afterwards. The end of autumn came, and the brig should have been in port; but nothing like the *Joanna* appeared in the channel between the sands. It was now really time to be uneasy. Joanna Jolliffe sat by the fire, and every gust of wind caused her a cold thrill. She had always feared and detested the sea; to her it was a treacherous, restless, slimy creature, glorying in the griefs of women. "Still," she said, "they *must* come!"

She recalled to her mind that Shadrach had said before starting that if they returned safe and sound, with success crowning their enterprise, he would go as he had gone after his shipwreck, and kneel with his sons in the church, and offer sincere thanks for their deliverance. She went to church regularly morning and afternoon, and sat in the most forward pew, nearest the chancel step. Her eyes were mostly fixed on that step, where Shadrach had knelt in the bloom of his young manhood; she knew to an inch the spot which his knees had pressed twenty winters before; his outline as he had knelt, his hat on the step beside him. God was good. Surely her husband must kneel there again: a son on each side as he had said; George just here, Jim just there. By long watching the spot as she worshipped became as if she saw the three returned ones there kneeling; the two slim outlines of her boys, the more bulky form between them; their hands clasped, their heads shaped against the eastern wall. The fancy grew almost to an hallucination—she could never turn her worn eyes to the step without seeing them there.

Nevertheless they did not come. Heaven was merciful, but it was not yet pleased to relieve her soul. This was her purgation for the sin of making them the slaves of her ambition. But it became more than purgation soon, and her mood approached despair. Months had passed since the brig had been due, but it had not returned.

Joanna was always hearing or seeing evidences of their arrival. When on the hill behind the port, whence a view of the open channel could be obtained, she felt sure that a little speck on the horizon, breaking the eternally level waste of waters southward, was the truck of the *Joanna's* mainmast. Or when indoors, a shout or excitement of any kind at the corner of the Town Cellar, where the High Street joined the quay, caused her to spring to her feet and cry: "'Tis they!"

But it was not. The visionary forms knelt every Sunday afternoon on the chancel step, but not the real. Her shop had, as it were, eaten itself hollow. In the apathy which had resulted from her loneliness and grief she had ceased to take in the smallest supplies, and thus had sent away her last customer.

In this strait Emily Lester tried by every means in her power to aid the afflicted woman; but she met with constant repulses.

"I don't like you! I can't bear to see you!" Joanna would whisper hoarsely when Emily came to her and made advances.

"But I want to help and soothe you, Joanna," Emily would say.

"You are a lady, with a rich husband and fine sons! What can you want with a bereaved crone like me!"

"Joanna, I want this: I want you to come and live in my house, and not stay in this dismal place any longer."

"And suppose they come and don't find me at home? You wish to separate me and mine! No, I'll stay here. I don't like you, and I can't thank you, whatever kindness you do me!"

However, as time went on Joanna could not afford to pay the rent of the shop and house without an income. She was assured that all hope of the return of Shadrach and his sons was vain, and she reluctantly consented to accept the asylum of the Lesters' house. Here she was allotted a room of her own on the second floor, and went and came as she chose, without contact with the family. Her hair grayed and whitened, deep lines channelled her forehead, and her form grew gaunt and stooping. But she still expected the lost ones, and when she met Emily on the staircase she would say morosely: "I know why you've got me here! They'll come, and be disappointed at not finding me at home and perhaps go away again; and then you'll be revenged for my taking Shadrach away from ye!"

Emily Lester bore these reproaches from the grief-stricken soul. She was sure—all the people of Havenpool were sure—that Shadrach and his sons had gone to the bottom. For years the vessel had been given up as lost. Nevertheless, when awakened at night by any noise, Joanna would rise from bed and glance at the shop opposite by the light from the flickering

118 lamp, to make sure it was not they.

It was a damp and dark December night, six years after the departure of the brig *Joanna*. The wind was from the sea, and brought up a fishy mist which mopped the face like moist flannel. Joanna had prayed her usual prayer for the absent ones with more fervor and confidence than she had felt for months, and had fallen asleep about eleven. It must have been between one and two when she suddenly started up. She had certainly heard steps in the street, and the voices of Shadrach and her sons calling at the door of the grocery shop. She sprang out of bed, and, hardly knowing what clothing she dragged on herself, hastened down Emily's large and carpeted staircase, put the candle on the hall table, unfastened the bolts and chain, and stepped into the street. The mist, blowing up the street from the quay, hindered her seeing the shop, although it was so near; but she had crossed to it in a moment. How was it? Nobody stood there. The wretched woman walked wildly up and down with her bare feet—there was not a soul. She returned and knocked with all her might at the door which had once been her own—they might have been admitted for the night, unwilling to disturb her till the morning. It was not till several minutes had elapsed that the young man who now kept the shop looked out of an upper window and saw the skeleton of something human standing below, half-dressed.

"Has anybody come?" asked the form.

"Oh, Mrs. Jolliffe, I didn't know it was you," said the young man kindly, for he was aware how her baseless expectations moved her. "No; nobody has come."

*A sudden fear seized Soapy that some dreadful enchant-
ment had rendered him immune to arrest.*

THE COP AND THE ANTHEM

O. Henry

On his bench in Madison Square, Soapy moved uneasily. When
wild geese honk high of nights, and when women without seal-
skin coats grow kind to their husbands, and when Soapy moves
uneasily on his bench in the park, you may know that winter is
near at hand.

A dead leaf fell in Soapy's lap. That was Jack Frost's card.
Jack is kind to the regular denizens of Madison Square, and
gives fair warning of his annual call. At the corners of four
streets he hands his pasteboard to the North Wind, footman of
the mansion of All Outdoors, so that the inhabitants thereof
may make ready.

Soapy's mind became cognizant of the fact that the time
had come for him to resolve himself into a singular Committee
of Ways and Means to provide against the coming rigor. And
therefore he moved uneasily on his bench.

The hibernatorial ambitions of Soapy were not of the highest. In them there were no considerations of Mediterranean
cruises, of soporific Southern skies or drifting in the Vesuvian
Bay. Three months on the Island was what his soul craved.
Three months of assured board and bed and congenial company, safe from Boreas and bluecoats, seemed to Soapy the essence of things desirable.

For years the hospitable Blackwell's had been his winter quarters. Just as his more fortunate fellow New Yorkers had bought their tickets to Palm Beach and the Riviera each winter, so Soapy had made his humble arrangements for his annual hegira to the Island. And now the time was come. On the previous night three Sabbath newspapers, distributed beneath his coat, about his ankles, and over his lap, had failed to repulse the cold as he slept on his bench near the spurting fountain in the ancient square. So the Island loomed big and timely in Soapy's mind. He scorned the provisions made in the name of charity for the city's dependents. In Soapy's opinion the Law was more benign than Philanthropy. There was an endless round of institutions, municipal and eleemosynary, on which he might set out and receive lodging and food accordant with the simple life. But to one of Soapy's proud spirit the gifts of charity are encumbered. If not in coin you must pay in humiliation of spirit for every benefit received at the hands of philanthropy. As Caesar had his Brutus, every bed of charity must have its toll of a bath, every loaf of bread its compensation of a private and personal inquisition. Wherefore it is better to be a guest of the law, which, though conducted by rules, does not meddle unduly with a gentleman's private affairs.

Soapy, having decided to go to the Island, at once set about accomplishing his desire. There were many easy ways of doing this. The pleasantest was to dine luxuriously at some expensive restaurant; and then, after declaring insolvency, be handed over quietly and without uproar to a policeman. An accommodating magistrate would do the rest.

Soapy left his bench and strolled out of the square and across the level sea of asphalt, where Broadway and Fifth Avenue flow together. Up Broadway he turned, and halted at a glittering café, where are gathered together nightly the choicest products of the grape, the silkworm, and the protoplasm.

Soapy had confidence in himself from the lowest button of

his vest upward. He was shaven, and his coat was decent and his neat, black, ready-tied four-in-hand had been presented to him by a lady missionary on Thanksgiving Day. If he could reach a table in the restaurant unsuspected, success would be his. The portion of him that would show above the table would raise no doubt in the waiter's mind. A roasted mallard duck, thought Soapy, would be about the thing—with a bottle of Chablis, and then Camembert, a demitasse and a cigar. One dollar for the cigar would be enough. The total would not be so high as to call forth any supreme manifestation of revenge from the café management; and yet the meat would leave him filled and happy for the journey to his winter refuge.

But as Soapy set foot inside the restaurant door the head waiter's eye fell upon his frayed trousers and decadent shoes. Strong and ready hands turned him about and conveyed him in silence and haste to the sidewalk and averted the ignoble fate of the menaced mallard.

Soapy turned off Broadway. It seemed that his route to the coveted Island was not to be an epicurean one. Some other way of entering limbo must be thought of.

At a corner of Sixth Avenue, electric lights and cunningly displayed wares behind plate glass made a shop window conspicuous. Soapy took a cobblestone and dashed it through the glass. People came running around the corner, a policeman in the lead. Soapy stood still, with his hands in his pockets, and smiled at the sight of brass buttons.

"Where's the man that done that?" inquired the officer excitedly.

"Don't you figure out that I might have had something to do with it?" said Soapy, not without sarcasm, but friendly, as one greets good fortune.

The policeman's mind refused to accept Soapy even as a clue. Men who smash windows do not remain to parley with the law's minions. They take to their heels. The policeman saw a man halfway down the block running to catch a car. With drawn club he joined in the pursuit. Soapy, with disgust in his heart, loafed along, twice unsuccessful.

On the opposite side of the street was a restaurant of no great pretensions. It catered to large appetites and modest purses. Its crockery and atmosphere were thick; its soup and napery thin. Into this place Soapy took his accusive shoes and telltale trousers without challenge. At a table he sat and consumed beefsteak, flapjacks, doughnuts, and pie. And then to the waiter he betrayed the fact that the minutest coin and himself were strangers.

"Now, get busy and call a cop," said Soapy. "And don't keep a gentleman waiting."

"No cop for youse," said the waiter, with a voice like butter cakes and an eye like the cherry in a Manhattan cocktail. "Hey, Con!"

Neatly upon his left ear on the callous pavement two waiters pitched Soapy. He arose, joint by joint, as a carpenter's rule opens, and beat the dust from his clothes. Arrest seemed but a rosy dream. The Island seemed very far away. A policeman who stood before a drugstore two doors away laughed and walked down the street.

Five blocks Soapy travelled before his courage permitted him to woo capture again. This time the opportunity presented what he fatuously termed to himself a "cinch." A young woman of a modest and pleasing guise was standing before a show window gazing with sprightly interest at its display of shaving mugs and inkstands, and two yards from the window a large policeman of severe demeanor leaned against a water plug.

It was Soapy's design to assume the role of the despicable and execrated "masher." The refined and elegant appearance of his victim and the contiguity of the conscientious cop encouraged him to believe that he would soon feel the pleasant official clutch upon his arm that would insure his winter quarters on the right little, tight little isle.

Soapy straightened the lady missionary's ready-made tie, dragged his shrinking cuffs into the open, set his hat at a killing cant and sidled toward the young woman. He made eyes at her, was taken with sudden coughs and "hems," smiled, smirked, and went brazenly through the impudent and contemptible litany of the "masher." With half an eye Soapy saw that the policeman was watching him fixedly. The young woman moved away a few steps, and again bestowed her absorbed attention upon the shaving mugs. Soapy followed, boldly stepping to her side, raised his hat and said:

"Ah there, Bedelia! Don't you want to come and play in my yard?"

The policeman was still looking. The persecuted young woman had but to beckon a finger and Soapy would be practically en route for his insular haven. Already he imagined he could feel the cozy warmth of the station house. The young woman faced him and, stretching out a hand, caught Soapy's coat sleeve.

"Sure, Mike," she said joyfully, "if you'll blow me to a pail of suds. I'd have spoke to you sooner, but the cop was watching."

With the young woman playing the clinging ivy to his oak, Soapy walked past the policeman, overcome with gloom. He seemed doomed to liberty.

At the next corner he shook off his companion and ran. He halted in the district where by night are found the lightest streets, hearts, vows, and librettos. Women in furs and men in greatcoats moved gaily in the wintry air. A sudden fear seized Soapy that some dreadful enchantment had rendered him immune to arrest. The thought brought a little of panic upon it, and when he came upon another policeman lounging grandly in front of a transplendent theater, he caught at the immediate straw of "disorderly conduct."

On the sidewalk Soapy began to yell drunken gibberish at the top of his harsh voice. He danced, howled, raved, and otherwise disturbed the welkin.

The policeman twirled his club, turned his back to Soapy, and remarked to a citizen:

"'Tis one of them Yale lads celebratin' the goose egg they give to the Hartford College. Noisy; but no harm. We've instructions to lave them be."

Disconsolate, Soapy ceased his unavailing racket. Would never a policeman lay hands on him? In his fancy the Island seemed an unattainable Arcadia. He buttoned his thin coat against the chilling wind.

In a cigar store he saw a well-dressed man lighting a cigar at a swinging light. His silk umbrella he had set by the door on entering. Soapy stepped inside, secured the umbrella, and sauntered off with it slowly. The man at the cigar light followed hastily.

"My umbrella," he said, sternly.

"Oh, is it?" sneered Soapy, adding insult to petit larceny. "Well, why don't you call a policeman? I took it. Your umbrella! Why don't you call a cop? There stands one on the corner."

The umbrella owner slowed his steps. Soapy did likewise, with a presentiment that luck would again run against him. The policeman looked at the two curiously.

"Of course," said the umbrella man—"that is—well, you know how these mistakes occur—I—if it's your umbrella I hope you'll excuse me—I picked it up this morning in a restaurant— if you recognize it as yours, why—I hope you'll—"

"Of course it's mine," said Soapy, viciously.

The ex-umbrella man retreated. The policeman hurried to assist a tall blonde in an opera cloak across the street in front of a streetcar that was approaching two blocks away.

Soapy walked eastward through a street damaged by improvements. He hurled the umbrella wrathfully into an excavation. He muttered against the men who wear helmets and carry clubs. Because he wanted to fall into their clutches, they seemed to regard him as a king who could do no wrong.

At length Soapy reached one of the avenues to the east where the glitter and turmoil was but faint. He set his face down this toward Madison Square, for the homing instinct survives even when the home is a park bench.

But on an unusually quiet corner Soapy came to a standstill. Here was an old church, quaint and rambling and gabled. Through one violet-stained window a soft light glowed, where, no doubt, the organist loitered over the keys, making sure of his mastery of the coming Sabbath anthem. For there drifted out to Soapy's ears sweet music that caught and held him transfixed against the convolutions of the iron fence.

The moon was above, lustrous and serene; vehicles and pedestrians were few; sparrows twittered sleepily in the eaves—for a little while the scene might have been a country churchyard. And the anthem that the organist played cemented Soapy to the iron fence, for he had known it well in the days when his life contained such things as mothers and roses and ambitions and friends and immaculate thoughts and collars.

The conjunction of Soapy's receptive state of mind and the influences about the old church wrought a sudden and wonderful change in his soul. He viewed with swift horror the pit into which he had tumbled: the degraded days, unworthy desires, dead hopes, wrecked faculties, and base motives that made up his existence.

And also in a moment his heart responded thrillingly to this novel mood. An instantaneous and strong impulse moved him to battle with his desperate fate. He would pull himself out of the mire; he would make a man of himself again; he would conquer the evil that had taken possession of him. There was time; he was comparatively young yet; he would resurrect his old eager ambitions and pursue them without faltering. Those solemn but sweet organ notes had set up a revolution in him. Tomorrow he would go into the roaring downtown district and find work. A fur importer had once offered him a place as driver. He would find him tomorrow and ask for the position. He would be somebody in the world. He would—

Soapy felt a hand laid on his arm. He looked quickly around into the broad face of a policeman.

"What are you doin' here?" asked the officer.

"Nothin'," said Soapy.

"Then come along," said the policeman.

"Three months on the Island," said the magistrate in the Police Court the next morning.

POINT OF VIEW

Are events told by someone in the story or by an outside observer? The reader answers this question by studying point of view, *the author's method of narration.*

Sometimes the narrator, or storyteller, is a character talking about himself or herself and using first-person pronouns (I, me). This is called the first-person point of view. "The £1,000,000 Bank Note" is written in the first person: "When I stepped ashore in London . . ." and so on.

Frequently the narrator is not one of the story's characters, and the narrator relates events by using third-person pronouns (he, she, they). *This is called the* third-person point of view; *the narrator seems to hover over and watch all the events.* When the narrator reads the minds of all the characters, the method is called the third-person omniscient point of view; *the narrator is omniscient, or all-knowing.* "The Lady or the Tiger?" has aspects of this method. When the narrator sees into the minds of only one or a few characters, the method is called limited omniscience.

When the narrator does not seem to see into any character's mind but just relates events, the method is called the third-person objective point of view. *It is almost like a newscaster speaking without any noticeable emotion or opinion.* "The Death of the Dauphin" makes use of this objective point of view.

Each point of view has advantages and limitations. First-person narratives are intensely personal but shaded by the narrator's prejudices and attitudes; third-person narratives are more flexible but more detached. The careful reader will look for these features to gain a richer appreciation of the author's method of channeling information to the reader.

When I stepped ashore in London my clothes were ragged and shabby, and I had only a dollar in my pocket.

THE £1,000,000 BANK NOTE

Mark Twain

When I was twenty-seven years old, I was a mining broker's clerk in San Francisco, and an expert in all the details of stock traffic. I was alone in the world, and had nothing to depend upon but my wits and a clean reputation; but these were setting my feet in the road to eventual fortune, and I was content with the prospect.

My time was my own after the afternoon board, Saturdays, and I was accustomed to put it in on a little sailboat on the bay. One day I ventured too far, and was carried out to sea. Just at nightfall, when hope was about gone, I was picked up by a small brig which was bound for London. It was a long and stormy voyage, and they made me work my passage without pay, as a common sailor. When I stepped ashore in London my clothes were ragged and shabby, and I had only a dollar in my pocket. This money fed and sheltered me twenty-four hours. During the next twenty-four I went without food and shelter.

About ten o'clock on the following morning, seedy and hungry, I was dragging myself along Portland Place, when a child that was passing, towed by a nursemaid, tossed a luscious big pear—minus one bite—into the gutter. I stopped, of course, and fastened my desiring eye on that muddy treasure. My mouth watered for it, my stomach craved it, my whole being begged for it. But every time I made a move to get it, some passing eye detected my purpose, and of course I straightened up, then, and looked indifferent, and pretended that I hadn't been thinking about the pear at all. This same thing kept happening and happening, and I couldn't get the pear. I was just getting desperate enough to brave all the shame, and to seize it, when a window behind me was raised, and a gentleman spoke out of it, saying:

"Step in here, please."

I was admitted by a gorgeous flunky, and shown into a sumptuous room where a couple of elderly gentlemen were sitting. They sent away the servant, and made me sit down. They had just finished their breakfast, and the sight of the remains of it almost overpowered me. I could hardly keep my wits together in the presence of that food, but as I was not asked to sample it, I had to bear my trouble as best I could.

Now, something had been happening there a little before, which I did not know anything about until a good many days afterward, but I will tell you about it now. Those two old brothers had been having a pretty hot argument a couple of days before, and had ended by agreeing to decide it by a bet, which is the English way of settling everything.

You will remember that the Bank of England once issued two notes of a million pounds each, to be used for a special purpose connected with some public transaction with a foreign country. For some reason or other only one of these had been used and canceled; the other still lay in the vaults of the bank. Well, the brothers, chatting along, happened to get to wondering what might be the fate of a perfectly honest and intelligent stranger who should be turned adrift in London without a friend, and with no money but that million-pound bank note, and no way to account for his being in possession of it. Brother A said he would starve to death; Brother B said he wouldn't. Brother A said he couldn't offer it at a bank or anywhere else, because he would be arrested on the spot. So they

went on disputing till Brother B said he would bet twenty
thousand pounds that the man would live thirty days, *anyway*,
on that million, and keep out of jail, too. Brother A took him
up. Brother B went down to the bank and bought that note.
Just like an Englishman, you see; pluck to the backbone. Then
he dictated a letter, which one of his clerks wrote out in a
beautiful round hand, and then the two brothers sat at the
window a whole day watching for the right man to give it to.

They saw many honest faces go by that were not intelligent
enough; many that were intelligent, but not honest enough;
many that were both, but the possessors were not poor enough,
or, if poor enough, were not strangers. There was always a defect, until I came along; but they agreed that I filled the bill all
around; so they elected me unanimously, and there I was, now,
waiting to know why I was called in. They began to ask me
questions about myself, and pretty soon they had my story. Finally they told me I would answer their purpose. I said I was
sincerely glad, and asked what it was. Then one of them
handed me an envelope, and said I would find the explanation
inside. I was going to open it, but he said no; take it to my
lodgings, and look it over carefully, and not be hasty or rash. I
was puzzled, and wanted to discuss the matter a little further,
but they didn't; so I took my leave, feeling hurt and insulted to
be made the butt of what was apparently some kind of a practical joke, and yet obliged to put up with it, not being in circumstances to resent affronts from rich and strong folk.

I would have picked up the pear, now, and eaten it before
all the world, but it was gone; so I had lost that by this unlucky
business, and the thought of it did not soften my feeling toward those men. As soon as I was out of sight of that house I
opened my envelope, and saw that it contained money! My
opinion of those people changed, I can tell you! I lost not a
moment, but shoved note and money into my vest pocket, and
broke for the nearest cheap eating house. Well, how I did eat!
When at last I couldn't hold any more, I took out my money

and unfolded it, took one glimpse and nearly fainted. Five millions of dollars! Why, it made my head swim.

I must have sat there stunned and blinking at the note as much as a minute before I came rightly to myself again. The first thing I noticed, then, was the landlord. His eye was on the note, and he was petrified. He was worshiping, with all his body and soul, but he looked as if he couldn't stir hand or foot. I took my cue in a moment, and did the only rational thing there was to do. I reached the note toward him, and said carelessly:

"Give me the change, please."

Then he was restored to his normal condition, and made a thousand apologies for not being able to break the bill, and I couldn't get him to touch it. He wanted to look at it, and keep on looking at it; he couldn't seem to get enough of it to quench the thirst of his eye, but he shrank from touching it as if it had been something too sacred for poor common clay to handle. I said:

"I am sorry if it is an inconvenience, but I must insist. Please change it; I haven't anything else."

But he said that wasn't any matter; he was quite willing to let the trifle stand over till another time. I said I might not be in his neighborhood again for a good while; but he said it was of no consequence, he could wait, and, moreover, I could have anything I wanted, anytime I chose, and let the account run as long as I pleased. He said he hoped he wasn't afraid to trust as rich a gentleman as I was, merely because I was of a merry disposition, and chose to play larks on the public in the matter of dress. By this time another customer was entering, and the landlord hinted to me to put the monster out of sight; then he bowed me all the way to the door, and I started straight for that house and those brothers, to correct the mistake which had been made before the police should hunt me up, and help me do it. I was pretty nervous, in fact pretty badly frightened, though, of course, I was no way in fault; but I knew men well enough to know that when they find they've given a tramp a million-pound bill when they thought it was a one-pounder, they are in a frantic rage against *him* instead of quarreling with their own nearsightedness, as they ought. As I approached the house my excitement began to abate, for all was quiet there, which made me feel pretty sure the blunder was not discovered yet. I rang. The same servant appeared. I asked for those gentlemen.

"They are gone." This in the lofty, cold way of that fellow's tribe.

"Gone? Gone where?"

"On a journey."

"But whereabouts?"

"To the Continent, I think."

"The Continent?"

"Yes, sir."

"Which way—by what route?"

"I can't say, sir."

"When will they be back?"

"In a month, they said."

"A month! Oh, this is awful! Give me *some* sort of idea of how to get word to them. It's of the last importance."

"I can't, indeed. I've no idea where they've gone, sir."

"Then I must see some member of the family."

"Family's away too; been abroad months—in Egypt and India, I think."

"Man, there's been an immense mistake made. They'll be back before night. Will you tell them I've been here, and that I will keep coming till it's all made right, and they needn't be afraid?"

"I'll tell them, if they come back, but I am not expecting them. They said you would be here in an hour to make inquiries, but I must tell you it's all right, they'll be here on time and expect you."

So I had to give it up and go away. What a riddle it all was!

134   I was like to lose my mind. They would be here "on time." What could that mean? Oh, the letter would explain, maybe. I had forgotten the letter; I got it out and read it. This is what it said:

> *You are an intelligent and honest man, as one may see by your face. We conceive you to be poor and a stranger. Enclosed you will find a sum of money. It is lent to you for thirty days, without interest. Report at this house at the end of that time. I have a bet on you. If I win it you shall have any situation that is in my gift—any, that is, that you shall be able to prove yourself familiar with and competent to fill.*

No signature, no address, no date.

Well, here was a coil to be in! You are posted on what had preceded all this, but I was not. It was just a deep, dark puzzle to me. I hadn't the least idea what the game was, nor whether harm was meant me or a kindness. I went into a park, and sat down to try to think it out, and to consider what I had best do.

At the end of an hour, my reasonings had crystallized into this verdict.

Maybe those men mean me well, maybe they mean me ill; no way to decide that—let it go. They've got a game, or a scheme, or an experiment, of some kind on hand; no way to determine what it is—let it go. There's a bet on me; no way to find out what it is—let it go. That disposes of the indeterminable quantities; the remainder of the matter is tangible, solid, and may be classed and labeled with certainty. If I ask the Bank of England to place this bill to the credit of the man it belongs to, they'll do it, for they know him, although I don't; but they will ask me how I came in possession of it, and if I tell the truth, they'll put me in the asylum, naturally, and a lie will land me in jail. The same result would follow if I tried to bank the bill anywhere or to borrow money on it. I have got to carry this immense burden around until those men come back, whether I want to or not. It is useless to me, as useless as a handful of ashes, and yet I must take care of it, and watch over it, while I beg my living. I couldn't *give* it away, if I should try, for neither honest citizen nor highwayman would accept it or meddle with it for anything. Those brothers are safe. Even if I lose their bill, or burn it, they are still safe, because they can stop payment, and the bank will make them whole; but meantime, I've got to do a month's suffering without wages or profit—unless I help win that bet, whatever it may be, and get that situation that I am promised. I *should* like to get that; men of their sort have situations in their gift that are worth having.

I got to thinking a good deal about that situation. My hopes began to rise high. Without doubt the salary would be large. It would begin in a month; after that I should be all right. Pretty soon I was feeling first-rate. By this time I was tramping the streets again. The sight of a tailor shop gave me a sharp longing to shed my rags, and to clothe myself decently once more. Could I afford it? No; I had nothing in the world but a million pounds. So I forced myself to go on by. But soon I was drifting back again. The temptation persecuted me cruelly. I must have passed that shop back and forth six times during that manful struggle. At last I gave in; I had to. I asked if they had a misfit suit that had been thrown on their hands. The fellow I spoke to nodded his head toward another fellow, and gave me no answer. I went to the indicated fellow, and he indicated another fellow with *his* head, and no words. I went to him, and he said:

" 'Tend to you presently."

I waited till he was done with what he was at, then he took me into a back room, and overhauled a pile of rejected suits, and selected the rattiest one for me. I put it on. It didn't fit, and wasn't in any way attractive, but it was new, and I was anxious to have it; so I didn't find any fault, but said with some

136 diffidence:

"It would be an accommodation to me if you could wait some days for the money. I haven't any small change about me."

The fellow worked up a most sarcastic expression of countenance, and said:

"Oh, you haven't? Well, of course, I didn't expect it. I'd only expect gentlemen like you to carry large change."

I was nettled, and said:

"My friend, you shouldn't judge a stranger always by the clothes he wears. I am quite able to pay for this suit; I simply didn't wish to put you to the trouble of changing a large note."

He modified his style a little at that, and said, though still with something of an air:

"I didn't mean any particular harm, but as long as rebukes are going, I might say it wasn't quite your affair to jump to the conclusion that we couldn't change any note that you might happen to be carrying around. On the contrary, we *can*."

I handed the note to him, and said:

"Oh, very well; I apologize."

He received it with a smile, one of those large smiles which goes all around over, and has folds in it, and wrinkles, and spirals, and looks like the place where you have thrown a brick in a pond; and then in the act of his taking a glimpse of the bill this smile froze solid, and turned yellow, and looked like those wavy, wormy spreads of lava which you find hardened on little levels on the side of Vesuvius. I never before saw a smile caught like that, and perpetuated. The man stood there holding the bill, and looking like that, and the proprietor hustled up to see what was the matter, and said briskly:

"Well, what's up? What's the trouble? What's wanting?"

I said: "There isn't any trouble. I'm waiting for my change."

"Come, come; get him his change, Tod; get him his

change."

Tod retorted: "Get him his change! It's easy to say, sir; but look at the bill yourself."

The proprietor took a look, gave a low, eloquent whistle, then made a dive for the pile of rejected clothing, and began to snatch it this way and that, talking all the time excitedly, and as if to himself:

"Sell an eccentric millionaire such an unspeakable suit as that! Tod's a fool—a born fool. Always doing something like this. Drives every millionaire away from this place, because he can't tell a millionaire from a tramp, and never could. Ah, here's the thing I'm after. Please get those things off, sir, and throw them in the fire. Do me the favor to put on this shirt and this suit; it's just the thing, the very thing—plain, rich, modest, and just ducally nobby; made to order for a foreign prince— you may know him, sir, his Serene Highness the Hospodar of Halifax; had to leave it with us and take a mourning suit be- cause his mother was going to die—which she didn't. But that's all right; we can't always have things the way we—that is, the way they—there! trousers all right, they fit you to a charm, sir; now the waistcoat; aha, right again! now the coat—Lord! look at that, now! Perfect—the whole thing! I never saw such a triumph in all my experience."

I expressed my satisfaction.

"Quite right, sir, quite right; it'll do for a makeshift, I'm bound to say. But wait till you see what we'll get up for you on your own measure. Come, Tod, book and pen; get at it. Length of leg, 32"—and so on. Before I could get in a word he had measured me, and was giving orders for dress suits, morning suits, shirts, and all sorts of things. When I got a chance I said:

"But, my dear sir, I *can't* give these orders, unless you can wait indefinitely, or change the bill."

"Indefinitely! It's a weak word, sir, a weak word. Eternally— *that's* the word, sir. Tod, rush these things through, and send

138 them to the gentleman's address without any waste of time. Let the minor customers wait. Set down the gentleman's address and—"

"I'm changing my quarters. I will drop in and leave the new address."

"Quite right, sir, quite right. One moment—let me show you out, sir. There—good day, sir, good day."

Well, don't you see what was bound to happen? I drifted naturally into buying whatever I wanted, and asking for change. Within a week I was sumptuously equipped with all needful comforts and luxuries, and was housed in an expensive private hotel in Hanover Square. I took my dinners there, but for breakfast I stuck by Harris's humble feeding house, where I had got my first meal on my million-pound bill. I was the making of Harris. The fact had gone all abroad that the foreign crank who carried million-pound bills in his vest pocket was the patron saint of the place. That was enough. From being a poor, struggling, little hand-to-mouth enterprise, it had become celebrated, and overcrowded with customers. Harris was so grateful that he forced loans upon me, and would not be denied; and so, pauper as I was, I had money to spend, and was living like the rich and the great. I judged that there was going to be a crash by and by, but I was in, now, and must swim across or drown. You see, there was just that element of impending disaster to give a serious side, a sober side, yes, a tragic side, to a state of things which would otherwise have been purely ridiculous. In the night, in the dark, the tragedy part was always to the front, and always warning, always threatening; and so I moaned and tossed, and sleep was hard to find. But in the cheerful daylight the tragedy element faded out and disappeared, and I walked on air, and was happy to giddiness, to intoxication, you may say.

And it was natural; for I had become one of the notorieties of the metropolis of the world, and it turned my head, not just a little, but a good deal. You could not take up a newspaper,

English, Scotch, or Irish, without finding in it one or more references to the "vest-pocket million-pounder" and his latest doings and sayings. At first, in these mentions, I was at the bottom of the personal gossip column; next, I was listed above the knights; next, above the baronets; next, above the barons, and so on, and so on, climbing steadily as my notoriety augmented, until I reached the highest altitude possible, and there I remained, taking precedence of all dukes not royal, and of all ecclesiastics except the primate of all England. But mind, this was not fame; as yet I had achieved only notoriety. Then came the climaxing stroke—the accolade, so to speak—which in a single instant transmuted the perishable dross of notoriety into the enduring gold of fame: *Punch* caricatured me! Yes, I was a made man, now; my place was established. I might be joked about still, but reverently, not hilariously, not rudely; I could be smiled at, but not laughed at. The time for that had gone by. *Punch* pictured me all aflutter with rags, dickering with a beefeater for the Tower of London. Well, you can imagine how it was with a young fellow who had never been taken notice of before, and now all of a sudden couldn't say a thing that wasn't taken up and repeated everywhere; couldn't stir abroad without constantly overhearing the remark flying from lip to lip, "There he goes; that's him!" couldn't take his breakfast without a crowd to look on; couldn't appear in an opera box without concentrating there the fire of a thousand lorgnettes. Why, I just swam in glory all day long—that is the amount of it.

You know, I even kept my old suit of rags, and every now and then appeared in them, so as to have the old pleasure of buying trifles, and being insulted, and then shooting the scoffer dead with the million-pound bill. But I couldn't keep that up. The illustrated papers made the outfit so familiar that when I went out in it I was at once recognized and followed by a crowd, and if I attempted to purchase, the man would offer me his whole shop on credit before I could pull my note on him.

140   About the tenth day of my fame I went to fulfill my duty to my flag by paying my respects to the American minister. He received me with the enthusiasm proper in my case, upbraided me for being so tardy in my duty, and said that there was only one way to get his forgiveness, and that was to take the seat at his dinner party that night made vacant by the illness of one of his guests. I said I would, and we got to talking. It turned out that he and my father had been schoolmates in boyhood, Yale students together later, and always warm friends up to my father's death. So then he required me to put in at his house all the odd time I might have to spare, and I was very willing, of course.

In fact I was more than willing; I was glad. When the crash should come, he might somehow be able to save me from total destruction; I didn't know how, but he might think of a way, maybe. I couldn't venture to unbosom myself to him at this late date, a thing which I would have been quick to do in the beginning of this awful career of mine in London. No, I couldn't venture it now; I was in too deep; that is, too deep for me to be risking revelations to so new a friend, though not yet clear beyond my depth, as *I* looked at it. Because, you see, with all my borrowing, I was carefully keeping within my means—I mean within my salary. Of course I couldn't *know* what my salary was going to be, but I had a good enough basis for an estimate in the fact that, if I won the bet, I was to have *choice* of any situation in that rich old gentleman's gift, provided I was competent—and I should certainly prove competent; I hadn't any doubt about that. And as to the bet, I wasn't worrying about that; I had always been lucky. Now, my estimate of the salary was six hundred to a thousand a year; say, six hundred for the first year, and so on up year by year, till I struck that upper figure by proved merit. At present I was only in debt for my first year's salary. Everybody had been trying to lend me money, but I had fought off the most of them on one pretext or another; so this indebtedness represented only

£300 borrowed money, the other £300 represented my keep and my purchases. I believed my second year's salary would carry me through the rest of the month if I went on being cautious and economical, and I intended to look sharply out for that. My month ended, my employer back from his journey, I should be all right once more, for I should at once divide the two years' salary among my creditors by assignment, and get right down to my work.

It was a lovely dinner party of fourteen. The Duke and Duchess of Shoreditch, and their daughter the Lady Anne-Grace-Eleanor-Celeste-and-so-forth-and-so-forth-de-Bohun, the Earl and Countess of Newgate, Viscount Cheapside, Lord and Lady Blatherskite, some untitled people of both sexes, the minister and his wife and daughter, and this daughter's visiting friend, an English girl of twenty-two, named Portia Langham, whom I fell in love with in two minutes, and she with me—I could see it without glasses. There was still another guest, an American—but I am a little ahead of my story. While the people were still in the drawing room, whetting up for dinner, and coldly inspecting the latecomers, the servant announced:

"Mr. Lloyd Hastings."

The moment the usual civilities were over, Hastings caught sight of me, and came straight with cordially outstretched hand; then stopped short when about to shake; and said with an embarrassed look:

"I beg your pardon, sir; I thought I knew you."

"Why, you do know me, old fellow."

"No! Are *you* the—the—"

"Vest-pocket monster? I am, indeed. Don't be afraid to call me by my nickname; I'm used to it."

"Well, well, well, this is a surprise. Once or twice I've seen your own name coupled with the nickname, but it never occurred to me that *you* could be the Henry Adams referred to. Why, it isn't six months since you were clerking away for Blake Hopkins in Frisco on a salary, and sitting up nights on an

142 extra allowance, helping me arrange and verify the Gould and Curry Extension papers and statistics. The idea of your being in London, and a vast millionaire, and a colossal celebrity! Why, it's the Arabian Nights come again. Man, I can't take it in at all; can't realize it; give me time to settle the whirl in my head."

"The fact is, Lloyd, you are no worse off than I am. I can't realize it myself."

"Dear me, it *is* stunning, now isn't it? Why, it's just three months today since we went to the Miners' restaurant—"

"No, the What Cheer."

"Right, it *was* the What Cheer; went there at two in the morning, and had a chop and coffee after a hard six hours' grind over those Extension papers, and I tried to persuade you to come to London with me, and offered to get leave of absence for you and pay all your expenses, and give you something over if I succeeded in making the sale; and you would not listen to me, said I wouldn't succeed, and you couldn't afford to lose the run of business and be no end of time getting the hang of things again when you got back home. And yet here you are. How odd it all is! How did you happen to come, and whatever *did* give you this incredible start?"

"Oh, just an accident. It's a long story—a romance, a body may say. I'll tell you all about it, but not now."

"When?"

"The end of this month."

"That's more than a fortnight yet. It's too much of a strain on a person's curiosity. Make it a week."

"I can't. You'll know why, by and by. But how's the trade getting along?"

His cheerfulness vanished like a breath, and he said with a sigh:

"You were a true prophet, Hal, a true prophet. I wish I hadn't come. I don't want to talk about it."

"But you must. You must come and stop with me tonight,

when we leave here, and tell me all about it."

"Oh, may I? Are you in earnest?" and the water showed in his eyes.

"Yes, I want to hear the whole story, every word."

"I'm so grateful! Just to find a human interest once more, in some voice or in some eye, in me and affairs of mine, after what I've been through here—Lord! I could go down on my knees for it!"

He gripped my hand hard, and braced up, and was all right and lively after that for the dinner—which didn't come off. No, the usual thing happened, the thing that is always happening under that vicious and aggravating English system—the matter of precedence couldn't be settled, and so there was no dinner. Englishmen always eat dinner before they go out to dinner, because *they* know the risks they are running; but nobody ever warns the stranger, and so he walks placidly into the trap. Of course nobody was hurt this time, because we had all been to dinner, none of us being novices except Hastings, and he having been informed by the minister at the time that he invited him that in deference to the English custom he had not provided any dinner. Everybody took a lady and processioned down to the dining room, because it is usual to go through the motions; but there the dispute began. The Duke of Shoreditch wanted to take precedence, and sit at the head of the table, holding that he outranked a minister who represented merely a nation and not a monarch; but I stood for my rights, and refused to yield. In the gossip column I ranked all dukes not royal, and said so, and claimed precedence of this one. It couldn't be settled, of course, struggle as we might and did, he finally (and injudiciously) trying to play birth and antiquity, and I "seeing" his Conqueror and "raising" him with Adam, whose direct posterity I was, as shown by my name, while *he* was of a collateral branch, as shown by *his,* and by his recent Norman origin; so we all processioned back to the drawing room again and had a perpendicular lunch—plate of sardines and a strawberry, and you group yourself and stand up and eat it. Here the religion of precedence is not so strenuous; the two persons of highest rank chuck up a shilling, the one that wins has first go at his strawberry, and the loser gets the shilling. The next two chuck up, then the next two, and so on. After refreshment, tables were brought, and we all played cribbage, sixpence a game. The English never play any game for amusement. If they can't make something or lose something—they don't care which—they won't play.

We had a lovely time; certainly two of us had, Miss Langham and I. I was so bewitched with her that I couldn't count my hands if they went above a double sequence; and when I struck home I never discovered it, and started up the outside row again, and would have lost the game every time, only the girl did the same, she being in just my condition, you see; and consequently neither of us ever got out, or cared to wonder why we didn't; we only just knew we were happy, and didn't wish to know anything else, and didn't want to be interrupted. And I *told* her—I did indeed—told her I loved her; and she— well, she blushed till her hair turned red, but she liked it; she *said* she did. Oh, there was never such an evening! Every time I pegged I put on a postscript; every time she pegged she acknowledged receipt of it, counting the hands the same. Why, I couldn't even say "Two for his heels" without adding, "*My*, how sweet you do look!" and she would say, "Fifteen two, fifteen four, fifteen six, and a pair are eight, and eight are sixteen—*do* you think so?"—peeping out aslant from under her lashes, you know, so sweet and cunning. Oh, it was just *too*-too!

Well, I was perfectly honest and square with her; told her I hadn't a cent in the world but just the million-pound note she'd heard so much talk about, and *it* didn't belong to me; and that started her curiosity, and then I talked low, and told her the whole history right from the start, and it nearly killed her, laughing. What in the nation she could find to laugh about, I couldn't see, but there it was; every half minute some new detail would fetch her, and I would have to stop as much as a minute and a half to give her a chance to settle down again. Why, she laughed herself lame, she did indeed; I never saw anything like it. I mean I never saw a painful story—a story of a person's troubles and worries and fears—produce just *that* kind of effect before. So I loved her all the more, seeing she could be so cheerful when there wasn't anything to be cheerful about; for I might soon need that kind of wife, you know, the way things looked. Of course I told her we should have to wait a couple of years, till I could catch up on my salary; but she didn't mind that, only she hoped I would be as careful as possible in the matter of expenses, and not let them run the least risk of trenching on our third year's pay. Then she began to get a little worried, and wondered if we were making any mistake, and starting the salary on a higher figure for the first year than I would get. This was good sense, and it made me feel a little less confident than I had been feeling before; but it gave me a good business idea, and I brought it frankly out.

"Portia, dear, would you mind going with me that day, when I confront those old gentlemen?"

She shrank a little, but said:

"N-o, if my being with you would help hearten you. But—would it be quite proper, do you think?"

"No, I don't know that it would; in fact I'm afraid it wouldn't. But, you see, there's so *much* dependent upon it that—"

"Then I'll go anyway, proper or improper," she said, with a beautiful and generous enthusiasm. "Oh, I shall be so happy to think I'm helping."

"Helping, dear? Why, you'll be doing it all. You're so beautiful and so lovely and so winning that with you there I can pile our salary up till I break those good old fellows, and they'll never have the heart to struggle."

Sho! you should have seen the rich blood mount, and her happy eyes shine!

"You wicked flatterer! There isn't a word of truth in what you say, but still I'll go with you. Maybe it will teach you not to expect other people to look with your eyes."

Were my doubts dissipated? Was my confidence restored? You may judge by this fact: privately I raised my salary to twelve hundred the first year on the spot. But I didn't tell her; I saved it for a surprise.

All the way home I was in the clouds, Hastings talking, I not hearing a word. When he and I entered my parlor, he brought me to myself with his fervent appreciations of my manifold comforts and luxuries.

"Let me just stand here a little and look my fill! Dear me, it's a palace; it's just a palace! And in it everything a body *could* desire, including cozy coal fire and supper standing ready. Henry, it doesn't merely make me realize how rich you are; it makes me realize, to the bone, to the marrow, how poor I am—how poor I am, and how miserable, how defeated, routed, annihilated!"

Plague take it! This language gave me the cold shudders. It scared me broad awake, and made me comprehend that I was standing on a half-inch crust, with a crater underneath. *I* didn't know I had been dreaming—that is, I hadn't been allowing myself to know it for a while back; but *now*—oh, dear! Deep in debt, not a cent in the world, a lovely girl's happiness or woe in my hands, and nothing in front of me but a salary which might never—oh, *would* never—materialize! Oh, oh, oh, I am ruined past hope; nothing can save me!

"Henry, the mere unconsidered drippings of your daily income would—"

"Oh, my daily income! Here, down with this hot Scotch, and cheer up your soul. Here's with you! Or, no—you're hungry; sit down and—"

"Not a bite for me; I'm past it. I can't eat, these days; but I'll drink with you till I drop. Come!"

"Barrel for barrel, I'm with you! Ready? Here we go! Now, then, Lloyd, unreel your story while I brew."

"Unreel it? What, again?"

"Again? What do you mean by that?"

"Why, I mean do you want to hear it *over* again?"

"Do I want to hear it *over* again? This *is* a puzzler. Wait; don't take any more of that liquid. You don't need it."

"Look here, Henry, you alarm me. Didn't I tell you the whole story on the way here?"

"You?"

"Yes, I."

"I'll be hanged if I heard a word of it."

"Henry, this is a serious thing. It troubles me. What did you take up yonder at the minister's?"

Then it all flashed on me, and I owned up, like a man.

"I took the dearest girl in this world—prisoner!"

So then he came with a rush, and we shook, and shook, and shook till our hands ached; and he didn't blame me for not having heard a word of a story which had lasted while we walked three miles. He just sat down then, like the patient, good fellow he was, and told it all over again. Synopsized, it amounted to this: He had come to England with what he thought was a grand opportunity; he had an "option" to sell the Gould and Curry Extension for the "locators" of it, and keep all he could get over a million dollars. He had worked hard, had pulled every wire he knew of, had left no honest expedient untried, had spent nearly all the money he had in the world, had not been able to get a solitary capitalist to listen to him, and his option would run out at the end of the month. In a word, he was ruined. Then he jumped up and cried out:

"Henry, you can save me! You can save me, and you're the only man in the universe that can. Will you do it? *Won't* you do it?"

"Tell me how. Speak out, my boy."

"Give me a million and my passage home for my 'option'! Don't, *don't* refuse!"

I was in a kind of agony. I was right on the point of coming out with the words, "Lloyd, I'm a pauper myself—absolutely penniless, and in *debt*!" But a white-hot idea came flaming through my head, and I gripped my jaws together, and calmed myself down till I was as cold as a capitalist. Then I said, in a commercial and self-possessed way:

"I will save you, Lloyd—"

"Then I'm already saved! God be merciful to you forever! If ever I—"

"Let me finish, Lloyd. I will save you, but not in that way; for that would not be fair to you, after your hard work, and the risks you've run. I don't need to buy mines; I can keep my capital moving, in a commercial center like London without that; it's what I'm at, all the time; but here is what I'll do. I know all about that mine, of course; I know its immense value, and can swear to it if anybody wishes it. You shall sell out inside of the fortnight for three millions cash, using my name freely, and we'll divide, share and share alike."

Do you know, he would have danced the furniture to kindling wood in his insane joy, and broken everything on the place, if I hadn't tripped him up and tied him.

Then he lay there, perfectly happy, saying:

"I may use your name! Your name—think of it! Man, they'll flock in droves, these rich Londoners; they'll *fight* for that stock! I'm a made man, I'm a made man forever, and I'll never forget you as long as I live!"

In less than twenty-four hours, London was abuzz! I hadn't anything to do, day after day, but sit at home, and say to all comers:

"Yes, I told him to refer to me. I know the man, and I know the mine. His character is above reproach, and the mine is worth far more than he asks for it."

Meantime, I spent all my evenings at the minister's with

Portia. I didn't say a word to her about the mine; I saved it for a surprise. We talked salary; never anything but salary and love; sometimes love, sometimes salary, sometimes love and salary together. And my! the interest the minister's wife and daughter took in our little affair, and the endless ingenuities they invented to save us from interruption, and to keep the minister in the dark and unsuspicious—well, it was just lovely of them!

When the month was up, at last, I had a million dollars to my credit in the London and County Bank, and Hastings was fixed in the same way. Dressed at my level best, I drove by the house in Portland Place, judged by the look of things that my birds were home again, went on toward the minister's and got my precious, and we started back, talking salary with all our might. She was so excited and anxious that it made her just intolerably beautiful. I said:

"Dearie, the way you're looking it's a crime to strike for a salary a single penny under three thousand a year."

"Henry, Henry, you'll ruin us!"

"Don't you be afraid. Just keep up those looks, and trust to me. It'll all come out right."

So as it turned out, I had to keep bolstering up *her* courage all the way. She kept pleading with me, and saying:

"Oh, please remember that if we ask for too much we may get no salary at all; and then what will become of us, with no way in the world to earn our living?"

We were ushered in by that same servant, and there they were, the two old gentlemen. Of course they were surprised to see that wonderful creature with me, but I said:

"It's all right, gentlemen; she is my future stay and helpmate."

And I introduced them to her, and called them by name. It didn't surprise them; they knew I would know enough to consult the directory. They seated us, and were very polite to me, and very solicitous to relieve her from embarrassment, and put her as much at her ease as they could. Then I said:

"Gentlemen, I am ready to report."

"We are glad to hear it," said *my* man, "for now we can decide the bet which my brother Abel and I made. If you have won for me, you shall have any situation in my gift. Have you the million-pound note?"

"Here it is, sir," and I handed it to him.

"I've won!" he shouted, and slapped Abel on the back. "*Now* what do you say, brother?"

"I say he *did* survive, and I've lost twenty thousand pounds. I never would have believed it."

"I've a further report to make," I said, "and a pretty long one. I want you to let me come soon and detail my whole month's history; and I promise you it's worth hearing. Meantime, take a look at that."

"What, man! Certificate of deposit for £200,000? Is it yours?"

"Mine. I earned it by thirty days' judicious use of that little loan you let me have. And the only use I made of it was to buy trifles and offer the bill in change."

"Come, this is astonishing! It's incredible, man!"

"Never mind, I'll prove it. Don't take my word unsupported."

But now Portia's turn was come to be surprised. Her eyes were spread wide, and she said:

"Henry, is that really your money? Have you been fibbing to me?"

"I have indeed, dearie. But you'll forgive me, *I* know."

She put up an arch pout, and said:

"Don't you be so sure. You are a naughty thing to deceive me so!"

"Oh, you'll get over it, sweetheart, you'll get over it; it was only fun, you know. Come, let's be going."

"But wait, wait! The situation, you know. I want to give you the situation," said my man.

"Well," I said, "I'm just as grateful as I can be, but really I don't want one."

"But you can have the very choicest one in my gift."

"Thanks again, with all my heart; but I don't even want *that* one."

"Henry, I'm ashamed of you. You don't half-thank the good gentleman. May I do it for you?"

"Indeed you shall, dear, if you can improve it. Let us see you try."

She walked to my man, got up in his lap, put her arm round his neck, and kissed him right on the mouth. Then the two old gentlemen shouted with laughter, but I was dumfounded, just petrified, as you may say. Portia said:

"Papa, he has said you haven't a situation in your gift that he'd take; and I feel just as hurt as—"

"My darling!—Is that your papa?"

"Yes, he's my steppapa, and the dearest one that ever was. You understand now, don't you, why I was able to laugh when you told me at the minister's, not knowing my relationships, what trouble and worry Papa's and Uncle Abel's scheme was giving you?"

Of course I spoke right up, now, without any fooling, and went straight to the point.

"Oh, my dearest dear sir, I want to take back what I said. You *have* got a situation open that I want."

"Name it."

"Son-in-law."

"Well, well, well! But, you know, if you haven't ever served in that capacity, you of course can't furnish recommendations of a sort to satisfy the conditions of the contract, and so—"

"Try me—oh, do, I beg of you! Only just try me thirty or forty years, and if—"

"Oh, well, all right; it's but a little thing to ask. Take her

152 along."

Happy, we two? There're not words enough in the unabridged to describe it. And when London got the whole history, a day or two later, of my month's adventures with that bank note, and how they ended, did London talk, and have a good time? Yes.

My Portia's papa took that friendly and hospitable bill back to the Bank of England and cashed it; then the bank canceled it and made him a present of it, and he gave it to us at our wedding, and it has always hung in its frame in the sacredest place in our home, ever since. For it gave me my Portia. But for it I could not have remained in London, would not have appeared at the minister's, never should have met her. And so I always say, "Yes, it's a million-pounder, as you see; but it never made but one purchase in its life, and *then* got the article for only about a tenth part of its value."

*Lifting his eyes to the dizzy altitude . . . the officer saw
an astonishing sight—a man on horseback riding down
into the valley through the air!*

A HORSEMAN IN THE SKY

Ambrose Bierce

One sunny afternoon in the autumn of the year 1861, a soldier
lay in a clump of laurel by the side of a road in Western Virginia. He lay at full length, upon his stomach, his feet resting
upon the toes, his head upon the left forearm. His extended
right hand loosely grasped his rifle. But for the somewhat methodical disposition of his limbs and a slight rhythmic movement of the cartridge box at the back of his belt, he might have
been thought to be dead. He was asleep at his post of duty. But
if detected he would be dead shortly afterward, that being the
just and legal penalty of his crime.

The clump of laurel in which the criminal lay was in the
angle of the road which, after ascending southward, a steep ac-
clivity to that point, turned sharply to the west, running along
the summit for perhaps one hundred yards. There it turned
southward again and went zigzagging downward through the
forest. At the salient of that second angle was a large flat rock,
jutting out from the ridge to the northward, overlooking the
deep valley from which the road ascended. The rock capped a
high cliff; a stone dropped from its outer edge would have
fallen sheer downward one thousand feet to the tops of the
pines. The angle where the soldier lay was on another spur of
the same cliff. Had he been awake, he would have commanded

a view not only of the short arm of the road and the jutting rock but of the entire profile of the cliff below it. It might well have made him giddy to look.

The country was wooded everywhere except at the bottom of the valley to the northward, where there was a small natural meadow, through which flowed a stream scarcely visible from the valley's rim. This open ground looked hardly larger than an ordinary dooryard, but was really several acres in extent. Its green was more vivid than that of the inclosing forest. Away beyond it rose a line of giant cliffs similar to those upon which we are supposed to stand in our survey of the savage scene, and through which the road had somehow made its climb to the summit. The configuration of the valley, indeed, was such that from our point of observation it seemed entirely shut in, and one could not but have wondered how the road which found a way out of it had found a way into it, and whence came and whither went the waters of the stream that parted the meadow two thousand feet below.

No country is so wild and difficult but men will make it a theater of war; concealed in the forest at the bottom of that military rattrap, in which half a hundred men in possession of the exits might have starved an army to submission, lay five regiments of Federal infantry. They had marched all the previous day and night and were resting. At nightfall they would take to the road again, climb to the place where their unfaithful sentinel now slept, and descending the other slope of the ridge, fall upon a camp of the enemy at about midnight. Their hope was to surprise it, for the road led to the rear of it. In case of failure their position would be perilous in the extreme; and fail they surely would should accident or vigilance apprise the enemy of the movement.

The sleeping sentinel in the clump of laurel was a young Virginian named Carter Druse. He was the son of wealthy parents, an only child, and had known such ease and cultivation and high living as wealth and taste were able to command in the mountain country of Western Virginia. His home was but a few miles from where he now lay. One morning he had risen from the breakfast table and said, quietly but gravely: "Father, a Union regiment has arrived at Grafton. I am going to join it."

The father lifted his leonine head, looked at the son a moment in silence, and replied: "Go, Carter, and, whatever may occur, do what you conceive to be your duty. Virginia, to which you are a traitor, must get on without you. Should we both live to the end of the war, we will speak further of the matter. Your mother, as the physician has informed you, is in a most critical condition; at the best she cannot be with us longer than a few weeks, but that time is precious. It would be better not to disturb her."

So Carter Druse, bowing reverently to his father, who returned the salute with a stately courtesy which masked a breaking heart, left the home of his childhood to go soldiering. By conscience and courage, by deeds of devotion and daring, he soon commended himself to his fellows and his officers; and it was to these qualities and to some knowledge of the country that he owed his selection for his present perilous duty at the extreme outpost. Nevertheless, fatigue had been stronger than resolution, and he had fallen asleep. What good or bad angel came in a dream to rouse him from his state of crime, who shall say? Without a movement, without a sound, in the profound silence and the languor of the late afternoon, some invisible messenger of fate touched with unsealing finger the eyes of his consciousness—whispered into the ear of his spirit the mysterious awakening word which no human lips have ever spoken, no human memory ever has recalled. He quietly raised his forehead from his arm and looked between the masking stems of the laurels, instinctively closing his right hand about the stock of his rifle.

His first feeling was a keen artistic delight. On a colossal pedestal, the cliff motionless at the extreme edge of the capping rock and sharply outlined against the sky, was an equestrian statue of impressive dignity. The figure of the man sat the figure of the horse, straight and soldierly, but with the repose of a Grecian god carved in the marble which limits the suggestion of activity. The gray costume harmonized with its aerial background; the metal of accouterment and caparison was softened and subdued by the shadow; the animal's skin had no points of highlight. A carbine, strikingly foreshortened, lay across the pommel of the saddle, kept in place by the right hand grasping it at the "grip"; the left hand, holding the bridle rein, was invisible. In silhouette against the sky, the profile of the horse was cut with the sharpness of a cameo; it looked across the heights of air to the confronting cliffs beyond. The face of the rider, turned slightly to the left, showed only an outline of temple and beard; he was looking downward to the bottom of the valley. Magnified by its lift against the sky and by the soldier's testifying sense of the formidableness of a near enemy, the group appeared of heroic, almost colossal, size.

For an instant Druse had a strange, half-defined feeling that he had slept to the end of the war and was looking upon a noble work of art reared upon that commanding eminence to commemorate the deeds of an heroic past of which he had been an inglorious part. The feeling was dispelled by a slight movement of the group; the horse, without moving its feet, had drawn its body slightly backward from the verge; the man remained immobile as before. Broad awake and keenly alive to the significance of the situation, Druse now brought the butt of his rifle against his cheek by cautiously pushing the barrel forward through the bushes, cocked the piece, and glancing through the sights, covered a vital spot of the horseman's breast. A touch upon the trigger and all would have been well with Carter Druse. At that instant the horseman turned his head and looked in the direction of his concealed foeman—seemed to look into his very face, into his eyes, into his brave, compassionate heart.

Is it, then, so terrible to kill an enemy in war—an enemy who has surprised a secret vital to the safety of one's self and comrades—an enemy more formidable for his knowledge than all his army for its numbers? Carter Druse grew deathly pale; he shook in every limb, turned faint, and saw the statuesque group before him as black figures, rising, falling, moving unsteadily in arcs of circles in a fiery sky. His hand fell away from his weapon, his head slowly dropped until his face rested on the leaves in which he lay. This courageous gentleman and hardy soldier was near swooning from intensity of emotion.

It was not for long; in another moment his face was raised from earth, his hands resumed their places on the rifle, his forefinger sought the trigger; mind, heart, and eyes were clear, conscience and reason sound. He could not hope to capture that enemy; to alarm him would but send him dashing to his camp with his fatal news. The duty of the soldier was plain: the man must be shot dead from ambush—without warning, without a moment's spiritual preparation, with never so much as an unspoken prayer, he must be sent to his account. But no—there is a hope; he may have discovered nothing—perhaps he is but admiring the sublimity of the landscape. If permitted, he may turn and ride carelessly away in the direction whence he came. Surely it will be possible to judge at the instant of his withdrawing whether he knows. It may well be that his fixity of attention—Druse turned his head and looked below, through the deeps of air downward, as from the surface to the bottom of a translucent sea. He saw creeping across the green meadow a sinuous line of figures of men and horses—some foolish commander was permitting the soldiers of his escort to water their beasts in the open, in plain view from a hundred summits!

Druse withdrew his eyes from the valley and fixed them again upon the group of man and horse in the sky, and again it was through the sights of his rifle. But this time his aim was at the horse. In his memory, as if they were a divine mandate, rang the words of his father at their parting, "Whatever may occur, do what you conceive to be your duty." He was calm now. His teeth were firmly but not rigidly closed; his nerves were as tranquil as a sleeping babe's—not a tremor affected any muscle of his body; his breathing, until suspended in the act of taking aim, was regular and slow. Duty had conquered; the spirit had said to the body: "Peace, be still." He fired.

At that moment an officer of the Federal force, who in a spirit of adventure or in quest of knowledge had left the hidden bivouac in the valley, and with aimless feet had made his way to the lower edge of a small open space near the foot of the cliff, was considering what he had to gain by pushing his exploration further. At a distance of a quarter mile before him, but apparently at a stone's throw, rose from its fringe of pines the gigantic face of rock, towering to so great a height above him that it made him giddy to look up to where its edge cut a sharp, rugged line against the sky. At some distance away to his right it presented a clean, vertical profile against a background of blue sky to a point half of the way down, and of distant hills hardly less blue thence to the tops of the trees at its base. Lifting his eyes to the dizzy altitude of its summit, the officer saw an astonishing sight—a man on horseback riding down into the valley through the air!

Straight upright sat the rider, in military fashion, with a firm seat in the saddle, a strong clutch upon the rein to hold his charger from too impetuous a plunge. From his bare head his long hair streamed upward, waving like a plume. His right hand was concealed in the cloud of the horse's lifted mane. The animal's body was as level as if every hoof stroke encountered the resistant earth. Its motions were those of a wild gallop, but even as the officer looked they ceased, with all the legs thrown sharply forward as in the act of alighting from a leap. But this was a flight!

Filled with amazement and terror by this apparition of a horseman in the sky—half-believing himself the chosen scribe of some new Apocalypse, the officer was overcome by the intensity of his emotions; his legs failed him and he fell. Almost at the same instant, he heard a crashing sound in the trees—a sound that died without an echo, and all was still.

The officer rose to his feet, trembling. The familiar sensation of an abraded shin recalled his dazed faculties. Pulling himself together, he ran rapidly obliquely away from the cliff to a point a half mile from its foot; thereabout he expected to find his man; and thereabout he naturally failed. In the fleeting instant of his vision, his imagination had been so wrought upon by the apparent grace and ease and intention of the marvelous performance that it did not occur to him that the line of march of aerial cavalry is directly downward, and that he could find the objects of his search at the very foot of the cliff. A half hour later he returned to camp.

This officer was a wise man; he knew better than to tell an incredible truth. He said nothing of what he had seen. But when the commander asked him if in his scout he had learned anything of advantage to the expedition, he answered:

"Yes, sir; there is no road leading down into this valley from the southward."

The commander, knowing better, smiled.

After firing his shot, Private Carter Druse reloaded his rifle and resumed his watch. Ten minutes had hardly passed when a Federal sergeant crept cautiously to him on hands and knees. Druse neither turned his head nor looked at him, but lay without motion or sign of recognition.

"Did you fire?" the sergeant whispered.

"Yes."

"At what?"

"A horse. It was standing on yonder rock—pretty far out. You see it is no longer there. It went over the cliff."

The man's face was white but he showed no other sign of emotion. Having answered, he turned away his face and said no more. The sergeant did not understand.

160   "See here, Druse," he said, after a moment's silence, "it's no
use making a mystery. I order you to report. Was there anybody on the horse?"

"Yes."

"Who?"

"My father."

The sergeant rose to his feet and walked away. "Good God!"
he said.

Until now he could not remember the time when he had not been dreading something.

PAUL'S CASE

Willa Cather

It was Paul's afternoon to appear before the faculty of the Pittsburgh High School to account for his various misdemeanors. He had been suspended a week ago, and his father had called at the principal's office and confessed his perplexity about his son. Paul entered the faculty room suave and smiling. His clothes were a trifle outgrown, and the tan velvet on the collar of his open overcoat was frayed and worn; but for all that, there was something of the dandy about him, and he wore an opal pin in his neatly knotted black four-in-hand, and a red carnation in his buttonhole. This latter adornment the faculty somehow felt was not properly significant of the contrite spirit befitting a boy under the ban of suspension.

Paul was tall for his age and very thin, with high, cramped shoulders and a narrow chest. His eyes were remarkable for a certain hysterical brilliancy, and he continually used them in a conscious, theatrical sort of way, peculiarly offensive in a boy. The pupils were abnormally large, as though he were addicted to belladonna, but there was a glassy glitter about them which that drug does not produce.

When questioned by the principal as to why he was there, Paul stated, politely enough, that he wanted to come back to school. This was a lie, but Paul was quite accustomed to lying;

162 found it, indeed, indispensable for overcoming friction. His teachers were asked to state their respective charges against him, which they did with such a rancor and aggrievedness as evinced that this was not a usual case. Disorder and impertinence were among the offenses named, yet each of his instructors felt that it was scarcely possible to put into words the real cause of the trouble, which lay in a sort of hysterically defiant manner of the boy's; in the contempt which they all knew he felt for them, and which he seemingly made not the least effort to conceal. Once, when he had been making a synopsis of a paragraph at the blackboard, his English teacher had stepped to his side and attempted to guide his hand. Paul had started back with a shudder and thrust his hands violently behind him. The astonished woman could scarcely have been more hurt and embarrassed had he struck at her. The insult was so involuntary and definitely personal as to be unforgettable. In one way and another he had made all his teachers, men and women alike, conscious of the same feeling of physical aversion. In one class he habitually sat with his hand shading his eyes; in another he always looked out of the window during the recitation; in another he made a running commentary on the lecture, with humorous intention.

His teachers felt this afternoon that his whole attitude was symbolized by his shrug and his flippantly red carnation flower, and they fell upon him without mercy, his English teacher leading the pack. He stood through it smiling, his pale lips parted over his white teeth. (His lips were continually twitching, and he had a habit of raising his eyebrows that was contemptuous and irritating to the last degree.) Older boys than Paul had broken down and shed tears under that baptism of fire, but his set smile did not once desert him, and his only sign of discomfort was the nervous trembling of the fingers that toyed with the buttons of his overcoat, and an occasional jerking of the other hand that held his hat. Paul was always smiling, always glancing about him, seeming to feel that people might be watching him and trying to detect something. This conscious expression, since it was as far as possible from boyish mirthfulness, was usually attributed to insolence or "smartness."

As the inquisition proceeded, one of his instructors repeated an impertinent remark of the boy's, and the principal asked him whether he thought that a courteous speech to have made a woman. Paul shrugged his shoulders slightly and his eyebrows twitched.

"I don't know," he replied. "I didn't mean to be polite or impolite, either. I guess it's a sort of way I have of saying things regardless."

The principal, who was a sympathetic man, asked him whether he didn't think that a way it would be well to get rid of. Paul grinned and said he guessed so. When he was told that he could go he bowed gracefully and went out. His bow was but a repetition of the scandalous red carnation.

His teachers were in despair, and his drawing master voiced the feeling of them all when he declared there was something about the boy which none of them understood. He added: "I don't really believe that smile of his comes altogether from insolence; there's something sort of haunted about it. The boy is not strong, for one thing. I happen to know that he was born in Colorado, only a few months before his mother died out there of a long illness. There is something wrong about the fellow."

The drawing master had come to realize that, in looking at Paul, one saw only his white teeth and the forced animation of his eyes. One warm afternoon the boy had gone to sleep at his drawing board, and his master had noted with amazement what a white, blue-veined face it was; drawn and wrinkled like an old man's about the eyes, the lips twitching even in his sleep, and stiff with a nervous tension that drew them back from his teeth.

His teachers left the building dissatisfied and unhappy; humiliated to have felt so vindictive toward a mere boy, to have uttered this feeling in cutting terms, and to have set each other on, as it were, in the gruesome game of intemperate reproach. Some of them remembered having seen a miserable street cat set at bay by a ring of tormentors.

As for Paul, he ran down the hill whistling the "Soldiers' Chorus" from *Faust,* looking wildly behind him now and then to see whether some of his teachers were not there to writhe under his lightheartedness. As it was now late in the afternoon and Paul was on duty that evening as usher at Carnegie Hall, he decided that he would not go home to supper. When he reached the concert hall the doors were not yet open and, as it was chilly outside, he decided to go up into the picture gallery—always deserted at this hour—where there were some of Raffaelli's gay studies of Paris streets and an airy blue Venetian scene or two that always exhilarated him. He was delighted to find no one in the gallery but the old guard, who sat in one corner, a newspaper on his knee, a black patch over one eye and the other closed. Paul possessed himself of the place and walked confidently up and down, whistling under his breath. After a while he sat down before a blue Rico and lost himself. When he bethought him to look at his watch, it was after seven o'clock, and he rose with a start and ran downstairs, making a face at Augustus, peering out from the cast room, and an evil gesture at the Venus de Milo as he passed her on the stairway.

When Paul reached the ushers' dressing room half a dozen boys were there already, and he began excitedly to tumble into his uniform. It was one of the few that at all approached fitting, and Paul thought it very becoming—though he knew that the tight, straight coat accentuated his narrow chest, about which he was exceedingly sensitive. He was always considerably excited while he dressed, twanging all over to the tuning of the strings and the preliminary flourishes of the horns in the music room; but tonight he seemed quite beside himself, and he teased and plagued the boys until, telling him that he was crazy, they put him down on the floor and sat on him.

Somewhat calmed by his suppression, Paul dashed out to the front of the house to seat the early comers. He was a model usher; gracious and smiling he ran up and down the aisles; nothing was too much trouble for him; he carried messages and brought programs as though it were his greatest pleasure in life, and all the people in his section thought him a charming boy, feeling that he remembered and admired them. As the house filled, he grew more and more vivacious and animated, and the color came to his cheeks and lips. It was very much as though this were a great reception and Paul were the host. Just as the musicians came out to take their places, his English teacher arrived with checks for the seats which a prominent manufacturer had taken for the season. She betrayed some embarrassment when she handed Paul the tickets, and a hauteur which subsequently made her feel very foolish. Paul was startled for a moment, and had the feeling of wanting to put her out; what business had she here among all these fine people and gay colors? He looked her over and decided that she was not appropriately dressed and must be a fool to sit downstairs in such togs. The tickets had probably been sent her out of kindness, he reflected as he put down a seat for her, and she had about as much right to sit there as he had.

When the symphony began Paul sank into one of the rear seats with a long sigh of relief, and lost himself as he had done before the Rico. It was not that symphonies, as such, meant anything in particular to Paul, but the first sigh of the instruments seemed to free some hilarious and potent spirit within him; something that struggled there like the genie in the bottle found by the Arab fisherman. He felt a sudden zest of life; the lights danced before his eyes and the concert hall blazed into unimaginable splendor. When the soprano soloist came on, Paul forgot even the nastiness of his teacher's being there and gave himself up to the peculiar stimulus such personages always had for him. The soloist chanced to be a German woman, by no means in her first youth, and the mother of many children; but she wore an elaborate gown and a tiara, and above all she had that indefinable air of achievement, that world-shine upon her, which, in Paul's eyes, made her a veritable queen of Romance.

• • •

After a concert was over Paul was always irritable and wretched until he got to sleep, and tonight he was even more than usually restless. He had the feeling of not being able to let down, of its being impossible to give up this delicious excitement which was the only thing that could be called living at all. During the last number he withdrew and, after hastily changing his clothes in the dressing room, slipped out to the side door where the soprano's carriage stood. Here he began pacing rapidly up and down the walk, waiting to see him come out.

Over yonder, the Schenley, in its vacant stretch, loomed big and square through the fine rain, the windows of its twelve stories glowing like those of a lighted cardboard house under a Christmas tree. All the actors and singers of the better class stayed there when they were in the city, and a number of the big manufacturers of the place lived there in the winter. Paul had often hung about the hotel, watching the people go in and out, longing to enter and leave schoolmasters and dull care behind him forever.

At last the singer came out, accompanied by the conductor, who helped her into her carriage and closed the door with a cordial *auf Wiedersehen* which set Paul to wondering whether she were not an old sweetheart of his. Paul followed the carriage over to the hotel, walking so rapidly as not to be far from the entrance when the singer alighted, and disappeared behind the swinging glass doors that were opened by a Negro in a tall hat and a long coat. In the moment that the door was ajar it seemed to Paul that he, too, entered. He seemed to feel himself go after her up the steps, into the warm, lighted building, into an exotic, tropical world of shiny, glistening surfaces and basking ease. He reflected upon the mysterious dishes that were brought into the dining room, the green bottles in buckets of ice, as he had seen them in the supper party pictures of the *Sunday World* supplement. A quick gust of wind brought the rain down with sudden vehemence, and Paul was startled to find that he was still outside in the slush of the gravel driveway; that his boots were letting in the water and his scanty overcoat was clinging wet about him; that the lights in front of the concert hall were out and that the rain was driving in sheets between him and the orange glow of the windows above him. There it was, what he wanted—tangibly before him, like the fairy world of a Christmas pantomime—but mocking spirits stood guard at the doors, and as the rain beat in his face, Paul wondered whether he were destined always to shiver in the black night outside, looking up at it.

He turned and walked reluctantly toward the car tracks. The end had to come sometime; his father in his nightclothes at the top of the stairs, explanations that did not explain, hastily improvised fictions that were forever tripping him up, his upstairs room and its horrible yellow wallpaper, the creaking bureau with the greasy plush collar box, and over his painted wooden bed the pictures of George Washington and John Calvin, and the framed motto "Feed my Lambs," which had been worked in red worsted by his mother.

Half an hour later Paul alighted from his car and went slowly down one of the side streets off the main thoroughfare. It was a highly respectable street, where all the houses were exactly alike, and where businessmen of moderate means begot and reared large families of children, all of whom went to Sabbath school and learned the shorter catechism, and were interested in arithmetic; all of whom were as exactly alike as their homes, and of a piece with the monotony in which they lived. Paul never went up Cordelia Street without a shudder of

168 loathing. His home was next to the house of the Cumberland minister. He approached it tonight with the nerveless sense of defeat, the hopeless feeling of sinking back forever into ugliness and commonness that he had always had when he came home. The moment he turned into Cordelia Street he felt the waters close above his head. After each of these orgies of living he experienced all the physical depression which follows a debauch; the loathing of respectable beds, of common food, of a house penetrated by kitchen odors; a shuddering repulsion for the flavorless, colorless mass of everyday existence; a morbid desire for cool things and soft lights and fresh flowers.

The nearer he approached the house, the more absolutely unequal Paul felt to the sight of it all: his ugly sleeping chamber; the cold bathroom with the grimy zinc tub, the cracked mirror, the dripping spiggots; his father, at the top of the stairs, his hairy legs sticking out from his nightshirt, his feet thrust into carpet slippers. He was so much later than usual that there would certainly be inquiries and reproaches. Paul stopped short before the door. He felt that he could not be accosted by his father tonight; that he could not toss again on that miserable bed. He would not go in. He would tell his father that he had no carfare and it was raining so hard he had gone home with one of the boys and stayed all night.

Meanwhile, he was wet and cold. He went around to the back of the house and tried one of the basement windows, found it open, raised it cautiously, and scrambled down the cellar wall to the floor. There he stood, holding his breath, terrified by the noise he had made, but the floor above him was silent, and there was no creak on the stairs. He found a soapbox, and carried it over to the soft ring of light that streamed from the furnace door, and sat down. He was horribly afraid of rats, so he did not try to sleep, but sat looking distrustfully at the dark, still terrified lest he might have awakened his father. In such reactions, after one of the experiences which made days and nights out of the dreary blanks of the calendar, when his senses were deadened, Paul's head was always singularly clear. Suppose his father had heard him getting in at the window and had come down and shot him for a burglar? Then, again, suppose his father had come down, pistol in hand, and he had cried out in time to save himself, and his father had been horrified to think how nearly he had killed him? Then, again, suppose a day should come when his father would remember that night, and wish there had been no warning cry to stay his hand? With this last supposition Paul entertained himself until daybreak.

The following Sunday was fine; the sodden November chill was broken by the last flash of autumnal summer. In the morning Paul had to go to church and Sabbath school, as always. On seasonable Sunday afternoons the burghers of Cordelia Street always sat out on their front stoops and talked to their neighbors on the next stoop, or called to those across the street in neighborly fashion. The men usually sat on gay cushions placed upon the steps that led down to the sidewalk, while the women, in their Sunday "waists," sat in rockers on the cramped porches, pretending to be greatly at their ease. The children played in the streets; there were so many of them that the place resembled the recreation grounds of a kindergarten. The men on the steps—all in their shirt sleeves, their vests unbuttoned—sat with their legs well apart, their stomachs comfortably protruding, and talked of the prices of things, or told anecdotes of the sagacity of their various chiefs and overlords. They occasionally looked over the multitude of squabbling children, listened affectionately to their high-pitched, nasal voices, smiling to see their own proclivities reproduced in their offspring, and interspersed their legends of the iron kings with remarks about their sons' progress at school, their grades in arithmetic, and the amounts they had saved in their toy banks.

On this last Sunday of November, Paul sat all the afternoon on the lowest step of his stoop, staring into the street, while his sisters, in their rockers, were talking to the minister's daughters next door about how many shirtwaists they had made in the last week, and how many waffles someone had eaten at the last church supper. When the weather was warm, and his father was in a particularly jovial frame of mind, the girls made lemonade, which was always brought out in a red-glass pitcher, ornamented with forget-me-nots in blue enamel. This the girls thought very fine, and the neighbors always joked about the suspicious color of the pitcher.

Today Paul's father sat on the top step, talking to a young man who shifted a restless baby from knee to knee. He happened to be the young man who was daily held up to Paul as a model, and after whom it was his father's dearest hope that he would pattern. This young man was of a ruddy complexion, with a compressed, red mouth, and faded, nearsighted eyes, over which he wore thick spectacles, with gold bows that curved about his ears. He was clerk to one of the magnates of a great steel corporation, and was looked upon in Cordelia Street as a young man with a future. There was a story that, some five years ago—he was now barely twenty-six—he had been a trifle dissipated, but in order to curb his appetites and save the loss of time and strength that a sowing of wild oats might have entailed, he had taken his chief's advice, oft reiterated to his employees, and at twenty-one had married the first woman whom he could persuade to share his fortunes. She happened to be the angular schoolmistress, much older than he, who also wore thick glasses, and who had now borne him four children, all nearsighted, like herself.

The young man was relating how his chief, now cruising in the Mediterranean, kept in touch with all the details of the business, arranging his office hours on his yacht just as though he were at home, and "knocking off work enough to keep two stenographers busy." His father told, in turn, the plan his corporation was considering, of putting in an electric railway plant at Cairo. Paul snapped his teeth; he had an awful apprehension that they might spoil it all before he got there. Yet he rather liked to hear these legends of the iron kings that were told and retold on Sundays and holidays; these stories of palaces in Venice, yachts on the Mediterranean, and high play at Monte Carlo appealed to his fancy, and he was interested in the triumphs of these cash boys who had become famous, though he had no mind for the cash-boy stage.

After supper was over and he had helped to dry the dishes, Paul nervously asked his father whether he could go to George's to get some help in geometry, and still more nervously asked for carfare. This latter request he had to repeat, as his father, on principle, did not like to hear requests for money, whether much or little. He asked Paul whether he could not go to some boy who lived nearer, and told him that he ought not to leave his schoolwork until Sunday; but he gave him the dime. He was not a poor man, but he had a worthy ambition to come up in the world. His only reason for allowing Paul to usher was that he thought a boy ought to be earning a little.

Paul bounded upstairs, scrubbed the greasy odor of the dishwater from his hands with the ill-smelling soap he hated, and then shook over his fingers a few drops of violet water from the bottle he kept hidden in his drawer. He left the house with his geometry conspicuously under his arm, and the moment he got out of Cordelia Street and boarded a downtown car, he shook off the lethargy of two deadening days and began to live again.

The leading juvenile of the permanent stock company which played at one of the downtown theaters was an acquaintance of Paul's, and the boy had been invited to drop in at the Sunday-night rehearsals whenever he could. For more than a year Paul had spent every available moment loitering about Charley Edwards's dressing room. He had won a place among Edwards's following not only because the young actor, who could not afford to employ a dresser, often found him useful, but because he recognized in Paul something akin to what churchmen term "vocation."

It was at the theater and at Carnegie Hall that Paul really lived; the rest was but a sleep and a forgetting. This was Paul's fairy tale, and it had for him all the allurement of a secret love. The moment he inhaled the gassy, painty, dusty odor behind the scenes, he breathed like a prisoner set free, and felt within him the possibility of doing or saying splendid, brilliant, poetic things. The moment the cracked orchestra beat out the overture from *Martha*, or jerked at the serenade from *Rigoletto*, all stupid and ugly things slid from him, and his senses were deliciously yet delicately fired.

Perhaps it was because, in Paul's world, the natural nearly always wore the guise of ugliness that a certain element of artificiality seemed to him necessary in beauty. Perhaps it was because his experience of life elsewhere was so full of Sabbath-school picnics, petty economies, wholesome advice as to how to succeed in life, and the inescapable odors of cooking, that he found this existence so alluring, these smartly clad men and women so attractive, that he was so moved by these starry apple orchards that bloomed perennially under the limelight.

It would be difficult to put it strongly enough how convincingly the stage entrance of that theater was for Paul the actual portal of Romance. Certainly none of the company ever suspected it, least of all Charley Edwards. It was very like the old stories that used to float about London of fabulously rich Jews, who had subterranean halls there, with palms, and fountains, and soft lamps and richly appareled women who never saw the disenchanting light of London day. So, in the midst of that smoke-palled city, enamored of figures and grimy toil, Paul had his secret temple, his wishing carpet, his bit of blue-and-white Mediterranean shore bathed in perpetual sunshine.

Several of Paul's teachers had a theory that his imagination

had been perverted by garish fiction, but the truth was that he
scarcely ever read at all. The books at home were not such as
would either tempt or corrupt a youthful mind, and as for
reading the novels that some of his friends urged upon him—
well, he got what he wanted much more quickly from music;
any sort of music, from an orchestra to a barrel organ. He
needed only the spark, the indescribable thrill that made his
imagination master of his senses, and he could make plots and
pictures enough of his own. It was equally true that he was not
stagestruck—not, at any rate, in the usual acceptation of that
expression. He had no desire to become an actor, any more
than he had to become a musician. He felt no necessity to do
any of these things; what he wanted was to see, to be in the atmosphere, float on the wave of it, to be carried out, blue
league after blue league, away from everything.

After a night behind the scenes, Paul found the schoolroom
more than ever repulsive; the bare floors and naked walls; the
prosy men who never wore frock coats, or violets in their but-
tonholes; the women with their dull gowns, shrill voices, and
pitiful seriousness about prepositions that govern the dative.
He could not bear to have the other pupils think, for a moment, that he took these people seriously; he must convey to
them that he considered it all trivial, and was there only by
way of a jest, anyway. He had autographed pictures of all the
members of the stock company which he showed his class-
mates, telling them the most incredible stories of his familiarity with these people, of his acquaintance with the soloists
who came to Carnegie Hall, his suppers with them and the
flowers he sent them. When these stories lost their effect, and
his audience grew listless, he became desperate and would bid
all the boys good-by, announcing that he was going to travel
for a while; going to Naples, to Venice, to Egypt. Then, next
Monday, he would slip back, conscious and nervously smiling;
his sister was ill, and he should have to defer his voyage until

spring.

Matters went steadily worse with Paul at school. In the itch to let his instructors know how heartily he despised them and their homilies, and how thoroughly he was appreciated elsewhere, he mentioned once or twice that he had no time to fool with theorems; adding—with a twitch of the eyebrows and a touch of that nervous bravado which so perplexed them—that he was helping the people down at the stock company; they were old friends of his.

The upshot of the matter was that the principal went to Paul's father, and Paul was taken out of school and put to work. The manager at Carnegie Hall was told to get another usher in his stead; the doorkeeper at the theater was warned not to admit him to the house; and Charley Edwards remorsefully promised the boy's father not to see him again.

The members of the stock company were vastly amused when some of Paul's stories reached them—especially the women. They were hardworking women, most of them supporting indigent husbands or brothers, and they laughed rather bitterly at having stirred the boy to such fervid and florid inventions. They agreed with the faculty and with his father that Paul's was a bad case.

· · ·

The eastbound train was plowing through a January snowstorm; the dull dawn was beginning to show gray when the engine whistled a mile out of Newark. Paul started up from the seat where he had lain curled in uneasy slumber, rubbed the breath-misted window glass with his hand, and peered out. The snow was whirling in curling eddies above the white bottomlands, and the drifts lay already deep in the fields and along the fences, while here and there the long dead grass and dried weed stalks protruded black above it. Lights shone from the scattered houses, and a gang of laborers who stood beside the track waved their lanterns.

Paul had slept very little, and he felt grimy and uncomfortable. He had made the all-night journey in a day coach, partly because he was ashamed, dressed as he was, to go into a Pullman, and partly because he was afraid of being seen there by some Pittsburgh businessman who might have noticed him in Denny & Carson's office. When the whistle awoke him, he clutched quickly at his breast pocket, glancing about him with an uncertain smile. But the little, clay-bespattered Italians were sleeping, the slatternly women across the aisle were in open-mouthed oblivion, and even the crumby, crying babies were for the nonce stilled. Paul settled back to struggle with his impatience as best he could.

When he arrived at the Jersey City station he hurried through his breakfast, manifestly ill at ease and keeping a sharp eye about him. After he reached the Twenty-third Street station, he consulted a cabman and had himself driven to a men's-furnishings establishment that was just opening for the day. He spent upward of two hours there, buying with endless reconsidering and great care. His new street suit he put on in the fitting room; the frock coat and dress clothes he had bundled into the cab with his linen. Then he drove to a hatter's and a shoe house. His next errand was at Tiffany's, where he selected his silver and a new scarf pin. He would not wait to have his silver marked, he said. Lastly, he stopped at a trunk shop on Broadway and had his purchases packed into various traveling bags.

It was a little after one o'clock when he drove up to the Waldorf, and after settling with the cabman, went into the office. He registered from Washington; said his mother and father had been abroad, and that he had come down to await the arrival of their steamer. He told his story plausibly and had no trouble, since he volunteered to pay for them in advance, in engaging his rooms; a sleeping room, sitting room, and a bath.

Not once, but a hundred times, Paul had planned this entry into New York. He had gone over every detail of it with Charley Edwards, and in his scrapbook at home there were pages of description about New York hotels, cut from the Sunday papers. When he was shown to his sitting room on the eighth floor he saw at a glance that everything was as it should be; there was but one detail in his mental picture that the place did not realize, so he rang for the bellboy and sent him down for flowers. He moved about nervously until the boy returned, putting away his new linen and fingering it delightedly as he did so. When the flowers came he put them hastily into water, and then tumbled into a hot bath. Presently he came out of his white bathroom, resplendent in his new silk underwear, and playing with the tassels of his red robe. The snow was whirling so fiercely outside his windows that he could scarcely see across the street, but within the air was deliciously soft and fragrant. He put the violets and jonquils on the taboret beside the couch, and threw himself down, with a long sigh, covering himself with a Roman blanket. He was thoroughly tired; he had been in such haste, he had stood up to such a strain, covered so much ground in the last twenty-four hours that he wanted to think how it had all come about. Lulled by the sound of the wind, the warm air, and the cool fragrance of the flowers, he sank into deep, drowsy retrospection.

It had been wonderfully simple; when they had shut him out of the theater and concert hall, when they had taken away his bone, the whole thing was virtually determined. The rest was a mere matter of opportunity. The only thing that at all surprised him was his own courage—for he realized well enough that he had always been tormented by fear, a sort of apprehensive dread that, of late years, as the meshes of the lies he had told closed about him, had been pulling the muscles of his body tighter and tighter. Until now he could not remember the time when he had not been dreading something. Even when he was a little boy it was always there—behind him, or before, or on either side. There had always been the shadowed corner, the dark place into which he dared not look, but from which something seemed always to be watching him—and Paul had done things that were not pretty to watch, he knew.

But now he had a curious sense of relief, as though he had at last thrown down the gauntlet to the thing in the corner.

Yet it was but a day since he had been sulking in the traces; but yesterday afternoon that he had been sent to the bank with Denny & Carson's deposit, as usual—but this time he was instructed to leave the book to be balanced. There was above two thousand dollars in checks, and nearly a thousand in the bank notes which he had taken from the book and quietly transferred to his pocket. At the bank he had made out a new deposit slip. His nerves had been steady enough to permit of his returning to the office, where he had finished his work and asked for a full day's holiday tomorrow, Saturday, giving a perfectly reasonable pretext. The bankbook, he knew, would not be returned before Monday or Tuesday, and his father would be out of town for the next week. From the time he slipped the bank notes into his pocket until he boarded the night train for New York, he had not known a moment's hesitation. It was not the first time Paul had steered through treacherous waters.

How astonishingly easy it had all been; here he was, the thing done; and this time there would be no awakening, no figure at the top of the stairs. He watched the snowflakes whirling by his window until he fell asleep.

When he awoke, it was three o'clock in the afternoon. He bounded up with a start; half of one of his precious days gone already! He spent more than an hour in dressing, watching every stage of his toilet carefully in the mirror. Everything was quite perfect; he was exactly the kind of boy he had always wanted to be.

When he went downstairs Paul took a carriage and drove up Fifth Avenue toward the Park. The snow had somewhat abated; carriages and tradesmen's wagons were hurrying soundlessly to and fro in the winter twilight; boys in woolen mufflers were shoveling off the doorsteps; the avenue stages made fine spots of color against the white street. Here and there on the corners were stands, with whole flower gardens blooming under glass cases, against the sides of which the snowflakes stuck and melted; violets, roses, carnations, lilies of the valley—somehow vastly more lovely and alluring that they blossomed thus unnaturally in the snow. The Park itself was a wonderful stage winter piece.

When he returned, the pause of the twilight had ceased and the tune of the streets had changed. The snow was falling faster, lights streamed from the hotels that reared their dozen stories fearlessly up into the storm, defying the raging Atlantic winds. A long, black stream of carriages poured down the avenue, intersected here and there by other streams, tending horizontally. There were a score of cabs about the entrance of his hotel, and his driver had to wait. Boys in livery were running in and out of the awning stretched across the sidewalk, up and down the red velvet carpet laid from the door to the street. Above, about, within it all was the rumble and roar, the hurry and toss of thousands of human beings as hot for pleasure as himself, and on every side of him towered the glaring affirmation of the omnipotence of wealth.

The boy set his teeth and drew his shoulders together in a spasm of realization; the plot of all dramas, the text of all romances, the nerve-stuff of all sensations was whirling about him like the snowflakes. He burnt like a faggot in a tempest.

When Paul went down to dinner the music of the orchestra came floating up the elevator shaft to greet him. His head whirled as he stepped into the thronged corridor, and he sank back into one of the chairs against the wall to get his breath. The lights, the chatter, the perfumes, the bewildering medley of color—he had, for a moment, the feeling of not being able to stand it. But only for a moment; these were his own people, he told himself. He went slowly about the corridors, through the writing rooms, smoking rooms, reception rooms, as though he were exploring the chambers of an enchanted palace, built and peopled for him alone.

When he reached the dining room he sat down at a table near a window. The flowers, the white linen, the many-colored wineglasses, the gay toilettes of the women, the low popping of corks, the undulating repetitions of the *Blue Danube* from the orchestra, all flooded Paul's dream with bewildering radiance. When the roseate tinge of his champagne was added— that cold, precious, bubbling stuff that creamed and foamed in his glass—Paul wondered that there were honest men in the world at all. This was what all the world was fighting for, he reflected; this was what all the struggle was about. He doubted the reality of his past. Had he ever known a place called Cordelia Street, a place where fagged-looking businessmen got on the early car; mere rivets in a machine, they seemed to Paul— sickening men, with combings of children's hair always hanging to their coats, and the smell of cooking in their clothes. Cordelia Street—Ah, that belonged to another time and country; had he not always been thus, had he not sat here night after night, from as far back as he could remember, looking pensively over just such shimmering textures and slowly twirling the stem of a glass like this one between his thumb and middle finger? He rather thought he had.

He was not in the least abashed or lonely. He had no especial desire to meet or to know any of these people; all he demanded was the right to look on and conjecture, to watch the pageant. The mere stage properties were all he contended for. Nor was he lonely later in the evening, in his lodge at the Metropolitan. He was now entirely rid of his nervous misgivings, of his forced aggressiveness, of the imperative desire to show himself different from his surroundings. He felt now that his surroundings explained him. Nobody questioned the purple; he had only to wear it passively. He had only to glance down at his attire to reassure himself that here it would be impossible for anyone to humiliate him.

He found it hard to leave his beautiful sitting room to go to bed that night, and sat long watching the raging storm from his turret window. When he went to sleep it was with the lights turned on in his bedroom; partly because of his old timidity, and partly so that, if he should wake in the night, there would be no wretched moment of doubt, no horrible suspicion of yellow wallpaper, or of Washington and Calvin above his bed.

Sunday morning the city was practically snowbound. Paul breakfasted late, and in the afternoon he fell in with a wild San Francisco boy, a freshman at Yale, who said he had run down for a "little flyer" over Sunday. The young man offered to show Paul the night side of the town, and the two boys went out together after dinner, not returning to the hotel until seven o'clock the next morning. They had started out in the confiding warmth of a champagne friendship, but their parting in the elevator was singularly cool. The freshman pulled himself together to make his train, and Paul went to bed. He awoke at two o'clock in the afternoon, very thirsty and dizzy, and rang for ice water, coffee, and the Pittsburgh papers.

On the part of the hotel management, Paul excited no suspicion. There was this to be said for him, that he wore his spoils with dignity and in no way made himself conspicuous. Even under the glow of his wine he was never boisterous, though he found the stuff like a magician's wand for wonder-building. His chief greediness lay in his ears and eyes, and his excesses were not offensive ones. His dearest pleasures were the gray winter twilights in his sitting room; his quiet enjoyment of his flowers, his clothes, his wide divan, his cigarette, and his sense of power. He could not remember a time when he had felt so at peace with himself. The mere release from the necessity of petty lying, lying every day and every day, restored his self-respect. He had never lied for pleasure, even at school; but to be noticed and admired, to assert his difference from other

Cordelia Street boys; and he felt a good deal more manly, more honest, even, now that he had no need for boastful pretensions, now that he could, as his actor friends used to say, "dress the part." It was characteristic that remorse did not occur to him. His golden days went by without a shadow, and he made each as perfect as he could.

On the eighth day after his arrival in New York he found the whole affair exploited in the Pittsburgh papers, exploited with a wealth of detail which indicated that local news of a sensational nature was at a low ebb. The firm of Denny & Carson announced that the boy's father had refunded the full amount of the theft and that they had no intention of prosecuting. The Cumberland minister had been interviewed, and expressed his hope of yet reclaiming the motherless lad, and his Sabbath-school teacher declared that she would spare no effort to that end. The rumor had reached Pittsburgh that the boy had been seen in a New York hotel, and his father had gone East to find him and bring him home.

Paul had just come in to dress for dinner; he sank into a chair, weak to the knees, and clasped his head in his hands. It was to be worse than jail, even; the tepid waters of Cordelia Street were to close over him finally and forever. The gray monotony stretched before him in hopeless, unrelieved years; Sabbath school, Young People's Meeting, the yellow-papered room, the damp dishtowels; it all rushed back upon him with a sickening vividness. He had the old feeling that the orchestra had suddenly stopped, the sinking sensation that the play was over. The sweat broke out on his face, and he sprang to his feet, looked about him with his white, conscious smile, and winked at himself in the mirror. With something of the old childish belief in miracles with which he had so often gone to class, all his lessons unlearned, Paul dressed and dashed whistling down the corridor to the elevator.

He had no sooner entered the dining room and caught the measure of the music than his remembrance was lightened by his old elastic power of claiming the moment, mounting with it, and finding it all sufficient. The glare and glitter about him, the mere scenic accessories had again, and for the last time, their old potency. He would show himself that he was game, he would finish the thing splendidly. He doubted, more than ever, the existence of Cordelia Street, and for the first time he drank his wine recklessly. Was he not, after all, one of those fortunate beings born to the purple, was he not still himself and in his own place? He drummed a nervous accompaniment to the Pagliacci music and looked about him, telling himself over and over that it had paid.

He reflected drowsily, to the swell of the music and the chill sweetness of his wine, that he might have done it more wisely. He might have caught an outbound steamer and been well out of their clutches before now. But the other side of the world had seemed too far away and too uncertain then; he could not have waited for it; his need had been too sharp. If he had to choose over again, he would do the same thing tomorrow. He looked affectionately about the dining room, now gilded with a soft mist. Ah, it had paid indeed!

Paul was awakened next morning by a painful throbbing in his head and feet. He had thrown himself across the bed without undressing, and had slept with his shoes on. His limbs and hands were lead heavy, and his tongue and throat were parched and burnt. There came upon him one of those fateful attacks of clearheadedness that never occurred except when he was physically exhausted and his nerves hung loose. He lay still, closed his eyes, and let the tide of things wash over him.

His father was in New York, "stopping at some joint or other," he told himself. The memory of successive summers on the front stoop fell upon him like a weight of black water. He had not a hundred dollars left; and he knew now, more than ever, that money was everything, the wall that stood between all he loathed and all he wanted. The thing was winding itself up; he had thought of that on his first glorious day in New

York, and had even provided a way to snap the thread. It lay
on his dressing table now; he had got it out last night when he
came blindly up from dinner, but the shiny metal hurt his eyes,
and he disliked the looks of it.

He rose and moved about with a painful effort, succumbing
now and again to attacks of nausea. It was the old depression
exaggerated; all the world had become Cordelia Street. Yet
somehow he was not afraid of anything, was absolutely calm;
perhaps because he had looked into the dark corner at last and
knew. It was bad enough, what he saw there, but somehow not
so bad as his long fear of it had been. He saw everything
clearly now. He had a feeling that he had made the best of it,
that he had lived the sort of life he was meant to live, and for
half an hour he sat staring at the revolver. But he told himself
that was not the way, so he went downstairs and took a cab to
the ferry.

When Paul arrived at Newark he got off the train and took
another cab, directing the driver to follow the Pennsylvania
tracks out of the town. The snow lay heavy on the roadways
and had drifted deep in the open fields. Only here and there
the dead grass or dried weed stalks projected, singularly black,
above it. Once well into the country, Paul dismissed the carriage and walked, floundering along the tracks, his mind a
medley of irrelevant things. He seemed to hold in his brain an
actual picture of everything he had seen that morning. He remembered every feature of both his drivers, of the toothless
old woman from whom he had bought the red flowers in his
coat, the agent from whom he had got his ticket, and all of his
fellow passengers on the ferry. His mind, unable to cope with
vital matters near at hand, worked feverishly and deftly at
sorting and grouping these images. They made for him a part
of the ugliness of the world, of the ache in his head, and the
bitter burning on his tongue. He stooped and put a handful of
snow into his mouth as he walked, but that, too, seemed hot.
When he reached a little hillside, where the tracks ran through

a cut some twenty feet below him, he stopped and sat down.

The carnations in his coat were drooping with the cold, he noticed, their red glory all over. It occurred to him that all the flowers he had seen in the glass cases that first night must have gone the same way, long before this. It was only one splendid breath they had, in spite of their brave mockery at the winter outside the glass; and it was a losing game in the end, it seemed, this revolt against the homilies by which the world is run. Paul took one of the blossoms carefully from his coat and scooped a little hole in the snow, where he covered it up. Then he dozed a while, from his weak condition, seemingly insensible to the cold.

The sound of an approaching train awoke him, and he started to his feet, remembering only his resolution, and afraid lest he should be too late. He stood watching the approaching locomotive, his teeth chattering, his lips drawn away from them in a frightened smile; once or twice he glanced nervously sidewise, as though he were being watched. When the right moment came, he jumped. As he fell, the folly of his haste occurred to him with merciless clearness, the vastness of what he had left undone. There flashed through his brain, clearer than ever before, the blue of Adriatic water, the yellow of Algerian sands.

He felt something strike his chest, and that his body was being thrown swiftly through the air, on and on, immeasurably far and fast, while his limbs were gently relaxed. Then, because the picture-making mechanism was crushed, the disturbing visions flashed into black, and Paul dropped back into the immense design of things.

CHARACTER

Part of the pleasure of reading short stories is the chance to meet characters from any era or environment. Sometimes we may even feel we know a story's characters better than we know the people around us, while at other times we recognize ourselves, as in a mirror.

To create this illusion of reality, the author selects aspects that reveal specific personality traits. A physical description, be it of complexion or the color of eyes or hair, helps the reader to learn something about a character very quickly. In the most dramatic method of depiction, the author places a character in a situation and lets the reader see him or her act and speak. The author may even let the reader eavesdrop on the character's thinking—something we cannot do in real life.

Why do some characters strike us as being more real than others? Part of the answer lies in how many dimensions of a character are revealed. If the author portrays only one or two of a character's traits, the character is flat. But if the author shows many dimensions and qualities of a character, the character is round. Characters are also said to be static or dynamic. Those that stay about the same are static; those that change (or are about to change) are dynamic. Flat characters are usually static; round characters are usually dynamic. In "Louisa," for example, Louisa is a round and dynamic character—as most main characters in short stories are—but Jonathan Nye is flat, static, and typical of anyone she would not want.

A short story does not allow for extensive character description. Every word is precious. The choices the author makes should clarify the character and reveal something about human nature.

"I have no reason to make my escape, and to kill me would do no harm; you killed me long ago."

GOD SEES THE TRUTH, BUT WAITS

Leo Tolstoy

Once upon a time there lived in the city of Vladimir a young tradesman named Aksenof. He had two shops and a house.

Aksenof had a ruddy complexion and curly hair; he was a very jolly fellow and a good singer. When he was young he used to drink too much, and when he was tipsy he was turbulent; but after his marriage he ceased drinking, and only occasionally had a spree.

One summer Aksenof was going to Nizhni, to the great fair. As he was about to bid his family good-by, his wife said to him:

"Ivan Dmitrievitch, do not start today. I dreamed that some misfortune befell you."

Aksenof laughed at her, and said:

"Are you still afraid that I shall go on a spree at the fair?"

His wife said:

"I myself know not what I am afraid of, but I had such a bad dream. You seemed to be coming home from town, and you took off your hat, and I looked, and your head was all gray."

Aksenof laughed.

"That means good luck. See, I am going now. I will bring you some rich remembrances."

And he bade his family farewell and set off.

When he had gone half his journey, he fell in with a tradesman who was an acquaintance of his, and the two stopped at
the same tavern for the night. They took tea together, and
went to sleep in adjoining rooms.

Aksenof did not care to sleep long. He awoke in the middle
of the night, and in order that he might get a good start while
it was cool, he aroused his driver and bade him harness up,
went down into the smoky hut, settled his account with the
landlord, and started on his way.

After he had driven about twenty-six miles, he again
stopped to get something to eat. He rested in the vestibule of
the inn, and when it was noon, he went to the doorstep and or-
dered the samovar prepared; then he took out his guitar and
began to play.

Suddenly a troika with a bell dashed up to the inn, and from
the carriage leaped an official with two soldiers. He came
directly up to Aksenof and asked:

"Who are you? Where did you come from?"

Aksenof answered without hesitation, and asked him if he
would like to have some tea with him.

But the official kept on with his questions:

"Where did you spend last night? Were you alone or with a
merchant? Have you seen the merchant this morning? Why
did you leave so early this morning?"

Aksenof wondered why he was questioned so closely, but he
told everything just as it was, and asked:

"Why do you put so many questions to me? I am not a thief
or a murderer. I am on my own business; there is nothing to
question me about."

Then the official called up the soldiers, and said:

"I am the police inspector, and I have made these inquiries
of you because the merchant with whom you spent last night
has been stabbed. Show me your things, and you men search
him."

They went into the tavern, brought in the trunk and bag,

and began to open and search them. Suddenly the police inspector pulled out from the bag a knife, and demanded:

"Whose knife is this?"

Aksenof looked and saw a knife covered with blood taken from his bag, and he was frightened.

"And whose blood is that on the knife?"

Aksenof tried to answer, but he could not articulate his words:

"I . . . I . . . don't . . . know. . . . I. . . . That knife . . it is . . . not mine. . . ."

Then the police inspector said:

"This morning the merchant was found stabbed to death in his bed. No one except you could have done it. The tavern was locked on the inside, and there was no one in the tavern except yourself. And here is the bloody knife in your bag, and your guilt is evident in your face. Tell me how you killed him and how much money you took from him."

Aksenof swore that he had not done it, that he had not seen the merchant after he had drunk tea with him, that the only money that he had with him—eight thousand rubles—was his own, and that the knife was not his.

But his voice trembled, his face was pale, and he was quivering with fright, like a guilty person.

The police inspector called the soldiers and commanded them to bind Aksenof and take him to the wagon.

When they took him to the wagon with his feet tied, Aksenof crossed himself and burst into tears.

They confiscated Aksenof's things and his money, and took him to the next city, and threw him into prison.

They sent to Vladimir to make inquiries about Aksenof's character, and all the merchants and citizens of Vladimir declared that Aksenof, when he was young, used to drink and was wild, but that now he was a worthy man. Then he was brought to trial.

He was sentenced for having killed the merchant and for

having robbed him of twenty thousand rubles.

Aksenof's wife was dumfounded by the event and did not know what to think. Her children were still small, and there was one at the breast. She took them all with her and journeyed to the city where her husband was imprisoned.

At first they would not grant her admittance, but afterward she got permission from the officials and was taken to her husband.

When she saw him in his prison garb, in chains, together with murderers, she fell to the floor, and it was a long time before she recovered from her swoon. Then she placed her children around her, sat down amid them, and began to tell him about their domestic affairs, and to ask him about everything that had happened to him.

He told her the whole story.

She asked, "What is to be done now?"

"We must petition the Czar. It is impossible that an innocent man should be condemned," he said.

The wife said that she had already sent in a petition to the Czar, but that the petition had not been granted. Aksenof said nothing, but was evidently very much downcast.

Then his wife said:

"You see, the dream I had, when I dreamed that you had become gray-headed, meant something, after all. Already your hair has begun to turn gray with trouble. You ought to have stayed at home that time."

And she began to tear her hair, and she said:

"Vanya, my dearest husband, tell your wife the truth: Did you commit that crime?"

Aksenof said:

"So you, too, have no faith in me!"

And he wrung his hands and wept.

Then a soldier came and said that it was time for the wife and children to go. And Aksenof for the last time bade his family farewell.

When his wife was gone, Aksenof began to think over all that they had said. When he remembered that his wife had also distrusted him, and had asked him if he had murdered the merchant, he said to himself:

"It is evident that no one but God can know the truth of the matter, and He is the only one to ask for mercy, and He is the only one from whom to expect it."

And from that time Aksenof ceased to send in petitions, ceased to hope, and only prayed to God. Aksenof was sentenced to be flogged, and then to exile with hard labor.

And so it was done.

He was flogged with the knout, and then, when the wounds from the whip were healed, he was sent with other exiles to Siberia.

Aksenof lived twenty-six years in the mines. The hair on his head had become white as snow, and his beard had grown long, thin, and gray. All his gaiety had vanished. He was bent, his gait was slow, he spoke little, he never laughed, and he spent much of his time in prayer.

Aksenof had learned while in prison to make boots, and with the money that he earned he bought *The Lives of the Saints* and used to read it when it was light enough in prison, and on holidays he would go to the prison church, read the Gospels, and sing in the choir, for his voice was still strong and good.

The authorities liked Aksenof for his submissiveness, and his prison associates respected him and called him "Grandfather" and the "man of God." Whenever they had petitions to be presented, Aksenof was always chosen to carry them to the authorities; and when quarrels arose among the prisoners, they always came to Aksenof and asked him to mediate.

Aksenof never received any letters from home, and he knew not whether his wife and children were alive.

One time some new convicts came to the prison. In the evening all the old convicts gathered around the newcomers, and began to ply them with questions as to the cities or villages from which this one or that one had come, and what their crimes were.

At this time Aksenof also was sitting on his bunk, near the strangers, and with bowed head was listening to what was said.

One of the new convicts was a tall, healthy-looking old man of sixty years, with a close-cropped gray beard. He was telling why he had been arrested. He said:

"And so, brothers, I was sent here for nothing. I unharnessed a horse from a postboy's sledge, and they caught me with it, and insisted that I was stealing it. But I said, 'I only wanted to go a little faster, so I whipped up the horse. And, besides, the driver was a friend of mine. It's all right,' I said. 'No,' said they, 'you were stealing it.' But they did not know what and where I had stolen. I have done things which long ago would have sent me here, but I was not found out; and now they have sent me here without any justice in it. But what's the use of grumbling? I have been in Siberia before. They did not keep me here very long, though."

"Where did you come from?" asked one of the convicts.

"Well, we came from the city of Vladimir; we are citizens of that place. My name is Makar, and my father's name was Semyon."

Aksenof raised his head and asked:

"Tell me, Semyonuitch, have you ever heard of the Aksenofs, merchants in Vladimir city? Are they alive?"

"Indeed, I have heard of them! They are rich merchants, though their father is in Siberia. It seems he was just like any of the rest of us sinners. And now tell me, Grandfather, what you were sent here for?"

Aksenof did not like to speak of his misfortunes. He sighed, and said:

"Twenty-six years ago I was condemned to hard labor on account of my sins."

Makar Semyonof said:

"But what was your crime?"

Aksenof replied, "So I must have deserved this."

But he would not give any further particulars. The other convicts, however, related why Aksenof had been sent to Siberia. They told how on the road someone had killed a merchant, and put the knife into Aksenof's luggage, and how he had been unjustly punished for this.

When Makar heard this, he glanced at Aksenof, slapped himself on the knees, and said:

"Well, now, this is wonderful! This is really wonderful! You have been growing old, Grandfather!"

They began to ask him what he thought was wonderful, and where he had seen Aksenof. But Makar did not answer; he only repeated:

"A miracle, boys! How wonderful that we should meet again here!"

And when he said these words, it occurred to Aksenof that perhaps this man might know who had killed the merchant. And he said:

"Did you ever hear of that crime, Semyonuitch, or did you ever see me before?"

"Of course I heard of it! The country was full of it. But it happened a long time ago. And I have forgotten what I heard," said Makar.

"Perhaps you heard who killed the merchant?" asked Aksenof.

Makar laughed, and said:

"Why, of course, the man who had the knife in his bag killed him. It would have been impossible for anyone to put the knife in your things and not have been caught doing it. For how could the knife have been put into the bag? Was it not standing close by your head? And you would have heard it, wouldn't you?"

As soon as Aksenof heard these words he felt convinced that this was the very man who had killed the tradesman. He stood up and walked away. All that night he was unable to sleep.

194 Deep melancholy came upon him, and he began to call back the past in his imagination.

He imagined his wife as she had been when for the last time she had accompanied him to the fair. She seemed to stand before him exactly as if she were alive, and he saw her face and her eyes, and he seemed to hear her words and her laugh.

Then his imagination brought up his children before him: one a boy in a little fur coat, and the other at his mother's breast.

And he imagined himself as he was at that time, young and happy. He remembered how he had sat on the steps of the tavern when they arrested him, and how he had played on his guitar, and how his soul was full of joy at that time.

And he remembered the place of execution where they had flogged him, and the executioner, and the people standing around, and the chains and the convicts, and all his twenty-six years of prison life, and he remembered his old age.

And such melancholy came upon Aksenof that he was tempted to put an end to himself.

"And all on account of this criminal!" said Aksenof to himself.

And then he began to feel such anger against Makar Semyonof that he almost lost himself, and was crazy with desire to pay off the load of vengeance. He repeated prayers all night, but could not recover his calm. When day came, he walked by Makar and did not look at him.

Thus passed two weeks. At night Aksenof was not able to sleep, and such melancholy had come over him that he did not know what to do.

One time during the night, as he happened to be passing through the prison, he saw that the soil was disturbed under one of the bunks. He stopped to examine it. Suddenly Makar crept from under the bunk, and looked at Aksenof with a startled face.

Aksenof was about to pass on so as not to see him, but Makar seized his arm, and told him how he had been digging a passage under the wall, and how every day he carried the dirt out in his bootlegs and emptied it in the street when they went out to work.

"If you only keep quiet, old man, I will get you out too. But if you tell on me, they will flog me; but afterward I will make it hot for you. I will kill you."

When Aksenof saw the man who had injured him, he trembled all over with rage, jerked his arm away, and said:

"I have no reason to make my escape, and to kill me would do no harm; you killed me long ago. But as to telling on you or not, I shall do as God sees fit to have me."

On the next day, when they took the convicts out to work, the soldiers discovered where Makar Semyonof had been digging in the ground. They began to make a search and found the hole. The chief came into the prison and asked everyone, "Who was digging that hole?"

All denied it. Those who knew did not name Makar, because they were aware that he would be flogged half to death for such an attempt.

Then the chief came to Aksenof. He knew that Aksenof was a truthful man, and he said:

"Old man, you are truthful. Tell me before God who did this."

Makar Semyonof was standing near, in great excitement, and he looked at the chief, but he dared not look at Aksenof.

Aksenof's hands and lips trembled, and it was some time before he could speak a word. He said to himself:

"If I shield him—but why should I forgive him when he has been my ruin? Let him pay for my sufferings! But shall I tell on him? They will surely flog him. But what difference does it make what I think of him? Will it be any the easier for me?"

Once more the chief demanded:

"Well, old man, tell the truth! Who dug the hole?"

Aksenof glanced at Makar Semyonof, and then said:

"I cannot tell, Your Honor. God does not bid me tell. I will not tell. Do with me as you please; I am in your power."

In spite of all the chief's efforts, Aksenof would say nothing more. And so they failed to find out who dug the hole.

On the next night, as Aksenof was lying in his bunk and was almost asleep, he heard someone come along and sit down at his feet.

He peered through the darkness and saw that it was Makar. Aksenof asked:

"What do you wish of me? What are you doing here?"

Makar Semyonof remained silent. Aksenof arose, and said:

"What do you want? Go away, or else I will call the guard."

Makar Semyonof bent close to Aksenof, and said in a whisper:

"Ivan Dmitrievitch, forgive me!"

Aksenof said:

"What have I to forgive you?"

"I killed the merchant and put the knife in your bag. And I was going to kill you too, but there was a noise in the yard. I thrust the knife in your bag, and slipped out of the window."

Aksenof said nothing, and he did not know what to say. Makar got down from the bunk, knelt on the ground, and said:

"Ivan Dmitrievitch, forgive me, forgive me, for God's sake. I will confess that I killed the merchant—they will pardon you. You will be able to go home."

Aksenof said:

"It is easy for you to say that, but how could I endure it? Where should I go now? My wife is dead! My children have forgotten me. I have nowhere to go."

Makar did not rise; he beat his head on the ground, and said:

"Ivan Dmitritch, forgive me! When they flogged me with the knout, it was easier to bear than it is now to look at you— and you had pity on me after all this—you did not tell on me. Forgive me, for Christ's sake! Forgive me, though I am a cursed villain!"

And the man began to sob.

When Aksenof heard Makar Semyonof sobbing, he himself burst into tears, and said:

"God will forgive you. Maybe I am a hundred times worse than you are!"

And suddenly he felt a wonderful peace in his soul. And he ceased to mourn for his home, and had no desire to leave the prison, but only thought of his last hour.

Despite what Aksenof had said, Makar Semyonof confessed his crime.

When the orders came to let Aksenof go home, he was dead.

"Prisoner, hear the sentence of the court. The court decides ... that you never hear the name of the United States again."

THE MAN WITHOUT A COUNTRY

Edward Everett Hale

I suppose that very few casual readers of the *New York Herald* of August 13th observed, in an obscure corner, among the *Deaths*, the announcement:

"Nolan. Died, on board U.S. Corvette *Levant*, Lat. 2° 11′ S., Long. 131° W., on the 11th of May, Philip Nolan."

I happened to observe it, because I was stranded at the old Mission-House in Mackinac, waiting for a Lake Superior steamer which did not choose to come, and I was devouring, to the very stubble, all the current literature I could get hold of, even down to the deaths and marriages in the *Herald*. My memory for names and people is good, and the reader will see, as he goes on, that I had reason enough to remember Philip Nolan. There are hundreds of readers who would have paused at that announcement, if the officer of the *Levant* who reported it had chosen to make it thus: "Died, May 11th, 'The Man Without a Country.' " For it was as "The Man Without a Country" that poor Philip Nolan had generally been known by the officers who had him in charge during some fifty years, as, indeed, by all the men who sailed under them. I dare say there is many a man who has taken wine with him once a fortnight, in a three years' cruise, who never knew that his name was "Nolan," or whether the poor wretch had any name at all.

There can now be no possible harm in telling this poor creature's story. Reason enough there has been until now, ever since Madison's administration went out in 1817, for very strict secrecy, the secrecy of honor itself, among the gentlemen of the navy who have had Nolan in successive charge. And certainly it speaks well for the esprit de corps of the profession and the personal honor of its members that to the press this man's story has been wholly unknown—and, I think, to the country at large also. I have reason to think, from some investigations I made in Naval Archives when I was attached to the Bureau of Construction, that every official report relating to him was burned when Ross burned the public buildings at Washington. One of the Tuckers, or possibly one of the Watsons, had Nolan in charge at the end of the war; and when, on returning from his cruise, he reported at Washington to one of the Crowninshields—who was in the Navy Department when he came home—he found that the department ignored the whole business. Whether they really knew nothing about it, or whether it was a *non mi ricordo*, determined on as a piece of policy, I do not know. But this I do know, that since 1817, and possibly before, no naval officer has mentioned Nolan in his report of a cruise.

But, as I say, there is no need for secrecy any longer. And now the poor creature is dead, it seems to me worthwhile to tell a little of his story, by way of showing young Americans of today what it is to be "A Man Without a Country."

Philip Nolan was as fine a young officer as there was in the "Legion of the West," as the Western division of our army was then called. When Aaron Burr made his first dashing expedition down to New Orleans in 1805, at Fort Massac, or somewhere above on the river, he met, as the devil would have it, this gay, dashing, bright young fellow, at some dinner party, I think. Burr marked him, talked to him, walked with him, took

200 him a day or two's voyage in his flatboat, and, in short, fascinated him. For the next year barrack life was very tame to
poor Nolan. He occasionally availed of the permission the
great man had given him to write to him. Long, high-worded,
stilted letters the poor boy wrote and rewrote and copied. But
never a line did he have in reply from the gay deceiver. The
other boys in the garrison sneered at him, because he sacri-
ficed in this unrequited affection for a politician the time
which they devoted to Monongahela, sledge, and high-low-
jack. Bourbon, euchre, and poker were still unknown. But one
day Nolan had his revenge. This time Burr came down the
river not as an attorney seeking a place for his office, but as a
disguised conqueror. He had defeated I know not how many
district attorneys; he had dined at I know not how many public dinners; he had been heralded in I know not how many
Weekly Arguses; and it was rumored that he had an army behind him and an empire before him. It was a great day—his arrival—to poor Nolan. Burr had not been at the fort an hour before he sent for him. That evening he asked Nolan to take him
out in his skiff, to show him a canebrake or a cottonwood tree,
as he said—really to seduce him; and by the time the sail was
over, Nolan was enlisted body and soul. From that time,
though he did not know it, he lived as "A Man Without a
Country."

What Burr meant to do I know no more than you, dear
reader. It is none of our business just now. Only, when the
grand catastrophe came, and Jefferson and the House of Virginia of that day undertook to break on the wheel all the possible Clarences of the then House of York by the great treason
trial at Richmond, some of the lesser fry in that distant Mississippi Valley, which was farther from us than Puget's Sound
is today, introduced the like novelty on their provincial stage,
and to while away the monotony of the summer at Fort
Adams, got up, for *spectacles*, a string of court-martials on the
officers there. One and another of the colonels and majors were

tried, and, to fill out the list, little Nolan, against whom, heaven knows, there was evidence enough—that he was sick of the service, had been willing to be false to it, and would have obeyed any order to march anywhere with anyone who should follow him, had the order only been signed, "By command of His Exc. A. Burr." The courts dragged on. The big flies escaped—rightly, for all I know. Nolan was proved guilty enough, as I say; yet you and I would never have heard of him, reader, but that, when the president of the court asked him at the close whether he wished to say anything to show that he had always been faithful to the United States, he cried out, in a fit of frenzy:

"D—n the United States! I wish I may never hear of the United States again!"

I suppose he did not know how the words shocked Colonel Morgan, who was holding the court. Half the officers who sat in it had served through the Revolution, and their lives, not to say their necks, had been risked for the very idea which he so cavalierly cursed in his madness. He, on his part, had grown up in the West of those days, in the midst of "Spanish plot," "Orleans plot," and all the rest. He had been educated on a plantation, where the finest company was a Spanish officer or a French merchant from Orleans. His education, such as it was, had been perfected in commercial expeditions to Vera Cruz, and I think he told me his father once hired an Englishman to be a private tutor for a winter on the plantation. He had spent half his youth with an older brother, hunting horses in Texas; and, in a word, to him "United States" was scarcely a reality. Yet he had been fed by "United States" for all the years since he had been in the army. He had sworn on his faith as a Christian to be true to "United States." It was "United States" which gave him the uniform he wore and the sword by his side. Nay, my poor Nolan, it was only because "United States" had picked you out first as one of her own confidential men of honor that "A. Burr" cared for you a straw more than for the flatboat men who sailed his ark for him. I do not excuse Nolan; I only explain to the reader why he damned his country, and wished he might never hear her name again.

He never did hear her name but once again. From that moment, September 23, 1807, till the day he died, May 11, 1863, he never heard her name again. For that half-century and more he was a man without a country.

Old Morgan, as I said, was terribly shocked. If Nolan had compared George Washington to Benedict Arnold, or had cried, "God save King George," Morgan would not have felt worse. He called the court into his private room, and returned in fifteen minutes, with a face like a sheet, to say:

"Prisoner, hear the sentence of the court. The court decides, subject to the approval of the President, that you never hear the name of the United States again."

Nolan laughed. But nobody else laughed. Old Morgan was too solemn, and the whole room was hushed dead as night for a minute. Even Nolan lost his swagger in a moment. Then Morgan added: "Mr. Marshal, take the prisoner to Orleans in an armed boat, and deliver him to the naval commander there."

The marshal gave his orders, and the prisoner was taken out of court.

"Mr. Marshal," continued old Morgan, "see that no one mentions the United States to the prisoner. Mr. Marshal, make my respects to Lieutenant Mitchell at Orleans, and request him to order that no one shall mention the United States to the prisoner while he is on board ship. You will receive your written orders from the officer on duty here this evening. The court is adjourned without delay."

I have always supposed that Colonel Morgan himself took the proceedings of the court to Washington City, and explained them to Mr. Jefferson. Certain it is that the President approved them—certain, that is, if I may believe the men who say they have seen his signature. Before the *Nautilus* got round from New Orleans to the northern Atlantic coast with the prisoner on board, the sentence had been approved, and he was a man without a country.

The plan then adopted was substantially the same which was necessarily followed ever after. Perhaps it was suggested by the necessity of sending him by water from Fort Adams and Orleans. The secretary of the navy—it must have been the first Crowninshield, though he is a man I do not remember—was requested to put Nolan on board a government vessel bound on a long cruise, and to direct that he should be only so far confined there as to make it certain that he never saw or heard of the country. We had few long cruises then, and the navy was very much out of favor; and as almost all of this story is traditional, as I have explained, I do not know certainly what his first cruise was. But the commander to whom he was entrusted— perhaps it was Tingey or Shaw, though I think it was one of the younger men—we are all old enough now—regulated the etiquette and the precautions of the affair, and according to his scheme they were carried out, I suppose, till Nolan died.

When I was second officer of the *Intrepid*, some thirty years after, I saw the original paper of instructions. I have been sorry ever since that I did not copy the whole of it. It ran, however, much in this way:

> Washington (with the date, which must
> have been late in 1807).

Sir—You will receive from Lt. Neale the person of Philip Nolan, late a lieutenant in the United States Army.

This person on his trial by court-martial expressed with an oath the wish that he might 'never hear of the United States again.'

The court sentenced him to have his wish fulfilled.

For the present, the execution of the order is entrusted by the President to this department.

You will take the prisoner on board your ship, and

keep him there with such precautions as shall prevent his escape.

You will provide him with such quarters, rations, and clothing as would be proper for an officer of his late rank, if he were a passenger on your vessel on the business of his government.

The gentlemen on board will make any arrangements agreeable to themselves regarding his society. He is to be exposed to no indignity of any kind, nor is he ever unnecessarily to be reminded that he is a prisoner.

But under no circumstances is he ever to hear of his country or to see any information regarding it; and you will specially caution all the officers under your command to take care that, in the various indulgences which may be granted, this rule, in which his punishment is involved, shall not be broken.

It is the intention of the government that he shall never again see the country which he has disowned. Before the end of your cruise you will receive orders which will give effect to this intention.

Resp'y yours,

W. SOUTHARD, for the

Sec'y of the Navy.

If I had only preserved the whole of this paper, there would be no break in the beginning of my sketch of this story. For Captain Shaw, if it was he, handed it to his successor in the charge, and he to his, and I suppose the commander of the *Levant* has it today as his authority for keeping this man in this mild custody.

The rule adopted on board the ships on which I have met "The Man Without a Country" was, I think, transmitted from the beginning. No mess liked to have him permanently, because his presence cut off all talk of home or of the prospect of return, of politics or letters, of peace or of war—cut off more than half the talk men like to have at sea. But it was always thought too hard that he should never meet the rest of us, except to touch hats, and we finally sank into one system. He was not permitted to talk with the men unless an officer was by. With officers he had unrestrained intercourse, as far as they and he chose. But he grew shy, though he had favorites: I was one. Then the captain always asked him to dinner on Monday. Every mess in succession took up the invitation in its turn. According to the size of the ship, you had him at your mess more or less often at dinner. His breakfast he ate in his own stateroom—he always had a stateroom—which was where a sentinel, or somebody on the watch, could see the door. And whatever else he ate or drank, he ate or drank alone. Sometimes, when the marines or sailors had any special jollification, they were permitted to invite "Plain Buttons," as they called him. Then Nolan was sent with some officer, and the men were forbidden to speak of home while he was there. I believe the theory was that the sight of his punishment did them good. They called him Plain Buttons, because, while he always chose to wear a regulation army uniform, he was not permitted to wear the army button, for the reason that it bore either the initials or the insignia of the country he had disowned.

I remember, soon after I joined the navy, I was on shore with some of the older officers from our ship and from the *Brandywine,* which we had met at Alexandria. We had leave to make a party and go up to Cairo and the Pyramids. As we jogged along (you went on donkeys then) some of the gentlemen (we boys called them "dons," but the phrase was long since changed) fell to talking about Nolan, and someone told the system which was adopted from the first about his books and other reading. As he was almost never permitted to go on shore, even though the vessel lay in port for months, his time, at the best, hung heavy; and everybody was permitted to lend him books, if they were not published in America and made no allusion to it. These were common enough in the old days, when people in the other hemisphere talked of the United

States as little as we do of Paraguay. He had almost all the foreign papers that came into the ship, sooner or later; only somebody must go over them first, and cut out any advertisement or
stray paragraph that alluded to America. This was a little cruel
sometimes, when the back of what was cut out might be as innocent as Hesiod. Right in the midst of one of Napoleon's battles, or one of Canning's speeches, poor Nolan would find a
great hole, because on the back of the page of that paper there
had been an advertisement of a packet for New York, or a
scrap from the President's message. I say this was the first time
I ever heard of this plan, which afterwards I had enough, and
more than enough, to do with. I remember it, because poor
Phillips, who was of the party, as soon as the allusion to reading was made, told a story of something which happened at the
Cape of Good Hope on Nolan's first voyage; and it is the only
thing I ever knew of that voyage. They had touched at the
Cape, and had done the civil thing with the English admiral
and the fleet, and then, leaving for a long cruise up the Indian
Ocean, Phillips had borrowed a lot of English books from an
officer, which, in those days, as indeed in these, was quite a
windfall. Among them, as the devil would order, was *The Lay
of the Last Minstrel*, which they had all of them heard of, but
which most of them had never seen. I think it could not have
been published long. Well, nobody thought there could be any
risk of anything national in that, though Phillips swore old
Shaw had cut out *The Tempest* from Shakespeare before he let
Nolan have it, because he said "the Bermudas ought to be ours,
and, by Jove, should be one day." So Nolan was permitted to
join the circle one afternoon when a lot of them sat on deck
smoking and reading aloud. People do not do such things so often now, but when I was young we got rid of a great deal of
time so. Well, it so happened that in his turn Nolan took the
book and read to the others; and he read very well, as I know.
Nobody in the circle knew a line of the poem, it was all magic
and chivalry, and was ten thousand years ago. Poor Nolan read

steadily through the fifth canto, stopped a minute and drank something, and then began, without a thought of what was coming:

> Breathes there the man, with soul so dead,
> Who never to himself hath said—

It seems impossible to us that anybody ever heard this for the first time; but all these fellows did then, and poor Nolan himself went on, still unconsciously or mechanically:

> This is my own, my native land!

Then they all saw something was to pay; but he expected to get through, I suppose, turned a little pale, but plunged on:

> Whose heart hath ne'er within him burned,
> As home his footsteps he hath turned
>   From wandering on a foreign strand?
> If such there breathe, go, mark him well.

By this time the men were all beside themselves, wishing there was any way to make him turn over two pages; but he had not quite presence of mind for that; he gagged a little, colored crimson, and staggered on:

> For him no minstrel raptures swell;
> High though his titles, proud his name,
> Boundless his wealth as wish can claim,
> Despite these titles, power, and pelf,
> The wretch, concentered all in self—

and here the poor fellow choked, could not go on, but started up, swung the book into the sea, vanished into his stateroom, "and by Jove," said Phillips, "we did not see him for two months again. And I had to make up some beggarly story to that English surgeon why I did not return his Walter Scott to him."

That story shows about the time when Nolan's braggadocio must have broken down. At first, they said, he took a very high tone, considered his imprisonment a mere farce, affected to enjoy the voyage, and all that; but Phillips said that after he came out of his stateroom he never was the same man again. He never read aloud again, unless it was the Bible or Shakespeare, or something else he was sure of. But it was not that merely. He never entered in with the other young men exactly as a companion again. He was always shy afterwards, when I knew him—very seldom spoke, unless he was spoken to, except to a very few friends. He lighted up occasionally—I remember late in his life hearing him fairly eloquent on something which had been suggested to him by one of Fléchier's sermons—but generally he had the nervous, tired look of a heart-wounded man.

When Captain Shaw was coming home—if, as I say, it was Shaw—rather to the surprise of everybody they made one of the Windward Islands, and lay off and on for nearly a week. The boys said the officers were sick of salt junk and meant to have turtle soup before they came home. But after several days the *Warren* came to the same rendezvous; they exchanged signals; she sent to Phillips and these homeward-bound men letters and papers, and told them she was outward bound, perhaps to the Mediterranean, and took poor Nolan and his traps on the boat back to try his second cruise. He looked very blank when he was told to get ready to join her. He had known enough of the signs of the sky to know that till that moment he was going "home." But this was a distinct evidence of something he had not thought of, perhaps—that there was no going home for him, even to a prison. And this was the first of some twenty such transfers, which brought him sooner or later into half our best vessels, but which kept him all his life at least some hundred miles from the country he had hoped he might never hear of again.

It may have been on that second cruise—it was once when he was up the Mediterranean—that Mrs. Graff, the celebrated Southern beauty of those days, danced with him. They had been lying a long time in the Bay of Naples, and the officers were very intimate in the English fleet, and there had been great festivities, and our men thought they must give a great ball on board the ship. How they ever did it on board the *Warren* I am sure I do not know. Perhaps it was not the *Warren*, or perhaps ladies did not take up so much room as they do now. They wanted to use Nolan's stateroom for something, and they hated to do it without asking him to the ball; so the captain said they might ask him, if they would be responsible that he did not talk with the wrong people, "who would give him intelligence." So the dance went on, the finest party that had ever been known, I dare say; for I never heard of a man-of-war ball that was not. For ladies they had the family of the American consul, one or two travelers who had adventured so far, and a nice bevy of English girls and matrons.

Well, different officers relieved each other in standing and talking with Nolan in a friendly way, so as to be sure that nobody else spoke to him. The dancing went on with spirit, and after a while even the fellows who took this honorary guard of Nolan ceased to fear any contretemps. Only when some English lady called for a set of "American dances," an odd thing happened. Everybody then danced contra dances. The black band, nothing loath, conferred as to what "American dances" were, and started off with "Virginia Reel," which they followed with "Money-Musk," which, in its turn in those days, should have been followed by "The Old Thirteen." But just as Dick, the leader, tapped for his fiddles to begin, and bent forward, about to say, " 'The Old Thirteen,' gentlemen and ladies!" as he had said, " 'Virginny Reel,' if you please!" and " 'Money-Musk,' if you please!" the captain's boy tapped him on the shoulder, whispered to him, and he did not announce the name of the dance; he merely bowed, began on the air and they all fell to—the officers teaching the English girls the figure, but not telling them why it had no name.

But that is not the story I started to tell. As the dancing went on, Nolan and our fellows all got at ease, as I said—so much so, that it seemed quite natural for him to bow to that splendid Mrs. Graff, and say:

"I hope you have not forgotten me, Miss Rutledge. Shall I have the honor of dancing?"

He did it so quickly that Shubrick, who was by him, could not hinder him. She laughed, and said:

"I am not Miss Rutledge any longer, Mr. Nolan; but I will dance all the same," just nodded to Shubrick, as if to say he must leave Mr. Nolan to her, and led him off to the place where the dance was forming.

Nolan thought he had got his chance. He had known her at Philadelphia and at other places had met her, and this was a godsend. You could not talk in contra dances, as you do in cotillions, or even in the pauses of waltzing; but there were chances for sounds, as well as for eyes and blushes. He began with her travels, and Europe, and Vesuvius, and the French; and then, when they had worked down, and had that long talking-time at the bottom of the set, he said boldly—a little pale, she said, as she told me the story, years after—

"And what do you hear from home, Mrs. Graff?"

And that splendid creature looked through him. Jove! how she must have looked through him!

"Home! Mr. Nolan! I thought you were the man who never wanted to hear of home again!" and she walked directly up the deck to her husband, and left poor Nolan alone, as he always was. He did not dance again.

I cannot give any history of him in order—nobody can now—and, indeed, I am not trying to. These are the traditions which I sort out, as I believe them, from the myths which have been told about this man for forty years. The lies that have been told about him are legion. The fellows used to say he was the "Iron Mask"; and poor George Pons went to his grave in the belief that this was the author of *Junius*, who was being punished for his celebrated libel on Thomas Jefferson. Pons was not very strong in the historical line. A happier story than either of these I have told is of the war. That came along soon after. I have heard this affair told in three or four ways—and indeed, it may have happened more than once. But which ship it was on I cannot tell. However, in one, at least, of the great frigate duels with the English, in which the navy was really baptized, it happened that a round shot from the enemy entered one of our ports square, and took right down the officer of the gun himself and almost every man of the gun's crew. Now you may say what you choose about courage, but that is not a nice thing to see. But as the men who were not killed picked themselves up, and as they and the surgeon's people were carrying off the bodies, there appeared Nolan, in his shirt sleeves, with the rammer in his hand, and, just as if he had been the officer, told them off with authority—who should go to the cockpit with the wounded men, who should stay with him—perfectly cheery, and with that way which makes men feel sure all is right and is going to be right. And he finished loading the gun with his own hands, aimed it, and bade the men fire. And there he stayed, captain of that gun, keeping those fellows in spirits, till the enemy struck—sitting on the carriage while the gun was cooling, though he was exposed all the time—showing them easier ways to handle heavy shot—making the raw hands laugh at their own blunders—and when the gun cooled again, getting it loaded and fired twice as often as any other gun on the ship. The captain walked forward, by way of encouraging the men, and Nolan touched his hat and said,

"I am showing them how we do this in the artillery, sir."

And this is the part of the story where all the legends agree:

that the commodore said,

"I see you do, and I thank you, sir; and I shall never forget this day, sir, and you never shall, sir."

And after the whole thing was over, and he had the Englishman's sword, in the midst of the state and ceremony of the quarterdeck, he said:

"Where is Mr. Nolan? Ask Mr. Nolan to come here."

And when Nolan came, the captain said:

"Mr. Nolan, we are all very grateful to you today; you are one of us today; you will be named in the dispatches."

And then the old man took off his own sword of ceremony, and gave it to Nolan, and made him put it on. The man told me this who saw it. Nolan cried like a baby, and well he might. He had not worn a sword since that infernal day at Fort Adams. But always afterwards, on occasions of ceremony, he wore that quaint old French sword of the commodore's.

The captain did mention him in the dispatches. It was always said he asked that he might be pardoned. He wrote a special letter to the secretary of war. But nothing ever came of it. As I said, that was about the time when they began to ignore the whole transaction at Washington, and when Nolan's imprisonment began to carry itself on because there was nobody to stop it without any new orders from home.

All that was near fifty years ago. If Nolan was thirty then, he must have been near eighty when he died. He looked sixty when he was forty. But he never seemed to me to change a hair afterwards. As I imagine his life, from what I have seen and heard of it, he must have been in every sea, and yet almost never on land. He must have known, in a formal way, more officers in our service than any man living knows. He told me once, with a grave smile, that no man in the world lived so methodical a life as he. "You know the boys say I am the Iron Mask, and you know how busy he was." He said it did not do for anyone to try to read all the time, more than to do anything else all the time; but that he read just five hours a day. "Then," he said, "I keep up my notebooks, writing in them at such and such hours from what I have been reading; and I include in these my scrapbooks." These were very curious indeed. He had six or eight, of different subjects. There was one of history, one of natural science, one which he called "Odds and Ends." But they were not merely books of extracts from newspapers. They had bits of plants and ribbons, shells tied on, and carved scraps of bone and wood, which he had taught the men to cut for him, and they were beautifully illustrated. He drew admirably. He had some of the funniest drawings there, and some of the most pathetic that I have ever seen in my life. I wonder who will have Nolan's scrapbooks.

Well, he said his reading and his notes were his profession and that they took five hours and two hours respectively of each day. "Then," said he, "every man should have a diversion as well as a profession. My natural history is my diversion." That took two hours a day more. The men used to bring him birds and fish, but on a long cruise he had to satisfy himself with centipedes and cockroaches and such small game. He was the only naturalist I ever met who knew anything about the habits of the housefly and the mosquito. All those people can tell you whether they are *Lepidoptera* or *Steptopotera;* but as for telling how you can get rid of them, or how they get away from you when you strike them—why, Linnaeus knew as little of that as John Foy, the idiot, did. These nine hours made Nolan's regular daily "occupation." The rest of the time he talked or walked. Till he grew very old, he went aloft a great deal. He always kept up his exercise and I never heard that he was ill. If any other man was ill, he was the kindest nurse in the world; and he knew more than half the surgeons do. Then if anybody was sick or died, or if the captain wanted him to on any other occasion, he was always ready to read prayers. I have remarked that he read beautifully.

My own acquaintance with Philip Nolan began six or eight years after the war, on my first voyage after I was appointed a midshipman. It was in the first days after our slave-trade treaty, while the reigning house, which was still the house of Virginia, had still a sort of sentimentalism about the suppression of the horrors of the Middle Passage, and something was sometimes done that way. We were in the South Atlantic on that business. From the time I joined, I believed I thought Nolan was a sort of lay chaplain—a chaplain with a blue coat. I never asked about him. Everything in the ship was strange to me. I knew it was green to ask questions, and I suppose I thought there was a Plain Buttons on every ship. We had him to dine in our mess once a week, and the caution was given that on that day nothing was to be said about home. But if they had told us not to say anything about the planet Mars or the Book of Deuteronomy, I should not have asked why; there were a great many things which seemed to me to have as little reason. I first came to understand anything about "The Man Without a Country" one day when we overhauled a dirty little schooner which had slaves on board. An officer was sent to take charge of her, and after a few minutes he sent back his boat to ask that someone might be sent him who could speak Portuguese. We were all looking over the rail when the message came, and we all wished we could interpret, when the captain asked who spoke Portuguese. But none of the officers did; and just as the captain was sending forward to ask if any of the people could, Nolan stepped out and said he should be glad to interpret, if the captain wished, as he understood the language. The captain thanked him, fitted out another boat with him, and in this boat it was my luck to go.

When we got there, it was such a scene as you seldom see, and never want to. Nastiness beyond account, and chaos run loose in the midst of the nastiness. There were not a great many of the Negroes; but by way of making what there were understand that they were free, Vaughan had had their handcuffs and anklecuffs knocked off, and, for convenience' sake, was putting them upon the rascals of the schooner's crew. The

Negroes were, most of them, out of the hold and swarming all round the dirty deck, with a central throng surrounding Vaughan and addressing him in every dialect and patois of a dialect, from the Zulu click up to the Parisian of Beledeljereed.

As we came on deck, Vaughan looked down from a hogshead, on which he had mounted in desperation, and said,

"For God's love, is there anybody who can make these wretches understand something? The men gave them rum, and that did not quiet them. I knocked that big fellow down twice, and that did not soothe him. And then I talked Choctaw to all of them together; and I'll be hanged if they understood that as well as they understood the English."

Nolan said he could speak Portuguese, and one or two fine-looking Kroomen were dragged out, who, as it had been found already, had worked for the Portuguese on the coast at Fernando Po.

"Tell them they are free," said Vaughan, "and tell them that these rascals are to be hanged as soon as we can get rope enough."

Nolan "put that into Spanish"—that is, he explained it in such Portuguese as the Kroomen could understand, and they in turn to such of the Negroes as could understand them. Then there was such a yell of delight, clinching of fists, leaping and dancing, kissing of Nolan's feet, and a general rush made to the hogshead by way of spontaneous worship of Vaughan as the deus ex machina of the occasion.

"Tell them," said Vaughan, well-pleased, "that I will take them all to Cape Palmas."

This did not answer so well. Cape Palmas was practically as far from the homes of most of them as New Orleans or Rio Janeiro was; that is, they would be eternally separated from home there. And their interpreters, as we could understand, instantly said, "*Ah, non Palmas*," and began to propose infinite other expedients in most voluble language. Vaughan was rather disappointed at this result of his liberality, and asked

216 Nolan eagerly what they said. The drops stood on poor Nolan's white forehead as he hushed the men down, and said:

"He says, 'Not Palmas.' He says, 'Take us home, take us to our own country, take us to our own house, take us to our own children and our own women.' He says he has an old father and mother, who will die, if they do not see him. And this one says he left his people all sick, and paddled down to Fernando to beg the white doctor to come and help them, and that these devils caught him in the bay just in sight of home, and that he has never seen anybody from home since then. And this one says," choked out Nolan, "that he has not heard a word from his home in six months, while he has been locked up in an infernal barracoon."

Vaughan always said he grew gray himself while Nolan struggled through this interpretation. I, who did not understand anything of the passion involved in it, saw that the very elements were melting with fervent heat, and that something was to pay somewhere. Even the Negroes themselves stopped howling as they saw Nolan's agony and Vaughan's almost equal agony of sympathy. As quick as he could get words, he said:

"Tell them yes, yes, yes; tell them they shall go to the Mountains of the Moon, if they will. If I sail the schooner through the Great White Desert, they shall go home!"

And after some fashion Nolan said so. And then they all fell to kissing him again, and wanted to rub his nose with theirs.

But he could not stand it long; and getting Vaughan to say he might go back, he beckoned me down into our boat. As we lay back in the stern sheets and the men gave way, he said to me: "Youngster, let that show you what it is to be without a family, without a home, and without a country. And if you are ever tempted to say a word or to do a thing that shall put a bar between you and your family, your home, and your country, pray God in His mercy to take you that instant home to His own heaven. Stick by your family, boy; forget you have a self, while you do everything for them. Think of your home, boy; write and send, and talk about it. Let it be nearer and nearer to your thought the farther you have to travel from it; and rush back to it when you are free, as that poor black slave is doing now. And for your country, boy," and the words rattled in his throat, "and for that flag," and he pointed to the ship, "never dream a dream but of serving her as she bids you, though the service carry you through a thousand hells. No matter what happens to you, no matter who flatters you or who abuses you, never look at another flag, never let a night pass but you pray God to bless that flag. Remember, boy, that behind all these men you have to do with, behind officers, and government, and people even, there is the country herself, your country, and that you belong to her as you belong to your own mother. Stand by her, boy, as you would stand by your mother, if those devils there had got hold of her today!"

I was frightened to death by his calm, hard passion; but I blundered out that I would, by all that was holy, and that I had never thought of doing anything else. He hardly seemed to hear me; but he did, almost in a whisper, say, "Oh, if anybody had said so to me when I was of your age!"

I think it was this half-confidence of his, which I never abused, for I never told this story till now, which afterwards made us great friends. He was very kind to me. Often he sat up, or even got up, at night to walk the deck with me when it was my watch. He explained to me a great deal of my mathematics, and I owe to him my taste for mathematics. He lent me books and helped me about my reading. He never alluded so directly to his story again; but from one and another officer I have learned, in thirty years, what I am telling. When we parted from him in St. Thomas harbor, at the end of our cruise, I was more sorry than I can tell. I was very glad to meet him again in 1830; and later in life, when I thought I had some influence in Washington, I moved heaven and earth to have him discharged. But it was like getting a ghost out of prison. They pretended there was no such man, and never was such a man. They will say so at the department now! Perhaps they do not know. It will not be the first thing in the service of which the department appears to know nothing!

There is a story that Nolan met Burr once on one of our vessels, when a party of Americans came on board in the Mediterranean. But this I believe to be a lie; or rather, it is a myth, *ben trovato*, involving a tremendous blowing-up with which he sunk Burr—asking him how he liked to be "without a country." But it is clear, from Burr's life, that nothing of the sort could have happened; and I mention this only as an illustration of the stories which get a-going where there is the least mystery at bottom.

So poor Philip Nolan had his wish fulfilled. I know but one fate more dreadful: it is the fate reserved for those men who shall have one day to exile themselves from their country because they have attempted her ruin, and shall have at the same time to see the prosperity and honor to which she rises when she has rid herself of them and their iniquities. The wish of poor Nolan, as we all learned to call him, not because his punishment was too great, but because his repentance was so clear, was precisely the wish of every Bragg and Beauregard who broke a soldier's oath two years ago, and of every Maury and Barron who broke a sailor's. I do not know how often they have repented. I do know that they have done all that in them lay that they might have no country—that all the honors, associations, memories, and hopes which belong to "country" might be broken up into little shreds and distributed to the winds. I know, too, that their punishment, as they vegetate through what is left of life to them in wretched Boulognes and Leicester Squares, where they are destined to upbraid each other till they die, will have all the agony of Nolan's, with the added pang that everyone who sees them will see them to despise and to execrate them. They will have their wish, like him.

For him, poor fellow, he repented of his folly, and then, like a man, submitted to the fate he had asked for. He never intentionally added to the difficulty of the delicacy of the charge of those who had him in hold. Accidents would happen; but they never happened from his fault. Lieutenant Truxton told me that, when Texas was annexed, there was a careful discussion among the officers, whether they should get hold of Nolan's handsome set of maps, and cut Texas out of it—from the map of the world and the map of Mexico. The United States had been cut out when the atlas was bought for him. But it was voted, rightly enough, that to do this would be virtually to reveal to him what had happened, or, as Harry Cole said, to make him think old Burr had succeeded. So it was from no fault of Nolan's that a great botch happened at my own table, when, for a short time, I was in command of the *George Washington* corvette, on the South American station. We were lying in the La Plata, and some of the officers, who had been on shore, and had just joined again, were entertaining us with accounts of their misadventures in riding the half-wild horses of Buenos Aires. Nolan was at table, and was in an unusually bright and talkative mood. Some story of a tumble reminded him of an adventure of his own, when he was catching wild horses in Texas with his brother Stephen, at a time when he must have been quite a boy. He told the story with a good deal of spirit—so much so that the silence which often follows a good story hung over the table for an instant, to be broken by Nolan himself. For he asked, perfectly unconsciously:

"Pray, what has become of Texas? After the Mexicans got their independence, I thought that province of Texas would come forward very fast. It is really one of the finest regions on earth; it is the Italy of this continent. But I have not seen or heard a word of Texas for near twenty years."

There were two Texan officers at the table. The reason he had never heard of Texas was that Texas and her affairs had been painfully cut out of his newspapers since Austin began his settlements; so that, while he read of Honduras and Tamaulipas, and, till quite lately, of California, this virgin province, in which his brother had traveled so far, and, I believe, had died, had ceased to be to him. Waters and Williams, the two Texas men, looked grimly at each other, and tried not to laugh. Edward Morris had his attention attracted by the third link in the chain of the captain's chandelier. Watrous was seized with a convulsion of sneezing. Nolan himself saw that something was to pay, he did now know what. And I, as master of the feast, had to say:

"Texas is out of the map, Mr. Nolan. Have you seen Captain Black's curious account of Sir Thomas Roe's welcome?"

After that cruise I never saw Nolan again. I wrote to him at least twice a year, for in that voyage we became even confidentially intimate; but he never wrote to me. The other men tell me that in those fifteen years he aged very fast, as well he might indeed, but that he was still the same gentle, uncomplaining, silent sufferer that he ever was, bearing as best he could his self-appointed punishment—rather less social, perhaps, with new men whom he did not know, but more anxious, apparently, than ever to serve and befriend and teach the boys, some of whom fairly seemed to worship him. And now it seems the dear old fellow is dead. He has found a home at last, and a country.

• • •

Since writing this, and considering whether or no I would print it, as a warning to the young Nolans and Vallandighams and Tatnalls of today of what it is to throw away a country, I have received from Danforth, who is on board the *Levant*, a letter which gives an account of Nolan's last hours. It removes all my doubts about telling this story.

To understand the first words of the letter, the non-professional reader should remember that after 1817 the position of every officer who had Nolan in charge was one of the

greatest delicacy. The government had failed to renew the order of 1807 regarding him. What was a man to do? Should he
let him go? What, then, if he were called to account by the department for violating the order of 1807? Should he keep him?
What, then, if Nolan should be liberated some day, and should
bring an action for false imprisonment or kidnaping against
every man who had had him in charge? I urged and pressed
this upon Southard, and I have reason to think that other officers did the same thing. But the secretary always said, as they
so often do at Washington, that there were no special orders to
give, and that we must act on our own judgment. That means,
"If you succeed, you will be sustained; if you fail, you will be
disavowed." Well, as Danforth says, all that is over now,
though I do not know but I expose myself to a criminal prose-
cution on the evidence of the very revelation I am making.

Here is the letter:

Levant, 2° 2′ S. @ 131° W.

Dear Fred: I try to find heart and life to tell you that
it is all over with dear old Nolan. I have been with him
on this voyage more than I ever was, and I can understand wholly now the way in which you used to speak of
the dear old fellow. I could see that he was not strong,
but I had no idea the end was so near. The doctor had
been watching him very carefully, and yesterday morning came to me and told me that Nolan was not so well,
and had not left his stateroom—a thing I never remembered before. He had let the doctor come and see him as
he lay there—the first time the doctor had been in the
stateroom—and he said he should like to see me. Oh,
dear! Do you remember the mysteries we boys used to
invent about his room, in the old *Intrepid* days? Well, I
went in, and there, to be sure, the poor fellow lay in his
berth, smiling pleasantly as he gave me his hand, but
looking very frail. I could not help a glance round,
which showed me what a little shrine he had made of

the box he was lying in. The Stars and Stripes were triced up above and around a picture of Washington, and he had painted a majestic eagle, with lightnings blazing from his beak and his foot just clasping the whole globe, which his wings overshadowed. The dear old boy saw my glance, and said, with a sad smile, "Here, you see, I have a country!" And then he pointed to the foot of his bed, where I had not seen before a great map of the United States, as he had drawn it from memory, and which he had there to look upon as he lay. Quaint, queer old names were on it, in large letters: "Indiana Territory," "Mississippi Territory," and "Louisiana Territory," as I suppose our fathers learned such things. But the old fellow had patched in Texas, too; he had carried his western boundary all the way to the Pacific, but on that shore he had defined nothing.

"Oh, Danforth," he said, "I know I am dying. I cannot get home. Surely you will tell me something now? Stop! Stop! Do not speak till I say what I am sure you know, that there is not in this ship, that there is not in America—God bless her!—a more loyal man than I. There cannot be a man who loves the old flag as I do, or prays for it as I do, or hopes for it as I do. There are thirty-four stars in it now, Danforth. I thank God for that, though I do not know what their names are. There has never been one taken away: I thank God for that. I know by that that there has never been any successful Burr. Oh, Danforth, Danforth," he sighed out, "how like a wretched night's dream a boy's idea of personal fame or of separate sovereignty seems, when one looks back on it after such a life as mine! But tell me—tell me something—tell me everything, Danforth, before I die!"

Ingham, I swear to you that I felt like a monster that I had not told him everything before. Danger or no danger, delicacy or no delicacy, who was I that I should have been acting tyrant all this time over this dear, sainted old man, who had years ago expiated, in his whole manhood's life, the madness of a boy's treason? "Mr. Nolan," said I, "I will tell you everything you ask about. Only, where shall I begin?"

Oh, the blessed smile that crept over his white face! And he pressed my hand and said, "God bless you! Tell me their names," he said, and he pointed to the stars on the flag. "The last I know is Ohio. My father lived in Kentucky. But I have guessed Michigan and Indiana and Mississippi—that was where Fort Adams is—they make twenty. But where are your other fourteen? You have not cut up any of the old ones, I hope?"

Well, that was not a bad text, and I told him the names, in as good order as I could, and he bade me take down his beautiful map and draw them in as I best could with my pencil. He was wild with delight about Texas, told me how his brother died there; he had marked a gold cross where he supposed his brother's grave was; and he had guessed at Texas. Then he was delighted as he saw California and Oregon; that, he said, he had suspected partly, because he had never been permitted to land on that shore, though the ships were there so much. "And the men," said he, laughing, "brought off a good deal besides furs." Then he went back—heavens, how far!—to ask about the *Chesapeake*, and what was done to Barron for surrendering her to the *Leopard*, and whether Burr ever tried again—and he ground his teeth with the only passion he showed. But in a moment that was over, and he said, "God forgive me, for I am sure I forgive him." Then he asked about the old war—told me the true story of his serving the gun the day we took the *Java*. Then he settled down more quietly, and very happily, to hear me tell in an hour the history of fifty years.

How I wished it had been somebody who knew something! But I did as well as I could. I told him of the English war. I told him about Fulton and the steamboat beginning. I told him about old Scott, and Jackson; told him all I could think about the Mississippi, and New Orleans, and Texas, and his own old Kentucky. And, do you think, he asked who was in command of the "Legion of the West." I told him it was a very gallant officer, named Grant, and that, by our last news, he was about to establish his headquarters at Vicksburg. Then, "Where was Vicksburg?" I worked that out on the map; it was about a hundred miles, more or less, above his old Fort Adams; and I thought Fort Adams must be a ruin now. "It must be at old Vicks's plantation," said he; "well, that is a change!"

I tell you, Ingham, it was a hard thing to condense the history of half a century into that talk with a sick man. And I do not now know what I told him—of emigration, and the means of it—of steamboats and railroads and telegraphs—of inventions and books and literature—of the colleges and West Point and the Naval School—but with the queerest interruptions that ever you heard. You see, it was Robinson Crusoe asking all the accumulated questions of fifty-six years.

I remember he asked, all of a sudden, who was President now; and when I told him, he asked if Old Abe was General Benjamin Lincoln's son. He said he met old General Lincoln, when he was quite a boy himself, at some Indian treaty. I said no, that Old Abe was a Kentuckian like himself, but I could not tell him of what family; he had worked up from the ranks. "Good for him!" cried Nolan; "I am glad of that. As I have brooded and wondered, I have thought our danger was in keeping up those regular successions in the first families." Then I got talking about my visit to Washington. I told him of meeting the Oregon Congressman, Harding; I told him about the Smithsonian and the exploring expedition; I told him about the Capitol—and the statues for the pediment—and Crawford's *Liberty*—and Greenough's *Washington.* Ingham, I told him everything I could think of that would show the grandeur of his country and its prosperity; but I could not make up my mouth to tell him a word about this infernal Rebellion!

And he drank it in, and enjoyed it as I cannot tell you. He grew more and more silent, yet I never thought he was tired or faint. I gave him a glass of water, but he just wet his lips, and told me not to go away. Then he asked me to bring the Presbyterian *Book of Public Prayer,* which lay there, and said, with a smile, that it would open at the right place—and so it did. There was his double red mark down the page; and I knelt down and read, and he repeated with me, "For ourselves and our country, O gracious God, we thank Thee that, notwithstanding our manifold transgressions of Thy holy laws, Thou hast continued to us Thy marvelous kindness"— and so to the end of that thanksgiving. Then he turned to the end of the same book, and I read the words more familiar to me: "Most heartily we beseech Thee with Thy favor to behold and bless Thy servant, the President of the United States, and all others in authority"—and the rest of the Episcopal collect. "Danforth," said he, "I have repeated those prayers night and morning, it is now fifty-five years." And then he said he would go to sleep. He bent me down over him and kissed me; and he said, "Look in my Bible, Danforth, when I am gone." And I went away.

But I had no thought it was the end. I thought he was tired and would sleep. I knew he was happy, and I wanted him to be alone.

But in an hour, when the doctor went in gently, he found Nolan had breathed his life away with a smile. He

226 had something pressed close to his lips. It was his father's badge of the Order of Cincinnati.

We looked in his Bible, and there was a slip of paper, at the place where he had marked the text:

"They desire a country, even a heavenly: wherefore God is not ashamed to be called their God: for he hath prepared for them a city."

On this slip of paper he had written:

"Bury me in the sea; it has been my home, and I love it. But will not someone set up a stone for my memory at Fort Adams or at Orleans, that my disgrace may not be more than I ought to bear? Say on it:

IN MEMORY OF
PHILIP NOLAN,
LIEUTENANT
IN THE ARMY OF
THE UNITED STATES

'He loved his country as no other man has loved her; but no man deserved less at her hands.' "

*"Then me an' your grandfather'll starve," said her
mother; "that's all there is about it. We can't neither of
us stan' it much longer."*

LOUISA

Mary Wilkins Freeman

"I don't see what kind of ideas you've got in your head, for my
part." Mrs. Britton looked sharply at her daughter, Louisa, but
she got no response.

Louisa sat in one of the kitchen chairs close to the door. She
had dropped into it when she first entered. Her hands were all
brown and grimy with garden mold; it clung to the bottom of
her old dress and her coarse shoes.

Mrs. Britton, sitting opposite by the window, waited, looking at her. Suddenly Louisa's silence seemed to strike her
mother's will with an electric shock; she recoiled, with an
angry jerk of her head. "You don't know nothin' about it. You'd
like him well enough after you was married to him," said she,
as if in answer to an argument.

Louisa's face looked fairly dull; her obstinacy seemed to cast
a film over it. Her eyelids were cast down; she leaned her head
back against the wall.

"Sit there like a stick if you want to!" cried her mother.

Louisa got up. As she stirred, a faint earthy odor diffused itself through the room. It was like a breath from a plowed field.

Mrs. Britton's little sallow face contracted more forcibly. "I
s'pose now you're goin' back to your potater patch," said she.

228 "Plantin' potaters out there jest like a man, for all the neighbors to see. Pretty sight, I call it."

"If they don't like it, they needn't look," returned Louisa. She spoke quite evenly. Her young back was stiff with bending over the potatoes, but she straightened it rigorously. She pulled her old hat farther over her eyes.

There was a shuffling sound outside the door and a fumble at the latch. It opened, and an old man came in, scraping his feet heavily over the threshold. He carried an old basket.

"What you got in that basket, Father?" asked Mrs. Britton.

The old man looked at her. His old face had the round outlines and naive grin of a child.

"Father, what you got in that basket?"

Louisa peered apprehensively into the basket. "Where did you get those potatoes, Grandfather?" said she.

"Digged 'em." The old man's grin deepened. He chuckled hoarsely.

"Well, I'll give up if he ain't been an' dug up all them potaters you've been plantin'!" said Mrs. Britton.

"Yes, he has," said Louisa. "Oh, Grandfather, didn't you know I'd jest planted those potatoes?"

The old man fastened his bleared blue eyes on her face, and still grinned.

"Didn't you know better, Grandfather?" she asked again.

But the old man only chuckled. He was so old that he had come back into the mystery of childhood. His motives were hidden and inscrutable; his amalgamation with the human race was so much weaker.

"Land sakes! Don't waste no more time talkin' to him," said Mrs. Britton. "You can't make out whether he knows what he's doin' or not. I've give it up. Father, you jest set them pertaters down, an' you come over here an' set down in the rockin' chair. You've done about 'nough work today."

The old man shook his head with slow mutiny.

"Come right over here."

Louisa pulled at the basket of potatoes. "Let me have 'em, Grandfather," said she. "I've got to have 'em."

The old man resisted. His grin disappeared, and he set his mouth. Mrs. Britton got up, with a determined air, and went over to him. She was a sickly, frail-looking woman, but the voice came firm, with deep bass tones, from her little lean throat.

"Now, Father," said she, "you jest give her that basket, an' you walk across the room, and you set down in that rockin' chair."

The old man looked down into her little, pale, wedge-shaped face. His grasp on the basket weakened. Louisa pulled it away, and pushed past out of the door, and the old man followed his daughter sullenly across the room to the rocking chair.

The Brittons did not have a large potato field; they had only an acre of land in all. Louisa had planted two thirds of her potatoes; now she had to plant them all over again. She had gone to the house for a drink of water; her mother had detained her, and in the meantime the old man had undone her work. She began putting the cut potatoes back in the ground. She was careful and laborious about it. A strong wind, full of moisture, was blowing from the east. The smell of the sea was in it, although this was some miles inland. Louisa's brown calico skirt blew out in it like a sail. It beat her in the face when she raised her head.

"I've got to get these in today somehow," she muttered. "It'll rain tomorrow."

She worked as fast as she could, and the afternoon wore on. About five o'clock she happened to glance at the road—the potato field lay beside it—and she saw Jonathan Nye driving past with his gray horse and buggy. She turned her back to the road quickly, and listened until the rattle of the wheels died away. At six o'clock her mother looked out of the kitchen window and called her to supper.

"I'm comin' in a minute," Louisa shouted back. Then she worked faster than ever. At half-past six she went into the house, and the potatoes were all in the ground.

"Why didn't you come when I called you?" asked her mother.

"I had to get the potatoes in."

"I guess you wa'n't bound to get 'em all in tonight. It's kind of discouragin' when you work, an' get supper all ready, to have it stan' an hour, I call it. An' you've worked 'bout long enough for one day in this damp wind, I should say."

Louisa washed her hands and face at the kitchen sink, and smoothed her hair at the little glass over it. She had wet her hair too, and made it look darker: it was quite a light brown. She brushed it in smooth straight lines back from her temples. Her whole face had a clear bright look from being exposed to the moist wind. She noticed it herself, and gave her head a little conscious turn.

When she sat down to the table her mother looked at her with admiration, which she veiled with disapproval.

"Jest look at your face," said she, "red as a beet. You'll be a pretty-lookin' sight before the summer's out, at this rate."

Louisa thought to herself that the light was not very strong, and the glass must have flattered her. She could not look as well as she had imagined. She spread some butter on her bread very sparsely. There was nothing for supper but some bread and butter and weak tea, though the old man had his dish of Indian-meal porridge. He could not eat much solid food. The porridge was covered with milk and molasses. He bent low over it, and ate large spoonfuls with loud noises. His daughter had tied a towel around his neck as she would have tied a pinafore on a child. She had also spread a towel over the tablecloth in front of him, and she watched him sharply lest he should spill his food.

"I wish I could have somethin' to eat that I could relish the way he does that porridge and molasses," said she. She had scarcely tasted anything. She sipped her weak tea laboriously.

Louisa looked across at her mother's meager little figure in its neat old dress, at her poor small head bending over the tea-cup, showing the wide parting in the thin hair.

"Why don't you toast your bread, Mother?" said she. "I'll toast it for you."

"No, I don't want it. I'd jest as soon have it this way as any. I don't want no bread, nohow. I want somethin' to relish—a herrin', or a little mite of cold meat, or somethin'. I s'pose I could eat as well as anybody if I had as much as some folks have. Mis' Mitchell was sayin' the other day that she didn't believe but what they had butcher's meat up to Mis' Nye's every day in the week. She said Jonathan he went to Wolfsborough and brought home great pieces in a market basket every week. I guess they have everything."

Louisa was not eating much herself, but now she took another slice of bread with a resolute air. "I guess some folks would be thankful to get this," said she.

"Yes, I s'pose we'd ought to be thankful for enough to keep us alive, anybody takes so much comfort livin'," returned her mother, with a tragic bitterness that sat oddly upon her, as she was so small and feeble. Her face worked and strained under the stress of emotion; her eyes were full of tears; she sipped her tea fiercely.

"There's some sugar," said Louisa. "We might have had a little cake."

The old man caught the word. "Cake?" he mumbled, with pleased inquiry, looking up, and extending his grasping old hand.

"I guess we ain't got no sugar to waste in cake," returned Mrs. Britton. "Eat your porridge, Father, an' stop teasin'. There ain't no cake."

After supper Louisa cleared away the dishes; then she put on her shawl and hat.

"Where you goin'?" asked her mother.

"Down to the store."

"What for?"

"The oil's out. There wasn't enough to fill the lamps this mornin'. I ain't had a chance to get it before."

It was nearly dark. The mist was so heavy it was almost rain. Louisa went swiftly down the road with the oilcan. It was a half mile to the store where the few staples were kept that sufficed the simple folk in this little settlement. She was gone a half hour. When she returned, she had besides the oilcan a package under her arm. She went into the kitchen and set them down. The old man was asleep in the rocking chair. She heard voices in the adjoining room. She frowned, and stood still, listening.

"Louisa!" called her mother. Her voice was sweet, and higher pitched than usual. She sounded the *i* in Louisa long.

"What say?"

"Come in here after you've taken your things off."

Louisa knew that Jonathan Nye was in the sitting room. She flung off her hat and shawl. Her old dress was damp, and had still some earth stains on it; her hair was roughened by the wind, but she would not look again in the glass. She went into the sitting room just as she was.

"It's Mr. Nye, Louisa," said her mother, with effusion.

"Good evenin', Mr. Nye," said Louisa.

Jonathan Nye half-arose and extended his hand, but she did not notice it. She sat down peremptorily in a chair at the other side of the room. Jonathan had the one rocking chair; Mrs. Britton's frail little body was poised anxiously on the hard rounded top of the carpet-covered lounge. She looked at Louisa's dress and hair, and her eyes were stony with disapproval, but her lips still smirked, and she kept her voice sweet. She pointed to a glass dish on the table.

"See what Mr. Nye has brought us over, Louisa," said she.

Louisa looked indifferently at the dish.

"It's honey," said her mother; "some of his own bees made

it. Don't you want to get a dish an' taste of it? One of them
little glass sauce dishes."

"No, I guess not," replied Louisa. "I never cared much
about honey. Grandfather 'll like it."

The smile vanished momentarily from Mrs. Britton's lips,
but she recovered herself. She arose and went across the room
to the china closet. Her set of china dishes was on the top
shelves, the lower were filled with books and papers. "I've got
somethin' to show you, Mr. Nye," said she.

This was scarcely more than a hamlet, but it was incorpo-
rated, and had its town books. She brought forth a pile of
them, and laid them on the table beside Jonathan Nye.
"There," said she, "I thought mebbe you'd like to look at
these." She opened one and pointed to the school report. This
mother could not display her daughter's accomplishments to
attract a suitor, for she had none. Louisa did not own a piano
or organ; she could not paint; but she had taught school ac-
ceptably for eight years—ever since she was sixteen—and in
every one of the town books was testimonial to that effect, in-
termixed with glowing eulogy. Jonathan Nye looked soberly
through the books; he was a slow reader. He was a few years
older than Louisa, tall and clumsy, long-featured and long-
necked. His face was a deep red with embarrassment, and it
contrasted oddly with his stiff dignity of demeanor.

Mrs. Britton drew a chair close to him while he read. "You
see, Louisa taught that school for eight year," said she, "an'
she'd be teachin' it now if Mr. Mosely's daughter hadn't grown
up an' wanted somethin' to do, an' he put her in. He was committee,' you know. I dun' know as I'd ought to say so, an' I
wouldn't want you to repeat it, but they do say Ida Mosely
don't give very good satisfaction, an' I guess she won't have no
reports like these in the town books unless her father writes
'em. See this one."

Jonathan Nye pondered over the fulsome testimony to
Louisa's capability, general worth, and amiability, while she

sat in sulky silence at the farther corner of the room. Once in a while her mother, after a furtive glance at Jonathan, engrossed in a town book, would look at her and gesticulate fiercely for her to come over, but she did not stir. Her eyes were dull and quiet, her mouth closely shut; she looked homely. Louisa was very pretty when pleased and animated, at other times she had a look like a closed flower. One could see no prettiness in her.

Jonathan Nye read all the school reports; then he arose heavily. "They're real good," said he. He glanced at Louisa and tried to smile; his blushes deepened.

"Now don't be in a hurry," said Mrs. Britton.

"I guess I'd better be goin'; Mother's alone."

"She won't be afraid; it's jest on the edge of the evenin'."

"I don't know as she will. But I guess I'd better be goin'." He looked hesitatingly at Louisa.

She arose and stood with an indifferent air.

"You'd better set down again," said Mrs. Britton.

"No, I guess I'd better be goin'." Jonathan turned towards Louisa. "Good evenin'," said he.

"Good evenin'."

Mrs. Britton followed him to the door. She looked back and beckoned imperiously to Louisa, but she stood still. "Now come again, do," Mrs. Britton said to the departing caller. "Run in anytime; we're real lonesome evenin's. Father he sets an' sleeps in his chair, an' Louisa an' me often wish somebody'd drop in. Folks round here ain't none too neighborly. Come in anytime you happen to feel like it, an' we'll both of us be glad to see you. Tell your mother I'll send home that dish tomorrer, an' we shall have a real feast off that beautiful honey."

When Mrs. Britton had fairly shut the outer door upon Jonathan Nye, she came back into the sitting room as if her anger had a propelling power like steam upon her body.

"Now, Louisa Britton," said she, "you'd ought to be ashamed of yourself—ashamed of yourself! You've treated him like a—hog!"

"I couldn't help it."

"Couldn't help it! I guess you could treat anybody decent if you tried. I never saw such actions! I guess you needn't be afraid of him. I guess he ain't so set on you that he means to ketch you up an' run off. There's other girls in town full as good as you an' better lookin'. Why didn't you go an' put on your other dress? Comin' into the room with that old thing on, an' your hair all in a frowse! I guess he won't want to come again."

"I hope he won't," said Louisa, under her breath. She was trembling all over.

"What say?"

"Nothin'."

"I shouldn't think you'd want to say anything, treatin' him that way, when he came over and brought all that beautiful honey! He was all dressed up, too. He had on a real nice coat—cloth jest as fine as it could be, an' it was kinder damp when he come in. Then he dressed all up to come over here this rainy night an' bring this honey." Mrs. Britton snatched the dish of honey and scudded into the kitchen with it. "Sayin' you didn't like honey after he took all that pains to bring it over!" said she. "I'd said I liked it if I'd lied uphill and down." She set the dish in the pantry. "What in creation smells so kinder strong an' smoky in here?" said she, sharply.

"I guess it's the herrin'. I got two or three down to the store."

"I'd like to know what you got herrin' for?"

"I thought maybe you'd relish 'em."

"I don't want no herrin's, now we've got this honey. But I don't know that you've got money to throw away." She shook the old man by the stove into partial wakefulness, and steered him into his little bedroom off the kitchen. She herself slept in one off the sitting rooms; Louisa's room was upstairs.

Louisa lighted her candle and went to bed, her mother's

236 scolding voice pursuing her like a wrathful spirit. She cried when she was in bed in the dark, but she soon went to sleep. She was too healthfully tired with her outdoor work not to. All her young bones ached with the strain of manual labor as they had ached many a time this last year since she had lost her school.

The Brittons had been and were in sore straits. All they had in the world was this little house with the acre of land. Louisa's meager school money had bought their food and clothing since her father died. Now it was almost starvation for them. Louisa was struggling to wrest a little sustenance from their stony acre of land, toiling like a European peasant woman, sacrificing her New England dignity. Lately she had herself split up a cord of wood which she had bought of a neighbor, paying for it in installments with work for his wife.

"Think of a schoolteacher goin' into Mis' Mitchell's house to help clean!" said her mother.

She, although she had been of poor, hardworking people all her life, with the humblest surroundings, was a born aristocrat, with that fiercest and most bigoted aristocracy which sometimes arises from independent poverty. She had the feeling of a queen for a princess of the blood about her schoolteacher daughter; her working in a neighbor's kitchen was as galling and terrible to her. The projected marriage with Jonathan Nye was like a royal alliance for the good of the state. Jonathan Nye was the only eligible young man in the place; he was the largest landowner; he had the best house. There were only himself and his mother; after her death the property would all be his. Mrs. Nye was an older woman than Mrs. Britton, who forgot her own frailty in calculating their chances of life.

"Mis' Nye is considerable over seventy," she said often to herself; "an' then Jonathan will have it all."

She saw herself installed in that large white house as reigning dowager. All the obstacle was Louisa's obstinacy, which her mother could not understand. She could see no fault in

Jonathan Nye. So far as absolute approval went, she herself was in love with him. There was no more sense, to her mind, in Louisa's refusing him than there would have been in a princess refusing the fairy prince and spoiling the story.

"I'd like to know what you've got against him," she said often to Louisa.

"I ain't got anything against him."

"Why don't you treat him different, then, I want to know?"

"I don't like him." Louisa said "like" shamefacedly, for she meant love, and dared not say it.

"*Like!* Well, I don't know nothin' about such likin's as some pretend to, an' I don't want to. If I see anybody is good an' worthy, I like 'em, an' that's all there is about it."

"I don't—believe that's the way you felt about—Father," said Louisa, softly, her young face flushed red.

"Yes, it was. I had some common sense about it."

And Mrs. Britton believed it. Many hard middle-aged years lay between her and her own love-time, and nothing is so changed by distance as the realities of youth. She believed herself to have been actuated by the same calm reason in marrying young John Britton, who had had fair prospects, which she thought should actuate her daughter in marrying Jonathan Nye.

Louisa got no sympathy from her, but she persisted in her refusal. She worked harder and harder. She did not spare herself indoors or out. As the summer wore on, her face grew as sunburnt as a boy's, her hands were hard and brown. When she put on her white dress to go to meeting on a Sunday, there was a white ring around her neck where the sun had not touched it. Above it her face and neck showed browner. Her sleeves were rather short, and there were also white rings above her brown wrists.

"You look as if you were turnin' Injun by inches," said her mother.

Louisa, when she sat in the meeting house, tried slyly to pull her sleeves down to the brown on her wrists; she gave a little twitch to the ruffle around her neck. Then she glanced across, and Jonathan Nye was looking at her. She thrust her hands, in their short-wristed, loose cotton gloves, as far out of the sleeves as she could; her brown wrists showed conspicuously on her white lap. She had never heard of the princess who destroyed her beauty that she might not be forced to wed the man whom she did not love, but she had something of the same feeling, although she did not have it for the sake of any tangible lover. Louisa had never seen anybody whom she would have preferred to Jonathan Nye. There was no other marriageable young man in the place. She had only her dreams, which she had in common with other girls.

That Sunday evening, before she went to meeting, her mother took some old wide lace out of her bureau drawer. "There," said she, "I'm goin' to sew this in your neck an' sleeves before you put your dress on. It'll cover up a little; it's wider than the ruffle."

"I don't want it in," said Louisa.

"I'd like to know why not? You look like a fright. I was ashamed of you this mornin'."

Louisa thrust her arms into the white dress sleeves peremptorily. Her mother did not speak to her all the way to meeting. After meeting, Jonathan Nye walked home with them, and Louisa kept on the other side of her mother. He went into the house and stayed an hour. Mrs. Britton entertained him, while Louisa sat silent. When he had gone, she looked at her daughter as if she could have used bodily force, but she said nothing. She shot the bolt of the kitchen door noisily. Louisa lighted her candle. The old man's loud breathing sounded from his room; he had been put to bed for safety before they went to meeting. Through the open windows sounded the loud murmur of the summer night, as if that, too, slept heavily.

"Good night, Mother," said Louisa, as she went upstairs; but her mother did not answer.

The next day was very warm. This was an exceptionally hot summer. Louisa went out early; her mother would not ask her where she was going. She did not come home until noon. Her face was burning; her wet dress clung to her arms and shoulders.

"Where have you been?" asked her mother.

"Oh, I've been out in the field."

"What field?"

"Mr. Mitchell's."

"What have you been doin' out there?"

"Rakin' hay."

"Rakin' hay with the men?"

"There wasn't anybody but Mr. Mitchell and Johnny. Don't, Mother!"

Mrs. Britton had turned white. She sank into a chair. "I can't stan' it nohow," she moaned. "All the daughter I've got."

"Don't, Mother! I ain't done any harm. What harm is it? Why can't I rake hay as well as a man? Lots of women do such things, if nobody round here does. He's goin' to pay me right off, and we need the money. Don't, Mother!" Louisa got a tumbler of water. "Here, Mother, drink this."

Mrs. Britton pushed it away. Louisa stood looking anxiously at her. Lately her mother had grown thinner than ever; she looked scarcely bigger than a child. Presently she got up and went to the stove.

"Don't try to do anything, Mother; let me finish getting dinner," pleaded Louisa. She tried to take the pan of biscuits out of her mother's hands, but she jerked it away.

The old man was sitting on the doorstep, huddled up loosely in the sun, like an old dog.

"Come, Father," Mrs. Britton called, in a dry voice, "dinner's ready—what there is of it!"

The old man shuffled in, smiling.

There was nothing for dinner but the hot biscuits and tea. The fare was daily becoming more meager. All Louisa's little hoard of school money was gone, and her earnings were very uncertain and slender. Their chief dependence for food through the summer was their garden, but that had failed them in some respects.

One day the old man had come in radiant, with his shaking hands full of potato blossoms; his old eyes twinkled over them like a mischievous child's. Reproaches were useless; the little potato crop was sadly damaged. Lately, in spite of close watching, he had picked the squash blossoms, piling them in a yellow mass beside the kitchen door. Still, it was nearly time for the pease and beans and beets; they would keep them from starvation while they lasted.

But when they came, and Louisa could pick plenty of green food every morning, there was still a difficulty: Mrs. Britton's appetite and digestion were poor; she could not live upon a green-vegetable diet; and the old man missed his porridge, for the meal was all gone.

One morning in August he cried at the breakfast table like a baby, because he wanted his porridge, and Mrs. Britton pushed away her own plate with a despairing gesture.

"There ain't no use," said she. "I can't eat no more garden sauce nohow. I don't blame poor Father a mite. You ain't got no feelin' at all."

"I don't know what I can do; I've worked as hard as I can," said Louisa, miserably.

"I know what you can do, and so do you."

"No, I don't, Mother," returned Louisa, with alacrity. "He ain't been here for two weeks now, and I saw him with my own eyes yesterday carryin' a dish into the Moselys', and I knew 'twas honey. I think he's after Ida."

"Carryin' honey into the Moselys'? I don't believe it."

"He was; I saw him."

"Well, I don't care if he was. If you're a mind to act decent now, you can bring him round again. He was dead set on you, an' I don't believe he's changed round to that Mosely girl as quick as this."

"You don't want me to ask him to come back here, do you?"

"I want you to act decent. You can go to meetin' tonight, if you're a mind to—I sha'n't go. I ain't got strength 'nough—an' 'twouldn't hurt you none to hang back a little after meetin', and kind of edge round his way. 'Twouldn't take more'n a look."

"Mother!"

"Well, I don't care. 'Twouldn't hurt you none. It's the way more'n one girl does, whether you believe it or not. Men don't do all the courtin'—not by a long shot. 'Twon't hurt you none. You needn't look so scart."

Mrs. Britton's own face was a burning red. She looked angrily away from her daughter's honest, indignant eyes.

"I wouldn't do such a thing as that for a man I liked," said Louisa, "and I certainly sha'n't for a man I don't like."

"Then me an' your grandfather'll starve," said her mother; "that's all there is about it. We can't neither of us stan' it much longer."

"We could—"

"Could what?"

"Put a—little mortgage on the house."

Mrs. Britton faced her daughter. She trembled in every inch of her weak frame. "Put a mortgage on this house, an' by an' by not have a roof to cover us! Are you crazy? I tell you what 'tis, Louisa Britton, we may starve, your grandfather an' me, an' you can follow us to the graveyard over there, but there's only one way I'll ever put a mortgage on this house. If you have Jonathan Nye, I'll ask him to take a little one to tide us along an' get your weddin' things."

"Mother, I'll tell you what I'm goin' to do."

"What?"

"I am goin' to ask Uncle Solomon."

"I guess when Solomon Mears does anythin' for us you'll know it. He never forgave your father about that wood lot, an' he's hated the whole of us ever since. When I went to his wife's funeral he never answered when I spoke to him. I guess if you go to him you'll take it out in goin'."

Louisa said nothing more. She began clearing away the breakfast dishes and setting the house to rights. Her mother was actually so weak that she could scarcely stand, and she recognized it. She had settled into the rocking chair, and leaned her head back. Her face looked pale and sharp against the dark calico cover.

When the house was in order, Louisa stole upstairs to her own chamber. She put on her clean old blue muslin and her hat, then she went slyly down and out the front way.

It was seven miles to her Uncle Solomon Mears's, and she had made up her mind to walk them. She walked quite swiftly until the house windows were out of sight, then she slackened her pace a little. It was one of the fiercest dog days. A damp heat settled heavily down upon the earth; the sun scalded.

At the foot of the hill Louisa passed a house where one of her girl acquaintances lived. She was going in the gate with a pan of early apples. "Hullo, Louisa," she called.

"Hullo, Vinnie."

"Where you goin'?"

"Oh, I'm goin' a little way."

"Ain't it awful hot? Say, Louisa, do you know Ida Mosely's cuttin' you out?"

"She's welcome."

The other girl, who was larger and stouter than Louisa, with a sallow, unhealthy face, looked at her curiously. "I don't see why you wouldn't have him," said she. "I should have thought you'd jumped at the chance."

"Should you if you didn't like him, I'd like to know?"

"I'd like him if he had such a nice house and as much money as Jonathan Nye," returned the other girl.

She offered Louisa some apples, and she went along the road eating them. She herself had scarcely tasted food that day.

It was about nine o'clock; she had risen early. She calculated how many hours it would take her to walk the seven miles. She walked as fast as she could to hold out. The heat seemed to increase as the sun stood higher. She had walked about three miles when she heard wheels behind her. Presently a team stopped at her side.

"Good mornin'," said an embarrassed voice.

She looked around. It was Jonathan Nye, with his gray horse and light wagon.

"Good mornin'," said she.

"Goin' far?"

"A little ways."

"Won't you—ride?"

"No, thank you. I guess I'd rather walk."

Jonathan Nye nodded, made an inarticulate noise in his throat, and drove on. Louisa watched the wagon bowling lightly along. The dust flew back. She took out her handkerchief and wiped her dripping face.

It was about noon when she came in sight of her Uncle Solomon Mears's house in Wolfsborough. It stood far back from the road, behind a green expanse of untrodden yard. The blinds on the great square front were all closed; it looked as if everybody were away. Louisa went around to the side door. It stood wide open. There was a thin blue cloud of tobacco smoke issuing from it. Solomon Mears sat there in the large old kitchen, smoking his pipe. On the table near him was an empty bowl; he had just eaten his dinner of bread and milk. He got his own dinner, for he had lived alone since his wife died. He looked at Louisa. Evidently he did not recognize her.

"How do you do, Uncle Solomon?" said Louisa.

"Oh, it's John Britton's daughter! How d'ye do?"

He took his pipe out of his mouth long enough to speak, then replaced it. His eyes, sharp under their shaggy brows, were fixed on Louisa; his broad bristling face had a look of stolid rebuff like an ox; his stout figure, in his soiled farmer dress, surged over his chair. He sat full in the doorway. Louisa, standing before him, the perspiration trickling over her burning face, set forth her case with a certain dignity. This old man was her mother's nearest relative. He had property and to spare. Should she survive him, it would be hers, unless willed away. She, with her unsophisticated sense of justice, had a feeling that he ought to help her.

The old man listened. When she stopped speaking he took the pipe out of his mouth slowly, and stared gloomily past her at his hay field, where the grass was now a green stubble.

"I ain't got no money I can spare jest now," said he. "I s'pose you know your father cheated me out of consider'ble once?"

"We don't care so much about money, if you have got something you could spare to—eat. We ain't got anything but garden stuff."

Solomon Mears still frowned past her at the hay field. Presently he arose slowly and went across the kitchen. Louisa sat down on the doorstep and waited. Her uncle was gone quite a while. She, too, stared over at the field, which seemed to undulate like a lake in the hot light.

"Here's some things you can take, if you want 'em," said her uncle, at her back.

She got up quickly. He pointed grimly to the kitchen table. He was a deacon, an orthodox believer; he recognized the claims of the poor, but he gave alms as a soldier might yield up his sword. Benevolence was the result of warfare with his own conscience.

On the table lay a ham, a bag of meal, one of flour, and a basket of eggs.

"I'm afraid I can't carry 'em all," said Louisa.

"Leave what you can't then." Solomon caught up his hat and went out. He muttered something about not spending any more time as he went.

Louisa stood looking at the packages. It was utterly impossible for her to carry them all at once. She heard her uncle shout to some oxen he was turning out of the barn. She took up the bag of meal and the basket of eggs and carried them out to the gate; then she returned, got the flour and ham, and went with them to a point beyond. Then she returned for the meal and eggs, and carried them past the others. In that way she traversed the seven miles home. The heat increased. She had eaten nothing since morning but the apples that her friend had given her. Her head was swimming, but she kept on. Her resolution was as immovable under the power of the sun as a rock. Once in a while she rested for a moment under a tree, but she soon arose and went on. It was like a pilgrimage, and the Mecca at the end of the burning, desertlike road was her own maiden independence.

It was after eight o'clock when she reached home. Her mother stood in the doorway watching for her, straining her eyes in the dusk.

"For goodness' sake, Louisa Britton! Where have you been?" she began. But Louisa laid the meal and eggs down on the step.

"I've got to go back a little ways," she panted.

When she returned with the flour and ham, she could hardly get into the house. She laid them on the kitchen table, where her mother had put the other parcels, and sank into a chair.

"Is this the way you've brought all these things home?" asked her mother.

Louisa nodded.

"All the way from Uncle Solomon's?"

"Yes."

Her mother went to her and took her hat off. "It's a mercy if you ain't got a sunstroke," said she, with a sharp tenderness. "I've got somethin' to tell you. What do you s'pose has happened? Mr. Mosely has been here, an' he wants you to take the school again when it opens next week. He says Ida ain't very well, but I guess that ain't it. They think she's goin' to get somebody. Mis' Mitchell says so. She's been in. She says he's carryin' things over there the whole time, but she don't b'lieve there's anything settled yet. She says they feel so sure of it they're goin' to have Ida give the school up. I told her I thought Ida would make him a good wife, an' she was easier suited than some girls. What do you s'pose Mis' Mitchell says? She says old Mis' Nye told her that there was one thing about it: if Jonathan had you, he wa'n't goin' to have me an' Father hitched on to him; he'd look out for that. I told Mis' Mitchell that I guess there wa'n't none of us willin' to hitch, you nor anybody else. I hope she'll tell Mis' Nye. Now I'm a-goin' to turn you out a tumbler of milk—Mis' Mitchell she brought over a whole pitcherful; says she's got more'n they can use—they ain't got no pig now—an' then you go an' lay down on the sittin'-room lounge, an' cool off; an' I'll stir up some porridge for supper, an' boil some eggs. Father'll be tickled to death. Go right in there. I'm dreadful afraid you'll be sick. I never heard of anybody doin' such a thing as you have."

Louisa drank the milk and crept into the sitting room. It was warm and close there, so she opened the front door and sat down on the step. The twilight was deep, but there was a clear yellow glow in the west. One great star had come out in the midst of it. A dewy coolness was spreading over everything. The air was full of birdcalls and children's voices. Now and then there was a shout of laughter. Louisa leaned her head against the doorpost.

The house was quite near the road. Someone passed—a man carrying a basket. Louisa glanced at him, and recognized Jonathan Nye by his gait. He kept on down the road toward the Moselys', and Louisa turned again from him to her sweet, mysterious, girlish dreams.

TONE

When we listen to someone, we pay attention to tone of voice, word choices, facial expressions, and gestures to figure out the speaker's attitude or feeling. When we read, we have to rely on fewer clues—the words in the story—to determine the author's tone, or attitude toward the subject.

Tone is often achieved through irony. There are several kinds of irony, but all involve contrasts. Sometimes a person says one thing and means another. The person who says, "You're wonderful!" but means just the opposite is using a form of irony; the person is speaking ironically. Another form of irony involves events that turn out the opposite of what is expected. For example, a thief might escape punishment and become wealthy and respected. Yet another form of irony occurs when the reader knows more than a character knows. For example, a character may say, "Oh, how she loves me," and the reader knows that this is not true.

Whether irony leads to humor or sadness, it is a device that provides only one clue to a story's tone. Among other tools at the author's disposal are exaggeration, word choice, and sentence length. In "A Work of Art" the narrator nearly stutters as he describes the scandalous sculpture. His nervousness is an exaggeration, a release.

Tone is frequently difficult to grasp, but it can be labeled simply. Playful, serene, ironic, whimsical, preachy, grim—these are words that can help the reader identify the author's tone. An understanding of tone will enable the attentive reader to enjoy all the pleasures of a story.

THE FATAL CRADLE

Otherwise, the Heart-Rending Story of Mr. Heavysides

Wilkie Collins

There has never yet been discovered a man with a grievance who objected to mention it. I am no exception to this general human rule. I have got a grievance, and I don't object to mention it. Compose your spirits to hear a pathetic story, and kindly picture me in your own mind as a baby five minutes old.

Do I understand you to say that I am too big and too heavy to be pictured in anybody's mind as a baby? Perhaps I may be—but don't mention my weight again, if you please. My weight has been the grand misfortune of my life. It spoiled all my prospects (as you will presently hear) before I was two days old.

My story begins thirty-one years ago, at eleven o'clock in the forenoon, and starts with the great mistake of my first appearance in this world, at sea, on board the merchant ship *Adventure*, Captain Gillop, five hundred tons' burden, coppered, and carrying an experienced surgeon.

In presenting myself to you (which I am now about to do) at that eventful period of my life when I was from five to ten minutes old, and in withdrawing myself again from your notice (so as not to trouble you with more than a short story) before the time when I cut my first tooth, I need not hesitate to admit that I speak on hearsay knowledge only. It is knowledge, however, that may be relied on, for all that. My information comes from Captain Gillop, commander of the *Adventure* (who sent it to me in the form of a letter); from Mr. Jolly, experienced surgeon of the *Adventure* (who wrote it for me—most unfeelingly, as I think—in the shape of a humorous narrative); and from Mrs. Drabble, stewardess of the *Adventure* (who told it me by word of mouth). Those three persons were, in various degrees, spectators—I may say astonished spectators—of the events which I have now to relate.

The *Adventure*, at the time I speak of, was bound out from London to Australia. I suppose you know without my telling you that thirty years ago was long before the time of the gold-finding and the famous clipper ships. Building in the new colony and sheep farming far up inland were the two main employments of those days, and the passengers on board our vessel were consequently builders or sheep farmers, almost to a man.

A ship of five hundred tons, well loaded with cargo, doesn't offer first-rate accommodation to a large number of passengers. Not that the gentlefolks in the cabin had any great reason to complain. There the passage money, which was a good round sum, kept them what you call select. One or two berths in this part of the ship were even empty and going a-begging, in consequence of there being only four cabin passengers. These are their names and descriptions:

Mr. Sims, a middle-aged man, going out on a building speculation; Mr. Purling, a weakly young gentleman, sent on a long sea voyage, for the benefit of his health; and Mr. and Mrs. Smallchild, a young married couple, with a little independence, which Mr. Smallchild proposed to make a large one by sheep farming.

This gentleman was reported to the captain as being very good company when on shore. But the sea altered him to a certain extent. When Mr. Smallchild was not sick, he was eating and drinking; and when he was not eating and drinking, he was fast asleep. He was perfectly patient and good-humored, and wonderfully nimble at running into his cabin when the qualms took him on a sudden; but as for his being good company, nobody heard him say ten words together all through the voyage. And no wonder. A man can't talk in the qualms; a man can't talk while he is eating and drinking; and a man can't talk when he is asleep. And that was Mr. Smallchild's life. As for Mrs. Smallchild, she kept her cabin from first to last. But you will hear more of her presently.

These four cabin passengers, as I have already remarked, were well enough off for their accommodation. But the miserable people in the steerage—a poor place at the best of times on board the *Adventure*—were all huddled together, men and women and children, higgledy-piggledy, like sheep in a pen, except that they hadn't got the same quantity of fine fresh air to blow over them. They were artisans and farm laborers who couldn't make it out in the Old Country. I have no information either of their exact numbers or of their names. It doesn't matter; there was only one family among them which need be mentioned particularly—namely, the family of the Heavysides. To wit, Simon Heavysides, intelligent and well-educated, a carpenter by trade; Susan Heavysides, his wife; and seven little Heavysides, their unfortunate offspring. My father and mother and brothers and sisters, did I understand you to say? Don't be in a hurry! I recommend you to wait a little before you make quite sure of that circumstance.

Though I myself had not, perhaps, strictly speaking, come on board when the vessel left London, my ill luck, as I firmly believe, had shipped in the *Adventure* to wait for me—and decided the nature of the voyage accordingly.

Never was such a miserable time known. Stormy weather came down on us from all points of the compass, with intervals of light, baffling winds or dead calms. By the time the *Adventure* had been three months out, Captain Gillop's naturally

252   sweet temper began to get soured. I leave you to say whether
it was likely to be much improved by a piece of news which
reached him from the region of the cabin on the morning of
the ninety-first day. It had fallen to a dead calm again; and the
ship was rolling about helpless, with her head all round the
compass, when Mr. Jolly (from whose facetious narrative I repeat all conversations exactly as they passed) came on deck to
the captain, and addressed him in these words:

"I have got some news that will rather surprise you," said
Mr. Jolly, smiling and rubbing his hands. (Although the expe-
rienced surgeon has not shown much sympathy for my trou-
bles, I won't deny that his disposition was as good as his name.
To this day no amount of bad weather or hard work can upset
Mr. Jolly's temper.)

"If it's news of a fair wind coming," grumbled the captain,
"that would surprise me on board this ship, I can promise
you!"

"It's not exactly a wind coming," said Mr. Jolly. "It's another cabin passenger."

The captain looked round at the empty sea, with the land
thousands of miles away, and with not a ship in sight—turned
sharply on the experienced surgeon—eyed him hard—changed
color suddenly—and asked what he meant.

"I mean there's a fifth cabin passenger coming on board,"
persisted Mr. Jolly, grinning from ear to ear—"introduced by
Mrs. Smallchild—likely to join us, I should say, toward evening—size, nothing to speak of—sex, not known at present—
manners and customs, probably squally."

"Do you really mean it?" asked the captain, backing away,
and turning paler and paler.

"Yes, I do," answered Mr. Jolly, nodding hard at him.

"Then I'll tell you what," cried Captain Gillop, suddenly
flying into a violent passion, "I won't have it! The infernal
weather has worried me out of my life and soul already—and I
won't have it! Put it off, Jolly—tell her there isn't room enough

for that sort of thing on board my vessel. What does she mean by taking us all in this way? Shameful! Shameful!"

"No! no!" remonstrated Mr. Jolly. "Don't look at it in that light. It's her first child, poor thing. How should *she* know? Give her a little more experience, and I dare say—"

"Where's her husband?" broke in the captain, with a threatening look. "I'll speak my mind to her husband, at any rate."

Mr. Jolly consulted his watch before he answered.

"Half-past eleven," he said. "Let me consider a little. It's Mr. Smallchild's regular time just now for squaring accounts with the sea. He'll have done in a quarter of an hour. In five minutes more he'll be fast asleep. At one o'clock he'll eat a hearty lunch, and go to sleep again. At half-past two he'll square accounts as before—and so on till night. You'll make nothing out of Mr. Smallchild, Captain. Extraordinary man—wastes tissue, and repairs it again perpetually, in the most astonishing manner. If we are another month at sea, I believe we shall bring him into port totally comatose.—Halloo! What do *you* want?"

The steward's mate had approached the quarterdeck while the doctor was speaking. Was it a curious coincidence? This man also was grinning from ear to ear, exactly like Mr. Jolly.

"You're wanted in the steerage, sir," said the steward's mate to the doctor. "A woman taken bad, name of Heavysides."

"Nonsense!" cried Mr. Jolly. "Ha, ha, ha! You don't mean—eh?"

"That's it, sir, sure enough," said the steward's mate, in the most positive manner.

Captain Gillop looked all around him in silent desperation; lost his sea legs for the first time these twenty years; staggered back till he was brought all standing by the side of his own vessel; dashed his fist on the bulwark, and found language to express himself in, at the same moment.

"This ship is bewitched," said the captain, wildly. "Stop!" he called out, recovering himself a little as the doctor bustled away to the steerage. "Stop! If it's true, Jolly, send her husband here aft to me. Damme, I'll have it out with one of the husbands!" said the captain, shaking his fist viciously at the empty air.

Ten minutes passed; and then there came staggering toward the captain, tottering this way and that with the rolling of the becalmed vessel, a long, lean, melancholy, light-haired man, with a Roman nose, a watery blue eye, and a complexion profusely spotted with large brown freckles. This was Simon Heavysides, the intelligent carpenter, with the wife and the family of seven small children on board.

"Oh! you're the man, are you?" said the captain.

The ship lurched heavily; and Simon Heavysides staggered away with a run to the opposite side of the deck, as if he preferred going straight overboard into the sea to answering the captain's question.

"You're the man—are you?" repeated the captain, following him, seizing him by the collar, and pinning him up fiercely against the bulwark. "It's your wife—is it? You infernal rascal! What do you mean by turning my ship into a lying-in hospital? You have committed an act of mutiny; or, if it isn't mutiny, it's next door to it. I've put a man in irons for less! I've more than half a mind to put *you* in irons! Hold up, you slippery lubber! What do you mean by bringing passengers I don't bargain for on board my vessel? What have you got to say for yourself, before I clap the irons on you?"

"Nothing, sir," answered Simon Heavysides, accepting the captain's strong language without a word of protest. "As for the punishment you mentioned just now, sir" continued Simon, "I wish to say—having seven children more than I know how to provide for, and an eighth coming to make things worse—I respectfully wish to say, sir, that my mind is in irons already; and I don't know as it will make much difference if you put my body in irons along with it."

The captain mechanically let go of the carpenter's collar;

the mild despair of the man melted him in spite of himself.

"Why did you come to sea? Why didn't you wait ashore till it was all over?" asked the captain, as sternly as he could.

"It's no use waiting, sir," remarked Simon. "In our line of life, as soon as it's over it begins again. There's no end to it that I can see," said the miserable carpenter, after a moment's meek consideration—"except the grave."

"Who's talking about the grave?" cried Mr. Jolly, coming up at that moment. "It's births we've got to do with on board this vessel—not burials. Captain Gillop, this woman, Mrs. Heavysides, can't be left in your crowded steerage in her present condition. She must be moved off into one of the empty berths—and the sooner the better, I can tell you!"

The captain began to look savage again. A steerage passenger in one of his "staterooms" was a nautical anomaly subversive of all discipline. He eyed the carpenter once more, as if he was mentally measuring him for a set of irons.

"I'm very sorry, sir," Simon remarked, politely—"very sorry that any inadvertence of mine or Mrs. Heavysides—"

"Take your long carcass and your long tongue forward!" thundered the captain. "When talking will mend matters, I'll send for you again. Give your own orders, Jolly," he went on, resignedly, as Simon staggered off. "Turn the ship into a nursery as soon as you like!"

Five minutes later—so expeditious was Mr. Jolly—Mrs. Heavysides appeared horizontally on deck, shrouded in blankets, and supported by three men. When this interesting procession passed the captain, he shrank aside from it with as vivid an appearance of horror as if a wild bull was being carried by him instead of a British matron.

The sleeping berths below opened on either side out of the main cabin. On the left-hand side (looking toward the ship's bowsprit) was Mrs. Smallchild. On the right-hand side, opposite to her, the doctor established Mrs. Heavysides. A partition of canvas was next run up, entirely across the main cabin. The smaller of the two temporary rooms thus made lay nearest the stairs leading on deck, and was left free to the public. The larger was kept sacred to the doctor and his mysteries. When an old clothes basket, emptied, cleaned, and comfortably lined with blankets (to serve for a makeshift cradle), had been in due course of time carried into the inner cabin, and had been placed midway between the two sleeping berths, so as to be easily producible when wanted, the outward and visible preparations of Mr. Jolly were complete; the male passengers had all taken refuge on deck; and the doctor and the stewardess were left in undisturbed possession of the lower regions.

While it was still early in the afternoon the weather changed for the better. For once in a way, the wind came from a fair quarter, and the *Adventure* bowled along pleasantly before it almost on an even keel. Captain Gillop mixed with the little group of male passengers on the quarterdeck, restored to his sweetest temper, and set them his customary example, after dinner, of smoking a cigar.

"If this fine weather lasts, gentlemen," he said, "we shall make out very well with our meals up here, and we shall have our two small extra cabin passengers christened on dry land in a week's time, if their mothers approve of it. How do you feel in your mind, sir, about your good lady?"

Mr. Smallchild (to whom the inquiry was addressed) had his points of external personal resemblance to Simon Heavysides. He was neither so tall nor so lean, certainly—but he, too, had a Roman nose, and light hair, and watery blue eyes. With careful reference to his peculiar habits at sea, he had been placed conveniently close to the bulwark and had been raised on a heap of old sails and cushions so that he could easily get his head over the ship's side when occasion required. The food and drink which assisted in "restoring his tissue," when he was not asleep and not "squaring accounts with the sea," lay close to his hand. It was then a little after three o'clock; and the snore with which Mr. Smallchild answered the captain's inquiry showed that he had got round again, with the regularity of clockwork, to the period of the day when he recruited himself with sleep.

"What an insensible blockhead that man is!" said Mr. Sims, the middle-aged passenger, looking across the deck contemptuously at Mr. Smallchild.

"If the sea had the same effect on you that it has on him," retorted the invalid passenger, Mr. Purling, "you would just be as insensible yourself."

Mr. Purling (who was a man of sentiment) disagreed with Mr. Sims (who was a man of business) on every conceivable subject, all through the voyage. Before, however, they could continue the dispute about Mr. Smallchild, the doctor surprised them by appearing from the cabin.

"Any news from below, Jolly?" asked the captain anxiously.

"None whatever," answered the doctor. "I've come to idle the afternoon away up here, along with the rest of you."

As events turned out, Mr. Jolly idled away an hour and a half exactly. At the end of that time Mrs. Drabble, the stewardess, appeared with a face of mystery, and whispered, nervously, to the doctor.

"Please to step below directly, sir."

"Which of them is it?" asked Mr. Jolly.

"*Both* of them," answered Mrs. Drabble emphatically.

The doctor looked grave; the stewardess looked frightened. The two immediately disappeared together.

"I suppose, gentlemen," said Captain Gillop, addressing Mr. Purling, Mr. Sims, and the first mate, who had just joined the party—"I suppose it's only fit and proper, in the turn things have taken, to shake up Mr. Smallchild? And I don't doubt but what we ought to have the other husband handy, as a sort of polite attention under the circumstances. Pass the word forward there for Simon Heavysides. Mr. Smallchild, sir! Rouse up! Here's your good lady—Hang me, gentlemen, if I know exactly how to put it to him."

258   "Yes. Thank you," said Mr. Smallchild, opening his eyes drowsily. "Biscuit and cold bacon, as usual—when I'm ready. I'm not ready yet. Thank you. Good afternoon." Mr. Smallchild closed his eyes again and became, in the doctor's phrase, "totally comatose."

Before Captain Gillop could hit on any new plan for rousing this imperturbable passenger, Simon Heavysides once more approached the quarterdeck.

"I spoke a little sharp to you, just now, my man," said the captain, "being worried in my mind by what's going on on board this vessel. But I'll make it up to you, never fear. Here's your wife in what they call an interesting situation. It's only right you should be within easy hail of her. I look upon you, Heavysides, as a steerage passenger in difficulties; and I freely give you leave to stop here along with us till it's all over."

"You are very good, sir," said Simon, "and I am indeed thankful to you and to these gentlemen. But please to remember, I have seven children already in the steerage—and there's nobody left to mind 'em but me. My wife has got over it uncommonly well, sir, on seven previous occasions—and I don't doubt but what she'll conduct herself in a similar manner on the eighth. It will be a satisfaction to her mind, Captain Gillop and gentlemen, if she knows I'm out of the way, and minding the children. For which reason, I respectfully take my leave." With those words Simon made his bow, and returned to his family.

"Well, gentlemen, these two husbands take it easy enough, at any rate!" said the captain. "One of them is used to it, to be sure; and the other is—"

Here a banging of cabin doors below, and a hurrying of footsteps, startled the speaker and his audience into momentary silence and attention.

"Ease her with the helm, Williamson!" said Captain Gillop, addressing the man who was steering the vessel. "In my opinion, gentlemen, the less the ship pitches the better, in the turn things are taking now."

The afternoon wore on into evening, and evening into night.

Mr. Smallchild performed the daily ceremonies of his nautical existence as punctually as usual. He was aroused to a sense of Mrs. Smallchild's situation when he took his biscuit and bacon; lost the sense again when the time came round for "squaring his accounts"; recovered it in the interval which ensued before he went to sleep; lost it again, as a matter of course, when his eyes closed once more—and so on through the evening and early night. Simon Heavysides received messages occasionally (through the captain's care), telling him to keep his mind easy; returned messages mentioning that his mind was easy, and that the children were pretty quiet, but never approached the deck in his own person. Mr. Jolly now and then showed himself; said, "All right—no news"; took a little light refreshment, and disappeared again as cheerful as ever. The fair breeze still held; the captain's temper remained unruffled; the man at the helm eased the vessel, from time to time, with the most anxious consideration. Ten o'clock came; the moon rose and shone superbly; the nightly grog made its appearance on the quarterdeck; the captain gave the passengers the benefit of his company; and still nothing happened. Twenty minutes more of suspense slowly succeeded each other—and then, at last, Mr. Jolly was seen suddenly to ascend the cabin stairs.

To the amazement of the little group on the quarterdeck, the doctor held Mrs. Drabble, the stewardess, fast by the arm, and without taking the slightest notice of the captain or the passengers, placed her on the nearest seat he could find. As he did this his face became visible in the moonlight, and displayed to the startled spectators an expression of blank consternation.

"Compose yourself, Mrs. Drabble," said the doctor, in tones of unmistakable alarm. "Keep quiet, and let the air blow over you. Collect yourself, ma'am—for heaven's sake, collect yourself!"

Mrs. Drabble made no answer. She beat her hands vacantly on her knees and stared straight before her, like a woman panic-stricken.

"What's wrong?" asked the captain, setting down his glass of grog in dismay. "Anything amiss with those two unfortunate women?"

"Nothing," said the doctor. "Both doing admirably well."

"Anything queer with their babies?" continued the captain. "Are there more than you bargained for, Jolly? Twins, for instance?"

"No! no!" replied Mr. Jolly, impatiently. "A baby apiece—both boys—both in first-rate condition. Judge for yourselves," added the doctor, as the two new cabin passengers tried their lungs below for the first time, and found that they answered their purpose in the most satisfactory manner.

"What the devil's amiss, then, with you and Mrs. Drabble?" persisted the captain, beginning to lose his temper again.

"Mrs. Drabble and I are two innocent people, and we have got into the most dreadful scrape that ever you heard of!" was Mr. Jolly's startling answer.

The captain, followed by Mr. Purling and Mr. Sims, approached the doctor with looks of horror. Even the man at the wheel stretched himself over it as far as he could to hear what was coming next. The only uninterested person present was Mr. Smallchild. His time had come round for going to sleep again, and he was snoring peacefully, with his biscuit and bacon close beside him.

"Let's hear the worst of it at once, Jolly," said the captain, a little impatiently.

The doctor paid no heed to his request. His whole attention was absorbed by Mrs. Drabble. "Are you better now, ma'am?" he asked anxiously.

"No better in my mind," answered Mrs. Drabble, beginning to beat her knees again. "Worse, if anything."

"Listen to me," said Mr. Jolly coaxingly. "I'll put the whole case over again to you, in a few plain questions. You'll find it all come back to your memory, if you only follow me attentively, and if you take time to think and collect yourself before you attempt to answer."

Mrs. Drabble bowed her head in speechless submission—and listened. Everybody else on the quarterdeck listened, except the impenetrable Mr. Smallchild.

"Now, ma'am!" said the doctor. "Our troubles began in Mrs. Heavysides's cabin, which is situated on the starboard side of the ship?"

"They did, sir," replied Mrs. Drabble.

"Good! We went backward and forward, an infinite number of times, between Mrs. Heavysides (starboard) and Mrs. Smallchild (larboard)—but we found that Mrs. Heavysides, having got the start, kept it—and when I called out, 'Mrs. Drabble! Here's a chopping boy for you; come and take him!'—I called out starboard, didn't I?"

"Starboard, sir—I'll take my oath of it," said Mrs. Drabble.

"Good again. 'Here's a chopping boy,' I said. 'Take him, ma'am, and make him comfortable in the cradle.' And you took him, and made him comfortable in the cradle, accordingly? Now where was the cradle?"

"In the main cabin, sir," replied Mrs. Drabble.

"Just so! In the main cabin, because we hadn't got room for it in either of the sleeping cabins. You put the starboard baby (otherwise Heavysides) in the clothes-basket cradle in the main cabin. Good once more. How was the cradle placed?"

"Crosswise to the ship, sir," said Mrs. Drabble.

"Crosswise to the ship? That is to say, with one side longwise toward the stern of the vessel, and one side longwise toward the bows. Bear that in mind—and now follow me a little further. No! no! Don't say you can't, and your head's in a whirl. My next question will steady it. Carry your mind on half an hour, Mrs. Drabble. At the end of half an hour you heard my voice again; and my voice called out, 'Mrs. Drabble! Here's another chopping boy for you; come and take him!'—and you came and took him larboard, didn't you?"

"Larboard, sir, I don't deny it," answered Mrs. Drabble.

"Better and better! 'Here is another chopping boy,' I said. 'Take him, ma'am, and make him comfortable in the cradle, along with number one.' And you took the larboard baby (otherwise Smallchild), and made him comfortable in the cradle along with the starboard baby (otherwise Heavysides), accordingly? Now what happened after that?"

"Don't ask me, sir!" exclaimed Mrs. Drabble, losing her self-control, and wringing her hands desperately.

"Steady, ma'am! I'll put it to you as plain as print. Steady! and listen to me. Just as you had made the larboard baby comfortable I had occasion to send you into the starboard (or Heavysides) cabin to fetch something which I wanted in the larboard (or Smallchild) cabin; I kept you there a little while along with me; I left you and went into the Heavysides cabin, and called to you to bring me something I wanted out of the Smallchild cabin, but before you got halfway across the main cabin I said, 'No; stop where you are, and I'll come to you'; immediately after which Mrs. Smallchild alarmed you, and you came across to me of your own accord; and thereupon I stopped you in the main cabin, and said, 'Mrs. Drabble, your mind's getting confused; sit down and collect your scattered intellects'; and you sat down and tried to collect them—"

("And couldn't, sir," interposed Mrs. Drabble, parenthetically, "Oh, my head! My head!")

—"And tried to collect your scattered intellects, and couldn't?" continued the doctor. "And the consequence was, when I came out from the Smallchild cabin to see how you were getting on, I found you with the clothes-basket cradle hoisted up on the cabin table, staring down at the babies inside, with your mouth dropped open, and both your hands twisted in your hair? And when I said, 'Anything wrong with either of those two fine boys, Mrs. Drabble?' you caught me by the coat collar, and whispered in my right ear these words, 'Lord save us and help us, Mr. Jolly, I've confused the two babies in my mind, and I don't know which is which!' "

"And I don't know now!" cried Mrs. Drabble hysterically. "Oh, my head! My head! I don't know now!"

"Captain Gillop and gentlemen," said Mr. Jolly, wheeling round and addressing his audience with the composure of sheer despair, "that is the Scrape—and if you ever heard of a worse one, I'll trouble you to compose this miserable woman by mentioning it immediately."

Captain Gillop looked at Mr. Purling and Mr. Sims. Mr. Purling and Mr. Sims looked at Captain Gillop. They were all three thunderstruck—and no wonder.

"Can't *you* throw any light on it, Jolly?" inquired the captain, who was the first to recover himself.

"If you knew what I have had to do below, you wouldn't ask me such a question as that," replied the doctor. "Remember that I have had the lives of two women and two children to answer for—remember that I have been cramped up in two small sleeping cabins, with hardly room to turn round in, and just light enough from two miserable little lamps to see my hand before me; remember the professional difficulties of the situation, the ship rolling about under me all the while, and the stewardess to compose into the bargain; bear all that in mind, will you, and then tell me how much spare time I had on my hands for comparing two boys together inch by inch—two boys born at night, within half an hour of each other, on board a ship at sea. Ha, ha! I only wonder the mothers and the boys and the doctor are all five of them alive to tell the story!"

"No marks on one or other of them that happened to catch your eye?" asked Mr. Sims.

"They must have been strongish marks to catch my eye in the light I had to work by and in the professional difficulties I had to grapple with," said the doctor. "I saw they were both straight, well-formed children—and that's all I saw."

"Are their infant features sufficiently developed to indicate a family likeness?" inquired Mr. Purling. "Should you say they took after their fathers or their mothers?"

"Both of them have light eyes, and light hair—such as it is," replied Mr. Jolly doggedly. "Judge for yourself."

"Mr. Smallchild has light eyes and light hair," remarked Mr. Sims.

"And Simon Heavysides has light eyes and light hair," rejoined Mr. Purling.

"I should recommend waking Mrs. Smallchild, and sending for Heavysides, and letting the two fathers toss up for it," suggested Mr. Sims.

"The parental feeling is not to be trifled with in that heartless manner," retorted Mr. Purling. "I should recommend trying the Voice of Nature."

"What may that be, sir?" inquired Captain Gillop with great curiosity.

"The maternal instinct," replied Mr. Purling. "The mother's intuitive knowledge of her own child."

"Aye, aye!" said the captain. "Well thought of. What do you say, Jolly, to the Voice of Nature?"

The doctor held up his hand impatiently. He was engaged in resuming the effort to rouse Mrs. Drabble's memory by a system of amateur cross-examination, with the unsatisfactory result of confusing her more hopelessly than ever.

Could she put the cradle back, in her own mind, into its original position? No. Could she remember whether she laid the starboard baby (otherwise Heavysides) on the side of the cradle nearest the stern of the ship, or nearest the bows? No. Could she remember any better about the larboard baby (otherwise Smallchild)? No. Why did she move the cradle on to the cabin table, and so bewilder herself additionally, when she was puzzled already? Because it came over her, on a sudden, that she had forgotten, in the dreadful confusion of the time, which was which; and of course she wanted to look closer at them,

and see; and she couldn't see; and to her dying day she should
never forgive herself; and let them throw her overboard, for a
miserable wretch, if they liked—and so on, till the persevering
doctor was wearied out at last, and gave up Mrs. Drabble, and
gave up, with her, the whole case.

"I see nothing for it but the Voice of Nature," said the captain, holding fast to Mr. Purling's idea. "Try it, Jolly—you can
but try it."

"Something must be done," said the doctor. "I can't leave
the women alone any longer, and the moment I get below they
will both ask for their babies. Wait here till you're fit to be
seen, Mrs. Drabble, and then follow me. Voice of Nature!"
added Mr. Jolly contemptuously as he descended the cabin
stairs. "Oh yes, I'll try it—much good the Voice of Nature will
do us, gentlemen. You shall judge for yourselves."

Favored by the night, Mr. Jolly cunningly turned down the
dim lamps in the sleeping cabins to a mere glimmer, on the
pretext that the light was bad for his patients' eyes. He then
took up the first of the two unlucky babies that came to hand,
marked the clothes in which it was wrapped with a blot of ink,
and carried it in to Mrs. Smallchild, choosing her cabin merely
because he happened to be nearest to it. The second baby (distinguished by having no mark) was taken by Mrs. Drabble to
Mrs. Heavysides. For a certain time the two mothers and the
two babies were left together. They were then separated again
by medical order; and were afterward reunited, with the difference that the marked baby went on this occasion to Mrs.
Heavysides, and the unmarked baby to Mrs. Smallchild—the
result, in the obscurity of the sleeping cabins, proving to be
that one baby did just as well as the other, and that the Voice
of Nature was (as Mr. Jolly had predicted) totally incompetent
to settle the existing difficulty.

"While night serves us, Captain Gillop, we shall do very
well," said the doctor, after he had duly reported the failure of
Mr. Purling's suggested experiment. "But when morning

comes, and daylight shows the difference between the children, we must be prepared with a course of some kind. If the two mothers below get the slightest suspicion of the case as it stands, the nervous shock of the discovery may do dreadful mischief. They must be kept deceived, in the interests of their own health. We must choose a baby for each of them when tomorrow comes, and then hold to the choice, till the mothers are well and up again. The question is, who's to take the responsibility? I don't usually stick at trifles—but I candidly admit that *I'm* afraid of it."

"I decline meddling in the matter, on the ground that I am a perfect stranger," said Mr. Sims.

"And I object to interfere, from precisely similar motives," added Mr. Purling, agreeing for the first time with a proposition that emanated from his natural enemy all through the voyage.

"Wait a minute, gentlemen," said Captain Gillop. "I've got this difficult matter, as I think, in its right bearings. We must make a clean breast of it to the husbands, and let *them* take the responsibility."

"I believe they won't accept it," observed Mr. Sims.

"And I believe they will," asserted Mr. Purling, relapsing into his old habits.

"If they won't," said the captain firmly, "I'm master on board this ship—and, as sure as my name is Thomas Gillop, *I'll* take the responsibility!"

This courageous declaration settled all difficulties for the time being; and a council was held to decide on future proceedings. It was resolved to remain passive until the next morning, on the last faint chance that a few hours' sleep might compose Mrs. Drabble's bewildered memory. The babies were to be moved into the main cabin before the daylight grew bright—or, in other words, before Mrs. Smallchild or Mrs. Heavysides could identify the infant who had passed the night with her. The doctor and the captain were to be assisted by

Mr. Purling, Mrs. Sims, and the first mate, in the capacity of witnesses; and the assembly so constituted was to meet, in consideration of the emergency of the case, at six o'clock in the morning, punctually.

At six o'clock, accordingly, with the weather fine, and the wind still fair, the proceedings began. For the last time Mr. Jolly cross-examined Mrs. Drabble, assisted by the captain, and supervised by the witnesses. Nothing whatever was elicited from the unfortunate stewardess. The doctor pronounced her confusion to be chronic, and the captain and the witnesses unanimously agreed with him.

The next experiment tried was the revelation of the true state of the case to the husbands.

Mr. Smallchild happened, on this occasion, to be "squaring his accounts" for the morning; and the first articulate words which escaped him in reply to the disclosure were, "Deviled biscuit and anchovy paste." Further perseverance merely elicited an impatient request that they would "pitch him overboard at once, and the two babies along with him." Serious remonstrance was tried next, with no better effect. "Settle it how you like," said Mr. Smallchild faintly. "Do you leave it to me, sir, as commander of this vessel?" asked Captain Gillop. (No answer.) "Nod your head, sir, if you can't speak." Mr. Smallchild nodded his head roundwise on his pillow—and fell asleep. "Does that count for leave to me to act?" asked Captain Gillop of the witnesses. And the witnesses answered, decidedly, Yes.

The ceremony was then repeated with Simon Heavysides, who responded, as became so intelligent a man, with a proposal of his own for solving the difficulty.

"Captain Gillop and gentlemen," said the carpenter, with fluent and melancholy politeness, "I should wish to consider Mr. Smallchild before myself in this matter. I am quite willing to part with my baby (whichever he is); and I respectfully propose that Mr. Smallchild should take *both* the children, and so make quite sure that he has really got possession of his own son."

The only immediate objection to this ingenious proposition was started by the doctor, who sarcastically inquired of Simon "what he thought Mrs. Heavysides would say to it?" The carpenter confessed that this consideration had escaped him, and that Mrs. Heavysides was only too likely to be an irremovable obstacle in the way of the proposed arrangement. The witnesses all thought so too; and Heavysides and his idea were dismissed together, after Simon had first gratefully expressed his entire readiness to leave it all to the captain.

"Very well, gentlemen," said Captain Gillop. "As commander on board, I reckon next after the husbands in the matter of responsibility. I have considered this difficulty in all its bearings, and I'm prepared to deal with it. The Voice of Nature (which you proposed, Mr. Purling) has been found to fail. The tossing up for it (which you proposed, Mr. Sims) doesn't square altogether with my notions of what's right in a very serious business. No, sir! I've got my own plan; and I'm now about to try it. Follow me below, gentlemen, to the steward's pantry."

The witnesses looked round on one another in the profoundest astonishment—and followed.

"Pickerel," said the captain, addressing the steward, "bring out the scales."

The scales were of the ordinary kitchen sort, with a tin tray on one side to hold the commodity to be weighed, and a stout iron slab on the other to support the weights. Pickerel placed these scales upon a neat little pantry table, fitted on the ball-and-socket principle, so as to save the breaking of crockery by swinging with the motion of the ship.

"Put a clean duster in the tray," said the captain. "Doctor," he continued, when this had been done, "shut the doors of the sleeping berths (for fear of the women hearing anything), and oblige me by bringing those two babies in here."

"Oh, sir!" exclaimed Mrs. Drabble, who had been peeping guiltily into the pantry—"oh, don't hurt the little dears! If anybody suffers, let it be me!"

"Hold your tongue, if you please, ma'am," said the captain. "And keep the secret of these proceedings, if you wish to keep your place. If the ladies ask for their children, say they will have them in ten minutes' time."

The doctor came in and set down the clothes-basket cradle on the pantry floor. Captain Gillop immediately put on his spectacles, and closely examined the two unconscious innocents who lay beneath him.

"Six of one and half a dozen of the other," said the captain. "I don't see any difference between them. Wait a bit, though! Yes, I do. One's a bald baby. Very good. We'll begin with that one. Doctor, strip the bald baby, and put him in the scales."

The bald baby protested—in his own language—but in vain. In two minutes he was flat on his back in the tin tray, with the clean duster under him to take the chill off.

"Weigh him accurately, Pickerel," continued the captain. "Weigh him, if necessary, to an eighth of an ounce. Gentlemen! Watch this proceeding closely; it's a very important one."

While the steward was weighing and the witnesses were watching, Captain Gillop asked his first mate for the logbook of the ship, and for pen and ink.

"How much, Pickerel?" asked the captain, opening the book.

"Seven pounds one ounce and a quarter," answered the steward.

"Right, gentlemen?" pursued the captain.

"Quite right," said the witnesses.

"Bald child—distinguished as Number One—weight, seven pounds one ounce and a quarter (avoirdupois)," repeated the captain, writing down the entry in the logbook. "Very good. We'll put the bald baby back now, Doctor, and try the hairy one next."

The hairy one protested—also in his own language—and also in vain.

"How much, Pickerel?" asked the captain.

"Six pounds fourteen ounces and three quarters," replied the steward.

"Right, gentlemen?" inquired the captain.

"Quite right," answered the witnesses.

"Hairy child—distinguished as Number Two—weight, six pounds and fourteen ounces and three quarters (avoirdupois)," repeated and wrote the captain. "Much obliged to you, Jolly—that will do. When you have got the other baby back in the cradle, tell Mrs. Drabble neither of them must be taken out of it till further orders; and then be so good as to join me and these gentlemen on deck. If anything of a discussion rises up among us, we won't run the risk of being heard in the sleeping berths." With these words Captain Gillop led the way on deck, and the first mate followed with the logbook and the pen and ink.

"Now, gentlemen," began the captain when the doctor had joined the assembly, "my first mate will open these proceedings by reading from the log a statement which I have written myself, respecting this business, from beginning to end. If you find it all equally correct with the statement of what the two children weigh, I'll trouble you to sign it, in your quality of witnesses, on the spot."

The first mate read the narrative, and the witnesses signed it, as perfectly correct. Captain Gillop then cleared his throat, and addressed his expectant audience in these words:

"You'll all agree with me, gentlemen, that justice is justice, and that like must to like. Here's my ship of five hundred tons, fitted with her spars accordingly. Say she's a schooner of a hundred and fifty tons, the veriest landsman among you, in that case, wouldn't put such masts as these into her. Say, on the other hand, she's an Indiaman of a thousand tons, would our spars (excellent good sticks as they are, gentlemen) be suitable for a vessel of that capacity? Certainly not. A schooner's spars to a schooner, and a ship's spars to a ship, in fit and fair proportion."

Here the captain paused, to let the opening of his speech sink well into the minds of the audience. The audience encouraged him with the parliamentary cry of "Hear! hear!" The captain went on:

"In the serious difficulty which now besets us, gentlemen, I take my stand on the principle which I have just stated to you. And my decision is as follows: Let us give the heaviest of the two babies to the heaviest of the two women; and let the lightest then fall, as a matter of course, to the other. In a week's time, if this weather holds, we shall all (please God) be in port; and if there's a better way out of this mess than *my* way, the parsons and lawyers ashore may find it, and welcome."

With those words the captain closed his oration; and the assembled council immediately sanctioned the proposal submitted to them, with all the unanimity of men who had no idea of their own to set up in opposition.

Mr. Jolly was next requested (as the only available authority) to settle the question of weight between Mrs. Smallchild and Mrs. Heavysides, and decided it without a moment's hesitation, in favor of the carpenter's wife, on the indisputable ground that she was the tallest and stoutest woman of the two. Thereupon the bald baby, "distinguished as Number One," was taken into Mrs. Heavysides's cabin; and the hairy baby, "distinguished as Number Two," was accorded to Mrs. Smallchild; the Voice of Nature, neither in the one case nor in the other, raising the slightest objection to the captain's principle of distribution. Before seven o'clock Mr. Jolly reported that the mothers and sons, larboard and starboard, were as happy and comfortable as any four people on board ship could possibly wish to be; and the captain thereupon dismissed the council with these parting remarks:

"We'll get the studding sails on the ship now, gentlemen, and make the best of our way to port. Breakfast, Pickerel, in half an hour, and plenty of it! I doubt if that unfortunate Mrs. Drabble has heard the last of this business yet. We must all lend a hand, gentlemen, and pull her through if we can. In other respects the job's over, so far as we are concerned; and the parsons and lawyers must settle it ashore."

• • •

The parsons and the lawyers did nothing of the sort, for the plain reason that nothing was to be done. In ten days the ship was in port, and the news was broken to the two mothers. Each one of the two adored her baby, after ten days' experience of it—and each one of the two was in Mrs. Drabble's condition of not knowing which was which.

Every test was tried. First, the test by the doctor, who only repeated what he had told the captain. Secondly, the test by personal resemblance; which failed in consequence of the light hair, blue eyes, and Roman noses shared in common by the fathers, and the light hair, blue eyes, and no noses worth mentioning shared in common by the children. Thirdly, the test of Mrs. Drabble, which began and ended in fierce talking on one side and floods of tears on the other. Fourthly, the test by legal decision, which broke down through the total absence of any instructions for the law to act on. Fifthly, and lastly, the test by appeal to the husbands, which fell to the ground in consequence of the husbands' knowing nothing about the matter in hand. The captain's barbarous test by weight remained the test still—and here am I, a man of the lower order, without a penny to bless myself with, in consequence.

Yes! I was the bald baby of that memorable period. My excess in weight settled my destiny in life. The fathers and mothers on either side kept the babies according to the captain's principle of distribution, in despair of knowing what else to do. Mr. Smallchild, who was sharp enough when not seasick, made his fortune. Simon Heavysides persisted in increasing his family, and died in the workhouse.

Judge for yourself (as Mr. Jolly might say) how the two boys born at sea fared in afterlife. I, the bald baby, have seen nothing of the hairy baby for years past. He may be short, like Mr. Smallchild—but I happen to know that he is wonderfully like Heavysides, deceased, in the face. I may be tall, like the carpenter—but I have the Smallchild eyes, hair, and expression, notwithstanding. Make what you can of that! You will find it come, in the end, to the same thing. Smallchild, junior, prospers in the world, because he weighed six pounds fourteen ounces and three quarters. Heavysides, junior, fails in the world, because he weighed seven pounds one ounce and a quarter. Such is destiny, and such is life. I'll never forgive *my* destiny as long as I live. There is my grievance. I wish you good morning.

... a little whispered word escaped her slightly parted lips. She said it over and over under her breath: "Free, free, free!"

THE STORY OF AN HOUR

Kate Chopin

Knowing that Mrs. Mallard was afflicted with a heart trouble, great care was taken to break to her as gently as possible the news of her husband's death.

It was her sister, Josephine, who told her, in broken sentences, veiled hints that revealed in half-concealing. Her husband's friend Richards was there, too, near her. It was he who had been in the newspaper office when intelligence of the railroad disaster was received, with Brently Mallard's name leading the list of "killed." He had only taken the time to assure himself of its truth by a second telegram, and had hastened to forestall any less careful, less tender friend in bearing the sad message.

She did not hear the story as many women have heard the same, with a paralyzed inability to accept its significance. She wept at once, with sudden, wild abandonment, in her sister's arms. When the storm of grief had spent itself she went away to her room alone. She would have no one follow her.

There stood, facing the open window, a comfortable, roomy armchair. Into this she sank, pressed down by a physical exhaustion that haunted her body and seemed to reach into her soul.

She could see in the open square before her house the tops of trees that were all aquiver with the new spring life. The delicious breath of rain was in the air. In the street below, a peddler was crying his wares. The notes of a distant song which someone was singing reached her faintly, and countless sparrows were twittering in the eaves.

There were patches of blue sky showing here and there through the clouds that had met and piled above the other in the west facing her window.

She sat with her head thrown back upon the cushion of the chair, quite motionless, except when a sob came up into her throat and shook her, as a child who has cried itself to sleep continues to sob in its dreams.

She was young, with a fair, calm face, whose lines bespoke repression and even a certain strength. But now there was a dull stare in her eyes, whose gaze was fixed away off yonder on one of those patches of blue sky. It was not a glance of reflection, but rather indicated a suspension of intelligent thought.

There was something coming to her and she was waiting for it, fearfully. What was it? She did not know; it was too subtle and elusive to name. But she felt it, creeping out of the sky, reaching toward her through the sounds, the scents, the color that filled the air.

Now her bosom rose and fell tumultuously. She was beginning to recognize this thing that was approaching to possess her, and she was striving to beat it back with her will—as powerless as her two white slender hands would have been.

When she abandoned herself, a little whispered word escaped her slightly parted lips. She said it over and over under her breath: "Free, free, free!" The vacant stare and the look of terror that had followed it went from her eyes. They stayed keen and bright. Her pulses beat fast, and the coursing blood warmed and relaxed every inch of her body.

She did not stop to ask if it were or were not a monstrous joy that held her. A clear and exalted perception enabled her to dismiss the suggestion as trivial.

She knew that she would weep again when she saw the kind, tender hands folded in death; the face that had never looked save with love upon her, fixed and gray and dead. But she saw beyond that bitter moment a long procession of years to come that would belong to her absolutely. And she opened and spread her arms out to them in welcome.

There would be no one to live for her during those coming years; she would live for herself. There would be no powerful will bending her in that blind persistence with which men and women believe they have a right to impose a private will upon a fellow creature. A kind intention or a cruel intention made the act seem no less a crime as she looked upon it in that brief moment of illumination.

And yet she had loved him—sometimes. Often she had not. What did it matter! What could love, the unsolved mystery, count for in face of this possession of self-assertion which she suddenly recognized as the strongest impulse of her being!

"Free! Body and soul free!" she kept whispering.

Josephine was kneeling before the closed door with her lips to the keyhole, imploring for admission. "Louise, open the door! I beg; open the door—you will make yourself ill. What are you doing, Louise? For heaven's sake open the door."

"Go away. I am not making myself ill." No; she was drinking in a very elixir of life through that open window.

Her fancy was running riot along those days ahead of her. Spring days, and summer days, and all sorts of days that would be her own. She breathed a quick prayer that life might be long. It was only yesterday she had thought with a shudder that life might be long.

She arose at length and opened the door to her sister's importunities. There was a feverish triumph in her eyes, and she carried herself unwittingly like a goddess of Victory. She clasped her sister's waist, and together they descended the stairs. Richards stood waiting for them at the bottom.

Someone was opening the front door with a latchkey. It was Brently Mallard who entered, a little travel-stained, composedly carrying his gripsack and umbrella. He had been far from the scene of accident, and did not even know there had been one. He stood amazed at Josephine's piercing cry; at Richards' quick motion to screen him from the view of his wife.

But Richards was too late.

When the doctors came they said she had died of heart disease—of joy that kills.

"This is beautiful, all right," he thought. "It would be a pity to throw it away. . . . And yet I dare not keep it. . . ."

A WORK OF ART

Anton Chekhov

Holding under his arm an object wrapped in a newspaper, Sasha Smirnov, the only son of his mother, walked nervously into the office of Doctor Koshelkov.

"Well, my dear boy," exclaimed the doctor warmly, "how do you feel today? What's the good news?"

Sasha began to blink with his eyes, put his hand over his heart, and stammered nervously:

"My mother sends her regards and begs to thank you. . . . I am my mother's only son, and you have saved my life . . . and we both hardly know how to thank you."

"Come, come, my young friend, let us not speak of it," interrupted the doctor, melting with pleasure. "I have only done what anybody else in my place would have done."

"I am the only son of my mother. . . . We are poor people and consequently we are not in a position to pay you for your trouble . . . and it makes it very embarrassing for us, Doctor, although both of us, Mother and I, who am the only son of my mother, beg of you to accept from us, a token of our gratitude, this object which . . . is an object of rare worth, a wonderful masterpiece in antique bronze."

The doctor made a grimace.

"Why, my dear friend," he said, "it is entirely unnecessary. I don't need this in the least."

"Oh, no, no," stammered Sasha. "I beg you, please accept it!"

He began to unwrap the bundle, continuing his entreaties in the meantime:

"If you do not accept this, you will offend both my mother and myself.... This is a very rare work of art ... an antique bronze. It is a relic left by my dead father. We have been prizing it as a very dear remembrance.... My father used to buy up bronze antiques, selling them to lovers of old statuary.... And now we continue in the same business, my mother and myself."

Sasha undid the package and enthusiastically placed it on the table.

It was a low candelabrum of antique bronze, a work of real art representing a group: On a pedestal stood two figures of women clad in the costume of Mother Eve and in poses that I have neither the audacity nor the temperament to describe. These figures were smiling coquettishly and in general gave one the impression that, were it not for the fact that they were obliged to support the candlestick, they would lean down from their pedestal and exhibit a performance which ... my dear reader, I am even ashamed to think of it!

When the doctor espied the present, he slowly scratched his head, cleared his throat and blew his nose.

"Yes, indeed, a very pretty piece of work," he mumbled. "But—how shall I say it—not quite ... I mean ... rather unconventional ... not a bit literary, is it? ... You know ... the devil knows...."

"Why?"

"Beelzebub himself could not have conceived anything more ugly. Should I place such a phantasmagoria upon my table I would pollute my entire home!"

"Why, Doctor, what a strange conception you have of art!" cried Sasha in offended tones. "This is a real masterpiece. Just look at it! Such is its harmonious beauty that just to contemplate it fills the soul with ecstasy and makes the throat choke down a sob! When you see such loveliness you forget all earthly things. . . . Just look at it! What life, what motion, what expression!"

"I quite understand all this, my dear boy," interrupted the doctor. "But I am a married man. Little children run in and out of this room and ladies come here continually."

"Of course," said Sasha, "if you look at it through the eyes of the rabble, you see this noble masterpiece in an entirely different light. But you certainly are above all that, Doctor, and especially when your refusal to accept this gift will deeply offend both my mother and myself, who am the only son of my mother. . . . You have saved my life . . . and in return we give you our dearest possession and . . . my only regret is that we are unable to give you the mate to this candelabrum."

"Thanks, friend, many thanks. . . . Remember me to your mother and . . . But for God's sake! You can see for yourself, can't you? Little children run in and out of this room, and ladies come here continually. . . . However, leave it here! There's no arguing with you."

"Don't say another word!" exclaimed Sasha joyously. "Put the candelabrum right here, next to the vase. By Jove, but it's a pity that I haven't got the mate to give you. But it can't be helped. Well, good-bye, Doctor!"

After the departure of Sasha, the doctor looked for a long time at the candelabrum and scratched his head.

"This is beautiful, all right," he thought. "It would be a pity to throw it away. . . . And yet I dare not keep it. . . . Hm! . . . Now who in the world is there to whom I can present or donate it?"

After long deliberation he hit upon a good friend of his, the lawyer Ukhov, to whom he was indebted for legal services.

"Fine!" chuckled the doctor. "Being a close friend of his, I cannot very well offer him money, and so I will give him this piece of indecency instead. . . . And he's just the man for it . . . single, and somewhat of a gay bird, too."

No sooner thought than done. Dressing himself, the doctor took the candelabrum and went to the home of Ukhov.

"Good morning, old chap!" he said. "I have come here to thank you for your trouble. . . . You will not take money, and I will therefore repay you by presenting you with this exquisite masterpiece. . . . Now say for yourself, isn't it a dream?"

As soon as the lawyer caught sight of it he was exhilarated with its beauty.

"What a wonderful work of art!" he laughed uproariously. "Ye gods, what conceptions artists will get in their heads! What alluring charm! Where did you get this little dandy?"

But now his exhilaration had oozed away and he became frightened. Looking stealthily toward the door, he said:

"But I can't accept it, old chap. You must take it right back."

"Why?" asked the doctor in alarm.

"Because . . . because . . . my mother often visits me, my clients come here . . . and besides, I would be disgraced even in the eyes of my servants."

"Don't say another word!" cried the doctor, gesticulating wildly. "You simply have got to accept it! It would be rank ingratitude for you to refuse it! Such a masterpiece! What motion, what expression. . . . You will greatly offend me if you don't take it!"

"If only this were daubed over or covered with fig leaves. . . ."

But the doctor refused to listen to him. Gesticulating even more wildly, he ran out of Ukhov's house in the thought that he was rid of the present.

When the doctor was gone the lawyer carefully examined the candelabrum, and then, just as the doctor had done, he began to wonder what in the world he could do with it.

"O very beautiful object," he thought. "It is a pity to throw it away, and yet it is disgraceful to keep it. I had best present it to someone ... I've got it! ... This very evening I'm going to give it to the comedian Shoshkin. The rascal loves such things, and besides, this is his benefit night. . . ."

No sooner thought than done. That afternoon the well-packed candelabrum was brought to the comedian Shoshkin.

That whole evening the dressing room of the comedian Shoshkin was besieged by men who hastened to inspect the present. And during all the time the room re-echoed with hilarious laughter which most closely resembled the neighing of horses.

If any of the actresses approached the door and said, "May I enter?" the hoarse voice of Shoshkin was immediately heard to reply:

"Oh, no, no, my darling, you mustn't. I am not dressed!"

After the performance the comedian shrugged his shoulders, gesticulated with his hands and said:

"Now what in the world am I to do with this? I live in a private apartment! I am often visited by actresses! And this isn't a photograph that one could conceal in a drawer!"

"Why don't you sell it?" suggested the wigmaker. "There is a certain old woman who buys up antique bronzes. . . . Her name is Smirnova. . . . You had better take a run over there; they'll show you the place all right, everybody knows her. . . ."

The comedian followed his advice.

Two days later Koshelkov, his head supported on his hand, was sitting in his office concocting pills. Suddenly the door was opened and into the office rushed Sasha. He was smiling radiantly and his breast heaved with joy. In his hands he held something wrapped in a newspaper.

"Doctor!" he cried breathlessly. "Imagine my joy! As luck would have it, I've just succeeded in getting the mate to your candelabrum! Mother is so happy! I am the only son of my mother. . . . You have saved my life."

And Sasha, quivering with thankfulness and rapture, placed a candelabrum before the doctor. The latter opened his mouth as if to say something, but uttered not a word. His power of speech was gone.

STUDY GUIDE
by
C. Beth Hansen
for
CLASSIC SHORT STORIES

A Note on the Study Guide "About the Author" and "About the Story" are intended to be used before the story, "Checking the Facts" and "Interpreting the Story" after the story. Each group of three stories is followed by "Be a Writer" and "Special Projects." "Further Reading" and "Audiovisual Resources" are at the end.

INTRODUCTION TO THE SHORT STORY

Like a magician, a storyteller holds an audience spellbound by creating a world of illusion and mystery. From prehistoric times to the present, people have told stories: through myths, legends, tales, parables, and songs. In modern times, especially in the United States, magazines have made stories readily available to nearly everyone.

The short story developed over many centuries; no single person sat down and invented it. However, several authors, whose works you can sample in this book, steered the short story along certain paths. In the 1800s Edgar Allan Poe said it should be read in a period from a half hour to two hours. It should be unified and intense (like a slow-motion close-up). France's Guy de Maupassant relied on a series of incidents to depict a character, but Russia's Anton Chekhov often revealed a character's traits in one powerful incident.

You will be introduced to some terms: *theme, setting, plot, point of view, character, tone.* Learning about these elements of the story can be like finding out how the magician's tricks are performed. But far from destroying the story's spell, knowing some of the storyteller's tricks can enhance your enjoyment.

THEME

THE DEATH OF THE DAUPHIN

About the Author

Alphonse Daudet (1840–1897) was born in southern France, a setting he used in many stories. Daudet moved to Paris when he was seventeen, and his writings captured the imagination of the literary world. He exhibited compassion and an eye for detail, with descriptions often derived from his notebooks filled with keen observations of persons and places.

About the Story

Daudet wrote this story while recovering from an illness. His writings from this period were called *Letters from My Mill* (1869), a reference to his convalescence in a farmhouse near an abandoned windmill.

In the story a little boy is dying, but he is a very special child. He is the dauphin, or male heir to the French throne, and he has never had a care in the world—until now. Can wealth and power help this prince? Can anyone or anything help him?

Checking the Facts

1. Where is the king as his son lies dying?
2. Name one action the boy orders to try to stop death.

3. What does Lorrain do after the dauphin speaks to him?
4. According to the prince, who is his cousin?
5. When does the dauphin cry?

Interpreting the Story

1. Why does the king cry? The queen? The dauphin?
2. Describe the people within the palace and their actions. Compare these to the townspeople and their actions. What does each group think of the dauphin?
3. In what ways is the prince like his father? Like his mother? Cite evidence from the story.
4. What is Daudet trying to tell his readers?

THE LADY OR THE TIGER?

About the Author

The American author Frank Stockton (1834–1902) first worked as a picture engraver. He proceeded from writing texts for his pictures to writing stories for children. He had several novels and short stories published during his eight-year tenure as an editor for a children's magazine. He left the magazine in 1881 to concentrate on his own writing, mainly for adults. Although Stockton's "A Tale of Negative Gravity" (1884) is considered one of the first science-fiction stories, "The Lady or the Tiger?" (1882) is the work he is most remembered for.

About the Story

Which is stronger, love or jealousy? And which will prevail when a princess has the power of life or death over a man? Look for hints in the story as to which emotion motivated the princess. This story's famous and unusual ending never fails to stir debates about the secrets of the human heart.

semified (Stockton coined this word) modified, halved.

barleycorn About one third of an inch.

epithalamic Nuptial; refers to a wedding song or poem.

determinate Firm and final.

moiety Part, or portion; half.

Checking the Facts

1. Describe the king's mood when something in his kingdom is not quite right.
2. Not every accused person decides his fate in the arena. Which ones do?
3. What do the king's subjects think of his method of administering justice?
4. Whom does the king love more than anyone else?
5. How does the princess learn what is behind each door?

Interpreting the Story

1. Most decisions are not life-and-death matters. What does the story tell you about the difficulty of making

any decision?

2. What do you think of the king's methods of administering justice? List the good points and the bad points of the system.
3. Does the princess point to the door hiding the lady or to the one hiding the tiger? Cite hints in the story. (Your class may want to debate this.)
4. Decide on an ending. Write a sentence that sums up the "finished" story's point, or its theme.

THE ARTIST OF THE BEAUTIFUL

About the Author

Few authors were as steeped in the American past as Nathaniel Hawthorne (1804–1864) was. A descendant of a judge at the Salem witchcraft trials, Hawthorne was both haunted and inspired by his Puritan heritage.

He sought his salvation in writing, and he learned his craft by constantly practicing it. After he graduated from college, he spent twelve years writing and rewriting, until he found critical success with a collection of stories, *Twice-Told Tales* (1837). His most famous work is the soul-searching novel *The Scarlet Letter* (1850).

About the Story

Taken from *Mosses from an Old Manse* (1846), this story involves a young watchmaker, the girl he loves, and the special gift he fashions for her. In his search for beauty, Owen Warland, the watchmaker, runs into obstacles that might shatter anybody's dream. By describing

Owen's quest, Hawthorne tells us something about our own hopes and ideals.

pinchbeck A copper and zinc mixture used to imitate gold, often in cheap jewelry.

Dutch toy Foreign or imported object, a negative reference based on trade rivalries.

main Sheer, utter; fully exerted.

'Change The Exchange, a place for transactions.

Queen Mab In Irish and English folklore, a fairy who brings forth dreams.

Albertus Magnus (1200–1280) German philosopher, church scholar; scientific genius accused of sorcery.

Friar (Roger) Bacon (1220?–1292?) English monk whose experiments earned him a reputation as a magician.

Washington Allston (1779–1843) American painter and author. Hawthorne refers to an unfinished work.

gripe To grip.

Checking the Facts

1. The townspeople praise Owen after he (a) marries Annie (b) invents a tiny watch (c) fixes the church clock (d) assists Robert Danforth.
2. After Annie accidentally ruins Owen's project, Owen (a) often drinks wine (b) moves to France (c) chuckles and starts over (d) throws things at her.
3. Owen makes the butterfly for Annie (a) because she asks him to make it (b) to add to her collection (c) as a

bridal gift (d) to repay a debt.

4. When the butterfly is destroyed, (a) Annie screams (b) Peter Hovenden laughs (c) Owen looks on calmly (d) all of the above.

Interpreting the Story

1. Tell how Robert Danforth, Peter Hovenden, and Annie oppose Owen's plans. Who is harshest? Why?
2. Why is Owen described as in a state of enjoyment even after the butterfly is destroyed?
3. If Annie and Owen had married, what kind of marriage do you think they would have had? Why?
4. Does Owen's persistence show strength of character or a form of obsession or madness? Explain.

☆ ★ ☆

Be a Writer

In "The Artist of the Beautiful," when Hawthorne describes Owen as being depressed he repeats a physical image: "He spent a few sluggish weeks with his head so continually resting in his hands. . . . The artist . . . could scarcely lift his head."

A. Write a paragraph with *several* physical signs showing Owen's "strange despair." It may help to picture Owen's walk, mouth, eyes, shoulders, and clothing.
B. Focusing on aspects of her physical appearance and her clothing, describe Annie on her wedding day.

G10 **A.** Divide "The Death of the Dauphin" into parts for speakers (narrator, dauphin, Lorrain, and so on) and give a dramatic reading of the story.

B. The public trials in "The Lady or the Tiger?" provide a bizarre entertainment for the people in the kingdom. Reread the schedule of events and then design, write, and neatly draw a pamphlet that could serve as a program for the audience on the day of the youth's trial.

SETTING

A WHITE HERON

About the Author

South Berwick, Maine, was the birthplace of Sarah Orne Jewett (1849–1909), and her writings celebrated the simple virtues she found there. She called her writings sketches, and in them she preserved the color and flavor of an era of rural New England life.

A Country Doctor (1884) and *The Country of the Pointed Firs* (1896) are her two most important works.

About the Story

In this 1886 story, young Sylvia's life on the farm with her grandmother is simple and serene. But her protected world is disturbed when a stranger comes, and she must make a choice as important as life itself. You may want to look at a picture of a heron before reading the story to appreciate the bird's rare and graceful beauty.

plaguy Annoying, troublesome.

bangeing A New England expression for lounging about, loitering.

hitch Get along together, as a team of horses would.

pettishly Fretfully, peevishly.

Note To portray the Maine dialect, Jewett replaced unpronounced letters with apostrophes. For example, *marsh* became "ma'sh," and *wanderer* became "wand'rer."

Checking the Facts

Answer *true* or *false* for each of the following.

1. Sylvia likes to chase and frighten boys.
2. While returning with the cow, Sylvia is startled by a bird's whistle.
3. The young man hunts mainly to get food.
4. Sylvia's first view of the sea is from a tree.
5. Although Sylvia sees the heron, the young man goes away disappointed.

Interpreting the Story

1. Would you have told the young man where the heron was? Could you have given up love or friendship to save a bird's life? Why or why not?
2. Imagine that Sylvia has moved back to her mother's home after the incident with the heron. Would she

still be "afraid of folks"? Why or why not?

3. How much easier or harder would Sylvia's decision have been if she had lived on the farm a shorter time? A longer time? Tell why in each case.

4. By her decision, Sylvia declares that certain beliefs are important to her. What are they?

THE PIT AND THE PENDULUM

About the Author

Edgar Allan Poe (1809–1849) did not quite invent the short story, but his suggested "rules" were like a patent for its form. Poe said a short story should be unified, able to be read in one sitting, and restricted as to time and place. It should create a single effect or interest.

Poe, who was orphaned as a child, was born in Boston and educated for a time in England. After college, he struggled to forge a future by writing—often publishing his own works. His tales and poems became known throughout the world, and readers today still enjoy his world of terror and mystery.

About the Story

Suffocating darkness. Slimy, cold walls. Rats. A nightmare? No, it is Poe's setting for horror and a gasping fight for survival.

Poe used the Spanish Inquisition, begun in 1478, as the backdrop for this story. The Inquisition was a Roman

Catholic tribunal set up to discover, punish, and prevent heresy. The Inquisition also became a political tool of Spain's King Ferdinand and Queen Isabella and was ultimately responsible for the exile, torture, or death of many of its victims.

Can a story's setting put a chill in the reader's heart? Listen to the narrator—and to the beating of his heart in a silent dungeon.

Hades   In mythology, the underworld of the dead.

autos-da-fé   Portuguese for "acts of faith." Refers to the Inquisition's showy sentencings or executions.

Toledo   City in central Spain that headed one of five inquisitorial districts.

Ultima Thule   The northernmost part of the habitable world; the extreme.

boots   Avails; in this case, "What use is it to tell?"

Checking the Facts

1. The narrator falls near the pit when (a) he is pushed (b) a rat scares him (c) he faints (d) he gets entangled in a piece of cloth.
2. The pendulum swings (a) with a hiss (b) more slowly each time (c) only once (d) through boiling water.
3. The prisoner escapes from the wrapping by (a) letting the blade cut it (b) getting rats to eat through it (c) ripping it by hand (d) losing weight.
4. The man finally (a) is rescued (b) burns to death (c) falls into the pit (d) is crushed.

Interpreting the Story

1. Throughout the story, what evidence is there that the narrator is being watched?
2. Could Poe have achieved such a feeling of horror with any other setting? If not, why not? If so, how?
3. Which sense (sight, hearing, or other) does Poe rely on most to create a mood of tension and fear?
4. Tell how the ending of the story weakens or strengthens the believability of the story.

THE OUTCASTS OF POKER FLAT

About the Author

Bret Harte (1836–1902) is most famous for the local color, or regional description, of his stories. He moved to California from the East when he was a teenager, and his experiences as tutor, miner, clerk, and reporter were later reflected in his writings. Harte's early successes with such stories as "The Luck of Roaring Camp" (1868) and "The Outcasts of Poker Flat" (1869) were rarely equaled. After serving in diplomatic posts in Germany and Scotland, he settled in London, where he spent his last years.

About the Story

How do you survive when people and places force you into a corner? Is it all a matter of luck or chance?

Watch how Harte uses setting to reveal the true personalities of five people stranded in a mountain pass in this vivid story of the newly settled West.

neat Leather made from cattle.

sluice Trough for collecting or washing ore.

Parthian Shot fired in retreat, a practice perfected by warriors of Parthia, an ancient Iranian empire.

castinets Castanets; called "bones" later in the story.

Covenanters Seventeenth-century Scottish Presbyterians who opposed union with the Church of England.

shift for myself Get along all right by myself.

chicken Little girl, little child.

argument Main subject, summary.

Mr. Pope Alexander Pope (1688–1744), British poet, translated the *Iliad*, a poem about the Trojan War (about 1100 B.C.) by Homer.

son of Peleus Achilles, a great warrior of ancient Greece.

Checking the Facts

1. Uncle Billy is (a) Poker Flat's mayor (b) a lawyer (c) a drunkard (d) a minister.
2. Which one of these is not ousted by the town? (a) John Oakhurst (b) Piney Woods (c) Mother Shipton (d) the Duchess.
3. The Innocent (a) teaches gambling (b) steals the supplies (c) marries the Duchess (d) heads back to Poker Flat.
4. Mother Shipton dies of (a) old age (b) pneumonia (c) bad whiskey (d) starvation.

Interpreting the Story

G16

1. How was John Oakhurst the "strongest and yet the weakest of the outcasts of Poker Flat"?
2. Choose one character. Tell whether the townspeople or the weather was the stronger force opposing that character. Give examples from the story.
3. If Harte had written the story today, what setting, or particular time and place, might he have chosen to show people being treated as outcasts? Explain.
4. How do you think Poker Flat's citizens would have reacted upon learning of the fate of the outcasts?

Be a Writer

A. Read the following passage by Sarah Orne Jewett and pay attention to her use of color.

> Sylvia could see the white sails of ships at sea, and the clouds that were purple and rose-colored and yellow at first began to fade away. Where was the white heron's nest in the sea of green branches . . . ?

1. Using a thesaurus, rewrite the passage by inserting a synonym for each color.
2. Describe a particular effect (cheerful sunny day or dreary rainy day) while describing the area immediately around your home. Use five or six colors, as Jewett did in the passage above.

B. Biographer Henry C. Merwin said Bret Harte wrote "as if the story were a message, to be delivered to the reader in the shortest possible time." Reread the first paragraph of "The Outcasts of Poker Flat." In sixty to seventy words, describe your entrance or your teacher's entrance into the classroom. Instead of a "Sabbath lull in the air," what will you choose? A "Monday-morning gloom"? The "festive air of our final day"?

Special Projects

A. Draw a detailed and accurate picture of the dungeon room of "The Pit and the Pendulum."
B. Write and perform a sixty-second radio advertisement aimed at getting someone your age to read one of the previous three stories.

PLOT

THE PIECE OF STRING

About the Author

Guy de Maupassant (1850–1893) was born in Normandy, a rural area of France cited in many of his stories.

As a young man, while serving as a government clerk, he realized he would much rather be a writer. For ten years he toiled to perfect his writing, discarding any piece of writing that did not meet his standards. His first published story, *"Boule de Suif"* ("Ball of Fat"), created a sensation. Maupassant went on to write nearly three hundred short stories marked by precise detail and unusual plots.

About the Story

G18 A man picks up a piece of string and finds himself accused of a crime. One seemingly minor action has changed his life. Published in 1883 as *"La Ficelle,"* this is a story of one man's conflict with society. But the truth speaks for itself—sometimes.

M'sieu' *Monsieur,* French for "mister."

Maître French for "master."

francs The chief French monetary unit.

Checking the Facts

1. Why does Hauchecorne pick up the string?
2. What announcement does the public crier make?
3. Who claims he saw Hauchecorne pick up the pocketbook?
4. After the farmhand returns the pocketbook, who at Jourdain's tavern believes Hauchecorne?
5. To whom does Hauchecorne call out on his deathbed?

Interpreting the Story

1. Describe Hauchecorne's attitude toward himself. How does this add to his problems?
2. Why does Hauchecorne go out of his way to tell his story to anyone he meets?
3. The climax is the story's moment of highest tension. At what point in this story does it become clear to the reader that Hauchecorne will never be believed?

4. If you were Hauchecorne, what would you have said or done to Malandain? To the crowd at Jourdain's? In each case tell why.

TO PLEASE HIS WIFE

About the Author

The British author Thomas Hardy (1840–1928) studied and trained to become an architect, but he became a designer of works of fiction, not buildings. Perhaps to protect himself from any possible embarrassment, Hardy submitted some of his early writings anonymously. As he gained success, he began to publish under his own name.

Hardy's writings stressed his characters' struggles against fate and nature. *The Return of the Native* (1878) and *Jude the Obscure* (1896) are among his most noted novels.

About the Story

Sometimes you know that "enough is enough," yet you cannot stop yourself. In this story, published in 1894 in a collection called *Life's Little Ironies*, Hardy explores a character's inability to control her ambition.

harbor-bar   A sandbar that protects a harbor.

collect of thanksgiving   A prayer.

presently   Soon, in a little while.

sixpenny   Inexpensive, about twelve cents.

bagman   Traveling salesman.

Jack   The hero of "Jack and the Beanstalk."

sovereigns, guineas   British gold coins.

truck (of the mainmast)   The top, where the flag is.

Checking the Facts

Write *true* on your paper for each accurate statement. Rewrite each false statement to make it true.

1. Shadrach Jolliffe is a stranger to Havenpool.
2. After she sees Shadrach kissing Emily, Joanna decides she cannot let him go.
3. Shadrach returns to sea because he loves it dearly.
4. Emily marries a rich widower and has two boys.
5. Joanna gladly moves in with Emily and her family.

Interpreting the Story

1. Critic Albert C. Baugh has accused Hardy of "loading the dice" against his characters and of "relying to an extravagant degree upon coincidence." For each of the following, decide whether the fact was either believable or too coincidental to be true. Tell how each strengthened or weakened the story.
   (a) Emily's taking residence across the street.
   (b) Emily's wealth and Joanna's poverty.
   (c) The loss of Shadrach and the boys.
2. At what point should Shadrach have opposed Joanna's greed? How could he have succeeded? If not, why not?

THE COP AND THE ANTHEM

About the Author

William Sydney Porter (1862–1910) used the pen name O. Henry. While confined in a federal prison on embezzlement charges, Porter wrote stories to support his daughter, and O. Henry was one of several pseudonyms he used. After his release from prison, O. Henry continued writing. Eventually he moved to New York City, the setting for many of his stories.

His trademark was the surprise ending. Although Maupassant, Stockton, and others used similar endings, it was O. Henry who became famous for them. His clever plots helped to make short stories popular for millions of new readers.

About the Story

Soapy, the *protagonist*, or main character, *wants* to be arrested. You will find out why in this unusual story.

O. Henry felt that everybody had a unique and unusual story to tell. *The Four Million*, the collection from which this story was taken, was O. Henry's way of saying New York City had a story for each person.

anthem   A song or hymn of praise.

pasteboard   Calling card.

hibernatorial   Referring to hibernation.

the Island   (Blackwell's) Now called Roosevelt Island, a place where people were detained for minor offenses.

G22 **the grape, the silkworm, and the protoplasm**   High-class wine, clothes, and people.

accusive   Accusing; one of several words O. Henry made up.

suds   Beer or ale.

transplendent   Beyond splendid.

lave them be   Leave them alone.

Checking the Facts

1. Why does Soapy want to be arrested?
2. Why isn't he arrested for breaking the window?
3. How do the waiters punish Soapy?
4. Where does the music come from when Soapy resolves to improve his life?
5. How is Soapy eventually arrested?

Interpreting the Story

1. Why, do you think, does Soapy prefer jail to charity?
2. O. Henry might have ended the story by having the "reformed" Soapy starting a job. Compare this with the story's actual ending. Which is better? Why?
3. Do you think Soapy will keep his promise to look for work—even after his winter stay in jail? Explain why you think his change in character is either temporary or permanent.

☆ ★ ☆

Be a Writer

In the first two paragraphs of "The Piece of String," Maupassant uses body shapes and clothing to describe the peasants: "Their long legs were twisted . . . . Their starched blue blouses, shining as though varnished. . . ."

Describe a group of people in contemporary terms by writing about body shapes and specialized clothing. *Hint:* You most likely would not describe a rock band in the same way you would depict a meeting of teachers. Or, to use another example, a soccer team would differ in appearance from a choir.

Special Projects

A. Each of the stories puts great importance on what happens (plot). Imagine you are a newscaster. Retell the events of the three preceding stories in a newscast. (Three students can be announcers.) Write your stories before "performing" them. Make sure you tell about events by putting the most important fact first; do *not* simply list items chronologically. Also, tell *only* the facts; leave out your opinion.

B. Perform (perhaps as a mime) the anthem-and-arrest scene of "The Cop and the Anthem." Use music.

POINT OF VIEW

THE £1,000,000 BANK NOTE

About the Author

Samuel Langhorne Clemens (1835–1910) was born in Florida, Missouri. His pen name, Mark Twain, was taken from a term used on the Mississippi River. Before he became an internationally known writer, he worked as a printer in Missouri, a steamboat pilot on the Mississippi, a prospector and miner in Nevada, and a journalist in California.

He is best known for his novels *The Adventures of Tom Sawyer* and *Adventures of Huckleberry Finn*. In these books Twain used the words, rhythms, and phrasings of common Americans. His humor and his use of the voices of everyday people are part of his legacy.

About the Story

A wager is made, Can a young man in a strange city survive for thirty days without any money—just a check worth several million dollars that nobody will cash?

Twain might have written this as an observer, a reporter. He didn't. Instead, he wrote it as a first-person account by one of the story's characters.

afternoon board The late listing of stock and commodity prices.

coil Mess, turmoil.

nobby Stylish, socially superior; wealthy.

Punch British satirical magazine.

Gould and Curry Extension Refers to a speculative venture in mining.

Arabian Nights Middle Eastern folk tales of adventure, love, and magic.

unabridged An unabridged dictionary.

Checking the Facts

1. How does the narrator get to London?
2. Where does the young man have his first success with the bank note?
3. How soon after the narrator meets Portia Langham does he fall in love with her?
4. Who asks the narrator for financial help?
5. What "situation," or job, does Henry Adams ask for?

Interpreting the Story

1. The story is told in the first person by a major character. If the story were told in the third person by an observer, why would the reader probably not know Henry Adams as well?
2. If a person wins a lot of money, his or her life can change *too* much—not necessarily for the better. Does the gift of the bank note make Henry a stronger or a weaker person? Explain.
3. Choose one incident from the story and tell how it shows that the rich and the poor are not treated alike. Was Twain right in his idea that the rich and the poor are treated differently?

G26 About the Author

Ambrose Bierce (1842–1914?) served in the Union Army during the Civil War. He fought valiantly in several battles, but he later referred to himself as "an assassin for my country." After the war, like Bret Harte and Mark Twain before him, he moved West and worked for magazines and newspapers.

His writings, such as his book of satirical and pessimistic definitions, *The Devil's Dictionary* (1911), were often sarcastic and cruel. He came to be known as "Bitter" Bierce. As a keen observer of war, he was a forerunner of Stephen Crane.

Bierce went to Mexico to cover a revolution. Last heard from in 1914, he was presumed killed, but his death remains a mystery.

About the Story

Set in the Civil War, this story vividly shows Bierce's brand of "savage irony," by which events take a grim and unexpected turn. For the most part, Bierce wrote the story through the eyes of an observer, but he allows us to share the main character's thoughts and feelings.

A young soldier is dozing while he is supposed to be a lookout. What he sees after he awakes, he will never forget.

grip The handle of a gun.

verge The edge, or rim.

deeps Depths, vast area.

Apocalypse   Refers to the biblical prophecy, in Revelation, of the end of the world, with Four Horsemen signifying war, famine, pestilence, and death.

Checking the Facts

1. Who tells Carter Druse to do his duty, even as a "traitor" to Virginia?
2. Why isn't Carter's mother told of his enlistment?
3. After he awakes, what does Carter see on the cliff?
4. What amazing sight does an officer fail to report?
5. Who is on the horse that Carter shoots?

Interpreting the Story

1. The endings of Bierce's stories have been called "often on the edge of the unbearable." Is that true of this story? Explain your opinion. What prior hint, or *foreshadowing*, is there of the ending?
2. What point is Bierce trying to make in this story? (*Hint:* Focus on the needs of duty and sacrifice.)
3. Suppose Bierce simply listed facts and did not reveal any character's thoughts. Could he have presented his theme as effectively? Why or why not?

PAUL'S CASE

About the Author

Willa Cather (1873–1947) was born in Virginia but spent her early years in Nebraska. After graduating from college, she worked as a reporter, then as a teacher in Pittsburgh. A book of poems, published in 1903, and a collection of short stories, published when Cather was thirty-two, established her writing career.

She often wrote of characters trying to find values, avoiding the artificial, and seeking the permanent.

About the Story

This story, taken from Cather's first collection of short stories, is about a young man who despises anything that is ordinary. Paul, the main character, finds it impossible to accept things as they are. He wants to escape from his life in Pittsburgh. As you read try to discover why Paul thought he was trapped.

four-in-hand Necktie.

Faust, Martha, Rigoletto, Pagliacci Titles of nine-teenth-century operas.

Carnegie Hall Refers to a concert hall in Pittsburgh.

Cumberland A Presbyterian sect.

waists Shirtwaists, or blouses.

iron kings Leaders of the iron and steel industries.

cash boys Messengers who handled money in a store.

purple High rank; royal garments.

Checking the Facts

Write *true* on your paper for each accurate statement. Rewrite each false statement to make it true.

1. Paul enjoys his job as a soloist at the opera.
2. Rather than face his father's questions, Paul spends the night in the basement.

3. Paul's father wants him to be like the young man who works as a clerk for an industrialist.
4. Paul spends a night on the town with a college student.
5. The hotel management in New York suspects Paul of being a thief from Pittsburgh.

Interpreting the Story

1. A clue to Paul's despair is his feeling that "all the world had become Cordelia Street." Why does Paul feel that way? Why does it depress him?
2. Cather tells the story from an omniscient, or all-knowing, point of view. We can read more than one character's thoughts. How do Paul's teachers feel after meeting with him?
3. The omniscient point of view gives us a glimpse of Paul's thoughts just before he dies. He regrets "the vastness of what he had left undone." What might Paul have tried to accomplish if he had decided to live? Were those things possible?
4. Paul's suicide indicates something distorted in his view of the world. Since Cather tells the story mostly through Paul's eyes, she limits the reader to his distorted viewpoint. But what choices does he *not* see? In what ways is his outlook warped? Give several examples from the story.

☆ ★ ☆

Be a Writer

A. Reread the paragraph in "A Horseman in the Sky" that begins as follows: "Druse withdrew his eyes from the valley and fixed them again upon the group of man and horse in the sky. . . ." Rewrite the entire paragraph in the first person, giving Carter Druse's thoughts. Begin by writing, "I withdrew my eyes from the valley. . . ." Show Carter's feelings and his reasons for his actions.

B. Teenagers' problems with parents and teachers can range from the trivial to the extremely serious (as in "Paul's Case"). Choose a problem, small or large, serious or funny, that you have had with an adult. Write a story about it in the third-person omniscient point of view, as Willa Cather might have done. Explain your attitude and the adult's. (*Example:* "She had not made her bed that morning; she had not felt like it. Her mother was furious when she discovered it. . . .")

Special Projects

A. Compose an illustration and caption for one of the stories in the point-of-view section.

B. Act out a skit showing Henry Adams trying to get change for a million pounds. Decide which characters to use, and arrange your own dialogue and staging.

CHARACTER

GOD SEES THE TRUTH, BUT WAITS

About the Author

Count Leo Tolstoy (1828–1910) was born of Russian aristocrats, but he was orphaned at an early age. Although Tolstoy was a writer, he was always involved in searching out ways to better the lives of the poor. He took up the peasants' cause, even to the point of starting a school and writing textbooks for their children.

His social and spiritual concerns were evident in his writings, which began with diaries he kept as a young man. *War and Peace* (1865–69) is his great life-embracing novel; many regard it as the world's greatest novel. It has hundreds of characters and a plot that weaves together their complex lives. *Anna Karenina* (1875–77) is another Tolstoy masterpiece.

About the Story

A man, Aksenof, is unjustly punished despite his protest of innocence. Watch how Aksenof responds and see if you can understand why he acts as he does.

Nizhni   Nizhni Novgorod, or Lower New Town.

rubles   Main currency of Russia.

Vanya   Nickname for Ivan.

knout   A whip with a leather lash, often intertwined with wire.

postboy   A postilion, or guide.

Note Russian names sometimes have more than one form. Thus, Makar's last name makes use of patronymics, forms (such as *-of*, *-itch*) that mean "son of." Therefore the son of Semyon is also known as Semyonof and Semyonuitch.

Checking the Facts

1. What reason does Aksenof's wife give for not wanting him to go on his journey?
2. Give one reason why Aksenof is accused of murdering the other merchant.
3. For how many years does Aksenof live in the mines?
4. What does Aksenof refuse to tell the chief? Why?
5. When does Aksenof find peace of soul?

Interpreting the Story

1. What trait of Aksenof do you admire most? Give examples from the story that show this trait. (For example, *piety;* shown by Aksenof's habit of prayer.)
2. For Tolstoy, characters are not all good or all bad. Name one weakness or failing of Aksenof; name one virtue or good action shown by Makar.
3. In your view, what is Tolstoy's theme, or message?

THE MAN WITHOUT A COUNTRY

About the Author

Edward Everett Hale (1822–1909) was the son of a Boston newspaper publisher. When he was eleven years old, he did his first writing for the paper. He was fond of saying that he was "cradled in the sheets of a newspaper." Hale, who considered school a "necessary nuisance," graduated from Harvard when he was seventeen. He taught school briefly, wrote for magazines, and became a Unitarian minister, later serving as chaplain of the United States Senate.

Hale's stories are sprinkled with many names and places and read like factual accounts. An optimistic social reformer, Hale was most concerned with the lessons his stories taught.

About the Story

Hale published this story in 1863 as a stirring call to patriotism for the Union during the Civil War.

The story begins in 1805 and tells of the plight of a man named Nolan. The narrator is Nolan's acquaintance, Fred Ingham. Nolan, it turns out, has made a terrible mistake, one that changed his whole life.

non mi ricordo Italian for "I don't remember"; something forgotten.

Aaron Burr Politician, third vice-president of the United States. Nolan is linked to a traitorous plot Burr was allegedly involved in. Burr was eventually tried and acquitted of treason.

Monongahela Whiskey made in western Pennsylvania.

sledge, high-low-jack Card games.

salt junk Dried salted beef.

contra dances Dances performed in two lines or in a square, with partners facing each other.

Iron Mask   Mysterious political prisoner in France in the late 1600s and early 1700s. A mask—probably black velvet, not iron—was put over his face as he was moved from prison to prison.

slave-trade treaty   In 1842 the United States and England began patrolling the African coast to try to stop the slave trade.

Middle Passage   The Atlantic Ocean portion of a slave's journey from Africa to America.

ben trovato   Italian for "well-founded but untrue."

Note   Hale uses many names and places—most are real; some are either obscure or made up. Although a biographical dictionary and a gazetteer would be helpful, they are not necessary to understand Hale's world.

Checking the Facts

1. What is Nolan's first reaction to his sentence?
2. For what courageous act is Nolan given a sword?
3. Whom does Nolan aid in returning to their country?
4. Who writes the letter to Ingham that tells of Nolan's last days?
5. As a last wish, what does Nolan want to know the names of?

Interpreting the Story

1. Why does Nolan curse the United States in court? (His reasons may have been political and personal.)

2. Why does the poem that Nolan reads aloud cause him to break down?
3. In what ways does Nolan change during his exile? *G35* Give at least two examples from the story.
4. According to the narrator's account, Nolan does not become bitter toward his country. Why not?
5. Could such a story occur today? Why or why not?

LOUISA

About the Author

Mary Eleanor Wilkins Freeman (1852–1930) was born in Massachusetts, whose changing towns and villages she used as settings for many stories. She wrote her earliest stories and poems for a Sunday-school magazine for children. However, Freeman's writings for adults were not published until she was in her thirties.

Her stories were often "psychological portraits" of strong-willed characters, usually women, who tried to do the painful but right thing.

About the Story

A young woman, Louisa, has the awesome burden of keeping her mother and grandfather from the brink of starvation. She could choose an easy solution, but her fierce independence and spirit of rebellion leave her only one acceptable choice.

frowse In a frizz, unkempt.

Mecca   Goal; alludes to city of Islamic pilgrimages.

G36   *Note*   Freeman often changed a word's form to imitate a regional pronunciation. For example, *potato* became "potater," *maybe* became "mebbe," and *scared* became "scart."

Checking the Facts

Write *true* or *false* for each statement.
1. Louisa had taught school since she was sixteen.
2. Jonathan Nye and Louisa want to elope.
3. Mrs. Britton thinks her family will gain financially if Louisa marries Jonathan.
4. The grandfather unknowingly damages the crops.
5. Louisa walks seven miles each way to her uncle's.

Interpreting the Story

1. Explain how Louisa saves or loses her dignity by begging her uncle for food.
2. Why do Louisa and her mother argue so much? In what ways do they agree more than they realize?
3. Louisa's mother is poor but a "born aristocrat" and very proud. Tell how Louisa does or does not understand this.
4. Does Louisa achieve "her own maiden independence" by carrying food from her uncle's? How does the entire story concern her goal of independence? Could she have gained her independence in any other way?

☆ ★ ☆

Be a Writer

A. Read this description of Solomon Mears in "Louisa."

> He took his pipe out of his mouth long enough to speak, then replaced it. His eyes, sharp under their shaggy brows, were fixed on Louisa; his broad bristling face had a look of stolid rebuff like an ox; his stout figure, in his soiled farmer dress, surged over his chair.

Describe a man or woman, real or imagined, as one of the following: timid, enraged, serene, or impatient. As Freeman did, make physical aspects, such as hair, complexion, hands, and clothes, express the emotion.

B. Write a short story in which the incidents of the story reveal one or two dominant traits of the main character. You may first want to identify for yourself the trait or traits you want to focus on. Therefore, if you concentrate on greed, for example, you might show a character acquiring item after item—only to find isolation and unhappiness.

Special Projects

A. In small groups act out one or more of the following from Hale's story: Nolan's trial; the reading the men gave of *The Lay of the Last Minstrel;* Nolan's dance with Mrs. Graff.

B. Report to your class on prison conditions in Tolstoy's Russia. (His novel *Resurrection* may offer some insights.) Compare those conditions to prison life in this country today.

THE FATAL CRADLE

About the Author

Wilkie Collins (1824–1889) was a British writer whose literary career began at twenty-four when he wrote a biography of his father, a famous landscape painter. But Collins became known for his fiction, and one account says that he was employed as a storyteller by a senior student at boarding school.

He succeeded. He made a mark as one of the developers of the detective and mystery novel, especially through such novels as *The Woman in White* (1860) and *The Moonstone* (1868).

About the Story

Published in the United States in 1873, this story has its own mystery about it. The narrator tells the reader to prepare for a "pathetic story" about a "grand misfortune." Your understanding of tone should tell you that you must decide, Does the narrator tell this story with a wink of the eye or in tears?

coppered   Coated with copper.

qualms   Nausea, faintness; seasickness.

Roman nose   Nose with a prominent bridge.

chopping   Large and vigorous; strapping.

spars   Poles that support or extend sails.

Indiaman   Merchant ship used in trade with India.

workhouse Workplace provided for the poor.

afterlife Later in life.

Checking the Facts

Complete the following phrases by writing the correct answer on your paper.

1. The narrator's last name is _____ .
2. _____ loses track of the babies.
3. An unsuccessful test of maternal instinct is called the "_____ of Nature."
4. The captain's solution is based on the _____ of the babies.
5. The child assigned to Mrs. _____ prospers later in life.

Interpreting the Story

1. What do you think of the captain's solution? How would you have settled the matter?
2. Remember that the narrator here is a character, and his thoughts are not necessarily the author's. What does the *narrator* say about destiny? Do you agree with him? Do you think Collins does? Explain.
3. Collins has the narrator close the story by saying, "I wish you good morning" to the reader. Is this a normal way to end a "heart-rending" story? From the very outset, Collins gives clues to how seriously we should take Heavysides and his grievance. Find two phrases or sentences, and tell how they show the lighter side of the narrator's "grand misfortune."

G40 About the Author

Kate Chopin (1851–1904) married, gave birth to six children in nine years, and became a widow before she turned to writing. According to one account, her doctor suggested that she use writing as a therapy to recover from grief over her husband's death. Her first short story was published when she was thirty-eight.

She wrote of what she knew: her childhood remembrances, her years on a plantation in Louisiana, her husband's death. Her novel *The Awakening* (1899) has been widely acclaimed.

About the Story

Originally entitled "Dream of an Hour," this story first appeared, in a magazine, in 1894. The story's main character, Mrs. Mallard, is shattered by news of her husband's death. Or is she? Pay attention to the narrator's tone to find the answer.

Checking the Facts

1. What physical ailment of Mrs. Mallard forces her sister to break the news very cautiously?
2. How does Richards learn of the railroad disaster?
3. What does Mrs. Mallard do at once upon hearing the report of her husband's death?
4. When does she plan to weep again for her husband?
5. Who enters through the front door?

Interpreting the Story

2. Mrs. Mallard experiences an uncontrollable feeling of freedom. Tell why you think the feeling is or is not natural for her under the circumstances.

3. Irony is often used to describe a situation in which the reader knows something that one or more of the characters do not. At the end of "The Story of an Hour" we are told that Mrs. Mallard died "of joy that kills." How is the tone of Chopin's last sentence ironic? Answer by choosing three characters and comparing the author's attitude toward Mrs. Mallard's death with each character's attitude.

A WORK OF ART

About the Author

The Russian writer Anton Chekhov (1860–1904) began writing humorous stories when he was nineteen to help support himself and his family. He continued to write as he went through medical school and after he received his degree. The success of his stories encouraged him to continue, and the world is forever grateful to him.

His nearly six hundred stories have secured a place for him as history's greatest short-story writer. He wrote "slices of life," illuminating characters through seemingly trivial incidents.

Chekhov was also a major playwright, and his works are still frequently performed. Among his most popular plays are *The Sea Gull* (1896), *The Three Sisters* (1901), and *The Cherry Orchard* (1904).

But the drama of any Chekhov piece is found chiefly in the ordinary lives of his characters, whose humor or sadness often derives from a failure to communicate.

About the Story

You are given a "work of art." But what do you do with a gift that makes you blush? Do you laugh or cry?

According to Chekhov, "conciseness is the sister of talent." He proves that here as he creates memorable characters in a few words.

Beelzebub The Devil.

benefit Benefit performance; performance for charity.

Checking the Facts

1. According to Sasha, why does he want to give the candelabrum to the doctor?
2. What excuse does the doctor give for not wanting the object in his living room?
3. To whom does the doctor give the candelabrum?
4. How do the comedian's friends react to it?
5. At the end, what does Sasha say he has brought the doctor?

Interpreting the Facts

1. Each character mentions somebody else as a reason for not keeping the gift. Is any character's excuse be-

lievable to you? Why or why not?

2. What would you do if the gift were given to you? Why?

3. The narrator refers to details of the candelabrum that he has "neither the audacity nor the temperament to describe." He says he is "even ashamed to think" of what the object suggests. This description gives a hint of Chekhov's tone, his attitude toward the predicament. Is the narrator really shocked? Is Chekhov as serious about the affair as his characters are? Explain.

4. Chekhov sometimes exaggerates his characters. Why? Give an example.

☆ ★ ☆

Be a Writer

A. "The Fatal Cradle" uses remarks in parentheses for humorous effect—as if the narrator were mumbling side comments or arguing with himself. For example, "In a week's time, if this weather holds, we shall all (please God) be in port." Describe a simple incident, such as waking up in the morning, and sprinkle it with a commentary of remarks in parentheses. For example, "The alarm sounded, and I fell out of bed (off to a fine morning!). . . ."

B. Tone is the result of the author's attitude toward the story. Write a simple scene using one tone. Then rewrite the same scene using a different tone. *Example:* A man slips and falls down. Tone 1: humorous, slapstick. Tone 2: sad, heart-tugging. *Example:* A girl turns down a date and spends the evening with a girl friend. Tone 1: The girl has done an admirable thing.

Tone 2: She has done a foolish thing.

C. Expand one of the pieces you wrote for **A** or **B** into a short story. As you write (and rewrite!) keep in mind that all authors make decisions about theme, setting, plot, point of view, character, and tone in their stories.

Special Projects

A. Decide on a tone for a particular story in this section. Then make a collage or do a painting that, to you, shows that feeling. *Examples:* mocking, mournful, lighthearted.

B. Choose one story from this book. Assume that the story is being made into a movie. The producer has asked you to find appropriate background music. In deciding what music to bring to class or to compose, keep the story's tone in mind. For example, you might find Bach organ music appropriate for Poe's story, ragtime piano music for "The Fatal Cradle."

☆ ★ ☆

Surveying the Short Story

You have seen that in reading a story you can focus on a particular element, such as theme or character. But you should recognize that *all* these elements merge uniquely in every story. This last section will help to increase your understanding and enjoyment by suggesting comparisons and conclusions. You might discuss the following points in class or use them as study or essay topics.

A. A story's title is your first link to the story. Which story titles did you find especially helpful or appropriate? Why? Would you have changed any titles? G45 Why?

B. For each of the following, choose a character and tell why you made the choice.

   1. A character who aroused your sympathy.

   2. A character who appealed to you or was likable.

   3. A character whom you found especially puzzling.

   4. A character whom you disliked.

C. Which story did you like most? In answering, show how the author's handling of *one* of the six story elements (theme, setting, and so on) added to your enjoyment.

D. Read a short story not found in this book. (The list of Further Reading offers suggestions.) Identify the point of view. If you were to change it, for example, from third person to first person, would the main character be better known or appear more distant? Would the narrator become more reliable? Less reliable? How? How would the plot be influenced?

E. According to the critic Wallace Stegner, Chekhov said that "writers should cut off the beginnings and endings of their stories, since it was there that they were most inclined to lie." Choose one story—in this collection or in your outside reading—and tell why you agree or disagree with Chekhov's theory. Give evidence from the story you have chosen.

Further Reading

Note For many authors, especially popular ones, such as Chekhov, Harte, O. Henry, Poe, and Twain, there are many collections available. Consult your library's card catalog for more extensive listings.

Bierce, Ambrose. *Can Such Things Be?* Ghost stories and military tales, many of which are found in other anthologies.

Cather, Willa. *Youth and the Bright Medusa.* Eight stories that deal with artistic sensibility and talent.

Chekhov, Anton. *The Portable Chekhov.* A comprehensive source for readers of Chekhov.

Chopin, Kate. *Bayou Folk.* Stories by Chopin with a distinctly Southern flavor.

Collins, Wilkie. *Short Stories of Wilkie Collins.* A collection of short writings by the British master.

Daudet, Alphonse. *Letters from My Windmill.* Sketches, often satiric or humorous, of French country life.

Freeman, Mary Wilkins. *A New England Nun and Other Stories.* Stories that often involve courageous women.

Hale, Edward Everett. *If, Yes, and Perhaps.* "The Man Without a Country" and other short pieces.

Hardy, Thomas. *Wessex Tales.* Hardy's "dreams of real people," including the popular "The Three Strangers."

Harte, Bret. *The Luck of Roaring Camp and Other Sketches.* Lively narratives of "roughing it" in the West.

Hawthorne, Nathaniel. *Twice-Told Tales.* Historical sketches and tales of New England life.

Henry, O. *The Four Million.* "The Gift of the Magi" and other favorites.

Jewett, Sarah Orne. *The Country of the Pointed Firs.* Twelve portraits of Maine life.

Maupassant, Guy de. *The Odd Number.* Thirteen tales by a master of plot and irony.

Poe, Edgar Allan. *The Portable Poe*. Tales, poems, letters, and criticism by Poe.

Stockton, Frank. *The Lady or the Tiger? and Other Stories.* G47
Twelve entertainments by Stockton.

Tolstoy, Leo. *The Death of Ivan Ilych and Other Stories.* Spiritually oriented stories by the Russian master.

Twain, Mark. *The Mysterious Stranger and Other Stories.* "The Man That Corrupted Hadleyburg" and "Luck" are among the gems by Twain in this volume.

Audiovisual Resources

Records and Cassettes

Bret Harte—Bettin. Spoken Arts. Record, cassette. Includes "The Outcasts of Poker Flat."

The Gift of the Magi and Other O. Henry Stories—Begley, Harris. Caedmon. Record, cassette. With "The Cop and the Anthem."

The Lady or the Tiger?—Anderson. Caedmon. Record, cassette. Includes "The Discourager of Hesitancy," a sequel.

The Man Without a Country—Robinson. Caedmon. Cassette.

De Maupassant Collection—Blake. Listening Library. 2 records. "The Piece of String" and others.

The Outcasts of Poker Flat and The Luck of Roaring Camp—Begley. Caedmon. Cassette.

The Pit and the Pendulum—Scourby. Spoken Arts. Record, cassette.

*Films (16mm)**

The Lady or the Tiger? by Frank Stockton. Encyclopaedia Britannica Educational Corp. 16 min, color. Stockton's story in a space-age setting.

The Man Without a Country. Eastman Kodak Company. 90 min, color. Cliff Robertson in starring role.

G48 *O. Henry's Full House.* Twentieth Century-Fox; Films, Inc. 111 min, b/w. Dramatizations of "The Cop and the Anthem" and three other stories.

The Outcasts of Poker Flat. Brandon Films, Audio Brandon Films. 81 min, b/w.

Paul's Case. Perspective Films. 53 min, color.

The Pit and the Pendulum. Association Films. 83 min, color. Vincent Price in a stirring performance.

A White Heron. Learning Corporation of America. 26 min, color.

A Work of Art. Brandon Films, Audio Brandon Films. 10 min, color or b/w. In Russian with English subtitles.

Filmstrips (35mm)*

The Cop and the Anthem. Brunswick Corp., Educational Record Sales. Filmstrip with captions, 50 frames, color.

The Man Without a Country. McGraw-Hill Films. Filmstrip with record, 55 frames, color.

The Outcasts of Poker Flat. Brunswick Corp., Educational Record Sales. Filmstrip with captions, 50 frames, color.

The Piece of String. Brunswick Corp., Educational Record Sales. Filmstrip with captions, 50 frames, color.

The Pit and the Pendulum. Brunswick Corp., Educational Record Sales. Filmstrip with captions, 40 frames, color.

---

* When two sources are listed, the first is the producer and the second is the distributor. To locate addresses of producers and distributors, use the *Index to 16mm Educational Films* and the *Index to 35mm Educational Filmstrips*, both published by the National Information Center of Educational Media at the University of Southern California. An alternate source of addresses is *Audiovisual Market Place*, published by R. R. Bowker Company. *The Educational Film Locator*, also published by Bowker, lists university libraries that are film rental centers. In addition, many of these audiovisual materials may be available through your local library.